Also in the Dreamland Series

(with Jim DeFelice)
DALE BROWN'S DREAMLAND: RETRIBUTION
DALE BROWN'S DREAMLAND: END GAME
DALE BROWN'S DREAMLAND: SATAN'S TAIL
DALE BROWN'S DREAMLAND: STRIKE ZONE
DALE BROWN'S DREAMLAND: RAZOR'S EDGE
DALE BROWN'S DREAMLAND: NERVE CENTER
DALE BROWN'S DREAMLAND

Titles by Dale Brown

SHADOW COMMAND • STRIKE FORCE
EDGE OF BATTLE • ACT OF WAR
PLAN OF ATTACK • AIR BATTLE FORCE
WINGS OF FIRE • WARRIOR CLASS
BATTLE BORN • THE TIN MAN
FATAL TERRAIN • SHADOW OF STEEL
STORMING HEAVEN • CHAINS OF COMMAND
NIGHT OF THE HAWK • SKY MASTERS
HAMMERHEADS • DAY OF THE CHEETAH
SILVER TOWER • FLIGHT OF THE OLD DOG

DALE BROWN'S

Dreamland
REVOLUTION

DALE BROWN and JIM DeFELICE

HARPER

An Imprint of HarperCollinsPublishers

This is a work of fiction. Names, characters, places, and incidents are products of the author's imagination or are used fictitiously and are not to be construed as real. Any resemblance to actual events, locales, organizations, or persons, living or dead, is entirely coincidental.

HARPER
An Imprint of HarperCollins*Publishers*
10 East 53rd Street
New York, New York 10022-5299

Copyright © 2008 by Air Battle Force, Inc.
ISBN 978-0-06-088947-0

First Harper paperback printing: November 2008

HarperCollins ® and Harper ® are registered trademarks of Harper-Collins Publishers.

Printed in the United States of America

Visit Harper paperbacks on the World Wide Web at
www.harpercollins.com

10 9 8 7 6 5 4 3 2 1

Dreamland: Duty Roster

Major General "Earthmover" Terrill

General Samson has been given a new portfolio by the Chairman of the Joint Chiefs of Staff—turn Dreamland into the country's top spec warfare command. He will *do* it—no matter how many eggheads he has to break in the process.

Lieutenant Colonel Tecumseh "Dog" Bastian

Dreamland's former commander finds himself in an uncomfortable position—under General Samson.

Major Jeffrey "Zen" Stockard

A top fighter pilot until a crash at Dreamland left him a paraplegic, Zen is in charge of the Flighthawks—while still looking for a cure for his paralysis.

Captain Breanna "Rap" Stockard

Zen's wife has seen him through his injury and rehabilitation. But can she balance her love for her husband with the demands of her career . . . and ambitions?

Major Mack "the Knife" Smith

Mack Smith is the best pilot in the world—and he'll tell you so himself. But getting ahead may mean taking a desk job . . . as Samson's chief of staff.

Captain Danny Freah

Danny commands Whiplash—the ground attack team that works with the cutting edge Dreamland aircraft and high-tech gear.

Jed Barclay

The young deputy to the National Security Advisor is Dreamland's link to the President. Barely old enough to shave, the former science whiz kid now struggles to master the intricacies of world politics.

Mark Stoner

A CIA officer who has worked with Dreamland before, Stoner has been sent to Romania on a special assignment—and now finds himself in the middle of much more than he bargained for.

Prelude:

Night Shivers

———

**Air Force High Technology Advanced
Weapons Center (Dreamland)
22 January 1998
0250 (all times local)**

BLACK SMOKE ENVELOPED THE FRONT OF THE MEGA-fortress, shrouding the aircraft in darkness. Wind howled through the open escape hatches.

Lt. Colonel Tecumseh "Dog" Bastian was alone on the flight deck. The rest of the crew had already ejected. Now it was too late for him to get out.

The plane's electronic controls had been fried by an electromagnetic pulse. Dog struggled to control it using the sluggish hydraulic backups. The smoke was so thick he couldn't even see the control panel immediately in front of him.

He pulled back on the stick, but the aircraft didn't respond. Instead, the right wing began tipping upward, threatening to throw the plane into a spin. Dog fought against it, struggling with the controls. Then suddenly the blackness cleared and he could see the aircraft carrier below.

It was on fire, but was going to still launch a plane.

The plane he had to stop.

He leaned on the stick, trying to muscle the nose of his aircraft toward his target. He was moving at over five hundred knots, and he was low, through a thousand feet, yet there was time to see each detail—the crew fueling the airplane, the sailors on the deck, the destroyer in the distance. . . .

I'm going to crash, he thought. This is it.

* * *

COLONEL BASTIAN ROLLED OVER ONTO HIS BACK IN THE bed, half awake, half still in the dream. His legs felt as if they had immense weights on them, pinned to earth by his oppressive unconscious.

The dream had been a nightmare, but it was more memory than invention. Dog had barely survived a similar encounter with the Chinese navy a week before. He'd been moments away from crashing into a carrier's flight deck to prevent the launch of a plane with a nuclear bomb when the Chinese finally stood down. He'd been flying the Megafortress on hydraulics, just like in the dream, and nearly lost control before pulling up so close he could have grabbed the ship's arrestor cables if he'd had the gear.

But the dream wasn't a perfect recreation of the incident either. It was better in some ways—less scary, not more. The billowing black smoke hadn't gotten in his way. There'd been antiaircraft fire—a lot of it. He couldn't see any people on the flight deck. And time certainly hadn't slowed down.

No, if anything, time had moved considerably faster than normal. Things had crowded together as he pushed the plane toward what he was sure would be his last moment.

But there was one element of the dream that was far darker than reality. He hadn't felt the fear he felt now, sitting up on the bed. He hadn't been afraid at all—he'd been too focused to be afraid, too consumed by his duty.

If Dog's girlfriend, Jennifer Gleason, had been here with him, he would probably have rolled next to her and fallen back to sleep, relaxed by her warmth. But she was on the other side of the country, at a hospital in New York, recovering from an operation on her kneecap. There was nothing to keep him in bed now, not warmth, not habit—Dog got up, flexing his shoulders against the stiffness of the night. The shadows of the room played tricks on his eyes, and he thought for a second that Jennifer was here after all. He saw the curve of her hip, the swell of her breast as she stood on the threshold. But the shadows gave way to solid objects: her robe hanging over his on the hanger behind the door.

Dog pulled on his pants, then two sweatshirts, grabbed his boots and stepped outside in his socks.

The cold desert air smacked his face as he leaned up against the wall of the house to put on his boots. It was good to feel cold—he'd been in the tropics and the Middle East so long he forgot what fifty degrees felt like, let alone 34 degrees.

Had it been a little later, Dog might have gone for a run. But it was too early for that, and besides, he wanted to *walk,* not run. Something about walking helped make his brain work.

He took short, easy steps up the path. By habit, he turned right, heading for the Taj Mahal—the unofficial name of Dreamland's command building —most of which was underground. After two steps he stopped, realizing he didn't want to go in that direction.

Dog no longer had an office at the Taj. In fact, he had no office at all, anywhere. A week ago he'd been commander of Dreamland, responsible not just for the base and its people, but for its many missions and, ultimately, its myriad programs. Now he was just a lieutenant colonel looking for a job, replaced as commander by a highly connected major general, Terrill Samson. The general had been assigned to bring Dreamland back into the fold of the regular military, and wanted no part of Tecumseh "Dog" Bastian, a man the brass thought of as a cowboy, at best. So he was now a knight without portfolio—not quite as bad as a man without a country, but close.

The cold air nipped at him. Dog pulled the hood on his sweatshirt over his head and tightened the strings to choke off the chill as he headed in the direction of the old boneyard—the graveyard of experiments past, where old aircraft came to sit out their remaining days, oxidizing in the sun. The first he saw was his favorite—an F-105 Thunderchief, which had most likely flown in Vietnam, surviving untold trials before safely returning its pilot home.

He'd never flown a Thud, but his first squadron commander had, and he'd spent long hours listening as Pappy talked about riding the Thunderchief up and down the Ho Chi Ming trail, "bombing the bejesus out of the commie rice eaters, and getting nothing but SA-2s up our tail pipes for thanks."

Dog stopped and smiled, thinking of Pappy. The funny thing was, he couldn't remember his real name.

Maybe even funnier—they called him Pappy because to the young bucks in the squadron, their leader was a grizzled old coot, one step from the retirement home.

Truth was, Pappy couldn't have been a day past forty. That didn't seem so very old to him anymore.

Amused by the turn his thoughts had taken, Dog laughed at himself, then continued walking.

I

Medal of Honor

JED BARCLAY HESITATED OUTSIDE THE DOOR, GLANCING down at his suit jacket and tie to make sure everything was in order. It was one of the personal "tricks" the speech therapist had given him: *Reassure yourself before a meeting that you look fantastic, hon, then you can proceed with confidence.*

Her precise, motherly voice rang in his ears as he took a slow, deep breath. The nearby Secret Service agent was probably choking back a laugh, he thought, not daring to glance in his direction.

"Jed, come on," said Jerrod Hale, the President's chief of staff, spotting him through the doorway. "They've already started."

"Yes, sir, I'm sorry."

Jed started inside with his head down, then heard the therapist's advice again: *Head up, stride with* purpose! *You belong where you're going.*

Even if it's the Oval office, she might have added—and undoubtedly would have if she'd known that his job as a deputy to the National Security Advisor often brought him here. He hadn't told her what his job was, and it appeared that the anonymous benefactor who arranged for his speech lessons hadn't told her.

Jed's boss, National Security Advisor Philip Freeman, nodded at him as he slipped into the room. President Kevin

Martindale gave him a nod as well, but then turned his attention back to the head of the Joint Chiefs of Staff, Admiral George Balboa, who was summing up the results of the U.S.'s successful intervention in the Indian-Pakistani War.

"So we now have peace between India and Pakistan. Total peace. For the moment." Balboa puffed out his words, punctuating his sentences with hard stops and short breaths as if they were darts. "The Navy has the situation under control. Entirely. Our two carriers are more than a match for the combatants. Medals are in order. My opinion."

"Oh, I think the Dreamland people deserve a *little* credit," said Arthur Chastain dryly. Chastain was the Secretary of Defense, and lately had been making little secret of his disdain for Balboa. Dreamland had, in fact, done most of the work, and had the casualties to prove it.

"Some credit. Some," admitted Balboa. "Terrill Samson is going to turn that place around."

"Samson is a good man," said Chastain. "But Dreamland doesn't need to be turned around. I admit Bastian is operating over his pay grade, but he's done a hell of a job."

Balboa made a face before continuing. His words came even faster, and in shorter bits. "I can envision a day where Dreamland works with Marines, SEALs, the whole nine yards."

"I think medals are a very good idea," said President Martindale. "An excellent idea." He rose from the desk. "And why hasn't Bastian been promoted?" he asked Chastain. "He deserves it."

"Ordinarily, sir, length of service is the most important criteria. Lieutenant Colonel Bastian—"

"The hell with that. He should be a general."

Balboa cut in. "Mr. President, with due respect. To go from lieutenant colonel to general, at a time when we're not at war—"

"Thanks to him," noted the President.

"Bypassing the normal process and making a lieutenant

colonel a general, I don't think it's a good idea, sir," said Chastain. "I like Bastian. I admire him. He's got a great future. But making him a general—"

"Roosevelt did it," said Martindale brightly.

"That was during the world war. And I don't believe that anyone went from lieutenant colonel to general without at least a few months as colonel," said Chastain. "Congress was also involved. They passed special legislation."

"There are promotion boards and processes," added Balboa. "If we disregard them, the entire service is harmed. We can't put one man above the entire military. It's not worth it, Mr. President."

Promotions were governed not only by tradition and service regulations, but by law. To become a full colonel, an officer usually had to spend twenty-two years in the military—and by law had to spend a minimum of three years in grade. Bastian failed on both counts. The law did allow what was unofficially called a "below the zone" promotion: One year before regular eligibility, a candidate might be elevated to the promotion list. But Chastain explained that Bastian had received a below the zone promotion to lieutenant colonel, and was therefore not eligible even for that consideration.

The criteria for promotion to flag officer rank—a general—was even more complicated. Congress limited the number of generals in the service. The Air Force was presently allotted 139 brigadier or one star generals; those ranks were not only full, but there was a long waiting list. In effect, a promotion was generally a replacement of a retiring general. No matter how capable he was, moving Lieutenant Colonel Bastian up to flag rank would provoke bad feelings—and require the approval of the Senate. The process would surely involve hearings, and given the recent criticism from some members of the Senate and congress that Dreamland was being used as the President's private army, that was something best avoided.

"Yes, all right, I'm sorry, gentlemen. Of course," said the President. "We have to think about the entire military. But

Bastian's promotion should be expedited. There *has* to be a way to get him to full colonel. He deserves it."

"That can be looked into," said Balboa.

"And the Congressional Medal of Honor, for what he did," said Martindale. "Clearly he earned that."

That was no exaggeration. Colonel Bastian had risked his life to stop a world war. His aircraft was under heavy fire and had been damaged by Chinese missiles, he'd outgunned several interceptors and at least one destroyer, he had his crew bail out, and then single-handedly dove his plane on that Chinese carrier, ready to sacrifice his life so the plane couldn't take off. He'd been seconds away from death when the Chinese stood down.

"If it weren't for Bastian," agreed Freeman, "we would be at war with the Chinese by now."

"I agree," said Chastain. "Frankly, that sort of honor is long overdue. All of the Dreamland people who were on that mission. The two pilots who were on that island . . . "

The Secretary of Defense looked at Jed, expecting him to supply their names.

"That would be Zen Stockard," he said. "Uh . . . um, M-Major Jeffrey Stockard and Cap-Captain Breanna Stockard."

Damn, he thought. He was still stuttering.

"I agree they should be recognized. Their efforts," said Balboa. "But of course, we do have provisions . . . regulations. A procedure."

"Follow the procedure," said Martindale. "But Bastian gets the Medal of Honor. And medals for the rest. Our heroes have to be recognized. Period. Next topic."

Northeastern Romania
1600

"THE GUARDS CHANGE AT TEN MINUTES TO MIDNIGHT. THE path to the pipe is wide open," said General Tomma Locusta. "You can make the attack without any interference."

"And no loss to your men," said the Russian.

Locusta nodded. The Russian was very good at stating the obvious.

"Sometimes eggs must be broken," said the Russian.

"Eggs are one thing, men another."

"As you wish," said the Russian. His name was Svoransky; he was a military attaché sent from Bucharest, the capital. He could not speak Romanian; the two men used English to communicate, the only language in common between them.

Locusta raised his binoculars, scanning farther across the valley toward the gas pipeline. Only the very top of its gunmetal-gray frame could be seen from here. Raised on metal stanchions, the huge metal pipe was part of an old network originally laid from Romania's own gas production wells. The government gas company had plans to bury the line eventually; until then, it was an easy and tempting target.

Which was what the Russian wanted.

"What is the interval between radio checks?" asked Svoransky.

"It is not necessary to worry about that," said Locusta, fearing he had given away too much information already. Svoransky was helping him, but it would be a mistake to believe that their interests were precisely the same.

A severe mistake. The Russians could never be trusted. Even Romania's fool of a president, Alin Voda, knew that.

Voda. Just thinking of him turned Locusta's stomach. He was a weakling, a democrat—part of the alleged liberalizing movement that aimed at bringing Romania into the twenty-first century. The movement was nothing but a cover for money grabbing capitalists who aimed at stealing Romania blind.

"Very good, then," said Svoransky. "I appreciate your showing me this in person."

Locusta nodded. He had taken the task on himself because he felt he could trust no one with it—not because he was afraid they would betray him, but because the soldiers in his command retained a strong dislike for Russians. Few Romanian soldiers, officers or enlisted, would have been able to countenance helping the Russians in this way. Locusta himself barely accepted it, and he was doing it so he could rid the country of its scoundrel democrats and return the strong hand it deserved.

"You are sure you have everything you need?" Svoransky asked. "Very sure? You must see to every detail—you do not want the government realizing who is truly behind the attacks."

The remark didn't deserve an answer, and Locusta made no reply. Instead he turned his glasses to the southeast, in the general direction the pipeline took from Bulgaria, through Turkey, and over to the far-off Caspian Sea. It was amazing to think that the gas would travel so many miles—and that it would go even farther still, to Austria, then Czechoslovakia, Germany, France, and Spain.

Of course, that wouldn't be the case once the attacks were finished. Western Europe would have to freeze—or buy from the Russians, which was what Svoransky wanted.

While stopping the flow of gas served Locusta's purposes as well, he did not want the pipeline damaged too severely. As soon as he was in charge of the government, the line would be repaired—and better guarded, most especially against the Russians. The revenues would be as handy for him as they were for Voda and his cronies.

"Tomorrow," said Svoransky. "Depend on it."

"We will," said Locusta, starting back toward the car.

**Allegro, Nevada
0610**

JEFF "ZEN" STOCKARD TAPPED THE SIDE OF THE POOL AND started back on his last lap, pushing hard enough to feel the strain in his shoulder muscles. The water was warm, and stank of chlorine. He closed his eyes and dove down, aiming for the bottom. He tapped it, then came up quickly, his thrusts so hard he nearly slammed against the end of the pool.

"You're looking good," said the lifeguard, standing nearby with a towel. They were the only two people in the large room that housed the gym's pool.

"Thanks, Pete." Zen put his arms on the edge of the pool and lifted himself out slowly, twisting his body around to sit on the side. Even though he'd grown friendly with the lifeguard—or trainer, which was his actual title—over the past six or seven months, Zen still felt self-conscious getting in and out of the pool, and especially getting into his wheelchair.

It wasn't the chair that bothered him; it was the looks of apprehension and pity from the people who saw him.

Not being able to use his legs did bother him, of course. It bothered him a great deal. But most days he had other things to focus on.

"Hey." The lifeguard squatted down. "You want to catch some breakfast? Coffee or something?"

"No, sorry. I'm supposed to meet Bree for breakfast before work."

Pete threw the towel over his shoulders. "I saw those news reports," he said. "God damn. You are a real hero. I'm really . . . it's amazing."

Zen laughed.

"No, I mean it. I ain't buttering you up, Zen. I'm really honored just to know you."

"Hey, I'm still the same guy," said Zen. He wasn't sure why he was laughing—maybe because he was nervous about being called a hero, or about being in the spotlight. "Still the same guy who pulls his pants on one bum leg at a time."

"You want me to get your chair?"

"If you could."

"Of course I can. God. Jeez, man, for you I'd do anything."

Zen began edging away from the pool. The flooring material was textured to provide a good grip for feet, which made it harder for him to move back. The lifeguard positioned the chair and helped him up.

"Hard to believe you could do all that and still be in a wheelchair," he said. "You guys really did stop a war."

"I guess we did."

"Maybe no one will ever go to war again, huh? If they know you guys will step in?"

"Somehow, I think that's wishful thinking, Pete," said Zen, starting for the locker room.

College Hospital, Nevada
0700

"WHAT ARE YOU DOING OUT OF BED?"

"I'm taking a walk," said Breanna Stockard.

"What are you doing out of bed?" repeated the doctor. Her name was Rene Rosenberg, and she was so short that Breanna—no giant herself—could look down at the top of her head and see speckles of gray in the roots of her hair.

"I seem to be taking a walk," repeated Breanna.

"You're dressed."

"Just about." Breanna turned slowly, surveying the room. She'd forgotten where her sweater was.

"Ms. Stockard—really, I insist that you rest. Have you had breakfast?"

"I need to move my legs before breakfast."

"The bathroom is behind you."

"I've already been."

"Then please, back in bed."

Breanna spotted the sweater on the chair under the television.

"I don't want you putting weight on that right leg," warned the doctor.

"You said the X rays were clean."

"Yes, but the ligaments and tendons in your knee were severely damaged."

"But not torn. Exercise is good," added Breanna, remembering the doctor's own words.

"Supervised exercise as part of a rehabilitation program, not jogging around the halls at seven in the morning."

"I was thinking I'd save the jogging for after breakfast."

Breanna shifted her weight back and forth. The ligament connecting the muscles and bones together had been severely strained, but not torn. Still, it did hurt enough for her to fight back a wince.

The doctor had her hands on her hips and a frown on her face. "Frankly, Breanna, I don't understand how you managed to avoid breaking your leg, let alone ripping the knee to shreds. How are your ribs?"

"Solid."

"And your head?"

"Still hard as a rock."

Dr. Rosenberg frowned. Breanna's lower right ribs were badly bruised. Her injuries had come after ejecting from her Megafortress, though their exact origin was something of a mystery—the doctors believed she had hit something, probably the bottom of the plane as she jumped, though Breanna thought it had happened much later, when she hit the water. She had a good memory of leaving the plane, jumping through the open hatchway in the Flighthawk bay with Zen. She could see him falling with her, diverted slightly by the slipstream of wind below the fuselage. His chute opened. She felt the tug of hers, looked up and saw the blossom above her . . .

The rest was a blank. Zen had found her in the water, pulled her onto a small atoll off the Indian coast, gotten her food and helped get them rescued.

"Breanna, really, you have to take it easy," said the doctor. "*Seriously,* Bree."

Something about the doctor's tone of voice—it was very unprofessional, almost pleading—caught Breanna off guard.

"I'm OK," she told her.

"You're not OK. You're getting better. And to keep getting better, you have to go slow. Bit by bit."

"My mother's been talking to you, hasn't she?"

A smile fluttered across Dr. Rosenberg's face. It didn't last—her professional mask was quickly put back in place, the lines of her mouth sloping downward slightly, as if she were ready to frown.

"The doctor did call and ask a few questions," admitted Rosenberg. "But you're my patient, and these are my concerns. A walk, with your cane, to stretch your legs," she added, retrieving the cane. "A short walk. With the cane. All right?"

Breanna took the cane and began making her way out of the room. Dr. Rosenberg walked at her side.

"I know it must be hard for you to throttle back," said the doctor as they stepped into the hallway. "You're a Type A personality. But sometimes —"

"She's A to Z," said Zen, stopping just before rolling into them.

"Hey," said Breanna.

"Where are you going?" said Zen. "I thought we were having breakfast."

"We are as soon as I work up an appetite."

Zen looked over at the doctor. "How's she doing?"

"I think she's aiming for a breakout." The doctor's grimace turned into a broad smile. Her manner changed; Breanna couldn't help thinking she was flirting with Zen, and felt a slight twinge of jealousy.

"You aimin' to bust outta this dump?" Zen asked her.

"Ain't no prison can hold me, Sheriff."

"Another two days. You were unconscious for an awfully long time," said Dr. Rosenberg. "Days."

"Two days. I was sleeping," insisted Breanna. It wasn't

clear what had happened to her; the neurologist believed she'd suffered a concussion, though the length of her "incident," as he called it, could also suggest a coma. She had no obvious sign of brain damage, and the series of tests failed to find anything subtle.

Her body was still somewhat depleted from exposure and dehydration, however, and it reminded her of it with a shake as she began walking down the hall. Determined not to let Zen or the doctor see, she gripped the top of the cane firmly, pausing just a moment.

The doctor missed it, but Zen didn't.

"Problem?" asked her husband.

"I'm waiting for you, slowpoke."

"That'll be the day."

"I'm going to leave you in the custody of your husband," said Rosenberg. "Jeff, she can make one circuit, then back to bed. Her knee really shouldn't be overstressed. And she should take those clothes off."

"I'll see what I can do about that."

Rosenberg, belatedly recognizing the double entendre, started to flush, then nodded and walked away.

"She's got a crush on you," Breanna told her husband.

"Who wouldn't?"

"You are *so* conceited."

"It's the chair. All babes fall for crips. Can't resist us."

Breanna's breakfast had arrived while they were out. Zen snickered at the overcooked croissant and told her he'd be right back. It took him more than a half hour to get to the cafeteria and back, but when he returned, he had a plate of bacon, a large helping of scrambled eggs, some home fries, toast, and a full carafe of coffee.

"What, no tomato juice?" said Breanna, pulling the cover off the plate of eggs.

"They're saving it for the Bloody Marys," Zen told her.

Breanna dug into the food greedily. The eggs were a little rubbery, but acceptable under the circumstances.

"All right, off with your clothes," growled Zen when she finished.

"What?"

"Doctor's orders." He smiled at her—then reached his fingers beneath her T-shirt. "What do you say?"

"They'll hear us out at the nurses' station."

"I'll close the door and put a do-not-disturb sign on it."

Zen's cell phone started to ring as he swung toward the door.

"You better answer that," she said.

"Why?"

"No one calls you on your cell phone unless it's an emergency."

"It's too early for an emergency."

"Jeff. What if it's my father?"

"You're legal age." Zen pulled out the phone, checked the number, then answered. "This is Zen. What's going on, cuz?"

Breanna could tell from her husband's voice that he was talking to Jed Barclay, his cousin and the President's liaison to Dreamland.

"Wow," he said, his eyes opening wide. "Here, tell Bree."

Breanna took the phone.

"Breanna how are you feeling?" asked Jed.

"A lot better than when I talked to you the other day. What's going on?"

"You guys are getting big-time medals. And your father, Colonel Bastian? The Medal of Honor. *No shit.*"

Dreamland
0728

MAJOR GENERAL TERRILL "EARTHMOVER" SAMSON took the last gulp of coffee from his cup, folded his arms and surveyed his office. The far wall was lined with photos of his past commands, along with a selection of pictures of him with superior officers, two Presidents, and a Hollywood movie star who'd visited his base to find out what pilots were really like. The wall to the right, until recently lined with bookshelves, now had framed commendations he'd received, along with a few oil paintings of the aircraft he'd flown. The furniture—which had arrived the day before—was sleek glass and chrome, very futuristic, just the right tone for Dreamland, Samson thought.

He wasn't quite done—he'd need a few models of aircraft to adorn his desk—but the office now bore his stamp.

The command itself would take a little longer. The first order of business was to organize Dreamland along traditional Air Force lines, which meant establishing a base command and a set of air wings to oversee the actual operations. To do that, he needed people. The base side was already taken care of: Colonel Marie Tassel was due at Dreamland in two weeks. She was a no-nonsense taskmaster who'd worked in the Inspector General's Office. Her job would be to run the physical plant, overseeing everything from day care for the dependents to purchasing paper clips, and Tassel was just anal enough to get the place shipshape in no time.

Samson had also chosen someone to head the science and engineering group—a military officer who would oversee the collection of civilian eggheads and hippies working on the high-tech toys Dreamland was famous for. Colonel John Cho was an engineer by training; he undoubtedly could speak their language while increasing their productivity. He'd also served as a tanker pilot early in his career and had done a stint with airlift. Cho was due in a few days, as soon as he finished up his present assignment at the Pentagon.

Filling the "action" side of things was trickier. Samson intended on establishing one wing to conduct combat operations and another to oversee experimental flights. But all the "good" colonels seemed to be taken.

Of course, he could slip a lieutenant colonel into one of

the slots, if he had the right man. But he didn't want to do that, and not simply because wing commander was generally a colonel's job. As long as he used rank as his first consideration, it was the perfect excuse to keep Bastian out of the position.

Not that Bastian was going to be a problem. He was going elsewhere. Soon. Sooner than soon. But just in case.

Samson looked at his desk, piled high with papers. The other thing he needed was a chief of staff.

Bastian, with an extremely limited man count and an even tighter budget, had functioned as his own chief of staff—thanks largely to the efforts of a chief master sergeant extraordinaire. But the chief was retiring, and in any event, Samson reflected, he wasn't here to do things on a shoestring. He needed a savvy major to sort things out for him—and run interference, he noted as his thoughts were interrupted by a loud knock at the door.

"Come," he commanded impatiently.

"General, Major Mack Smith, sir. You asked me to stop by, sir."

Mack walked into the office as if he owned it. He had the cocky smile that Samson instantly recognized as the particular disease of a fighter jock. Tall, well-built, and with a somewhat boyish face, Smith looked like he stepped out of a Hollywood movie. He reeked of arrogance—without waiting for permission, he pulled over a chair and sat down.

"Did I say you should *sit*, Major?"

"Sir, no sir."

Mack jumped quickly to his feet. He was still grinning, but his quickness was a good sign, thought Samson. He tried to remember who the hell Mack Smith was: He'd met so many people over the past few days that he was drawing a blank.

"The general is having a little trouble placing me," said Mack, his voice now obsequious. "We met, sir, on Diego Garcia."

Smith? Not the head of the special operations ground unit, the pararescuers with counterterror training—that was a black captain, Danny Freah.

Smith?

"General, if I may—I served under you sir, briefly, in the Fourth Air Force."

The Fourth Air Force? God, that took him back.

"I was a second lieutenant, sir," added Mack. "Young and impressionable. You showed me the way."

"Go on," said Samson.

Mack barely needed the prompting. He recited a service record that would have made Jimmy Doolittle jealous—a record that Samson wouldn't have believed had he not read the after-action reports involving Dreamland under the so-called "Whiplash orders"—actions directed by the President.

An F-15 pilot in the Gulf War with a kill, serious time as a test pilot, a stint as a foreign air force advisor, combat operations on two continents, with a dozen kills to his name—the man was definitely going places in the Air Force. He was just the sort Samson wanted under him.

And maybe a *perfect* chief of staff.

"That's enough, Major," said Samson, interrupting. "As I recall, you were looking for some help finding a new assignment."

"Uh, yes sir."

"An active wing—something that will help you move ahead."

"I'd appreciate that, General." Mack gave him a big smile.

"I can certainly do that. Have a seat, Major. Would you like some coffee?"

"Yes, sir. Thank you, sir."

"There's a pot in the outer office. Refill mine, too."

Mack hopped to. Samson leaned back in his chair. Smith had been Bastian's copilot on his last mission. Ordered by Bastian to jump into the water—with characteristically misplaced bravado, Bastian had been planning to crash his plane into a Chinese carrier—the major had pulled the crew together and gotten them rescued.

That was all very well and good—the men would respect him—but if he'd been Bastian's copilot, he might be too close to him.

"So tell me, Major, what do you think of Major Catsman?" he asked when Mack returned with the coffee.

Mack made a face as he sat down.

"Problem?"

"She's OK."

Catsman had been Bastian's executive officer. Samson had thought of making her his chief of staff, but some of her comments over the past few days convinced him that would be a mistake.

"You can be candid," Samson told Mack. "She's not a very good officer?"

"Oh, she's a great officer," said Mack. "Very good at what she does. Just . . . well, I wouldn't want to speak out of turn."

Samson raised his hand. "This is completely off the record, Major. Just chatter between us."

"Well, yes sir. She does seem pretty close to Colonel Bastian, don't you think?"

"An affair?"

"Oh no, no, nothing like that," said Mack. "She just—you know the old saying about looking through the world with rose-shaded glasses? Well, Major Catsman has Bastian-shaded glasses, if you know what I mean."

Samson nodded. "She tried to convince me I should talk Ray Rubeo out of quitting."

"Dr. Ray? Pshew. Good riddance."

"Good riddance?"

Mack shrugged. "He wasn't exactly a team player. You know what I mean? We're still off the record, sir?"

"Yes, yes, of course," said Samson.

Rubeo was the civilian scientist who had headed the science department. Samson eagerly accepted his resignation after making it clear that eccentric eggheads had no future in his command.

"Tell me, Mack, what do you think of Danny Freah?" said Samson.

"Captain Freah? Head of base security, head of Whiplash. Our top Spec Warfare guy. A-number-one. Close to Bastian, but dependable even so. He's done a hell of a lot with the Whiplash kids. Still impressionable. With the right mentor, he could go all the way."

Samson began quizzing Mack about the other personnel at the base. Mack had a strong opinion about each one of them. It didn't take long for Samson to realize that Mack Smith knew where all the bodies were buried—and where a few more might to be dumped.

"Mack, have you given any thought to your next assignment?" asked the general, once more interrupting him. "I mean *real* thought?"

"Excuse me, sir, as I'd said earlier, I did, and not to repeat myself but—"

"No, no, Mack. *Real* thought." Samson rose from his chair and walked over to the wall with his photographs. "Some men plan things out very far in advance. Others just let them happen."

Mack got up from the chair and walked over behind the general.

"Did you ever meet Curtis LeMay?" asked Samson, pointing at the photo of himself and the famous Air Force general who had served during World War II and the Cold War.

"Gee, no, sir."

"Richard Nixon. Tragic figure," said Samson, pointing to another photo. "Not so tragic as LBJ. That's after he left the presidency. I'm a captain in that photo. Freshly promoted."

"The general hasn't changed a bit," said Mack.

Samson smirked. Yes, Mack would do very well as chief of staff. After he was broken in.

"You flew Boners, sir?" asked Mack, staring at another shot.

Samson frowned. Though "boner" was a common nickname for the B-1B bomber—it came from spelling out B-1—he didn't particularly like it.

"I've had plenty of stick time in the B-1," he said, "among other planes. I was one of the first B-1B squadron leaders. A pretty plane."

"Yes sir, real pretty."

"To get where I am, you need a few things, Mack. Some important things."

"Luck, General?"

"I'm anything but lucky, Major."

If he was lucky, thought Samson, he'd have been given a full command like Centcom or the Southern Command, posts he coveted, rather than Dreamland.

"You need experience, you need ambition, you need good postings," continued the general. "And you need friends. Mentors. The Air Force is very political, Mack. Very. Even for someone like you, with a great record, who you know can determine how far you go."

"I'll bet."

"I've been blessed with a number of very important mentors—men, and a few women as well, whom I've met on the way up. Admiral Balboa, for one."

"Sure. You probably know a lot of people."

Samson could see that Mack wasn't quite getting it. The general went back to his desk and had another sip of coffee. "I'm looking for a chief of staff," he said bluntly. "I'm hoping you'll be interested."

"Chief of staff? A desk job?"

"An important hands-on position," said Samson. "A right-hand man."

"Gee, General, I hadn't really thought of taking something like that."

"Mmmm." Samson pressed his lips together.

"Can I, uh, think it over?"

"Of course, Mack." He rose to dismiss him—and hide his displeasure. "Let's say, twenty-four hours?"

"Um, uh—yes, sir. Thank you, sir."

"No, thank you, Mack." Samson stared at him a moment. When Mack didn't move, he added, "Dismissed," and went back to work on his papers.

Northeastern Romania, near the border with Moldova 1803

MARK STONER PULLED THE HOOD OF HIS SWEATSHIRT OVER his head as he got out of the Fiat, then zipped his winter coat against the cold. He closed the door of the car, slipping his hand into his coat pocket as he walked along the road, his fingers gripping the .45 caliber Colt automatic in his pocket, an old but trusted friend.

Making his way along the crumbling asphalt of the highway shoulder, he reached the start of a dirt path that twisted down through the woods. He paused as if to tie his shoe, dropping to his knee and looking around, making sure he wasn't being followed or watched. The sun had already set, but the woods were thin and he had a good, clear view of his surroundings. Satisfied he was alone, Stoner rose and started down the trail. He walked slowly so he could listen for any sound that seemed out of place.

After twenty yards the path veered sharply to the right. Stoner stopped again, once more checking around carefully, though this time he didn't bother with a pretense. The terrain dropped off precipitously to the left, giving a good view of the valley and, not coincidentally, of the gas pipeline that ran nearby.

Stoner had never been here before, but he had examined satellite photos of the area, and everything seemed vaguely familiar. That, he knew, was dangerous—familiarity made you assume things you shouldn't assume. It was better to be a stranger, as he was to Romania. A stranger trusted no one, took nothing for granted.

Stoner was a professional stranger. His actual job was as a paramilitary officer, assigned to the CIA's operations directorate. He was literally a stranger to Romania, having been pressed into service here barely a week before, following the death of another officer. The man had been murdered by rebels in a town twenty miles to the south, and was in fact the third CIA employee killed in the troubled northeastern quarter of Romania over the past year. Stoner had been sent to find out what the hell was going on.

Thirty yards after the sharp bend, the trail disintegrated into a pile of a large boulders, the result of a landslide that had occurred several years before. Though he had a good view of the rocks and the drop-off beyond, Stoner took his time approaching them, stopping and starting, aware that it would be an easy place for an ambush. When he finally reached the rocks, the last light of the sun was nearly gone. He dropped to his haunches, then unzipped his coat and took out his night-vision binoculars.

The gas line ran on the opposite side of the valley, roughly a mile and a half from where he was. The pipe was at least thirty years old, originally built to take gas from nearby wells down to the southwest, toward Bucharest, the Romanian capital. Those wells had stopped producing roughly a decade before, and the pipes sat unused until Inogate—the European oil and gas network—realized they were almost perfectly positioned to join a network of pipelines from Turkey to Austria and Central Europe.

Almost perfectly placed. A hundred fifty miles to the southwest would have been much better. But these pipes were here already, which meant not only could their construction costs be avoided, but so could the web of environmental regulations and political maneuvering that went hand in hand with construction in Europe, even in a country like Romania, which had only recently emerged from behind the Iron Curtain. A detour of a few hundred miles was nothing to the gas itself, and it had the side benefit of promising future economic development in an area where it was sorely needed.

But the pipeline was also a tempting target for the Romanian rebels who'd sought refuge in the north after being chased from the more urban south. They were communists, young hard-liners angry over the country's flowering democracy and nascent capitalism.

It was more complicated than that—it was *always* more complicated than that—but the nuances weren't important to Stoner. He leaned back against the rocks. Observing the pipeline was just a sideline tonight. The rebels had yet to make a serious or successful attack on it. Their targets thus far had been political—police stations, a mayor's house, several town halls. The effectiveness of their attacks vacillated wildly.

All of which, in his opinion, made them unlikely candidates to have murdered the CIA officers. As did the fact that no communiqués—no e-mails or phone calls to radio stations—had followed the deaths.

Which was one reason he was going to meet one of them tonight.

Stoner checked his watch. He had an hour to get to the village and meet his guide across the border, in Moldova. He turned and started for the car.

Dreamland
0809

DOG CRANED HIS HEAD, WATCHING AS THE B-1B/L ROCKETED off the runway. The big jet—a highly modified version of the B-1—pitched its nose almost straight upward, riding a wave of thrust through the light curtain of clouds. For a brief moment the aircraft's black hull engulfed the rising sun, blotting it out in an artificial eclipse. Then it was beyond the yellow orb, streaking toward the first mission checkpoint at 20,000 feet.

Though he no longer commanded Dreamland, Dog was still one of the few pilots checked out to fly nearly every plane on the base. Hoping to keep himself busy until fresh orders arrived, he'd volunteered to take a spot in the test rotation whenever needed, and was due to take the stick in Dreamland's other B-1B in a few hours.

"Purty little beast, eh, Colonel?" asked Al "Greasy Hands" Parsons, sidling up to Dog with a satisfied look on his face.

"You sound almost sentimental, Chief. Like it's one of your babies."

"It is. I love airplanes, Colonel. More like lust, really."

Dog lost sight of the aircraft as it twisted toward Range 6B. A few seconds later the air shook with a sonic boom.

"Of course, some of 'em are purtier than others," continued Parsons. "The B-1—I always liked that plane. Pain in the you-know-what to keep running, when we first got her, anyway. Par for the course. But she's a sleek little beast."

"I wouldn't call her little."

"Compared to a B-52, she is," said Parsons. He whistled. "I remember, I thought the B-36 was big." He whistled again. "Then the first day I saw the Superfortress, man, that shrunk everything."

Dog shaded his eyes, straining to catch a glimpse of the B-1B/L and its laser test shots.

"It'll be over here," said Greasy Hands, pointing in the direction of the range.

Sure enough, a white funnel appeared on the horizon. Two more followed. A laser mounted in the belly of the aircraft had fired and struck a series of ground targets on the range, striking them while flying faster than the speed of sound.

"Looked good from here," said Parsons. "But then again, it always does. Buy you breakfast, Colonel?"

A week ago Dog would have felt guilty lingering here to watch the test, even from the distance. But now, Samson's appointment as Dreamland's new commander meant there was no mountain of papers waiting for him back at the office, no personnel matters to settle, no experiments to oversee.

"I could use a cup of coffee," he told Parsons. "So tell me a little bit about the B-36, Chief. It was before my time."

"You're not implying I'm old, are you, Colonel?"

Dog chuckled. The two men turned in the direction of the Taj.

GREASY HANDS HAD JUST BEGUN TO WAX ELOQUENT ABOUT the sound six 3,800-horsepower Pratt & Whitney engines and four GE turbojets made on takeoff when Major Natalie Catsman ran into the combined mess hall, the large cafeteria that served Dreamland personnel regardless of rank.

"Colonel, Zen just told me the news," she said breathlessly. "Congratulations."

"What news?" said Dog.

"We all knew it—now the world will know it, too."

"What news?" Dog asked again.

"Listen up everyone." Catsman turned around. "Colonel Bastian is getting the Congressional Medal of Honor!"

"What?" said Dog, dumbfounded.

"It's true," said Zen, rolling into the room with a wide grin on his face.

Dog looked around the room, not exactly sure what was going on.

"You're getting the Medal of Honor," Zen told him as he came close. "Jed just told me. Bree's on the phone. She wants to congratulate you."

"The Medal of Honor?"

"Hot damn, congratulations, Colonel!" said Greasy Hands Parsons, slapping Colonel Bastian on the back.

As if by some hidden signal, everyone in the cafeteria rose and began to applaud. Dog, not sure what to say—not even sure that this was in fact happening—opened his mouth, but then closed it.

The Medal of Honor?
The Medal of Honor.

II

An Honor and Privilege

Northeastern Romania,
near the border with Moldova
1933

THE GUN WAS AN OLD REVOLVER, A RUGER BLACKHAWK, a good gun but an odd one to find in northeastern Romania.

And not one particularly welcome when it was pointed at his head.

"Put the pistol down," said Stoner. His hand was in his pocket, his own .45 aimed at the Romanian's chest.

"You are Stoner?" the man with the gun asked.

"You think anybody else is going to be standing out in the middle of this fucking road at this hour?"

The man glanced to his right, looking at his companion. It was a half second of inattention, a momentary, reflexive glance, but it was all Stoner needed. He leaped forward, grabbing and pushing the man's arm up with his left hand while pulling out his own gun with his right. The Romanian lost his balance; Stoner went down to the ground with him, pistol pointed at the man's forehead. The Romanian's gun flew to the side.

"Identify yourself, asshole." Stoner pushed the muzzle of the weapon against the man's forehead.

The Romanian couldn't speak. His companion took a step closer.

"You come any closer, he's fucking dead!" Stoner yelled.

"He doesn't speak English," said the man on the ground.

"Tell him, you jackass. Tell him before I blow your brains out. Then I'll shoot him, too."

In a nervous voice, the Romanian urged his friend to remain calm.

"Now tell me who the hell you are," said Stoner.

Though they were dressed in civilian clothes, Stoner knew the man and his companion had to be the two soldiers sent to help him sneak across the border, but there was a point to be made here. Pulling a gun on him was completely unacceptable.

"I am Deniz. He is Kyiv. He does not speak no English," added the man on the ground. "We were to help you."

"Yeah, I know who the hell you are." Stoner jumped up, taking a step back. "You're going to check me out, you do it from a distance. You don't walk right up to me and draw your gun. You're lucky I didn't shoot you."

Deniz gave a nervous laugh, then reached for his pistol. Stoner kicked it away, then scooped it up.

"This is your only weapon?" he asked.

Deniz shrugged.

"What's he carrying?"

"No gun. The captain said—"

"No gun?"

"We are to pretend we're civilians," said Deniz. "No uniform, no rifle. Not even boots."

Idiot, thought Stoner. "You know where we're going?" he asked.

Deniz nodded.

Stoner looked at them. Deniz was twenty, maybe, taller than he was but at least fifty pounds lighter. Kyiv was a pudge of a man, his age anywhere from fifteen to thirty-five. He looked like a baker who liked his work a little too much, not a fighter.

Neither would be much help if things got rough. On the other hand, Stoner not only didn't know the area, but knew only a few phrases in Romanian.

"Kyiv knows the border very well," said Deniz, trying to reassure him. "Part of his family lives there. Yes?"

He repeated what he had said in Romanian for Kyiv, who nodded and said something in Romanian.

"The girls are better on the other side," added Deniz. "We go there often. No guns. Not needed."

Stoner frowned, then led them to his car, parked off the road behind some brush.

"You know how to use these, I assume," he said, opening the trunk and handing them each an AK-47.

"It is not dangerous where we are going," said Deniz.

"It's always dangerous," said Stoner, pressing the rifle on him. "Don't kid yourself."

He took his own gun—another AK-47, this one a paratrooper's model with a folding metal stock—and doled out banana magazines to the others

"This is the spot," he said, unfolding the satellite photo he'd brought. "The GPS coordinates are for this barn."

Deniz took the paper, turning it around several times as he looked at it. Then he handed it to his companion. The two men began talking in Romanian.

"He knows the barn," said Deniz finally. "Five kilometers from the border. The woman who owned it died two years ago. A neighbor mows the field."

"Who owns it now?"

Kyiv didn't know.

"The rebels have been quiet this week," said Deniz as Stoner adjusted his knapsack. "We have become a very silent area."

"That's good to know."

"We could take your car," added the Romanian.

"No. We walk."

Taking the car would mean they'd have to pass through a Moldovan as well as a Romanian military checkpoint, and their procedures required them to keep track of every car or truck passing through by recording the license plate. Even if it wasn't likely there would be trouble, Stoner didn't want the trip recorded. Besides, going on foot would make it easier to survey the area and avoid an ambush or double-cross. Five kilometers wasn't much to walk.

"We drive over many times," said Deniz.

"Walking's good for you. You should be able to do five kilometers inside an hour without a pack."

The soldier frowned. Neither man seemed in particularly good shape. Stoner assumed their training regime was far from the best.

They walked in silence for about fifteen minutes, the pace far slower than what would have been required to do five kilometers in an hour. Even so, Stoner had to stop every so often to let them catch up.

"Why are we going?" asked Deniz after they had crossed the border.

"We're meeting someone."

"A rebel or a smuggler?"

Stoner shrugged. Deniz chortled.

"A smuggler," guessed Deniz.

"Why do you care?"

"Curious. The captain told us an American needs a guide. That's all we know," answered the Romanian.

"That's more than you should."

Kyiv said something. His tone was angry, and Stoner looked at Deniz for an explanation.

"The smugglers are the men with the money," said Deniz. "They throw cash around. My friend thinks it's disgusting."

"And you?"

"I just want what they want."

Deniz gave him a leering smile. Stoner had been planning on giving the men a "tip" after they returned; now he wasn't so sure he'd bother.

"Tell me about the rebels," he said. "They don't scare you?"

"Criminals." Deniz spit. "Clowns. From the cities."

He added something Romanian that Stoner didn't understand.

"They are dogs," explained Deniz. "With no brains. They make an attack, then run before we get there. Cowards. There are not many."

"How many is not many?"

Deniz shrugged. "A thousand. Two, maybe."

The official government estimates Stoner had seen ranged from five to ten thousand, but the Bucharest CIA station chief guessed the number was far lower, most likely under a thousand if not under five hundred. What the rebels lacked in numbers, the Romanian army seemed to make up for in incompetence, though in fairness it was far harder to deal with a small band of insurgents bent on destruction than a regular army seeking to occupy territory.

"You speak English pretty well," Stoner told Deniz, changing the subject.

"In Bucharest, all learn it. TV. It is the people here who don't need it." He gestured toward Kyiv. "If you live all of your life in the hills, there is not a need."

"I see."

"On the computer—Internet—everything good is English."

"Probably," said Stoner."

"Someday, I go to New York."

"Why New York?"

"My cousin lives there. Very big opportunity. We will do business, back and forth. There are many things I could get in New York and sell here. Stop!"

He put his hand across Stoner's chest. Stoner tensed, worrying for a moment that he might have sized the men up wrong.

"There is a second Moldovan border post there," said Deniz, pointing to a fence about a hundred meters away. "A backup. If you don't want to be seen, we must go this way through the field."

"Lead the way."

Dreamland
22 January 1998
0935

FOLDED, THE MAN/EXTERNAL SYNTHETIC SHELL KINETIC Integrated Tool—better known as MESSKIT—looked like a nineteenth century furnace bellows with robot arms.

Unfolded, it looked like the remains of a prehistoric, man-sized bat.

"And you think this thing is going to make me fly?" asked Zen, looking at it doubtfully.

"It won't take you cross-country," said scientist Annie Klondike, picking it up from the table in the Dreamland weapons lab where she'd laid it out. "But it will get you safely from the plane to the ground. Think of it as a very sophisticated parachute."

Zen took the MESSKIT from her. It was lighter than he'd thought it would be, barely ten pounds. The arms were made of a carbon-boron compound, similar to the material used in the Dreamland Whiplash armored vests. The wings were made of fiber, but the material felt like nothing he'd ever touched—almost like liquid steel.

Six very small, microturbine engines were arrayed above and below the wing. Though no bigger than a juice glass, together the engines could provide enough thrust to lift a man roughly five hundred feet in the air. In the MESSKIT, their actual intention was to increase the distance an endangered pilot could fly after bailing out, and to augment his ability to steer himself as he descended.

"You sure this thing will hold me?"

"Prototype holds me," said Danny.

"Yeah, but you're a tough guy," joked Zen. "You fall on your head, the ground gets hurt."

"It's much stronger than nylon, Zen, and you've already trusted your life to that," said Annie.

A white-haired grandmother whose midwestern drawl softened her sometimes sardonic remarks, Annie ran the ground weapons lab at Dreamland. MESSKIT was a "one-off"—a special adaptation of one of the lab's exoskeleton projects. Exoskeletons were like robotic attachments to a soldier's arms and legs, giving him or her the strength to lift or carry very heavy items. The MESSKIT's progenitor was intended to help paratroopers leaving aircraft at high altitude, allowing them to essentially fly to a target miles away.

Annie and some of the other techies had adapted the design after hearing about the problems Zen had had on his last mission using a standard parachute. If MESSKIT was successful, others would eventually be able to use it to bail out of high-flying aircraft no matter what altitude they were at or what the condition of the airplane. MESSKIT would allow an airman to travel for miles before having to land. If Zen had had it over India, he might have been able to fly far enough to reach an American ship and safety when his plane was destroyed. And because it was powered, the MESSKIT would also have allowed him to bail out safely from the Megafortress after the ejection seat had already been used.

"Try it on," urged Danny, who'd served as the lab's guinea pig and done some of the testing the day before. "You put it on like a coat."

"What's with these arms? What am I, an octopus?"

"You put your hands in them. Your fingers slide right in. See?"

"Yours, maybe."

"Starship can test it just as well," said Danny.

"I got it," snapped Zen. "You don't need to use reverse psychology on me."

"Now would I do that?"

Zen gave the MESSKIT to Danny to hold and wheeled himself to the side of the table. He maneuvered himself out of the wheelchair and onto a backless bench, then held up his arms.

"I am rea-dy for the operation, Doc-tor," he said in a mock Frankenstein monster voice.

Once on, the gear felt like a cross between football pads and a jacket with a thin backpack attached. His hands fit into metallic gloves. Bar grips extended from the side "bones" of the suit; they looked a bit like silver motorcycle throttles, with buttons on the end.

"Comfortable?" Danny asked.

"Different," said Zen.

Annie was looking over the device, adjusting how it sat on his back. Zen moved back and forth, twisting his torso.

"Here, press the left-hand button once and pick this up," said Danny, bringing over a twenty pound dumbbell.

Zen could curl considerably more than twenty pounds with either hand, but he was amazed at how light the weight felt.

Danny laughed. "Don't throw it. You should see it on boost. You can pick up a car."

He was exaggerating—but only slightly. The MESSKIT used small motors and an internal pulley system to help leverage the wearer's strength.

The more Zen fidgeted with the suit, the more he saw its possibilities. Annie and the rest of the development team might think of it as a way to help him get out of a stricken Megafortress. But Zen realized that a similar device with artificial legs instead of wings could help him walk.

Like a robot, maybe, but still . . .

"So when do we test it?" he asked.

"It looks like a good fit," said Annie, tugging down the back as if she were a seamstress. "We can set up the gym and go at it tomorrow."

"Why not today?" he asked. "Why not right now?"

The others exchanged a glance, then Danny started to laugh.

"Told you," he said.

"Come on," said Zen. "Let's get to work."

Dreamland
0935

THE NEWS ABOUT LIEUTENANT COLONEL BASTIAN'S MEDAL of Honor hit General Samson like the proverbial ton of bricks. The more he thought about it, the more he felt as if a house had fallen on him.

Though his first reaction was to swell with pride.

Samson had seen combat himself in his younger days, and he knew how tenuous courage on the battlefield could be. He also knew that for a soldier to get the Medal of Honor while managing somehow to survive was extremely difficult—luck really, since by definition the sort of selfless act the honor required meant death in nearly every case.

Samson had been on the mission that the President was citing Dog for.

Well, in the theater at least—and even a vague association provided at least a modicum of reflected glory. A commander takes responsibility for all that his people do, good and bad; personal feelings toward Dog aside, the colonel's success reflected well on his commanding officer, no matter how far removed from the actual event.

But as Samson thought about the implications, his mood quickly sank. For one thing, he wanted Bastian gone from Dreamland, and the medal would make it harder to push him out. It might even be impossible if Bastian decided to fight.

Worse, what if Bastian put his hand up to become wing commander? How could he refuse a Medal of Honor winner?

Bastian wasn't a full colonel, and wing commanders almost always were. But hell, the guy had held a post a major general now commanded, *and* had won a Medal of Honor in combat—only a supercilious prig would deny him the post if he truly wanted it.

How did Bastian get the medal, anyway? Samson wondered. Wasn't the process normally begun with a recommendation from his commander? In what drunken stupor had he written that recommendation?

Samson's phone rang. He picked it up, and heard his chief civilian secretary, Chartelle Bedell, tell him in her singsong voice that Admiral Balboa was on the line.

"Samson," he said, pushing the button to make the connection.

"General. Congratulations are in order," said Balboa. "Your command is to receive an armful of medals for the action off India and Pakistan."

"We heard rumors, Admiral. I was wondering, though. Usually—"

"The order comes directly from the commander in chief," continued Balboa. "And as a matter of fact, he wants to meet with the personnel in question personally. As soon as possible."

"Sir, I—"

"You have a problem with that, Samson?"

"Of course not, Admiral. We'd be honored to have the President here. The security arrangements—"

"Make them. There'll be no press. The President happens to be on his way to the coast for some conference or other and wants to personally shake Colonel Bastian's hand. It's his idea, Terrill. He loves to press the flesh. You know that. I'm surprised he's not more concerned about germs."

"Well yes, sir, of course."

"You can expect him first thing in the morning. Throw out the red carpet."

"Tomorrow?" asked Samson, but it was too late—Balboa had already hung up the phone.

Northeastern Romania
2031

THE ATTACK ON THE GAS LINE WAS MADE SEVERAL HOURS earlier than General Locusta expected, and his first reaction was genuine surprise and anger. Locusta was in the small house used as his army corps headquarters, having a late tea with some of his officers, when word came. The news was delivered by a Romanian army private who'd driven from the attack site five miles away; the man had sprinted from the parking area and barely caught his breath before delivering the news.

"Where?" demanded Locusta. "Have they been repulsed?"

"They are gone, General," said the man. "We have had two casualties."

"Two?"

The private nodded.

"How many guerrillas were killed?"

The man shook his head. While that was probably a good thing—had the men been killed, it was very possible their true identities would have been discovered—Locusta was furious. The Russian had promised him none of his men would be harmed. The general had practically gift wrapped the pipeline for him, and he responded by killing two of his men.

That was what came from working with the Russians.

"General?" the private prodded him.

"The pipeline is broken?" asked Locusta.

"There was an explosion. Our captain was ordering the line closed as I left."

"I will inspect it myself." Locusta turned to one of his captains. "Send a message to the capital immediately. Tell them to shut the entire line down. As a precaution. Add that the situation is under control for the moment and I am on my way personally to inspect the site."

**Dreamland
1034**

"COMFORTABLE, ZEN?" ASKED ANNIE, TALKING TO HIM through the radio in the test helmet.

"I'm just about to nod off," he replied.

"I'll bet. We're counting down from five. Here we go. Five, four . . . three . . . "

Zen flexed his arms. He was sitting on a high-tech aluminum step ladder—it looked more elaborate than the models you'd find in a hardware store, but that was essentially what it was. Besides the MESSKIT, he was wearing a harness attached by very thick rubber straps and nylon safety ties to anchors on the "gym" ceiling, walls, and floor. Thick cushion pads covered nearly every surface in the hangarlike room; the only spaces left unprotected were small clear plastic panels for video cameras and various sensors, and the window of the control room, protected by a webbed net that hung across the open space.

Zen took a last look across at the control room—it was at about eye level, ten feet off the ground—and thought to himself that it would be just his luck to be propelled into the netting like a school of mackerel if the experiment went haywire.

"Ladder away," said Annie, continuing the countdown.

The metal seat that had been supporting him slid back. Zen didn't move—his weight was now entirely supported by the safety harnesses, which were quickly checked by the computer monitoring the test.

"Green light on ladder retrieve," said one of the techies in the control room.

Behind him, the ladder's "closet" opened and the ladder began folding itself away. But Zen was too focused on the MESSKIT to pay any attention. The device seemed to barely weigh anything.

"We're ready any time you are, Zen," said Annie.

"Opening the umbrella," he said, extending his arms before pushing the button on the control in his left hand.

The wings unfolded with a loud thump, the sort of sound a book makes falling off a desk. Zen was tugged upward gently. He pushed his arms back, spreading his wings—the skeleton and its small bat wings moved easily.

Zen worked left and right, just getting used to the feel, while Annie and the others in the control room monitored the device. After a few minutes, the tension on the suspension straps holding him off the floor was eased. Zen settled about six inches, then another six; he flapped his arms playfully, not trying to fly, but testing the safety equipment to make sure everything was still in order.

"All right, the safety harnesses are working," said Annie. "We're going to give you some breeze. If you're ready."

"Let 'er rip," Zen said, and leaned forward, anticipating the next set of tests as some of the giant cushions on the wall slid upward to reveal small louvered slots.

"Two knots, then five," said Annie.

Even at two knots, the effect of the wind on the wings was immediately noticeable. Zen pushed his hands down as the wind hit his face; the microsensors in the MESSKIT's skeleton transferred his movements to the small motors that controlled the wing's surface, and suddenly he was pitched downward. The guide ropes and harness kept him from going too far forward, but the shift was still an abrupt enough to catch him by surprise.

"Wow," he said. "I'm flying."

"Not yet, Major," said Annie dryly. "Maybe by the end of the day."

Dreamland
1345

THE ENGINEERS WHO TRANSFORMED THE B-1B INTO Dreamland B-1B/L Testbed 2 had left the throttle controls to the left of each pilot's position, but otherwise there was little similarity between the aircraft's cockpit and that of its "stock" brethren. A sleek glass panel replaced the 1970s-era gauges, dials, and switches that had once faced the pilots. The panel layout was infinitely configurable and could be changed by voice command to different presets adapted to a specific mission or pilot. The electronics behind the panel were even more radically different. Dreamland B-1B/L Testbed 2 could simultaneously track 64,237 targets and potential threats anywhere in the world. The number was related to the processing capacity of the chips used in the radar and computers but was still somewhat arbitrary. Ray Rubeo's answer, when Dog asked him why that number was chosen, had been, "They had to stop somewhere."

Gathering the data through the Dreamland communication network—and eventually through standard military systems— the plane's advanced flight computer could not only keep tabs on any potential enemy in the world, but provide the pilot with a comprehensive plan to evade detection or destroy the enemy before it knew the plane was targeting it.

Or the computer could do it all itself, without human help—or interference. Which was what today's test was all about.

"Ready any time you are, Colonel," said the copilot, Marty "Sleek Top" Siechert. A civilian contractor, a former Marine Corps aviator who'd returned to flying fast jets after working as a mid-level manager at McDonnell Douglas, Siechert's nickname came from his bald head, which looked like a polished cue ball.

Not that Dog could see it. Both men were dressed in full flight gear, with g suits and brain buckets, even though the cabin was fully pressurized.

"Let's get this pony into the air," said Dog, putting his hand on the throttle.

Dreamland B-1B/L Testbed 2—more commonly and affectionately known as *Boomer*—rocked as her engines revved to life. The four General Electric F101-GE-102 engines she was born with had been replaced by new GE models that were about seventy percent more powerful and conserved much more fuel. Unlike the Megafortress, the B-1B was a supersonic aircraft to begin with, and thanks to its uprated engines, had pushed out over Mach 2.4 in level flight—probably a record for a B-1B, though no one actually kept track. More impressive— at least if you were paying the gas bill—*Boomer* could fly to New York and back at just over the speed of sound with a full payload without needing to be refueled.

"I have 520 degrees centigrade on engines three and four," said Sleek Top.

"Roger that," replied Dog. The temperature readings were an indication of how well the engines were working. "Five twenty. I have 520 one and two."

They ran through the rest of the plane's vitals, making sure the plane was ready to takeoff. With all systems in the green, Dog got a clearance from the tower and moved down the ramp to the runway.

"Burners," he told Sleek Top as he put the hammer down.

The afterburners flashed to life. The plane took a small step forward, then a second; the third was a massive leap. The speed bar at the right of Dog's screen vaulted to 100 knots; a half breath later it hit 150.

"We're go," said Dog as the airplane passed 160 knots, committing them to takeoff.

The plane's nose came up. *Boomer* had used less than 3,000 feet of runway to become airborne.

Like the stock models, the B-1B/L's takeoff attitude was limited to prevent her long tail from scraping, and the eight-degree angle made for a gentle start to the flight. Gentle but not slow—she left the ground at roughly 175 knots, and within a heartbeat or two was pumping over 300.

Dog checked the wing's extension, noting that the computer had set them at 25 degrees, the standard angle used for routine climb-outs. Like all B-1s, *Boomer*'s wings were adjustable, swinging out to increase lift or maneuverability and tucking back near the body for speed and cruising efficiency. But unlike the original model, where the pilots pulled long levers to manually set the angle, *Boomer*'s wings were set automatically by the flight computer even when under manual control. The pilot could override using voice commands, but the computer had first crack at the settings.

The wings' geometry capitalized on improvements made possible by the use of the carbon composite material instead of metal. The goal of these improvements had been to reduce weight and improve performance, but as a side benefit the new wings also made the plane less visible on radar.

They were also, of course, considerably more expensive to manufacture than the originals, a problem the engineers were finding difficult to solve.

It was also a problem that Dog no longer had to worry about or even consider. All he had to do was finish his climb-out to 35,000 feet and get into a nice, easy orbit around Range 14a.

"Way marker," said his copilot. "We're looking good, Colonel. Ready for diagnostics."

"Let 'em rip," said Dog.

The B-1Bs flown by the Strategic Air Command were crewed by four men: pilot, copilot, and two weapons systems operators. *Boomer* had places for only the pilot and copilot, with the weapons handled by the copilot, with help from the threat and targeting computer. The arrangement was under review. Experience with the Megafortress had shown that under combat conditions, dedicated weapons handlers could be beneficial. There was plenty of room for them on the flight deck, but the additional cost in terms of money and manpower might not be justifiable.

Indeed, Dog wasn't entirely sure the presence of the pilot and copilot could be justified. The Unmanned Bomber project, though still far from an operational stage, demonstrated that a potent attack aircraft could be flown effectively anywhere in the world from a bunker back in the States. The next generation of Flighthawks—the robot fighters that worked with the Megafortress as scouts, escorts, and attack craft—would contain equipment allowing them to do just that, though they still needed to be air-launched.

The next generation of Flighthawks was very much on Dog's mind as the diagnostics were completed, because the afternoon's test session was a mock dogfight between a pair of Flighthawks and the B-1. The aim of the test was to put *Boomer*'s airborne laser through its paces, but of course from the pilots' point of view, the real goal was to wax the other guy's fanny.

Dog wondered if the computers thought like that.

"*Boomer*, this is Flighthawk control. *Hawk One* and *Two* are zero-five minutes from the range. What's your status?"

"Rarin' for a fight, Starship," responded Dog. "Are you ready, Lieutenant?"

"Ready to kick your butt," said Starship.

Dog laughed. Starship—Lieutenant Kirk "Starship" Andrews—seemed to have broken out of his shell a bit thanks to his temporary assignment with the Navy. In fact, he'd done so well there that the commander he'd been assigned to, Captain Harold "Storm" Gale, had tried to keep him. Considering Storm's general attitude that Air Force personnel rated lower than crustaceans on the evolutionary scale, his attachment to Starship was high praise.

"I didn't mean any disrespect, sir," added Starship hastily.

"No offense taken," said Dog. "Let's see how you do, Lieutenant."

Dog and Sleek Top turned over control to the computer and settled back to watch how *Boomer* did. The tests began quietly, with the two Flighthawks making a head-on approach at *Boomer*'s altitude. The B-1's radar tracked them easily, identified them as threats, presented itself with several options for striking them, then worked out the solution most likely to succeed.

The computer system used to guide the Flighthawks—known as C^3—already did this, but the task was considerably more difficult for a laser-armed ship. While in sci fi flicks lasers regularly blasted across vast tracts of space to incinerate vessels moving just under the speed of light, back on earth lasers had not yet developed such abilities—and might not ever. The laser weapon aboard the B-1 fired a focused beam of high-energy light that could burn a hole through most materials known to man, assuming it stayed focused on its target long enough.

And that was the rub. Both *Boomer* and its airborne targets were moving at high rates of speed, and while there *might* be some circumstances under which the B-1B/L could count on getting off a sustained blast of ten or more seconds, dogfight conditions meant that blast length would often be measured in microseconds.

For the laser to be a practical air-to-air weapon, its enemy's specific vulnerabilities had to be targeted and then hit repeatedly. That was where the computer did most of its number crunching. It was able to assess the typical vulnerabilities of its opponent, prepare what was called a "shooting plan" to exploit those vulnerabilities, and then direct the laser fire as both aircraft moved at the speed of sound. And it could change that plan as the battle progressed.

For example, if the B-1 was tangling with a MiG-27, the computer would realize that the motors the MiG used to adjust its wings in flight were extremely heat sensitive. Depending on the orientation of the two planes, the computer would target those motors, crippling his enemy. As the MiG slowed down to cope with the malfunction, the computer would then fire a series of blasts on the port wing fuel tank, aiming not to punch holes in the wing, but to create a series of hot spots in the tank, which would disrupt the fuel flow, slowing the plane down. For the coup de grace, the computer would ignite the antiair missile on the plane's right wing spar, in effect having the MiG destroy itself.

This would all happen in a span of seconds. While the human controlling the weapon could approve each individual targeting stage, ideally he would simply tell the computer to take down the bandit, and he could then worry about something else.

A MiG-27, though relatively fast, was an easy target, since it was big, conventionally flown, and most important of all, well-known. The Flighthawks, by contrast, were much more difficult opponents. Not only had they been designed to minimize some of the traditional vulnerabilities, but their lack of a pilot removed one of the laser weapon's neatest tricks—blasting the cockpit with heat and making the enemy pilot extremely uncomfortable.

"We're ready," declared Sleek Top as they finished the first battery of tests. "Clear computer to engage in encounter."

"You feeling lucky yet?" Dog asked Starship.

"Don't need luck, Colonel."

"Let's do it."

The Flighthawks swung east, preparing to make their attack. The Flighthawks—officially, U/MF-2/c, which stood for "unmanned fighter 2, block c"—were about the size of a Honda Civic and were equipped with cannons. They were slower than the B-1B/L but more maneuverable.

On the first test, everyone followed a prepared script. The two Flighthawks passed a quarter mile to the east. The computer picked them up without trouble, adjusted *Boomer*'s speed to get longer shots on their engines, and then recorded a simulated hit.

"Two birds down," reported the copilot.

"Hear that, Starship?" said Dog. "You're walking home."

"I always walk home, Colonel. Ready for test two?"

"Have at it."

The Flighthawks banked behind *Boomer* and began to close, aiming to shoot their cannons at the fat radar dome at the plane's tail. This was a more realistic attack scenario, and was further complicated by Starship's handling of the planes—he kept them jinking and jiving as they approached, making it difficult for *Boomer* to lock its laser. The fact that there were two targets made things even more complicated, as the computer had trouble deciding which of the two aircraft provided a better target and kept reordering its plan of attack.

"I'm tempted to do an override," said Sleek Top, who could have solved the computer's problem by designating one of the planes as primary target.

"Let's see how it does."

The words were barely out of Dog's mouth when the laser fired, recording a simulated hit on *Hawk One*. It took nearly thirty seconds, but it recorded a fatal strike on *Hawk Two* as well.

Then the fun began.

"On to test three, Colonel," said Starship.

"Anytime you're ready, son."

The Flighthawks dove toward the earth. Test three was entirely free-form—Starship could do anything he wanted, short of actually hitting *Boomer*, of course.

"Tracking," reported Sleek Top.

Dog could see the two aircraft in the radar display; they were about a mile off his wing. They changed course and headed toward Glass Mountain, at the very edge of the test range.

"Why's he running away?" Sleek Top asked.

"He's not. He's going to get lost in the ground clutter. He wants us to follow, hoping we'll be impatient."

"Are we going to?"

Had Dog been flying the plane, he would have: It was more macho to beat the other guy in the battle he chose. But the B-1's computer made the right decision, at least by the playbook it had been taught—don't get suckered into the battlefield the other guy wants you to fight. It maintained its position.

"He's off the scope."

"Mmmmm," said Dog.

Boomer increased the distance between itself and its adversary. Starship would be able to track his position and would soon realize that he wasn't biting.

What would he do then?

"Here we come," said Sleek Top. He read out the course and

heading of the first contact, *Hawk One,* which was streaking toward them from the west.

"So where's the other?" asked Dog.

"Still in the bushes somewhere."

The computer abruptly threw the plane on its left wing, plunging toward the earth—just as the second Flighthawk appeared on his screen to the east, almost directly below him.

"How the hell did he do that?"

Dog resisted the temptation to grab the stick as the big airplane pulled to its left. Too late, *Boomer*'s computer realized it had been suckered—*Hawk One,* flying directly behind *Hawk Two* so its radar profile couldn't been seen, had snuck onto the laser ship's tail.

"Bang, bang, you're dead," said Starship as the computer recorded a fatal blast from the Flighthawk.

"Damn," said Sleek Top.

Actually, the computer had done very well. Only Starship's skill—and the young man's battle-tested cleverness—had defeated it.

"What do you say, best two out of three?" said Sleek Top.

"I have a better idea," said Starship. "Go to manual controls."

That was a gauntlet Dog couldn't resist—though he checked to make sure they still had plenty of time on the range.

"You're on," said the colonel, circling around as the Flight-hawks disappeared again.

"I'd like to see him try that again."

"He won't," said Dog.

Actually, Starship tried something similar. Having learned that he could fool most radars by flying the Flighthawks extremely close together, he lined *Hawk One* and *Two* back up and then came at *Boomer* from above. Dog, thinking Starship was trying to sneak one of the UM/Fs in at him off the deck—another favorite trick to avoid radar—realized what was going on a fraction of a second too late. As *Hawk Two* came onto his tail, he pushed his nose down, outaccelerating it before Starship could fire.

Then he banked hard, flattened the plane out, and turned the tables on the Flighthawk as it started to recover.

"Fire," he told Sleek Top calmly.

"Can't get a lock—he's jinking and jiving too much."

"Stay on him," said Dog. His own hard g maneuvers were part of the problem, as his free-form flight path made it hard for the laser to get a bead on its enemy. Dog put his nose straight down, trying to turn into *Hawk Two* and give Sleek Top a better shot. But before he could get his nose where he wanted it, the other Flighthawk started its own attack run, and Dog found himself between both of them. He pushed hard left, felt the aircraft starting to invert—then got an idea and pushed her hard in the other direction. *Boomer* wobbled slightly, fierce vortexes of wind buffeting her wings, but it held together and followed his commands. Dog jammed his hand on the throttle, accelerating and turning his belly toward *Hawk One*.

"Locked!" said Sleek Top.

"Fire!" answered Dog. "Don't wait for me."

The computer gurgled something in his ear—a warning saying that flight parameters were being exceeded. Dog ignored the warning, rolling *Boomer*'s wings perpendicular to the earth. For two or three seconds his belly was exposed to *Hawk Two*.

Two or three seconds was all the computer needed.

"Splash *Hawk Two*," shouted Sleek Top, his normally placid voice alive with the excitement of the contest.

"Where's *Hawk One*?"

"Still tracking. Our left. Parallel."

The laser had not been able to stay with Starship's evasive maneuvers, and now Dog found himself in trouble. The B-1 had used up much of its flight energy, and to prevent itself from becoming merely a falling brick, had to spread its wings. That was a dead giveaway to Starship that his adversary was weak, and the fighter jock did what all fighter jocks are bred from birth to do—he went for the jugular. He pulled *Hawk One* onto Dog's tail, aiming the cannon in his nose at the big tail filling his gun screen. Dog ducked and rolled, trying to trade altitude for enough speed to get away.

While he managed to keep *Hawk One* from getting a clean shot, he couldn't set one up for himself either. The Flight-hawk kept closing, angling to stay above the laser's angle of fire. Finally, there was only one way to extricate himself: Dog reached for the throttle and lit his afterburners, out-accelerating the smaller craft.

Or running away, depending on your point of view.

"I'd say that's a draw," said Starship over the radio.

"Draw my foot," answered Sleek Top "We got one of yours."

"I kept you from accomplishing your mission," said Star-ship smugly.

"Our mission was to shoot you down."

Dog laughed. He was going to miss these guys when he left Dreamland.

Northwestern Moldova, near the Romanian border 2345

STONER PUT HIS HEAD DOWN AND HELD HIS BREATH AS THE truck passed a few yards away. There was a hole in its muf-fler, and the engine coughed every fifth or sixth revolution, chuttering and sending smoke out from the side. The noise drowned out the sound from the second truck, and was so loud Stoner wasn't sure there were any others behind them. He waited a few seconds, then raised his head cautiously. There were no other vehicles.

"Smugglers," said Deniz, the Romanian army corporal.

"What are they taking across?"

"This way, nothing. They can come back from our country with anything. Food. Medicine." He paused and smiled. "Women."

Stoner couldn't tell whether that was meant to be a joke.

"How do they pass the checkpoints?"

"Twenty euros. I tell you, we could have driven."

Stoner got up from behind the stone wall. Deniz whistled to Kyiv, the other Romanian soldier, who came out from behind the tree where he'd been hiding. The three men resumed their walk along the dirt road. It had taken nearly three hours for them to cover five kilometers, largely because Stoner was being overly cautious, stopping even when he heard aircraft passing overhead. Being late, he knew, was not as big a problem as not arriving at all.

The long trek had given him more time to judge his guides. As soldiers, they were more competent than he'd thought at first, good at spotting possible ambush points and wary enough to plot escape routes before moving through fields they weren't already thoroughly familiar with. He trusted them, to a point, but knew that if they were captured by guerrillas, it wouldn't take much for them to give him away.

Deniz said something to Kyiv and the two men laughed. Stoner frowned, figuring it was probably some sort of joke at his expense.

"We are almost there. We stay on the road unless we hear something," said Deniz, gesturing. "Two hundred meters."

Stoner grunted, thinking, watching. He had a pair of night vision goggles in his pack, but there was more than enough light from the moon to see along the road and well into the nearby fields. The steeple of a church stood up on the right, marking a hamlet. Two houses sat near a bend in the road ahead. Otherwise, the way was clear.

Even though there were no lights shining in the windows or smoke coming from the chimneys, Stoner had Kyiv lead them into a field opposite the two houses so they could pass without taking any risks. The field connected with another; a narrow farm lane ran north along the end of this second field, separated from a neighboring farm by a thick row of trees.

Stoner put his night vision glasses on as he walked, growing warier as the shadows in the distance multiplied. But nothing was stirring.

The detours cost them another fifteen minutes. Finally, he saw the ramshackle barn where he was supposed to meet his contact. It stood above the field on the opposite side of the road, its foundation built into the crest of the hill.

He scanned the building carefully, then shook his head.

"So?" asked Deniz.

"I don't see anyone."

"No?"

Stoner turned his view to the nearby field. It too was empty.

The Romanians watched him silently. They weren't joking any more, nor whispering. For most of the night they'd left their rifles slung lazily over their shoulders. Now they held the guns with both hands, ready.

Stoner began moving to his right, keeping the barn in sight. The dirt and dead grass had heaved up with the evening frost, and it crunched as he walked. After he'd gone about thirty yards, he stopped and once again carefully examined the barn and nearby fields.

No one.

Slowly, he made his way up the hill, the two Romanian soldiers trailing behind him. About five yards from the barn, Stoner saw a shadow on the ground in front of it. He froze, steadied his gun.

"Champagne," he said loudly.

The shadow moved, revealing itself as a man with a rifle.

"Champagne," repeated Stoner. He curled his finger against the AK's trigger, slowly starting to apply pressure.

"Parlez-vous français?" said the shadow. Do you speak French?

That wasn't the agreed upon phrase, and the accent was so un-French that Stoner had trouble understanding it.

"Champagne," he said again.

"Vin blanc," answered the shadow. White wine.

That was the right answer, but the delay made Stoner wary. Had it been just a human mistake, or a giveaway that something was wrong?

"I don't speak French," said Stoner in very slow Russian.

"Anglaise?" responded the man.

Was it a trick? The contact would surely expect him to speak English.

It had to be a trick.

"You don't speak Russian?" said Stoner.

The man again asked, in English, whether they could use that language.

Stoner exhaled very slowly. He had to either trust the man—or shoot him. Doing nothing was more dangerous than either.

"I can speak English," said Stoner.

The shadow took two steps forward. Though his voice was deep, he stood barely five feet tall, and had a scraggly beard that matched his thin body. He stopped abruptly, spotting the other two men a few yards behind Stoner.

"They're with me." Stoner gestured with his left hand. His right continued to hold the gun, his trigger finger still ready to plunge.

"This way, we go," said the man, pointing to his right.

Stoner let him start. His stomach had tightened into a boulder. They walked eastward across the field, down to a narrow creek, then began following it northward. His escorts fell farther and farther behind; twice Stoner stopped for them.

"You trust him?" asked Deniz when he caught up the second time.

Of course not, thought Stoner. But he only shrugged.

After about a half hour of walking, the stream entered a

culvert under a paved road. The stream was wider here; and while it remained shallow, it was more than four feet across.

"Wait," said the man who had met them. He put up his hand.

Stoner nodded. The man went up the embankment to the road.

"I don't trust him," said Deniz when he caught up again. "What is he doing?"

Stoner shook his head. The elaborate precautions made sense—if a man was going to betray his comrades, he would have to expect himself to be betrayed.

"Maybe we should find some cover," suggested Deniz. "To cover you."

"Do it," said Stoner.

He'd already spotted two good places on the right bank of the stream, both protected on three sides by large rocks or thick tree trunks. The Romanians saw them as well and moved toward them.

"Where are your friends?" the man asked when he returned. He looked around nervously.

"They're here. Where is the man I'm to meet?"

"A house. Two hundred meters." He pointed to the right.

"Lead the way."

The man shook his head. "I'm not to go. Not your friends either. Only you."

Stoner looked into his face. He had the face of a man who'd been beaten many times. He seemed more nervous than before.

"All right," said Stoner. "Deniz, I'm going up the road. Stay with our friend."

"Yes," Deniz called out from his hiding spot.

Stoner began walking. The setup seemed too elaborate for an ambush, but he couldn't be sure. He tried focusing on his mission, tried pushing away the fear.

He dropped to his knee when he reached the road, scanning carefully. The house stood very close to the road, just beyond a curve ahead. It was tiny, barely bigger than a garden shed would be back in the States. The woods thickened to his right, but there was a hill on his left and a clear field. He went up the hill, approaching the house from the back.

The cold ate through his coat. He opened his mouth, flexing his jaw muscles. The tendons were so stiff they popped, as if he were cracking his knuckles.

A dim light shone through the two rear windows of the house. Stoner walked up slowly, moving his head back and forth as he tried to see through them.

Nothing.

He was almost to the back of the building when he heard a footstep on the gravel in front of him. Dropping to his knee, he waited.

"Who's there?" said a woman's voice.

"Champagne," said Stoner, trying not to sound surprised that his contact was a woman.

"Vin blanc."

"Take two steps forward."

The woman did so, walking out from the path near the corner of the building. She had a submachine gun in her hands.

"Why are you armed?" Stoner asked. His own rifle was aimed at her chest.

"It is not safe here to be without a weapon. Not for me. Nor you," she added.

"Put your gun down," he told her.

"And you yours."

"All right." But he waited until she had placed hers on the ground and stood again.

"You are the American?" asked the woman. Her English was accented, but not as heavily as Deniz's or the man who had led him here.

"Yes."

"You're more than an hour late."

"It took a while to get across the border."

The woman's answer was cut short by a scream and the sound of gunfire back near the road.

Stoner scooped up his rifle. The woman already had her gun and was running. He aimed at her, then realized she was running toward the field.

"This way!" she yelled. "Come on!"

Before he could answer, a hail of bullets rang out from the woods, whizzing over his head.

Dreamland
1434

ANNIE KLONDIKE BENT OVER ZEN AS HE FINISHED HIS checks. He was sitting on a folding metal stool, which had been pressed into service as a kind of launching pad so he didn't have to start by sitting on the ground. His wheelchair was unsuitable, and the standard suits were always used standing up.

"Now listen, Jeff, no kidding," said Annie in her sternest voice. "We've done a lot today. If you're the least bit tired—"

"I'm fine," he told her, pulling on his Whiplash smart helmet, equipped with full communications gear and a video display in the visor. He reached back near his ear to the small set of controls embedded in the base, activating the integral communications set.

Danny Freah was standing a few feet away, wearing his own exoskeleton test unit. The Exo3 was fully integrated with a battle suit; its bulletproof armor was twice as thick as the regular units used by the Whiplash troopers, enough to prevent penetration by 35mm cannon rounds, though a round that large was likely to cause considerable internal damage since the suit wasn't big enough to diffuse all of the shell's kinetic energy. Some facets of the suit had not yet been implemented; it would eventually be equipped with LED technology to make its wearer invisible in the sky. But otherwise it was very similar to MESSKIT. Danny had taken it for over a dozen flights already.

"Helmet on," he said.

Zen could tell he was getting a kick out of playing pilot. "Hat's on," he replied.

"Go to ten percent," Danny told him.

Zen looked down at his right hand, then pushed the button he was holding with his thumb. The microjet engines in the back of the MESSKIT powered to life. They were relatively quiet, making a sound similar to a vacuum cleaner at about fifty paces.

Zen slowly twisted the control, moving the engines carefully to five percent total output, then to seven, and finally to ten. As the number 10 flashed in his visor indicator, his wings tugged him gently off the stool.

"You're looking good," said Danny. "Let's go to seventeen."

As he said that, Danny pushed his throttle and held out his arms. He rose abruptly. Zen tried the same thing, but without Danny's experience, he started moving backward rather than up. He pitched both hands down, as he'd practiced in the gym. This brought him forward abruptly, but he was able to back off into a hover without too much difficulty.

The designers had worked hard to make the unit and its controls as intuitive as possible, but the feel of flying still took some getting used to. Zen slipped his power up two degrees and found that pushing his head forward helped him stay in place as he rose.

His helmet's visor projected an altitude reading in the lower right corner, showing that he was 4.112 meters off the ground.

"How's it feel?" asked Danny.

"Like I'm on an amusement park ride."

Danny laughed.

The sensation also reminded Zen of the zero gravity exercises he'd gone through early in the Flighthawk program, when the developers were trying to get a handle on how difficult it would be for someone in a plane maneuvering at high speed to control the Flighthawks. He didn't feel exactly weightless, but the exoskeleton relieved what would have felt like a great deal of pressure on his shoulder muscles. He thought about this as he and Danny rose to fifty and then a hundred feet, practicing emergency procedures. Zen had a small, BASE-style parachute on his chest, just in case; the chute was designed to deploy quickly at low altitude if anything went wrong.

Confident that he could handle an emergency, he started putting the MESSKIT through its paces, accelerating across the marked course, then gliding into a circular holding pattern.

"You're getting pretty good with this," said Danny as they completed a figure eight. "You sure you haven't flown before?"

"Ha ha."

"How are your arms?"

"They don't feel bad at all."

"The thing to worry about are cramps," said Danny. "When we were first starting the experiments, Boston cramped up so badly we had to replace him in the program."

Danny was referring to Sergeant Ben "Boston" Rockland, another member of the Whiplash special operations team. Zen got plenty of upper body exercise, and felt confident that whatever strain the MESSKIT was putting on his shoulders was minimal. His real concern was what he would do if he had a bad itch.

"All right, let's do a few sprints, then see how you are at landing," said Danny.

"Last one to the flag is a rotten egg," said Zen.

He leaned forward and twisted his throttle. The wind rushed passed his helmet—but so did Danny. Zen pitched his body down farther, then felt as if he was going to fall into a loop. He backed off, slowing immediately. He looked up, and saw that Danny had already crossed the finish line.

But Danny didn't have any time to gloat.

"Captain, we have an automated alarm going off on Access Road 2," said one of the security lieutenants, breaking into the frequency. "I have an aerial en route and hope to have a visual in thirty seconds. Maybe a car accident."

An "aerial" was a small UAV, or unmanned aerial vehicle, used for surveillance.

"Go ahead and scramble the response team," said Danny.

"They're out at Test Area 12, covering a broken leg."

"Call Team 2," said Danny.

"They're standing by for the fighter exercises. They're already covering three ranges."

Because of the distances involved, not to mention the danger inherent in the base's experiments, Dreamland procedures called for a pararescue team to stand by near the range whenever live exercises were being held. The recent deployment and a ramp-up in Dreamland's research activities had stretched the available personnel, and there were times, such as now, when only two full teams were immediately available.

"Stand by," said Danny.

"Problem?" asked Zen, who'd heard the conversation over the radio.

"Maybe a car accident out on Road 2."

"Why don't we go check it out?" said Zen.

"Just what I was thinking. But—"

Zen knew what that *but* meant. He didn't bother to answer, pushing his head forward and sliding the power reading to 15.

"Major, I really believe you should wait until you're fully checked out," said Annie from the ground.

"Thank you," Zen replied, as if she'd paid him a compliment.

There were four access roads to Dreamland, but only Road 1, which ran from Nellis Air Base, was paved. The others were hard-packed dirt, or as his wife Breanna liked to say, hard-packed holes with rocks scattered in between. But even though it was about as smooth as a battered washboard, Road 2 was often used by base personnel as a shortcut. Not only was it a few miles shorter than Road 1, but its horrible conditions restricted traffic to those in the know, lowering the wait at the security post where it entered the main road. That could save as much as an hour during the busy times of the day.

Road 2 came off the southeastern end of the base perimeter and ran due south for a mile and half before jogging lazily east. Zen started in that direction, then increased his speed as Danny shot ahead.

"Security Command, this is Freah. I'm on my way via Exo3. Major Stockard is with me. Alert the perimeter system—I don't feel like being shot down."

Friend or foe identifiers in the gear would prevent the Razor antiair lasers from firing on them, but any uncleared flight over the perimeter fence would elicit an armed response from the robot Ospreys, which would force them to land or simply shoot them down.

The surveillance UAV zipped ahead from the west, dropping into a hover over the road three miles from the perimeter fence. The small aircraft—its rotors would have tucked neatly under the deck of a household lawn mower—was flying about twenty feet below Zen. It looked like a hive supported by a swarm of bees.

"Car is upside down," reported the security supervisor.

"Roger that, I see it on my screen," said Danny. "I have a smart helmet. Have the aerial back off."

"McDaniels and Percival are en route from the guard station. They're ten minutes away."

"Roger that."

A FORD EXPLORER LAY ON ITS ROOF ABOUT THIRTY YARDS from the side of the road.

"Zen, check your fuel," said Danny as they approached.

"It says ten minutes, plus reserve."

"When you hit reserve, go back."

Of course Danny wanted him to go back, Zen thought—he couldn't be useful on the ground. "We'll take it as it comes," he replied. "I'm going to check the area and see if anyone was thrown out."

"Roger that. Good idea."

DANNY WAITED FOR THE UAV TO BACK OFF BEFORE TUCKing his arms into a U-shape and sliding his power down. He settled onto the dusty road about fifteen feet from the spot where the Explorer had gone off. The truck had traveled a good distance before stopping, and the marks in the desert made it look as if it had flipped at least twice.

Dropping to his knees, Danny unlatched the wing assembly to keep it from getting damaged. Then he hopped up and ran to the wreck.

The front of the SUV was crushed. He could smell gasoline as he got down on his hands and knees to peer inside. The driver was suspended in her seat, wedged against the roof and wheel, a deflated air bag wrapped against her face and torso. He couldn't tell if she was alive.

The driver's side window had been smashed, but the metal was so mangled it was impossible to reach her. He went around to the other side. There was a bit more room there, but it was still a very tight squeeze just to get his hand in.

Danny smelled gasoline as he groped with his fingers, trying to reach her neck and get a pulse. He snaked his arm back out, then took off his helmet, hoping he could reach in farther without it. As he started to slide his hand inside the car, he saw the woman move her head.

Alive!

He grabbed his helmet.

"Security Command, this is Danny Freah. I have a very injured woman trapped in the vehicle. Send Team 2 immediately. Order the test ranges closed down."

"Roger that, Captain."

"Give them a sitrep. Tell them to be ready with the Jaws of Life."

"Yeah, roger, roger, Cap. I'm on it."

The Jaws of Life was a special tool that worked like a hydraulic pry bar; in this case, it would be used to pull the squashed door away from the cab so the victim could be extricated. Danny took a step back from the wreck, frustrated that he had to wait, even for a few minutes, and worried that the gasoline he smelled meant there was a dangerous leak.

He could use the exoskeleton to help him open the door. He crouched back down by the vehicle, trying to find a grip.

"What's going on?" asked Zen, who was hovering above.

"Trying to get her out," grunted Danny.

His first try failed: The mechanical hand gripped the metal of the crushed door so hard that it gave way as he pulled it off.

"Need help?" asked Zen.

"If I can figure out how to open the car without breaking it into pieces, I'll be fine."

"Maybe I can hold one side," suggested Zen.

"I'm afraid that we'll end up jostling it too much," said Danny. "Hang on."

He pushed his left arm against the crushed top of the car, and then positioned his right against the door. The smell of gasoline was strong now. The car radio was on—he worried that the slightest spark would set off a fire or explosion.

"One, two, three, push," he told himself aloud, flexing his arms. The sensors in the exoskeleton felt the resistance and ramped up the power to help. It was designed to supply a slow, gradual push—moving too fast under certain circumstances could pull his body apart.

The crushed car parts moved about eight inches apart before the carbon skeleton began to pull through the metal.

"I think I'm almost there," Danny said, repositioning himself.

* * *

WHAT ZEN THOUGHT WAS A BODY TURNED OUT TO BE A TIRE, which had left the SUV as it careened off the road. He turned to the north and did a slow circuit around the wreck, making sure he hadn't missed anything. The bumper and part of the fender had fallen off, and there was glass back near the road. A man's jacket had tumbled out as well.

Hearing Danny talking to himself, Zen came back over the SUV.

"Danny, you need help down there?"

"Think I got it," grunted the captain.

Zen saw the security team's black SUV driving up the road in the distance, dust spewing behind it. A moment later he heard the heavy beat of an Osprey approaching. He backed off, watching cautiously as the aircraft landed on the other side of the road and disgorged its team of pararescuers. He'd never felt quite so intimidated by the aircraft's huge rotors before.

BY THE TIME THE PJS REACHED THE TRUCK, DANNY FREAH had pried the vehicle open enough to lean in and examine the driver. She was breathing, with an irregular though strong pulse.

While the PJs went to work stabilizing her body and removing her from the wreck, Danny walked to the back, trying to find the source of the gas leak. The roof of the car, now the closest part to the ground, was soaked with fuel.

He bent down, then heard a groan from inside.

He thought at first that it was the driver. But a second groan sounded more male than female. He stepped back, took out his small LED flashlight, then went back and peered inside. He saw a leg on the back floor.

His stomach turned.

Then the leg moved and Danny jumped back. It took a second before he realized the leg hadn't been amputated by the crash and that he was seeing someone trapped under the car, his leg sticking out through a rear sunroof.

"We got another back there!" shouted one of the PJs.

"Yeah, I see him!" yelled Danny. "He's trapped underneath. His leg is moving."

Trying to clear his head from the gas fumes, Danny walked a few feet from the wreck. Watching the PJs set the driver out on a stretcher, he recognized her as one of the women who worked in the all-ranks cafeteria. He knew she had at least one kid at home.

"She's pretty bad, Captain," said the sergeant in charge of the rescue team, Gabe McManus. "We need to get her over to the med center stat."

"Go," said Danny.

"What about the other guy?"

"We're going to have to lift the truck to get him. That'll take a while," said Danny. "We'll need to hook the Osprey up. Let's save her first."

McManus nodded. The others had already immobilized the driver and lifted her gently onto a stretcher.

It would take at least ten minutes for another Osprey to arrive, and a good ten if not more after that to secure a chain and lift the truck safely. Twenty minutes wasn't a lifetime—but it might be to the trapped man.

"Maybe we can jack the truck up with the gear in the Jimmy," McManus said.

"Ground's kind of loose," said Danny. "I'd worry about it slipping."

"Yeah," agreed the sergeant. "But it might do that when we hook up the Osprey, too. Car looks like it's kind of perched on some of the rocks there—slip a bit too much and he's in even worse trouble."

McManus dropped flat and peered underneath. "All we really need is about two feet," he said. "We might be able to get a couple of guys on the side, lift gently—"

"I have a better idea," said Danny.

* * *

Zen saw Danny standing next to the truck. He looked like he was trying to gauge whether he could push it over. "What are you doing?" he asked.

"We have another guy underneath. I think I can use the arm to lift it."

"You want help?"

"I don't know. Maybe."

Zen came over slowly, his power at seven percent. "We can lift it straight up," he said.

"We're going to have to pull up together," Danny told him.

"Just tell me what to do."

Danny explained how to use the skeleton's fingers as clamps, then coached him on slowly revving the power. They'd have to work as a team, each clamped on one side of the vehicle.

The ease Zen had felt just a few moments before had evaporated. He jerked to the side, unable to get into the right position. His legs dangled uselessly below him. He forced his arms closer together, slipping back on the power. Sweat poured out of his body. It wasn't the heat, though it was plenty hot. His nerves were melting.

It's easy, he told himself. *We're going to save this guy, save his legs. Don't let him end up like me.*

His own feet were touching the ground. He edged closer to the SUV, trying to find a good place to grip.

"Got it, Zen?" asked Danny.

"Hold on. I'm still new at this."

Zen hooked his arm under the chassis and found a solid hold for the body. The finger extensions on his arm seemed too weak to hold, and left part of his hand bare—he could feel the grease and grime from the chassis.

I hope I don't crush my hand, he thought.

"Ready," he told Danny.

"Ramp up slow, real slow. On three. One, two . . . "

Zen twisted his wrist as gently as he could, as saw the

power move up to 15, then 20. The exoskeleton was straining, but the SUV didn't budge. He twisted his hand on the throttle, fighting the urge to rev it as high as it could go.

"That's it, keep steady!" said Danny. "*Steady!* Just hold it there. You OK, Zen?"

"Yeah, I got it."

The PJs scrambled to brace the man and get him out. Zen could hear them talking through their radios. They were near the victim—he was conscious, answering them, complaining about his legs.

At least he felt pain. That was a good sign.

A tone sounded in Zen's helmet. He was into his fuel reserves.

"Danny—"

"Yeah, I heard it. Let's move it, you guys. McManus—you have two minutes."

It took nearly three. Zen and Danny held the truck up together for another minute and a half; by then it was too late for Zen to fly back. Instead, he fluttered down to the ground, exhausted, landing ignobly in a heap. Before he could say anything, two of the PJs grabbed him and hustled him into the back of the security Jimmy.

"Way to go, Major," said the man on his left as they slid him into the back.

"Yeah," said Zen. "Thanks."

The truck started to move. The passenger they'd pulled out was laying on a flat board across the folded-down seat, his ride cushioned by four large balloonlike buffers. The truck moved slowly down the road, avoiding the worst of the potholes.

"Major, am I going to be all right?" the passenger asked.

Zen glanced at the parajumper behind him. He was a certified combat medic, the closest thing to a doctor you could find on the front line, and more experienced in dealing with trauma injuries than many emergency room specialists. The

PJ made a slight movement with his eyes, signaling to Zen that he didn't know.

"Yeah, kid," he said. "I think you're going to be cool. I'm pretty sure you are."

"Wow, that's a relief," said the young man.

Zen recognized him as a maintainer, one of the engine specialists responsible for the EB-52 power plants. A crew dog who'd worked on his aircraft many times, he was sure.

"I wasn't wearing my seat belt," he continued. "We went off the road—there was a jackrabbit or something weird. I bounced up and down and the top flew open. The next thing I knew, it felt like the whole world was sitting on top of me and I was being pulled apart. I am gonna make it, right?"

"You'll make it," said Zen.

"My legs are kinda numb."

Zen glanced up at the PJ, who now had a pained expression on his face. He'd been prodding the young man's foot with a pin, apparently getting no response.

"They gave you painkillers," Zen said. "I'm surprised your head's not numb."

"As long as I can walk."

"Just close your eyes and relax now," said the pararescue man, resting his hand gently on the young man's chest. "We'll be at the med center in a few minutes."

**Northwestern Moldova,
near the Romanian border
23 January 1998
0134**

STONER FOUGHT THE URGE TO RETURN FIRE, KNOWING IT would just give away their position. He lay still, gun ready, waiting as the bullets continued to fly. The cold seeped up through his jacket into his chest; his pants grew damp with the chill.

Finally, the rounds slacked off. Stoner waited, expecting more.

The ground smelled vaguely like cow dung. He funneled his breath through his mouth as slowly and silently as he could, worried that his breath might be visible in the moonlight. Finally, when he hadn't heard any gunfire for a few minutes, he began edging to his right. He raised his head ever so slightly as he moved, trying to see down the hill.

There were two shadows near the road, but by the time he spotted them they were moving toward the cottage and he didn't have a clear shot. He waited until their shapes had been consumed by the cottage then got up and ran down the hill toward the road.

Meanwhile, two flashlights played across the windows of the cottage. There was more gunfire, this time muted—a nervous gunman firing inside the house, Stoner thought.

The woman he'd come to meet was somewhere near the ridge, but he wasn't sure where; he'd lost track of her when the shooting began. He felt certain she wasn't in the building, but if she was, there was nothing he was going to do about it now. Stoner edged further down the hill, aiming to find a place where he could easily ambush the gunmen when they came out of the house. As he did, however, he sighted a shadow moving along the road. He held his breath as it disappeared in a clump of trees.

His night goggles were in his ruck, but he was afraid getting them out would be too noisy: the trees were less than twenty years away.

If there was just one man by the road, he would take him out as quietly as possible, then turn his attention back to the cottage. If there were more . . .

If there were more he would have to fight his way through them.

No. It would be better to simply leave.

He could do that, but it would mean giving up on his contact.

Wasn't she just a lure, though? Wasn't this an elaborate ambush?

Stoner transferred the AK-47 to his left hand, then reached with his right to his knife scabbard. Killing a man with a knife was not an easy thing, a fact Stoner knew from unfortunate experience: Some years back, he'd failed in his one attempt to do so, sneaking up on a border guard between China and Vietnam. He'd put his knife on the man's throat, but his pull hadn't been deep enough; the man had managed to shout an alarm before a second slash of the knife, this one deeper, killed him.

Stoner worked his fingers around the knife's hilt, trying to get the right grip. Only when he was sure he had it did he start working his way in the man's direction.

The cigarette tip flared again, then faded. Twenty yards was a long way to cross without being seen or heard. Stealth and speed had to be balanced against each other. Stoner bent his legs slightly as he walked, lowering his center of gravity, hoping that the way the trees threw their shadows would keep him hidden. He got to within ten yards, then five, then three—less than the distance across a kitchen.

He slid the rifle down. All or nothing now.

Two yards. The man lowered his head, cupping his hands, lighting another cigarette.

He was alone.

Stoner sprang forward. He grabbed the man's mouth with his left hand, while his right rode up and across the man's neck—too high, but with enough force that the mistake could be overcome. He pushed his knee into the man's back and rammed the knife hard across flesh that suddenly felt like jelly. Stoner pulled back with his left hand and plunged the knife across his neck a second time, the blade slicing through the windpipe and into the vertebrae. Stoner pushed his knee hard against the man's back, felt no resistance; he stabbed one more time, then let his victim fall away.

Even as the man hit the ground, Stoner reset his attention on the cottage, where the flashlights were now joined in an X near the outside wall. He scooped up his rifle, then grabbed the dead man's gun and began moving along the road.

If they saw a shadow coming from this direction, they would think it was their companion. The illusion would last only until they shouted to him. He wouldn't be able to answer, except with his gun.

Stoner stopped and undid the top of his backpack. Taking out the night glasses he put them on. The building, the night, turned silvery green. The men had gone back inside.

Stoner began trotting along the road, trotting then running, adrenaline pumping. He turned up a dirt path that led to the cottage's side door.

One of the flashlight beams appeared at the edge of the building. Stoner went down to his knee, ready to fire.

The beam grew longer, moving slowly back and forth across the yard.

Where was the other man? Or men?—He'd seen two flashlights, but there could always be another.

Stoner turned his head in the other direction quickly, making sure no one was coming across the front of the barn.

The man with the flashlight rounded the corner. He was dressed in fatigues, but Stoner couldn't see any insignia or other sign that he was a soldier instead of a guerrilla. He had an AK-47 in his right hand, the flashlight in his left.

As the flashlight swung in his direction, Stoner fired a three-shot burst that took the man square in the chest.

The man's companion began shouting from behind the cottage as his friend fell. Stoner raced up the hill, then threw himself down as bullets began flying from the corner of the building. Stoner fired back, then got up into a crouch to swing to his right and flank the gunman.

A fresh burst of bullets cut him off. Stoner hunkered against the ground.

The man took a step out from the corner of the building. Stoner began to fire as the man reared back and threw something, then disappeared behind the building again.

A grenade.

Stoner saw it arc to his right. He threw himself leftwards, tumbling against the hillside, hoping to get as much distance between himself and the explosion as he could.

**Dreamland
1534**

WITH THE DOGFIGHT SESSION OVER, DOG AND SLEEK TOP put *Boomer* through a series of calmer tests, pushing her around the test range as special instruments recorded stresses on her frame and that of the laser housing. While the session was important—in many ways far more critical than the computer's dogfight was—it was nonetheless routine, and Dog found himself struggling to stay focused on his job. He thought of his lover, Jennifer, who'd had her knee operated on back East and would be staying with her sister in New Jersey for at least another two weeks. He thought of his daughter, Breanna, who'd been injured as well. He'd seen her the night before at the hospital. She looked so small in the bed, so fragile. For some reason, it made him think of all the time with her he'd missed when she was growing up.

Leaving, the hospital, he'd run into her mother. Surprisingly, he didn't feel any animosity toward her, and—uncharacteristically, he thought—she didn't display any toward him. Like the specialists who'd seen her, Bree's mother was baffled by the "coma-like unconsciousness" she'd suffered after landing, but she was very optimistic about her prognosis.

Dog's thoughts circled with the plane, until finally it was time to land. He let Sleek Top take the stick, and the copilot brought the plane in for a textbook perfect landing, taxiing right into the B-1 development hangar without help from either of the waiting tractors. Downstairs, Dog and Sleek Top prepared separate briefs on the mission, answering questions for the engineers who'd been monitoring the tests.

No matter how routine the pilots considered it, the geeks always had something to talk about, and it was going on 1900—7:00 P.M. in civilian time—before they were satisfied enough to let Sleek Top and Dog go.

"Probably wore them out with our duhs," said Sleek Top as they rode up the elevator from the offices in the bunker directly below the underground hangar area. He mimicked one of the engineers' voices: " 'What did it feel like at thirty percent power as you came through the turn?' A lot like forty percent power, only slower, son."

Dog laughed.

"They haven't been up in the plane," Sleek Top continued, his tone more serious. "You should have some jump seats rigged and take them aloft."

"That's a good idea, Sleek. But it's not my call."

"It's your base."

"Not anymore."

"It'll always be your base," said the test pilot as the door opened.

General Samson was standing across the vestibule. It wasn't clear that he'd heard Sleek Top's comment—the elevator doors were sealed pretty tight—but Dog had a feeling he had.

So did Sleek Top. He grimaced, gave the general a wave, then strode quickly away.

"Colonel Bastian, a word," said Samson.

Dog followed him to the far end of the hangar ramp. Gently sloped, the wide expanse of concrete led to a large blast-proof hangar where the B-1s were kept. It looked like the ramp of a very wide parking garage.

Before he'd come to Dreamland, Dog had been in awe of generals—if not the men (and women), then at least the office. Part of his attitude had to do with his respect for the Air Force and tradition, but a larger part stemmed from his good fortune he'd had of working for some extremely good men, especially during the Gulf War.

Dreamland had changed that. While he wouldn't call himself cynical, he had a much more balanced view now. He realized that the process of rising to the upper ranks had a lot to do with politics—often a lot more than anything else.

Colonel Bastian had met some inept generals in his day. Samson wasn't one of them. He was capable, though bullheaded and cocky—characteristics critical to a combat pilot, but not particularly winsome in a commander, especially at a place like Dreamland.

"B-1 is a hell of a plane," said Samson, walking in the direction of *Boomer*. "I commanded a squadron of them for SAC."

"Yes, sir. I think you mentioned that."

"I don't know about some of these mods, though." Samson stopped short and put his hands on his hips. "Airborne lasers?"

"Going to be a hell of a weapon."

"Once it's perfected—that's the rub, isn't it? You know how many iron bombs one laser would buy once it's in production, Tecumseh?"

Dog actually did know, or at least could have worked it out, but the question was clearly rhetorical; Samson didn't wait for an answer.

"And having a computer fly it—that was your test today, wasn't it?"

"Yes, sir."

"I don't like it." Samson practically spat on the ground as he spoke. "What we need are more planes and pilots. Not more gadgets. Widgets, I call them. They can't replace pilots."

Dog couldn't help but smile.

"Problem, Colonel?"

"You sound a little like my old boss, General Magnus,"

said Dog. "When he started. By the time he moved on, he was pushing for all the high tech he could get."

"I know Magnus. Good man. Had to retire. Couldn't play the Washington system."

That was probably correct, thought Dog—a point in Magnus's favor.

"But Magnus isn't here. I am," added Samson. He turned his gaze back to the aircraft. It seemed to Dog that he wished he were back in the pilot's seat again—back as a captain flying missions.

Who didn't? That was the best part of your career. Though it was a rare officer who understood it at the time.

"This airborne tactical laser can change a lot of things," said Dog. "It'll revolutionize ground support. With some more work, the laser will do a credible job as an antifighter weapon as well. And to do all that, it needs a pretty powerful computer to help the pilots fly and target the enemy."

"I don't need a sales pitch," said Samson sharply. Then he added, in a tone somewhat less gruff, "We've gotten off to a bad start, you and I. But I don't think it's necessary that we be enemies. In a way—in a lot of ways—you remind me of myself when I was your age. Ambitious. Tough. A bit strong willed—but that's a plus."

Dog didn't say anything. He knew that Samson was trying to be magnanimous, though to his ears the general sounded like an ass.

"Congratulations on your Medal of Honor," added Samson. "You've heard about it, I understand. You earned it, Bastian. You and the others did a hell of a job. Hell of a job. Made us all proud."

"Thank you, sir."

"The President is coming. Or at least, I hope he can squeeze us into his schedule. I have made a request—I'm sure I'm going to get him here. Maybe as early as tomorrow."

"Tomorrow?"

Samson waved his hand as if brushing away a fly. "I still

have to do some paperwork—you know, there are going to be hoops with this medal thing, so don't expect too much too quickly. But I thought it would be nice for the President to show his respect, and admiration."

"You don't have to go to any trouble. I don't— Medals don't really mean that much."

";The hell they don't!" Samson practically shouted. "They mean everything. They remind us how we should carry ourselves. What we're about!"

Out of the corner of his eye, Dog saw that some of the aircraft maintainers were staring at them.

"So, Colonel, as I said, we've gotten off to a bad start, you and I," added Samson.

"Yes, sir."

"Is there anything you'd like to say?"

Dog wasn't exactly sure what Samson was expecting, though he was clearly expecting something.

"*Lieutenant* colonel?" said Samson. "Is there anything you'd like to say?"

In normal conversation, a lieutenant colonel was always called a colonel; as far as Dog was concerned, the only reason Samson would use his full rank now was to put him in his place—which was made all the more obvious by the emphasis he put on the word.

"Not really, General."

"Excuse me?" said Samson, raising his voice.

"I have nothing I want to say. Thank you. I didn't expect a medal, but I'm very honored. Flattered. Humbled, really."

"You don't want to apologize for anything?"

"For getting off on the wrong foot?"

"For not showing respect."

Dog stiffened. He didn't have anything to apologize for. Samson was just playing bs games, throwing his weight around.

"If the general feels an apology is warranted for anything," he said coldly, "then I apologize."

Samson scowled, pressing his lips together and furling his eyebrows out.

"I was wondering when you'd want me to run down the main projects and personnel with you," said Dog, trying to move the conversation past its sticking point. "I can make myself available at any—"

"That won't be necessary," snapped Samson, stalking back up the ramp toward the exit.

GENERAL SAMSON WAS SO ANGRY, HIS LOWER LIP STARTED to tremble by the time he reached his waiting SUV. He'd offered the idiot the chance to apologize, to start fresh, and the jerk had all but spat in his face.

A cowboy, out of control, with no respect for anyone. From first to last.

Last, as far as Samson was concerned. Medal of Honor or not, the sooner Bastian was gone from Dreamland, the better.

Northwestern Moldova,
near the Romania border
23 January 1998
0155

MARK STONER HAD HEARD SEVERAL EXPLOSIONS IN HIS life, but none quite like this.

The grenade the gunman had thrown blew up with the sound a pumpkin makes when it hits the pavement. Part of the explosive packed beneath the hard metal shell failed to explode, whether because of manufacturing defects or poor storage during the fifty-some years since. But more than enough explosive did ignite to shred the metal canister and send splinters hurtling through the air in every direction, red hot metal spat from a dragon's mouth.

Stoner caught a small piece in his right side. There was no pain at first, just a light flick as if someone had tapped him there with a pen or a ruler. And then it began to burn. This was a fire on the inside of his skin, a flame that stayed in place rather than spreading, and was all the more intense because of it. His body twisted away from the pain. He couldn't breathe for a second. He lost his grip on his rifle.

The man who'd thrown the grenade came down the hill toward him, his flashlight waving over the ground.

Stoner reached for his gun but couldn't find it. He grabbed to the left, reached farther, found the barrel and began pulling it over. The flashlight's beam moved closer to him. He slid his hand along the rifle, trying to reach the trigger, but it was too late—the guerrilla's light hit him.

An assault rifle barked—a long, sustained burst, a thick run of death.

But the bullets didn't hit Stoner. They hadn't been aimed at him. They struck the man with the flashlight, cutting a dotted line across his back. The holes the bullets made were so close together, he was nearly severed in two.

A minute later the woman he'd come to meet stood over him, AK-47 in hand.

"You are the man who answered the message," she said.

"Yes."

"Where did they hit you?"

He rolled over and showed her.

She knelt down. "It's shrapnel only. It has to be taken out. The wound can be cauterized."

"Yeah." He unsheathed his knife. "Do it."

"It will hurt very much."

"No shit."

She frowned. "There is blood all over this knife."

"I killed one of them near the road."

"Well then, let us get someplace where I can clean it and start a fire."

"No one's going to be looking for them?" Stoner asked as she helped him up.

"They may. It will be best to do this quickly."

* * *

HER NAME WAS SORINA VIORICA. SHE WAS ROMANIAN. SHE called herself a freedom fighter. Stoner tried not to scoff.

A good idea, considering she had his knife in her hands and was poking out the grenade shard as she spoke.

"This government has done very little for the people, the poor people," she insisted, slipping the tip of the knife into his side as they sat on the floor of the house. She'd started a small fire nearby, and smoke curled in his nose. "The people are left to fend like animals as the fat get fatter. Hold still. You must hold still."

The tip of knife blade struck something underneath the metal, and a sharp pain ran through his abdomen, all the way to his fingers and toes. He felt faint.

"Out," she said, turning to the fire. "Now for the part that will hurt."

Stoner pulled his T-shirt up into his mouth and bit down, waiting as Sorina Viorica heated the knife in the fire. It was an old method of dealing with a wound—cauterizing it, basically burning the flesh so it would no longer bleed or spread an infection.

Effective, but extremely painful.

Stoner dug his fingers into his face as the pain wracked his body. His heart pumped fiercely; his head felt as if it would explode. His whole body writhed in agony. He swam in it, awash in pain.

"Are you still with me?" she asked.

"Oh yeah." The words were a relief. He pushed up.

"I have to wrap it."

"Yeah, yeah."

She stood up and took off the heavy coat she was wearing, removed a thick shirt and then stripped off a T-shirt. She had another beneath it, but he could see the outline of her breasts, loose against her body.

"This is just to keep dirt away from it," she said as she wrapped it around his torso. "There shouldn't be further problems. But you'll have to have it seen to."

"Yeah."

Stoner took a long, deep breath, trying to pull his thoughts back to the present, trying to push his mind past the pain.

"We should go," he told her. "This isn't safe."

Sorina looked up suddenly, as if she'd heard something outside. "Yes," she told him.

"I brought two men with me, as guides over the border. They're with the man who showed me here."

"Let's go, then."

Stoner got up slowly and followed her out of the cottage. He was in a kind of shock, his mind pushed back behind a wall of thick foam. It had separated itself from the rest of his body, from some, though not all, of the pain. He felt like he had a hole in his side; though the grenade fragment was gone, it felt as if it was still there, and on fire. He told himself he was lucky—absurdly lucky—to be hit by only a splinter and not the full force of the grenade, to be nabbed lightly in a part of his body where he could still walk, still use his arms, his head, his eyes. He told himself he was lucky and that he had to use that luck—that if he didn't move, he was a dead man.

Stoner went out into the night like an animal, his only instinct survival. He followed Sorina Viorica down the opposite side of the hill, holding his gun in his left hand, breathing hard. His midsection seemed to be twisting away from the rest of his body, a tourniquet that squeezed itself. The pain lessened ever so slightly and began to feel . . . not good, but familiar in a way that told him he could survive it.

When they reached a small stream, they turned left, back toward the road. After a hundred yards or so, Sorina stopped.

"I'm sorry I'm moving so fast. Catch your breath."

"I'm OK," said Stoner, though he was thankful for the rest.

"They were after me, not you," she said as he leaned back against the tree. "They have been trying to kill me for several days."

"Who are they?"

"Russians. Are you ready?"

"Sure."

Stoner pushed off from the tree. Russians. He wanted to know more, suspected that they were to blame for the deaths, thought for sure they were pulling the strings. But he couldn't ask the questions he needed to ask. He had to walk first, had to get back over the border, away.

"Those were Russians that shot at us?" he managed.

Sorina was too far ahead even to hear. The pain flared. Stoner hooked his thumb into his T-shirt and stuffed the end into his mouth, biting hard. He tried thinking of her breasts, tried thinking of anything but the pain. He knew he was going to make it, but he had to push through, keep his legs moving and his lungs breathing.

Sorina Viorica stopped about fifty feet from the road. Stoner remembered his night goggles, but they were gone, along with his backpack. He rubbed his eyes, staring at the darkness across the road.

"You left them there?" Sorina said, pointing.

"Yeah."

"What was your code?"

"There was none."

Stoner gathered his strength, then whistled. There was no answer. He tried again.

"Maybe I'm not loud enough," he said.

Sorina didn't answer. She started to the right, trotting toward a small copse of trees that bordered the road. Stoner fell steadily behind.

"Wait here," she said when he reached her.

"You can't go alone."

"I'll be fine. You just wait."

He slumped against one of the trees, too weak to protest. Sorina ran to the right, starting to slide around the spot where he'd left his escorts, flanking them carefully.

Was it possible this was all an elaborate setup? But if so, to what end?

Blame the Russians, not the guerrillas.

That made no sense.

So the Russians were involved.

Stoner had a satellite phone with him, a "clean" device that couldn't be traced to the CIA. He took it out and waited as it powered up. A single number was programmed in: a voice mail box that the Agency could check for emergency messages. Otherwise there were no presets to give him away if captured.

He pressed the combination. The phone dialed itself. A voice in Spanish told him no one was home but that he was free to leave a message.

"This is Stoner. I'm over the border. There was an ambush. I'm OK. I'm coming back. The Russians are involved somehow. My contact is a woman. Her name is Sorina Viorica."

The words came out as a series of croaks, like a hoarse frog. He needed water. He pressed the End Transmit button and put the phone away.

A few minutes later a shadow appeared before him. He started to raise his rifle, then realized it was Sorina Viorica.

"They're dead," she said.

"Who?"

"Your men. And Claude. Come."

Stoner followed her across the road. Claude, the guide who had met him at the barn, lay near the water. A bullet had shattered his temple. The two Romanian soldiers had fallen together a few yards away. Their bodies were riddled with bullets. Both of their guns were still loaded; they'd never had a chance to fire.

Or maybe they'd tried to surrender and the bastards killed them anyway.

Sorina was looking through the woods, examining the ground.

"There may be more than the three we killed. It's hard to tell," she said. "They usually work in three-man teams, but two together, so there would be six together."

"Spetsnaz?" said Stoner.

"I don't know the name, just that they're Russian."

"OK."

"If there is another team tracking us, they will be vicious. Where's your car?"

"On the other side of the border."

"That far? You walked?"

"I didn't want to get stopped."

"You couldn't bribe the guards?"

"It didn't seem like a good idea at the time. Especially if I was coming back with you."

She frowned at him.

"You wanted to talk. It's not safe to do it here."

"You think I'm going to let you turn me into the military?"

"I'm not going to turn you into the military."

She was holding her rifle on him.

Stoner kept talking. "If I was going to do something stupid like that, I wouldn't have come back to the house for you," he said. "Your message said that you had mutually beneficial information, and that we could work out a deal. That's why I came."

"With two soldiers."

"I needed guides over the border. I don't speak the language. I left them here—if I was going to ambush you, I would have."

"I don't know."

"Your people killed two Americans," added Stoner. "Maybe you killed them yourself."

"We haven't killed any Americans. Not even spies. It is the Russians. They have taken over the movement."

Stoner stared at the barrel of the AK-47. The moonlight turned the rifle's black metal silver, as if it were a ghost's gun, as if he were imagining everything happening.

"You didn't patch me up to shoot me now," he said.

"How do you know?"

"You've already made your decision to help," Stoner told her. "They're after you. It's all you can do."

"I can do many things."

"You have to trust me."

"I trust no one."

Stoner nodded. "But you take chances."

"Like you?"

"Like me."

She lowered her weapon. "I will go," she told him. "But I will talk only to you, not the army, or to the government. They are all corrupt."

Stoner rose slowly. "What about them?"

She shook her head.

"You want to just leave them on the ground?"

"Of course."

"Even your man?"

"Very possibly he was the one who betrayed me."

Dreamland
22 January 1998
1700

ALL THAT REMAINED WAS TO TEST THE MESSKIT THE WAY it was meant to be used—from an airplane.

A C-130 configured for airborne training and recertification was used as the test plane. Danny joked that they ought to requisition an office chair with casters and use it to launch Zen into the air: They'd push him off the plane's ramp and see what happened.

Zen didn't think the joke was particularly funny, but the actual jump was nearly that informal: He put one arm around Danny and the other around Boston, and the next thing he knew, he was flying through the air, propelled with the others as they leaped off the ramp.

Within seconds he was free. It didn't feel as if he was falling, exactly, nor with the MESSKIT not yet deployed could he say that he was flying. He was skydiving, something he'd never *really* done, even before he lost the use of his legs. His head seemed to be moving through a wind tunnel, with his arms and the rest of his body playing catch-up.

His heart was bringing up the rear, pumping furiously to keep pace.

A small light blinked at the left-hand side of his helmet's visor. Activated by the abrupt change in altitude, the MESSKIT's system monitor was sensing the external conditions. Zen had ten seconds to take control either by voice or manually, or the system would assume that its pilot had been knocked unconscious by the force of the ejection and would then automatically fly him to the ground.

"Zen zero one, MESSKIT override to manual," he said.

The light stopped blinking. In its place, a ghosted grid appeared in front of his eyes. Numbers floated at the left, a compass and GPS coordinate points appeared on the right.

He was at 21,135 feet, and falling.

"Deploy wing kit at two-zero angels," Zen said.

The computer had to calculate whether this was practical before answering. It was another safety measure to prevent the MESSKIT from opening in unsafe conditions. Zen was also wearing a reserve parachute with an automated activation device set to open if his rate of fall exceeded eighty-three feet per second.

DEPLOYMENT IN 17.39 SECONDS flashed on the screen.

Zen pushed forward, doing his best to get into the traditional frog posture used by a skydiver. He spread his arms, as if trying to fly.

Unlike a parachute, the MESSKIT's wing deployment did not jerk him up by the shoulders or torso. Instead of a tug, he felt as if the wind had suddenly filled in below him, holding him up. He reached his hands up, the handlelike holders springing open below his wrists.

And now he was a bird—a very, very high flying one, but a

bird nonetheless. He could steer by shifting his weight, or by pushing hard against the tabs at the ends of each handle.

At first, he didn't think either method did very much. Then he realized that the compass in his visor was moving madly. He eased up, leveling into straight flight.

The view was spectacular, many times more impressive than anything he'd seen from the cockpit of an F-15, let alone the video the Flighthawks fed him. All of Dreamland spread before him; beyond it, all of Nevada, all the way to the Sierra Nevada Mountains. Las Vegas was to his left; to his right . . . well, from this vantage point, it looked like Canada. The sun hung low over the desert, casting a pinkish light against the mountains, a beautiful shade that any painter would trade his soul to recreate.

The normal rate of fall in a modern parachute was in the vicinity of eighteen feet per second. But because it was more glider than parachute, the MESSKIT could descend very slowly—he was currently gliding downward at a rate of just over nine feet per second. Of course, that meant trading descent for linear progress, as Annie had put it—or flying. He soon found that by shifting his weight forward slightly, the pressure from his arms directed the MESSKIT's airfoil to slow his descent even further.

"Hey, Zen, you're headed toward the end of the range," said Danny over the radio. Both he and Boston were using traditional parachute rigs. They'd waited to deploy them until after Zen's wings had expanded and it was clear he was under control. Now they were falling off to his right, well below him.

"I forgot you guys were here," said Zen.

"Don't forget to come down," said Danny. "And somewhere in Nevada, all right? I have some things to do tonight, and I don't want to fish you out of the Pacific."

"Oh, I'll come down," said Zen, starting a turn to stay inside the test area. "I know one thing."

"What's that?"

"I'm going again. And again after that. I can't wait to see a full sunset from up here."

Northeastern Romania
23 January 1998
0550

AMONG THE ITEMS STONER HAD STOCKPILED IN THE TRUNK of his rented Nexia was a medical kit. He pulled out a bottle of hydrocodone and chased five pills with his bottled water. Then, to counteract the effects of the synthetic codeine—the dose was two and half times a full-strength prescription—he took two capsules of Adderall, an amphetamine.

He pulled on a spare shirt and jacket, holding his breath against the pain. It was going to take a while for the codeine to kick in. Even then, all it would do was take the edge off.

"Can you drive?" he asked Sorina Viorica. "I can if I have to, but probably we'd be better if you did."

"I can drive," she said.

"We have to go south. To Bucharest."

She frowned. "I'm not going to your embassy."

"I wasn't going to take you there. I have an apartment. You'll be safe. The GPS unit—"

"I know the way," she said.

Stoner slipped the seat to the rear, adjusting it so he could lean his head back and get a more comfortable. The seat belt sat right over his wound, but he managed to bunch his jacket to the side and relieve most of the pressure on it. The drugs didn't seem to have much of an effect at first, but after twenty minutes or so he realized his mouth was hanging open and his upper body was starting to feel numb. He pushed back up in the seat, wincing at the pain yet grateful that it helped wake him up.

A few minutes later, Sorina braked hard to avoid rear-ending a car stopped around a curve. There was a checkpoint ahead, soldiers checking IDs.

She started to put the car into reverse.

"Don't," said Stoner, putting his hand on the shifter. He fought against the shock of pain. "They already see us."

"I don't have identification."

"I'll deal with it."

"No."

"You're going to have to trust me," he told her.

"This isn't a question of trust."

Stoner reached beneath his belt to the small pouch where he kept his ID and took out his diplomatic passport, along with a folded letter. He considered taking out money as well, but decided against it—better to play the arrogant American with nothing to hide, impatient at the delay.

"You're my interpreter. You work for the embassy."

"My name?"

"Pick something you'll remember. And I can pronounce."

"Jon. It was my father's name."

"That's a last name?"

"Yes. Call me Ms. Jon."

Stoner undid his seat belt and brought his seat back up to horizontal. The line moved slowly. They were three cars from the front.

"You are sure of this?" said Sorina Viorica.

"We have no choice. If you get out, they'll probably start shooting. They'll hunt you down."

She frowned, probably thinking it wouldn't be that hard to get away.

Stoner noticed a bloodstain on his pants as they pulled near the soldiers, but it was too late to do anything. He folded his hands down against it and put an annoyed look on his face as the two soldiers peered into the car.

The sun was just rising, and it was dark inside the vehicle; the man on Stoner's side shone a flashlight around, hitting Stoner's eyes. He had to fight the reflex to cover his eyes with his hands.

The man on the driver's side rapped on the window. When

Sorina Viorica opened it, he told her in Romanian that they must hand over their IDs.

Stoner didn't wait for the translation.

"Here," he told Sorina, giving her the passport with his left hand. "Tell him we're in a hurry. If I'm late, you're going to be fired."

Something flickered in the man's face. Stoner realized he spoke English.

So did Sorina Viorica, though she pretended she didn't.

"You have to be patient," she said to Stoner. "They are just doing their job. Things are different in our country. You cannot be an arrogant American. It is an insult."

"I don't care. If I'm not in Bucharest by seven, the ambassador will have a fit."

"I told you, we're not going to make it."

"Then you'll be finding another way to feed your kid, whether your husband was killed by the guerrillas or not. I didn't hire you for charity."

Sorina Viorica began explaining to the soldier that her boss was an American on official business and due in the capital.

The soldier grabbed his passport and the letter from the defense ministry saying that Stoner was to be given free passage and professional courtesies. The letterhead impressed the soldier, though he tried not to show it.

"You work for a jerk," the soldier told Sorina.

"My boy is only three. I work where I can," she said. "What's going on?"

"The rebels attacked the pipeline last night."

"No!"

"They did some damage. Not much." He flipped through the passport. "And your identity—"

"Get the damn flashlight out of my face," Stoner snarled, rolling down the window and leaning out. "I'll have you busted down to private!" he shouted. "And if you are a private, I'll get you into a latrine!"

"I'm sorry," Sorina told the soldier near her. "These Americans."

She turned to Stoner. "Please. Just relax. Please relax. There's no sense getting angry. He's doing his job. Please. He probably has a family."

"What's his name? Get his goddamn name. I want to have him on report. I'm going to tell the ambassador this is why I was late. Get his name."

Sorina pushed back in the seat, glancing toward heaven and muttering something Romanian.

"Get his *name!*"

"You can go," said the soldier at her window, handing back Stoner's passport. "I'm sorry for you."

"Get his name!" demanded Stoner.

Sorina Viorica stepped on the gas.

Neither of them spoke for a full minute.

"That checkpoint was not normal," she said finally. "There was an attack last night, on the pipeline."

"I see."

"But there couldn't have been."

"Why not?"

"We decided six months ago that we wouldn't. That is not what we want. It must have been the Russians."

"Right."

"It's true," she said sharply. "And besides, I know."

"If your friends tried to kill you, what makes you think they'd tell you what they were doing?"

"My friends didn't try to kill me. It was the Russians. The movement itself—it's dwindled. Those who remain are misfits."

"How do you know they were Russians who attacked us?" asked Stoner.

"Their boots were new. None of our people have new boots. Not even a year ago. And now—the only ones left are misfits."

An interesting point, thought Stoner. A very interesting point.

College Hospital, Nevada
22 January 1998
1950

"I DON'T KNOW WHY I TOLD THE KID THAT. I DON'T KNOW why I said *anything*."

Breanna watched as Zen wheeled himself backward across the room. It had been a long time since she'd seen him so agitated, so angry with himself.

"God, Bree. Why couldn't I keep my mouth shut? What if he *doesn't* walk?"

"I don't think it's going to be that bad, Zen," she told him. "I'm sure the doctors will be able to do something."

Zen shook his head. "I saw the looks on their faces when we brought him into the base. I've seen that look. God, I've seen that look."

"Jeff, you can't get so down on yourself. It's not up to you whether he walks or not. God, if anyone would understand—"

"He's not going to understand."

"I mean, if anyone could understand what he's going through, it would be you. It is you. Jeff?"

But Zen had already rolled out of her room.

Northeastern Romania
23 January 1998
0900

BY 9:00 A.M., GENERAL LOCUSTA HAD PROVIDED BUCHAREST with a full report of the bombing of the gas pipeline. Two rebels had been killed, he claimed—not exactly a lie, since he did have two bodies to present, though Locusta knew that the men had been left by the Russian special forces troops that launched the attack.

He downplayed his own losses, though he had already ordered full military honors for both men killed.

The damage to the pipeline was minimal, Locusta assured Bucharest; it would be repaired within days and there would be minimal disruption of the gas supplies.

Locusta was playing a dangerous game. The attack was part of a payoff for Russian cooperation in the coming coup, cooperation that would include the use of an assassin against the defense minister when the time came. It was also meant to convince the government to send the last units he felt he needed to assure himself victory when he moved against the president.

But it could also backfire and encourage Bucharest to sack him. Even though he'd been warning for weeks that an attack might be imminent, and even though he'd claimed that he didn't have the necessary troops for the growing threat, there was still a possibility that he could be blamed for failing to stop the attack, and be replaced by someone else.

If that happened, all of his preparations would be lost. At the very best, he'd be back where he was two years before: commander of a single division, not the leader of an army corps three times the size. All of the connections he had carefully cultivated among the old-timers—the hard-liners shut out by the new government—would be lost. Those men valued strength, and the scent of weakness and failure would send them running.

So when the phone didn't ring at precisely 9:00 A.M.—the time set for Locusta to speak to the president about the incident—the general began to grow nervous. He fidgeted with his feet, a habit he'd had since he was a boy. Pushing them together under the desk, he began jerking his legs up and down, tapping his soles lightly together. At 9:05 he rose from his desk and walked around the office, trying to remain nonchalant and work off his growing anxiety.

By 9:10, he was worried, wondering if he should place the call himself.

He decided not to. President Voda's office had made the appointment, and made it clear that the president would call him. To short-circuit the process would be a concession, however subtle, to a man he despised.

The phone finally rang at 9:17. Locusta waited until the third ring before answering.

"General Locusta."

"Please hold for the president."

Another three minutes passed before President Voda came on the line.

"Tomma, tell me what is going on," said Voda abruptly.

"The pipeline is secure—for now. We have shot two guerrillas. With more men, I can prevent future problems."

"More men—you always ask for more men "

"Unfortunately, last night proves I am right."

"I see estimates that the guerrillas are faltering."

Locusta sighed. He knew that the guerrillas' movement was in fact growing smaller, partly because of his efforts, but also because the leftists were naturally weaklings. But it did him absolutely no good to admit this.

"Yes, yes, I suppose the events of last night are proof of what the situation is," said Voda finally. "I will get you your men. But—no operations over the border. Not at this time."

Though he had made suggestions in the past, Locusta had no plans to launch any operations now. He would, though, soon. When he was in *full* command.

"Did you hear me, General?"

"If we have a specific target, Mr. President, I think you might reconsider."

"When you have a target, you will review it with me. I will decide."

"Yes, Mr. President. But if we have to stay on defense, the additional men will be critical."

"You'll have them. You'll get whatever you need."

The president continued to speak. He was concerned about the situation. He didn't want news of it to get out; he didn't want Romania to appear weak. Locusta agreed—though he knew that the Russians would already be leaking it.

Then the president surprised him.

"I am considering asking the U.S. to assist us," said Voda.

"The Americans?" said Locusta, caught off guard.

"Politically, it would have been difficult a few weeks ago, but now that they are riding a wave of popularity, it is something that could be managed. You've been asking for more aircraft—they can provide some."

"I don't need the Americans to chase down these bandits."

"Our own air force is useless," said the president coldly.

Locusta couldn't argue with that. He suspected, however, that Voda wanted the Americans involved as much for political reasons as military ones. Voda's grand plan called for Romania to join NATO: another foolish move, borne from weakness, not strength.

"Their aircraft will help you track the guerrillas," said the president. "I will inform you if they agree."

The line went dead. Locusta stared at the phone for a second, then slammed it down angrily. The president was an ass.

The Americans would complicate everything if they came.

**Approaching Dreamland
0550**

PRESIDENT MARTINDALE WATCHED OUT THE WINDOW OF *Air Force One* as the hulking black jet drew parallel to the wings. It was a sleek jet—a B-1, Martindale thought, though he would be the first to admit that he wasn't an expert on aircraft recognition. It had the general shape of a fighter but was much too large to be one—nearly as long, in fact, as the EB-52 Megafortress riding beside it.

He recognized the EB-52 very well, of course. No other aircraft had ever been so closely identified with an administration before. It was ironic, Martindale thought; he certainly considered himself a man of peace—not a dove, exactly, but the last politician who would have chosen a weapon of war as his personal token. Yet he'd called out the military more than anyone since Roosevelt.

And much more effectively, he hoped.

Most of his critics didn't exactly see it that way. He didn't much mind the congressmen in the other party criticizing him. It was their job, after all. But when people in his own party questioned his motives in stopping the war between China, India, and Pakistan—that flabbergasted him.

And of course, they loved to claim he used Dreamland as his own secret air force and army.

Dreamland's reorganization under Major General Samson would stop some of those wagging tongues, integrating the command back into the regular military structure. But Martindale didn't want the baby thrown out with the bathwater, as the old saying went. Dreamland was the future. Samson's real task, as far as he was concerned, was to make the future happen now.

"Are those planes an escort?" asked the Secretary of State, Jeffrey Hartmann. "Or are they checking us out?"

"Probably a little bit of both," laughed Martindale, sitting back in his seat.

"If we can get back to the Romanian issue before we land," said Secretary of Defense Chastain. "It's a very serious situation. Europe is depending on natural gas for winter heating. If that pipeline is destroyed, we'll have chaos."

"No, not chaos," said Hartmann. "The Russians can provide an adequate supply. They have over the past few years."

"At prices that have been skyrocketing," said Chastain. "Prices that will mean a depression, or worse."

"You're exaggerating," said Hartmann.

"The Russians see the pipeline as a threat," said Chastain. "They're dancing in the Kremlin as we speak."

"I don't see them involved in this," said the Secretary of State. "They'll exploit it, yes. That's the Russian way. Take any advantage you can get. But they're not going to back guerrillas."

"Don't be naive," said Chastain. "Of course they are."

"They have enough trouble with the Chechens."

"I think the situation is critical," said Philip Freeman, the National Security Advisor. "Gas prices are just one facet. If the Russians are involved, their real goal may be to split NATO. They certainly want to keep the other Eastern European countries from joining. Look at how they're setting the prices: NATO members pay more. We've seen the pressure with Poland. The Romanian pipeline makes that harder to do."

"You're jumping to conclusions," said Hartmann. "There's no evidence that the Russians are involved. I doubt they are."

There was a knock at the door of the President's private cabin. Martindale nodded, and the Secret Service man who was standing nearby unlatched it. A steward appeared.

"Mr. President, the pilot advises that he is on final approach."

"Very good. Buckle up, gentlemen. We're about to land."

DESPITE THE FACT THAT HE ACTED AS DREAMLAND'S LI- aison, Jed Barclay had been to the base only a handful of times over the past two years. He'd never been there with the President, however, and so was surprised by the pomp and circumstance the secret base managed: Not only had a pair of Megafortresses and EB-52s escorted them in, but a half-dozen black special operations Osprey MV-22s hovered alongside Air Force One as the 747 taxied toward the hangar area. Six GMC Jimmy SUVs raced along on either side of the big jet, flanking it as it approached the small stage set up just beyond the access apron. The entire area was ringed by security vehicles and weapons. Mobile antiaircraft missiles stood shoulder-to-shoulder with Razor antiaircraft lasers. There were antipersonnel weapons as well—large panels of nonlethal, hard plastic balls were strategically placed on the outskirts of the audience area, along with an array of video cameras and other sensors. Given how difficult it was to get to Dreamland, the gear was obviously intended to impress the President and his party.

Not that normal security was neglected. As a precaution, the President's stop at Dreamland was unannounced, and in fact would only be covered by the three pool journalists who were traveling in *Air Force One*. Their access—and even that of most of the White House staffers and cabinet members— would be limited to the immediate runway area where the ceremony was to take place.

The reporters wore expressions of awe as they walked down the rolling stairway from *Air Force One*. It was the first time they'd seen most if not all of the aircraft and weaponry in person.

Nearly all of Dreamland had assembled in the hangar area, with video feeding those with essential jobs elsewhere in the complex. The Whiplash security people, dressed in their black battle gear, ringed the crowd, though there was no need for crowd control in the traditional sense: While thrilled by the visit, the Dreamlanders were hardly the types who might start a riot.

Jed slipped down the steps, nodded at one of the men—the sergeant called Boston, whom he'd met before—then moved along the audience tape, catching up to the President and his party, who were met a few yards from the steps by General Samson. The general's hands moved energetically, visual exclamation marks as he told the President how grateful he and his entire command were for the visit. As he spoke, Samson smiled in the direction of the pool reporters, who'd been ushered to the opposite side of the President by the assistant press liaison. Jed couldn't quite hear what Samson was saying, but knew enough from dealing with him that the word the general would be using most often would be "I."

"Jed!"

Jed heard Breanna above the din of the crowd and the canned Hail to the Chief music being projected from the onstage sound system. It took a few moments to locate her; he was shocked to see her sitting in a wheelchair under a freestanding canopy at the far right of the reception line.

He knew she'd been injured during her ordeal off the Indian coast, but somehow it was impossible to reconcile the image he saw before him. Breanna was athletic and outgoing, a beautiful woman who'd made him jealous of his cousin the first time they met—or would have had he been capable of feeling anything but awe toward his older cousin.

Now she looked gaunt, her face peeling from sunburn, her eyes blackened like a prize fighter's after a title bout.

"The chair is just temporary," she said, rising as he drew near. Her smile was the same, though her lips were blistered. "They're really babying me. I only strained my knee. It's embarrassing."

"Hey, Bree," he said.

He kissed her on the cheek, folding his arms around her for a hug. Then he pulled back abruptly, remembering that he was out in public.

Breanna sat back down.

"Zen is up on the stage, guiding the Flighthawks for the display," she said. "My dad is with him. They're going to let the President take the controls for a spin."

"He'll like that."

Samson had finished his little welcoming speech and was accompanying the President down the line of officers in their direction.

"Look at me, I'm nervous," said Breanna, holding up her hand to show him it was shaking.

"So who is this lovely lady?" President Martindale asked. "Jed, are you going to introduce me?"

"This is, um, see, my sister-in-law, Breanna Stockard," he said.

"Captain Stockard, one of our best pilots," said Samson, a half step behind the President.

"An honor to meet you, Mr. President," said Breanna.

She pulled her arm up to salute. Martindale smiled and put out his hand to shake.

"Captain, it's an honor and a pleasure for me to meet you. You, your husband, your fellow pilots and crew—the world owes you a debt of gratitude. It's beyond words, frankly. I'm the one who's honored."

Martindale, of course, was a consummate politician—no one could become President otherwise. But his words sounded sincere, and Jed believed they were. Martindale was extremely proud of the fact that he had averted nuclear catastrophe on his watch. And he was grateful for the people who had made it happen.

"We have a lot of good people here, Mr. President," said Breanna.

"Some of the best. And you'll be getting more. Right, General?"

"Yes, sir, Mr. President. With your help, of course."

"Now where the hell is Dog?" said the President, turning around and looking. "He's responsible for all this."

A look flashed across Samson's face that made Jed think he was going to have a heart attack, but the general quickly recovered.

"Lieutenant Colonel Bastian is up on the stage with our Flighthawk pilot," said Samson, a little stiffly. "We planned a surprise for you, sir. We thought you might like to take the stick of one of the Flighthawks."

Martindale glanced over at Jed, as if to check if it was OK. Not knowing what else to do, Jed nodded.

"I'd love it, Terrill. Let's do it."

Bucharest, Romania
1550

STONER TOOK SORINA VIORICA BACK TO THE SAFE HOUSE in the student quarter near the university in the center of Bucharest. The apartment was a dreary, postwar railroad flat on the second story of a building whose gray bricks seemed to ooze dirt. But its nondescript look was part of its appeal. Out of the way, it could be easily secured. The door and frame had been replaced with wood-covered steel that looked old, but would stand up against a battering ram. There was only one window, located at the rear of the building. It was blocked by a steel gate that could only be unlocked from the inside.

Sorina kept her arms folded across her chest as Stoner showed her through the place. The furniture was bare. There was a television, but no telephone Internet connection—it would be too easy to track communications.

"This is my prison?" said Sorina when they reached the back room.

"It's not a prison."

"Oh, it's a resort. My mistake."

Stoner laughed. His wound had stopped pounding; he'd been able to back off on the drugs. He sat down in one of the thick upholstered chairs. The fabric covering it was a green and brown plaid, long faded from whatever dull glory it once had.

"And what do you expect me to do here?" asked Sorina, still standing.

"Tell me more about the Russians."

She didn't respond. Stoner thought he knew what was going on inside her head—it was a kind of traitor's regret, trying to pull back from what she'd already decided to do.

He had to reel her in gently.

"We can get something to eat," he suggested.

"I'm not hungry."

"If you dye your hair, you won't be recognized," he told her. "You may not be recognized now."

She bent her lip into a sarcastic smile. Stoner was fairly confident she wouldn't be recognized in Bucharest, but he had limited means of finding out, and so for now would have to trust her judgment. She'd insisted on taking back roads to get here, then doubled back several times to make sure they weren't being followed.

"You want me to go out and get you some food?" he asked. "For later."

Sorina shrugged, then added. "So I am a prisoner?"

"No, you can leave right now if you want. Leave whenever you want."

She frowned.

"Unless you'd rather go to the embassy."

"No. I am not going there at all."

That was a relief, actually: once there, she became a potential problem.

"And what are you doing?" she asked.

"I'll get this looked at." He gestured toward his side. "And I have to talk to some people. I'll be back tomorrow."

"When?"

"Afternoon, maybe. I don't know."

"What if I'm not here?"

"I'll be disappointed."

She laughed. It had an edge to it; if Stoner hadn't been convinced earlier that she was tough, that she was deadly, the laugh would have told him everything he needed to know.

"Well, then I'm leaving," she said abruptly, and turned and walked through the rooms and out the door.

He knew she was testing him, but he wasn't sure what answer she was looking for. He remained in the chair—too tired to move, too beat up. He stayed there for ten minutes, fifteen; he stayed until he decided that if he didn't get up, he'd fall asleep.

Stoner walked warily through the apartment, not sure if

she was hiding somewhere. The door to the landing was open about halfway; he pulled it back slowly and stepped out.

The stairs were empty. He locked the door, then put the key under the ragged mat in front of the apartment.

If she was watching from nearby, she did a good job hiding herself.

"SO THE RUSSIANS ARE DEFINITELY INVOLVED?"

"She claims they were. The guerrillas were wearing new boots, newer clothes. Whether they were Russian or not, I have no idea."

"Is she going to give you more information?"

Stoner shrugged. The station chief, a slightly overweight Company veteran named Russ Fairchild, frowned. Stoner wasn't sure whether to interpret his displeasure as being aimed at him or the woman.

"But the Russians are definitely involved?" repeated Fairchild.

"That's what she claims."

"If you got her to tell you where the main guerrilla camps are, that'd be quite a feather in your cap."

"Yeah," said Stoner, though he was thinking that he didn't need any more feathers in his cap.

"Who are the Russians?"

"From the description, it's Spetsnaz," said Stoner, referring to the special forces group that was run under the Russian Federalnaya Sluzhba Bezopasnosti, or FSB, the successor to the KGB. "She gave me two names on the way down. First names."

"Useless," said Fairchild. "And probably false."

"Yeah."

"Still, this is all good work. Promising. Langley will like it," added Fairchild, referring to CIA headquarters. "When are you seeing her again?"

"Soon." Stoner hadn't told him how the visit had ended; he saw no point in saying she might already be long gone. If she'd run away, it'd be obvious soon enough.

"The Russians would have only killed George and Sandra if they put a priority on the mission," said Fairchild. "If George and Sandra were close to something."

Stoner didn't think that was true at all. From his experience with the FSB, most of the agents would kill for nearly no reason. Like the KGB before it, the Russian spy agency had a reputation as one of the most professional in the world. But they were killers at heart. Fairchild, a decade older than he was, might view the spy game as a gentleman's art, but in Stoner's experience it was a vicious business.

"I'll tell the Romanians what happened to their men," said Fairchild, rising. "Don't sweat it."

"OK."

"Their guns weren't fired at all?"

Stoner shook his head.

"I may make them . . . I may make them sound a little braver than they were."

Who knew how brave they'd been at the end? They did, and their killers. What did it matter, really?

"Sure," said Stoner. "Say they saved my life."

Bacau, Romania
1600

GENERAL LOCUSTA MADE SURE THE DOOR TO HIS OFFICE was closed before he picked up the phone. The call was from General Karis, leader of the Romanian Third Division outside Bucharest.

"Still having trouble with the rebels, I hear," said Karis as soon as he picked up. "Nothing too serious, I hope."

"I can deal with the rebels. At the moment, they're useful."

"So I would guess. You're getting even more men?"

"I've been promised."

"You have to move soon. There are rumblings."

Locusta cleared his throat, but Karis did not take the hint.

"Some of our backers think an even stronger hand is needed," said Karis. "By failing to deal the rebels a death blow—"

"I told you. I am dealing with the rebels."

"The gas line will be very valuable once you are in charge. The revenue."

"I would not want anyone to overhear you speaking like this," said Locusta, finally losing his patience.

"There is no problem on my side. Is there on yours?"

Locusta needed Karis—it would be extremely difficult if not impossible to move on the capital if his troops opposed him. He also trusted him; they had been friends for years, and his fellow general hated President Voda even more than he did. Still, Locusta found Karis's impatient arrogance hard to stomach. He'd always been headstrong, and while it would be unfair to call him impetuous, he showed less caution than Locusta felt he should.

"There are no problems," Locusta assured him. "But we must be careful."

"Yes. So?"

"I am almost ready," said Locusta.

"The Americans?"

"They can be dealt with."

"Good. We are ready. But you must move quickly."

The general hung up without adding that he was moving as quickly as he could.

Dreamland
0700

DOG STEPPED BACK AS THE PRESIDENT SETTLED INTO THE big chair next to Zen and began manipulating the control stick. No kid with a computer game on Christmas morning had a broader smile than Martindale's as he took over control of the plane, pushing it into a climb straight overhead.

Dog asked himself if he truly deserved the Medal of Honor. Only a few dozen members of the Air Force had ever won one. Nearly all, he knew, had given their lives in combat.

He'd been prepared to do that as well—he'd come very close, within a few feet, but survived.

Death wasn't a criteria for the medal. But he somehow felt he was an imposter, a pretender who didn't deserve it.

The President rose from his chair, turning the aircraft back over to Zen to land. People began to applaud. Dog's thoughts continued to drift. Breanna was wheeled up. He smiled at her, then glanced at Zen, who was beaming himself. They were good kids.

Old enough to have kids themselves by now. Though for some reason he wasn't exactly looking forward to being called *Grandpa*.

"The country, the world, owe you a great deal," said the President, beginning his speech. "I can't tell you how proud, how very proud and honored I am to be here."

JED FELT THE VIBRATION OF HIS BLACKBERRY JUST AS the crowd began to applaud. He pulled it out and thumbed up the message. It was from Colonel Hash, the NSC's military liaison.

AMNIA UPDATE URGENT/ALERT FREEMAN ASAP

Jed slipped the BlackBerry back into his pocket and immediately began sidling toward the side of the audience area. He tried to appear nonchalant, pasting a bored expression on his face before double-timing up the boarding ladder.

The communications officer aboard *Air Force One* nodded at him as he went into the small compartment and sat down at the machine reserved for NSC use. Jed punched in his passwords and waited a few seconds while the computer connected him with his secure account.

The CIA had forwarded a report from one of its officers in the field, Mark Stoner, and endorsed by the Romanian station chief. Stoner had made contact with a member of the Romanian "resistance movement." The source claimed that the attack on the pipeline the night before had not been authorized by the rebels' governing committee. She believed that it had been either instigated or made directly by Russian special forces units. She also blamed the Russians for the murders of three CIA officers in the country over the past several months.

CREDIBLE WITNESS. SHE APPEARS TO HAVE BEEN PURSUED BY RUSSIAN SPECIAL FORCES IN MOLDOVA. REPORTS A SPLIT IN GUERRILLA LEADERSHIP. CLAIMS DWINDLING GUERRILLA NUMBERS, BOASTED BY RUSSIAN SPETSNAZ TROOPS. I AM IN THE PROCESS OF GATHERING FURTHER INFORMATION.

There was additional information from the ambassador at Bucharest, indicating that the damage to the Romanian pipeline would be fixed within a few days. The Romanian government had tried to keep a lid on information about the attack, but someone claiming to be a spokesman for the guerrillas had posted photos on the Web earlier that day and contacted the Romanian and German media.

And the country's president, Alin Voda, had called the ambassador on his personal line and requested American air assistance "to hunt the criminals before they make their next attack."

Jed backed out of his account and went to find his boss.

"I KNOW THERE HAVE BEEN A LOT OF RUMORS ABOUT A Medal of Honor for Colonel Bastian," said President Martindale, wrapping up his speech. "Let me just say this—they're true."

The audience, which had applauded politely a few times as Martindale spoke, erupted with a loud and unanimous hurrah. He stepped back and gestured to Dog, signaling that he should step forward to the mike.

"I really don't deserve this honor," said Dog, taking the microphone and addressing the others at the base. "You do. You all do. You've made my time here fantastic. Mr. President, there's no better command on the face of the earth."

"We have another update from Romania," whispered Philip Freeman, stepping up toward the President. "It may interest you."

"Let's discuss it on the plane."

"Yes, sir."

A few minutes later, aboard *Air Force One,* the President listened to Jed review the message from the CIA.

Meanwhile, a quick scan of the networks and news wire services showed that the energy market was already reacting to the news of the attack. Natural gas prices had shot up nearly thirty percent, and petroleum futures were trading ten dollars higher—which would have an impact on America as well as Europe.

"We have to deal with this forcefully," said Martindale. "If the Russians think they can get away without consequence, they'll continue to attack."

"That's only from one source," protested Secretary of State Hartmann. "And a prejudiced one."

"I don't see what a guerrilla would gain by blaming the Russians," said Chastain.

"We're not there—we don't know what the politics are."

"Regardless, we have to take a stand immediately," said Martindale. "If only to calm the energy markets. I'm not going to suck my thumb like Carter and the others during the oil embargo. We're protecting that gas line."

"Sending aircraft could backfire," said Hartmann. "If the Russians are truly involved, they may use it as an excuse to up their assistance."

"They don't need an excuse," said Chastain.

"We do have to be careful about the border situation," said Freeman. "Especially Moldova. They've asked to join NATO as well."

"They backed off that six months ago," noted Chastain. "The Russians have been courting them."

"If our forces got across the border, that will drive them into Russia's arms," said Freeman. "And even if we're willing to write them off, if other countries think we're backing Romania in a secret war against Moldova rather than the guerrillas, that will damage our hopes of getting them into NATO. Germany for one will object."

"Agreed," said the President. "But if we handle this correctly, we'll help our cause."

"Perhaps," admitted Hartmann.

"We'll send air support," said the President. "Moldova is absolutely off-limits, but if we send the right people, that won't be a problem."

It was obvious who the President had in mind.

"Jed, get General Samson up here," added Martindale. "And Dog. I want to talk to them personally."

GENERAL SAMSON STRODE PURPOSEFULLY INTO THE PRESIdent's conference room aboard *Air Force One*. It wasn't nearly as big or as elaborate as he thought it would be—fabric-covered walls stood behind two oversized couches on either side of a low conference table. Still, it was the *President's* conference room.

Samson nodded at Martindale, who was on the phone, then at Secretary of Defense Arthur Chastain, National Security Advisor Philip Freeman—and Lieutenant Colonel Bastian.

Bastian?

What the hell was he doing here?

"Philip, explain what's going on," said Martindale, covering the phone's mouthpiece. "I'll be right with you."

Samson listened as the National Security Advisor explained the situation in Romania.

"I'm sure Dreamland can supply planes to track ground movements," said Samson when he was finished. "And the Whiplash boys can give some close-air support lessons. I'll have a deployment plan ready no later than the end of the month."

"You're not quite understanding," said Freeman. "This has top priority."

Samson wasn't sure what Freeman was implying. Deploying to a place like Romania took a great deal of preparation. Two weeks worth of planning was nothing, especially given the present state of his staff. He was still filling positions.

But he sensed excuses weren't what Freeman or Chastain, much less the President himself, wanted.

"By the end of next week, certainly," he said. "I already have a few things in mind."

"General, we'd like you to be on the ground in a day or two," said Arthur Chastain.

"A day or two?"

"The Whiplash orders call for *immediate* deployment," said Freeman.

"Of course. Once we have a plan in place."

No one said anything. Samson felt about as comfortable as a skunk in church. Sweat began percolating under his collar.

He shot a sideways glance at Dog. Bastian must be loving this.

Why the hell was he here, anyway?

The President finished his phone call. "Gentlemen, are we set?" he asked.

The others looked at Samson.

"I just wanted to make sure," started Samson. "The— expediency of the mission. You're asking for us . . . well sir, let me put it this way. We can of course deploy immediately.

Tomorrow if you wish. But with a little more preparation, we—"

"Yes, tomorrow, of course," said Martindale. "Dog—Colonel Bastian—you'll be going?"

Dog cleared his throat. "That would be up to the general, sir. I'm at his disposal."

Clever, thought Samson, as Martindale turned his gaze back toward him.

But the assignment might be just the thing to get Bastian out from under his hair while he continued reorganizing the base. Yes, it would work very nicely.

"If Colonel Bastian is available, it would be great to have him on the mission," said Samson. "I'll need an experienced deputy at the scene, so to speak. I can't think of anyone better to lead the mission there. Assuming that's all right with you, Mr. President."

"General, that's perfect." Martindale rose and extended his hand, in effect dismissing him. "I look forward to a long working relationship with you. Carry on."

III

Killers of Children

**Iasi Airfield,
northeastern Romania
24 January 1998
1600**

THE FIELD AT IASI WAS FAIRLY LONG, BUT THE APPROACH was not. Between the nearby mountains and the possibility of handheld antiaircraft missiles, aircraft had to drop precipitously and then veer sharply to the west to land. For all his experience in the Megafortress, Dog broke into a sweat as his copilot, Lieutenant Kevin Sullivan, read off his altitude.

But he loved it.

"You're right on beam, Colonel," said Sullivan.

"Hang tight, boys," said Dog, swinging Dreamland EB-52 *Bennett* onto the airstrip with a crisp turn.

Like all Megafortresses, the *Bennett* was named for a Medal of Honor winner—Captain Steven L. Bennett, who in 1972 had saved innumerable lives supporting Marines overrun by Viet Cong, then given his own life so his copilot/observer would live, crash-landing his aircraft rather than ejecting when the other man's gear failed.

Dog was eligible to have a Megafortress named after him as well, but he'd already decided to do without that honor for the time being. He didn't quite feel up to the standards Captain Bennett and the others had set.

"You still have the touch, Colonel!" said Sullivan as they rolled to a stop on the far end of the concrete.

Despite the long flight, Sullivan was his usual overenthusiastic self, bouncing in his seat as they secured the aircraft. When they were done, the copilot practically danced off the flight deck. Dog followed him down, waiting as Zen lowered himself into his wheelchair using the special lift attached to the EB-52's ladder.

Dog had debated whether to take Zen on the mission, given his recent ordeal off the coast of India. But not having him along on a mission was almost inconceivable, and Dog didn't even bother arguing when Zen volunteered.

Breanna, however, was another matter.

"Your daughter's never going to forgive you for leaving her home," Zen told him as they headed toward a pair of cars near the edge of the runway apron.

"She should blame the doctors, not me," Dog told him. "They say she needs rest."

"Hey, I'm just the messenger," said Zen. "Personally, I agree."

Two Romanian enlisted men and a major were standing in front of a boxy-looking Romanian-built Dacia near the hangar. The men snapped to attention as Dog and Zen approached. Dog gave a quick but sharp salute in return.

"You are Colonel Bastian?" asked the major.

"That's right." Dog extended his hand.

"I am General Petri's aide. I'm to take you to him immediately."

"Sounds good."

The major looked at Zen. Dog knew exactly what he was thinking: What was a man in a wheelchair doing on the mission?

"This is Major Jeff Stockard. Everyone calls him Zen," said Dog. "He's my second in command on the mission. He's in charge of the Flighthawks—the unmanned aircraft that will actually provide support."

Zen stuck out his hand. The Romanian major took it warily.

"This our ride?" Dog asked, pointing to the car.

"Yes," said the major. He glanced again at Zen.

"Don't worry about me," Zen told him. "I can just hold onto the bumper. Tell the driver to try and avoid the potholes, though, all right?"

DOG WAS NOT A TALL MAN, BUT HE HAD A GOOD SIX OR seven inches over Romanian Air Force General Boris Petri, a gray-haired, hollow-cheeked man whose crisp uniform gave a hint of starch to the tiny office where he met the two Dreamland officers. Petri's English was serviceable, but to ensure that there were no mistakes in communication he called in one of his aides, a lieutenant whose brother was a star soccer player on the Romanian national team. The general was so proud of the connection that he mentioned it not once but twice as they waited for him to arrive. In the meantime, he offered Dog tea and brandy, sloshing them together in large cups that, to Dog's palate, held considerably more brandy than tea.

Once the lieutenant arrived, the talk turned serious, with the general briefing them not only about the guerrilla situation, but the air force in general. He seemed somewhat apologetic and defensive at the same time, noting that the Romanian air force was in the process of rebuilding itself and that it would soon be capable of defeating its enemies.

Dog slipped into diplomatic mode, assuring the general that his mission was first of all symbolic, demonstrating not the deficiencies of the Romanians but rather the country's strategic importance to Europe and the United States. Working with the Romanians would be of considerable value to the Dreamland contingent, he explained, since Dreamland's mission had recently been expanded to help in similar situations across the globe.

"It will be some time before our air force is ready to work with yours," said Petri.

"I understood there was a squadron of MiG-21s at Bacau."

"A squadron, yes." The general gave him a sad smile. "All but one of the planes is grounded because of a lack of spare parts. And there is no one there to fly the plane. The pilots have been shipped south to train on our new aircraft. Lamentably, those are not suitable for ground attack."

The new planes were four MiG-29s, front-line interceptors that could, in fact, be used in an attack role if their owner so chose. But for a variety of reasons—most especially the fact that the planes were deemed too precious to be risked in dangerous ground attacks—the MiGs were currently stationed at Borcea-Fetesti, far out of harm's way. The Romanians equipped them solely with air-to-air missiles; they had no ground attack weapons aside from iron bombs, and their pilots weren't even trained for the ground support role.

Officially, the Aviatez Militaire Romane had forty MiG-21s, older but still useful aircraft that would do reasonably well as ground support planes, at least during the day. But as Petri pointed out, only a minuscule number, less than a handful, were in any shape to fly. Romania even lacked attack helicopters; a few of its French-built Pumas had been fitted with .50 caliber machine guns that were fired from the right passenger door, but they were no substitute for actual gunships.

It didn't take a genius to realize that the country would have been much better off using the money it had spent on the MiG-29s for some lesser but more practical aircraft that could have been used in a counterinsurgency role, something like the American OA-10 Bronco, or surplus Russian Su-24s or Su-25s, all older planes that could be used for ground support. The left-over money could have been used for new parts and training for the MiGs they did have. But Dog wasn't there to offer that kind of advice, and General Petri wasn't in a position to implement it.

"You haven't finished your tea," said the translator when the general wound down his briefing.

"I'm a little tea'd out," said Dog, rising. "I'd like to arrange to meet with the commander of the ground forces as soon as possible."

"The general had hoped General Locusta would be here by now," said the translator. "Maybe within the hour. Certainly no later than dinner."

"Then with your permission, I'll get my people straightened out."

"Very good, Colonel."

Petri sprang up from his seat. "It's an honor to be working with a hero like you," he said, not bothering with his translation.

"Well, thank you," said Dog, embarrassed. "I hope I can live up to your expectations."

WHILE DOG AND ZEN WERE MEETING WITH THE AIR FORCE general, the Dreamland MC-17 arrived carrying the Whiplash ground team, the Dreamland mobile command trailer, and an Osprey. Danny Freah had already set up security perimeters and launched a pair of low-observable dirigibles as eye-in-the-sky monitors.

A second balloon system would be used to provide protection against rocket and mortar attacks: Four balloons would be lofted above the four corners of the aircraft and used to anchor an explosive net above them. The two layers of the net were meant to catch projectiles as they descended toward the aircraft, and small explosives would detonate the warheads, destroying them before they damaged the plane.

The system had never been used in the field before, and though its chief engineer had come along to oversee its deployment, the Whiplashers were having trouble setting it up. The wind proved stronger and more complicated than the computer model could handle, and even the scientist had taken to cursing at the screen.

"We'll get it, Colonel," he said, without looking up. "Growing pains."

Dog smiled and gave him a pat on the back. Dreamland had gained quite a reputation for coming up with cutting edge technology, but in the colonel's opinion, its real ability was dealing with growing pains. That was what Dreamland was all about—taking things from the laboratory and putting them in the field, where the *real* tests took place. An old saying held that no battle plan survived first contact with the enemy; the words were doubly true when it came to technology.

A convoy of four Land Rovers and a black Mercedes with flags flying from its bumpers approached the security zone around the Megafortresses. Two Whiplash troopers, dressed in full battle gear, stopped the lead truck; within seconds, Danny's radio was squawking.

"A General Locusta wants to visit," Danny told Dog. "His people are kind of pissed that we won't let them through."

"Let's go make nice," said Dog, heading toward the stopped convoy.

GENERAL TOMMA LOCUSTA FUMED AS HE SAT IN THE REAR of his Mercedes staff car. It was bad enough that he had to accept assistance from the U.S. Air Force, but now the arrogant bastards were preventing him from moving freely on a Romanian base.

An American officer appeared at the window, dressed in a pilot's flight suit.

"Lower the window," Locusta told his driver.

"General Locusta? I'm Lieutenant Colonel Tecumseh Bastian," said the man, bending toward him. "A lot of people call me Dog. I'm in charge of the people here."

"No, Colonel," replied Locusta. "You are in charge of the Americans here. Not the Romanians."

Dog smiled, leaning his hands on the car. "Yes, sir. That's true. I understand we're going to be working with you."

"You're going to be working *for* me," said Locusta. "To provide support."

"We'll do whatever we can. I wonder if you'd like to huddle for a few minutes and start making some arrangements?"

"What's the word, 'huddle'?"

"Excuse me, General. Your English is so good I just forgot for a minute that you weren't a native speaker. I meant, should we sit down somewhere and talk about the arrangements for our working together? And if you're available, I'd like to introduce you to some of my people, and show you some of the hardware."

Locusta realized the American was trying to be nice to him, but it was too late as far as he was concerned. To a man, the Americans were arrogant blowhards who acted as if everything they touched turned to gold.

"My headquarters right now is just being set up. It's rather sparse," added Dog, who gestured toward a small trailer next to a hangar. "But it would give us a place to talk out of the cold."

"Let's go," said Locusta.

"Sir, the one thing I'd ask is that your people stay with you if they're inside our protective corridor. A lot of the security is automated and I don't want any accidents."

"Then see that there are no accidents," said Locusta, rapping the seat back to tell his driver to move on.

DOG TURNED AND LOOKED AT DANNY, ROLLING HIS EYES. Zen, sitting behind them, barely suppressed his laughter.

"Guess we got off on the wrong foot, huh, Dog?" said Zen as they started toward the trailer.

"Ah, he's probably not that bad," replied Dog.

"No worse than Samson."

Dog ignored the comment. "We are guests in his country," he said. "If the tables were turned, we'd probably be a little prickly."

"You're bucking for the diplomatic corps," said Zen.

Dog laughed. "Maybe I am."

"He's just trying to prove he doesn't have a problem with *all* generals," said Danny.

"Samson's your boss now, Danny. And yours too, Zen," said Dog. While he didn't like Samson, the hint of disrespect in their voices bothered him. "You better remember that."

"I understand chain of command," said Danny. "I have no problem with that."

"It's generals I don't like," said Zen.

"Then you better not become one," snapped Dog.

He was still irritated when he reached the trailer. General Locusta stood there impatiently, waiting with a dozen aides. The entire contingent started to follow him up the steps.

"The thing is, General, I'm not sure everybody is going to fit inside," said Dog when he realized what was happening. "I'd suggest that maybe you choose—"

"My aides will stay with me."

"Yes, sir."

Not counting the communications specialist in the back compartment, twelve people could fit in the trailer, but it was a squeeze. Sixteen was uncomfortably tight. Locusta had twenty men with him.

Worse, the trailer had only recently been powered up— which meant the environmental system hadn't finished heating it. This wasn't a problem at first, since the body heat from the crowd quickly raised the temperature. But then the system had to switch into cooling mode. It couldn't react fast enough, and the small space overheated.

Dog tried to ignore the rising temperature. He concentrated on the paper map the general's aides had spread on the table. It showed the mountains and valley farm area to the south where the guerrillas had been operating. Filled with small agricultural communities, the area had been mostly peaceful since the end of World War II.

"Here is the pipeline," said General Locusta, taking over the briefing. "The network runs through here, along this valley, then to the west. It must be protected at all costs. We have forward camps here, here, and here."

Locusta jabbed his finger at a succession of small red squares.

"These mountains here, 130 kilometers from the border—south of Bacau, where our main base is—that is where we have had the most trouble."

"Where was the pipeline attacked the other day?" asked Danny.

"Here, west of Braila, south of Route 25."

"That's pretty far from where you say the guerillas have been operating."

"I considered complaining to them," said the general sarcastically.

The general's brusque manner softened, but only slightly, as Danny explained how his ground team would train soldiers to act as forward air controllers, working with the Megafortress and Flighthawk crews. The Romanians, he said, would be in charge; the Dreamland people would work alongside them, taking the same risks.

When the general's aides began making suggestions about how and where the training should be conducted, Dog noticed the corners of Locusta's mouth sagging into a bored frown.

"General, why don't you and I inspect some of the aircraft that will be available to support you?" he suggested. "We can let these men sort out the other issues and arrangements."

"All right," said Locusta, even though his frown deepened.

LOCUSTA'S APPREHENSION GREW AS THE AMERICAN colonel showed off the Megafortress and its robot planes, the Flighthawks. He'd known the technology would be impressive, of course, but when he was shown a computer demonstration tape from an earlier mission, he was amazed by the ability of the radar to find ground forces and by the robot planes that would attack them. A Megafortress and two Flighthawks could do the work of an entire squadron of fighters.

They were potent weapons, and could certainly help him fight the guerrillas. But they could also upset his plans to take over the country if he wasn't careful.

"General, I'm looking forward to a strong working relationship," Dog told him as they walked back to his car. Locusta's aides were already waiting.

"Yes," said Locusta. "Just remember, Colonel—you are here to assist us. Not take over."

"I only want to help you."

Locusta nodded, then got into the car.

Allegro, Nevada
0908

BREANNA PRACTICALLY LEAPED TO THE PHONE.

"Hello, hello," she said.

"Hello, hello yourself," said Zen.

His voice sounded tired and distant, but it was good to hear it anyway.

"Lover, how are you?" she asked.

"Missing you."

"Mmmm. And I miss you." She fell into the chair, closed her eyes and listened as her husband told her about his first day in Romania.

"We're sleeping in a hangar, dormitory-style," said Zen. "Sully has the bunk next to me. And he snores."

"Wish I could tuck you in."

"Me too. The mayor came around a little while ago. He offered us a hotel, but Danny vetoed it. Security. He's like a Mother Hen."

"Danny's only watching out for you."

"He's just being paranoid. The people have been pretty good. The commanding general is a hard case, but your father handled him perfectly. Aside from that, Romania is beautiful. It's real peaceful. Mountains nearby, a lot of farms."

"You sound like a travelogue."

"Beats the hell out of where we've been lately."

"Thank God for that."

Zen admitted that he might change his opinion as time went on, though only because she wasn't there. He wouldn't say anything directly about the mission because they were on an open line, but when he mentioned off-handedly that he'd be flying in the morning, she felt her heart jump a little.

"So what did you do today?" he asked finally.

"Zen, it's barely past nine here. There's a what, ten hour time difference?"

"Yeah. It's 1912 here. But let me just guess," he added. "You've done your workout, vacuumed, straightened out the kitchen, and had about four cups of coffee."

"Five. I also did the laundry."

Zen laughed. "How's your knee?"

"Pretty solid. I'm up to the third bar of resistance on the machine."

"I'm glad the doctor told you to take it easy."

"I don't remember her saying that."

"You liar."

"No, really. And I am taking it easy. I am."

"You are taking it easy for you," he conceded.

"I wish I were with you."

"You can't be on every deployment."

"And you can?"

"Don't get mad."

"I'm not—well, maybe a little."

Neither one of them spoke. She knew Zen was right—she wasn't taking it easy, and she wasn't going to take it easy. It wasn't in her nature. But it wasn't in his, either.

"Hey, I love you, you know," he said finally. "A lot."

"And I love you too, baby."

"Maybe when this whole thing is done, we'll take a real vacation."

"OK."

"Maybe here," he said, laughing. "Place does look beautiful, at least from the air."

Dreamland
1006

BE CAREFUL WHAT YOU WISH FOR . . .

Mack Smith had heard his mother say that a million times growing up. And damned if it wasn't one of the few things she'd said that turned out to be true.

Working as General Terrill Samson's chief of staff meant working . . . and working . . . and working, 24/7. Samson believed in delegating—and with much of his staff and subordinate officers still en route to Dreamland from previous posts, he was the delegate de jour.

There was another saying his mother had used all the time: Stuff rolls downhill.

Except she didn't say "stuff."

Mack was contemplating just how far downhill he was when his office phone rang. The light signaled that the call was an internal one—from the general's office.

"General wants to talk to you," said Chartelle Bedell, the general's civilian secretary.

The first time Chartelle had said that to him, Mack called him back on the intercom. It was a mistake he wouldn't make again.

"I'll be in before you can put down the phone," he told her, jumping up from his desk and double-timing his way down the hall.

Chartelle gave him a big smile as he walked in. Mack smiled back. She wasn't much to look at, but she had been with the general for several years and knew how to read his moods. Mack knew it was essential to have a good spy in the bullpen—the office outside the general's—and while he hadn't completely won her over yet, he figured he would soon.

"There you are, Smith," said Samson after he knocked and was buzzed inside. "Every day down here it's something else."

"Yes, sir. That's the way it is here," replied Mack.

"Not under my command, it's not."

"No sir, of course. You're really on your way to turning it around."

Samson frowned. Mack felt his stomach go a little sour. The vaunted Mack Smith charm never seemed to work with the old man.

"The B-1 laser program," said the general, as if the mere mention explained what he had on his mind.

"Yes, sir. Good plane."

"It has its plusses and minuses, Smith," said Samson. "You were a fighter jock. I flew them. Don't forget."

"Yes, sir," said Mack. The general's use of the past tense when referring to his profession irked him, but it wasn't the sort of thing he could mention.

"What the *hell* happened to the test schedule of these planes?" demanded Samson. "They're two months behind. Two months."

Two months wasn't much in the scheme of things, especially on a complicated project like the laser B-1. And in fact, depending on how you looked at the program, it was actually ahead of schedule; most of the delays had to do with the ground-attack module, which was being improved from a baseline simply because the engineers had realized late in the day that they could do so without adding additional cost. The rest of the delay was mainly due to the shortage of pilots—the plane had to be flown for a certain number of hours before its different systems were officially certified.

Mack tried explaining all of this, but Samson was hardly in a receptive mood.

"The laser is the problem, isn't it, Mack?"

"The laser segment is ahead of schedule, sir. As I was saying, the plane is actually ready—"

"Because if it is, we should just shelve it. Some of this new age crap—it just adds unnecessary complication. If the force is going to be lean and mean, we need weapons that are lean and mean. Low maintenance. Sometimes cutting edge toys are just that—toys."

"Well yes sir, but I think you'll find that the laser segment is, um, moving along nicely."

"Then what the *hell* is the holdup?"

"There's a problem with pilots," he said. "A shortage."

"Fix it, Mack."

Finding qualified pilots—and they had to be military pilots, preferably Air Force, with the requisite security clearances, to say nothing of their abilities—wasn't exactly easy. But he knew of one pilot, albeit a fighter jock, who was available.

Himself.

"You know, I wouldn't mind taking the stick now and again myself," said Mack. "In the interim. This way—"

"Major, if my chief of staff has enough time to get into the seat of a test aircraft, then I'm not giving him enough work to do."

"Yes, sir, that's what I was thinking."

Mack was back in his office a half hour later when he was surprised by a knock on the door.

"It's open."

"Hey Mack, how goes things for the new chief of staff?" said Breanna. She entered with a noticeable limp, but that was a vast improvement over the wheelchair he'd seen her in the other day.

"Bree! How are you?" He got up, intending to give her a light peck on the cheek in greeting. Then he remembered General Samson's order against "unmilitary shows of affection" and stopped cold. Thrusting his hand out awkwardly, he asked how she was.

"I feel great," said Breanna. "Mind if I sit down?"

"Sure. Sit. Sit."

Mack had once had the hots for Breanna, but that was long over. She was a bit too bossy and conceited for his taste, so he'd passed her along to Zen.

Her body made it easy to overlook those shortcomings, however. Her face—it was like looking at a model.

"How do you like being chief of staff?" Breanna asked.

"It's great. I have my thumb on the pulse of the base," he said, "I've solved several problems already. We're turning this place around, the general and I."

A frown flickered across Breanna's face. "I heard that you need more test pilots on the B-1 laser program," she said.

"Uh, yeah."

"I'm here to volunteer."

"Uh—"

"You need pilots. I've flown *Boomer* a couple of times."

"You were heading the unmanned bomber project."

"So? You still need a pilot. And UMB isn't scheduled for more test flights for another three months. If that," Breanna added, "because I hear that General Samson wants to cut it."

She'd heard correctly. General Samson's priorities for the base and its projects emphasized manned programs, with only a few exceptions. He also tended to favor improvements to traditional weapons systems, like the development of smart microbombs, over what he called "gee-whiz toys" like the airborne lasers that had yet to prove themselves.

"Maybe it'll get cut, maybe not," said Mack. "Ultimately, it may not be up to the general."

"He has a lot of say."

"True."

"So, when do I fly?" asked Breanna.

"Um—"

"Tomorrow's not too soon for me."

"Wait a second, Bree. Yeah, I need pilots, but—"

"What's the but?"

"You're supposed to be in the hospital, aren't you?"

"No. I was released the other day."

"That doesn't mean you're ready to fly."

"Look. I'm fine." Breanna got up from her chair and did a little dance in front of his desk.

"I'm tempted. I'm really tempted," said Mack. "But you came in here with a limp."

"Did I?"

"And what about that concussion or coma or whatever you had?"

"Doctors didn't find anything wrong."

"I don't know."

"What do you need to say yes?"

"Medical clearance, for one thing."

"Done."

"Oh yeah? Let's see the medical report."

"I haven't bothered to schedule it yet. I will."

"Fine. No problem," said Mack. "A clean bill of health, and then you're back in the cockpit."

"Not a problem."

"A doctor has to say you can fly."

"Of course."

"A flight surgeon, not a veterinarian."

"Hard-de-har-har."

"McMichaels," said Mack, naming the toughest doctor on the base. McMichaels had once threatened to ground him for a sore bicep.

"I like Mickey."

"Good then. It's a deal."

Bucharest, Romania
2005

STONER SLID HIS WATCH CAP LOWER ON HIS HEAD, COVERING his ears and about half of his forehead. Then he turned the corner and walked to the apartment building where he'd left Sorina Viorica. He had his head down but was watching out of the corners of both eyes, making sure he wasn't being followed or watched.

The building's front door was ajar. Stoner pushed in, wearing an easy nonchalance to camouflage his wariness. He double-pumped up the stairs to the second floor, then went directly to the apartment door and knocked.

No answer.

Stoner surveyed the hall and nearby stairs, making sure he was alone, then turned back and knocked again.

He'd left the key under the mat, but there was no sense checking for it—she would either open the door for him or he would leave.

Stoner took a deep breath. If she wasn't here, he'd get to work trying to commandeer information about the Russian Spetsnaz, flesh out that angle. Eventually he'd put together a program either to stop them or expose them. The station chief had already made it clear anything like that would need to get approved back in Washington, but Stoner didn't think he'd have trouble getting something approved if he linked it to the dead officers.

He'd spent the day rereading the police reports and visiting the places where they'd died. Nothing he'd seen convinced him that the Russians were involved. Or vice versa.

There was a sound at the door. Stoner saw a shadow at the eyeglass. A moment later Sorina Viorica opened the door.

"I didn't think you were coming back," she told him.

"I got tied up with some things."

"Come in."

He walked inside. Sorina Viorica put her head out the door, checking the hall before coming back in.

"Your lock is better than I expected," she told him, walking to the kitchen. "But I don't know if the door would last."

"It will. Long enough for you to get out."

"Not even the army would be so stupid to come in the front way without watching the back. And the police are not as stupid as the army," said Sorina. A small pot of coffee sat on the back burner of the stove. She held it up. "Want some?"

"Sure."

"The stove is hard to start."

She ducked down, watching the igniter click futilely. Stoner examined the curves of her body. The austere toughness of her personality was matched by her athletic compactness.

The burner caught with a loud hush, a blue flame extending nearly a foot over the stove before settling down.

"You should get it fixed," Sorina said, putting the pot on.

"I'll tell the landlord."

She opened a drawer and took out a pair of scissors. "While we are waiting," she said, handing them over, "give me a haircut."

"A haircut?"

"I need one." She pulled out one of the chairs and turned it around, then sat so her breasts were squeezed against the chair back.

"I'm not much of a barber."

"Just cut it straight. Lop it off."

Stoner took some of her hair. For some reason it felt softer than he'd expected. "How much?" he asked, moving the scissors along its length.

"Above my ears. Short. That's easy."

"Are you sure you want me to do this?"

"Yes."

He worked on it for more than an hour, each cut as tentative as the first. They stopped twice, to check his progress and to drink their coffee. About halfway through, Sorina reached into her pocket and pulled out a pack of cigarettes. She had to light it from the stove; Stoner thought the flame would singe her face when it caught.

When he was done, she took the scissors and went to the bathroom. After about five minutes she came out with her hair neatly trimmed.

"How does it look?" she asked.

"I liked it better long."

Sorina Viorica smiled for the first time since they'd met.

"I am going to take a shower. When I am done, we can go for a walk."

THEY WALKED UP TOWARD THE BOULEVARD CAROL I, around the Piata C.A. Rosetti circle. Stoner watched the expressions of the people they passed, carefully looking for some sign that Sorina Viorica was recognized.

"I'm invisible here," she told him. "To the citizens—they don't know who I am."

"What about the police?"

She shrugged. "That I won't test."

They ate in a coffeehouse that served small sandwiches. Sorina ate hers in only a few minutes.

"Want another?" asked Stoner.

She shook her head, though he could tell she was still hungry.

"That is why we struggle," she said, pointing with her gaze across the room.

An old woman sat over a cup of tea. Her shoes were held together by string; her coat had a series of small rips on the sleeve and back.

"Before this government, people were helped," said Sorina Viorica. "But I don't expect you to understand. Your streets are filled with homeless."

Stoner called over the waiter. "I would like to buy the woman there a sandwich."

The waiter frowned, acting as if he didn't understand English—though he'd understood when Stoner ordered earlier.

"Here," said Stoner, pressing several bills into his hand. "Get her something good."

"Should I be impressed?" Sorina Viorica asked after the waiter left.

"Impressed?"

"By your generosity. Or was it part of an act?"

"It is what it is."

"Even the people who should understand, don't," said Sorina, changing her tact. "You saw the waiter's expression. Yet he is not that much different than her."

"Nor are we."

She smirked. "When the revolution comes, then we will see who's different."

"I'd keep my voice down if I were you."

"This is the student quarter. If I can't talk of revolution here, where can I?"

Sorina Viorica spent the next half hour doing just that, explaining to Stoner that all her movement wanted—originally—was equity and peace for everyone.

"That wasn't the case under Ceausescu," Stoner said.

"No. He was a dictator. A devil."

"So you want to return to that?"

She shook her head.

"There are elections now," said Stoner.

"They are a front for the old line. The hard-liners, the military—they are the ones really in control."

"Then change it by voting. Not by violence."

"Will your country let us?"

"It's not up to us. It's up to you. To Romanians."

Sorina Viorica's face grew sad. "Our movement is dead. It has been hijacked. And if by some miracle we were to win, we would be a vassal again, a slave to Russia. They are all my enemies."

Stoner waited for her to continue, but she didn't. Whatever her personal story was—and he suspected there was a great deal to it—she didn't share. The CIA files had a single reference to her, because she'd been on a Romanian government watch list. She had relatives in Arad, a city near Hungary, but apparently her parents both died when she was young.

After they ate, they walked for a while through University Square. Sorina said no more about the movement. Instead, she told Stoner some of the history of the city— the old history, each building evoking a different period— nineteenth century, eighteenth century, seventeenth, sixteenth.

"You want me to betray them," she said as they walked up the steps to the apartment.

"You said they were your enemies. And that the only ones left were misfits, and criminals."

She took the key out of her pocket.

"They want to kill you," he said. "You could get revenge."

"You don't know me very well, do you, Mr. Stoner?" she said, and closed the door behind her.

Dreamland
1156

MICKEY MCMICHAELS TUCKED THE BELL END OF HIS stethoscope into his jacket pocket.

"I can't say you're in bad health, Breanna," said the flight surgeon. "You're in great health. But . . . Your knee doesn't hurt you?"

Breanna shook her head.

"Not even a twinge?"

She shrugged.

"No broken bones. Contusions are fading," he admitted. "Ribs, not even tender."

"So what's the hang-up?"

"You were very dehydrated, you had a concussion, twisted knee, bruised ribs—"

"You're going to ground me for a few bruises?"

Dr. McMichaels pursed his lips. "Your knee is not back to normal. And as for that coma or whatever it was—"

"I've had two CAT scans that say I'm fine. Give me another."

"I may."

"X-ray my whole body. Do any test you want. Just give me my ticket to fly."

"You have to take it slow, Breanna. You have to give your body time to heal."

"It's healed. It's so healed it's starting to atrophy."

"I appreciate that you're bored. But you have to heal. And I have to do my job."

"Do it. Tell me what I have to do to get back in the air."

McMichaels sighed. For a second, Breanna thought she had worn him down. Then he shook his head.

"I'm not ready to say you can fly. You need more of a recovery period."

Breanna suddenly felt very angry. "I'm going to come back to you every day until you clear me."

"That's up to you."

Tears welled in her eyes. She turned and walked out of the office as quickly as she could, arms swinging, her cheeks flushed with anger and embarrassment. She was sure that if she were a man, they'd let her back in the air. Mack, Zen, her father—they'd all gotten in the cockpit with injuries more severe than hers. Hell, Zen was *paralyzed* and he was allowed to fly.

The thing that frosted her most of all—the doctors were taking out their own ignorance, their own mistakes, on her. They all wanted to believe she'd been in a coma or had major brain trauma. Well *fine*, except there was zero evidence—zero—of any brain damage. Of any abnormality whatsoever.

So, because they were wrong, they were taking it out on her.

Breanna stalked down the hall and up the ramp to the entrance to the med building, trying to contain her anger. She fixed her eyes on the ground as she passed the security station, too furious even to say hello. The cold outside air bit at her face as soon as she cleared the doorway; the tears she'd been holding back let loose.

She wiped them as best she could as she started in the direction of her on-base apartment. She was almost there when she spotted a knot of people coming out of the entrance, laughing and talking; she turned abruptly, not wanting to be seen crying. Quickening her pace, she found herself walking toward the hangar area. She pushed her fingers around her eyes, rubbing out the moisture.

But she didn't want to go into the hangars or the offices beneath them either. The only thing left seemed to be to go back home to their condo in Allegro.

Once again she turned, this time in the direction of the helicopter landing pad and the parking lot at Edwards.

"Hey, Bree, how's it going?" yelled Marty Siechert as she changed direction.

Breanna briefly debated with herself whether to stop, but it was difficult for her to be impolite with anyone, and Sleek Top had been a friend for a while.

"Hi, Sleek, how are you?"

"What's up?" The former Marine-turned-civilian test pilot bent his head to the side, as if the change in angle would give him a better view of her face. "Your face looks raw."

"I've been out in the cold."

"Where you headed?"

"Probably home."

"You talk to Mack about flying the B-1s or what?"

"Yes, I did." Her lower lip started to tremble. She stopped abruptly.

"You all right?"

Her emotions felt like the lava in a volcano, surging toward the top. She nodded, and bit her teeth against her lips.

"Hey, how about we go get some lunch?" suggested Sleek Top.

"I don't know."

"Off base. I know a quiet lunch place. Kind of a dump, but the food's good. Italian."

"All right," she said. "Sure."

AS SLEEK TOP HAD SAID, MAMA'S WAS A BIT OF A DUMP, but the portions were large and the marinara sauce couldn't be beat. Breanna stayed away from the wine, as did Sleek Top, who was going to fly later that night.

"I don't know why I was so upset. I acted—I was like a little girl who had her toys taken away," said Breanna.

She'd calmed considerably. While she was still deeply disappointed about not being allowed to fly, she was also disappointed in herself. Showing emotion had been unprofessional. It wasn't like her.

"You've been through a lot," said Sleek Top. "Everything that's happened to you in the last few weeks? God, Bree, we all thought you and Zen were . . . dead."

"But we weren't."

"Maybe you should slow down a bit," he told her. "You know. Take a couple of weeks . . . "

His voice trailed off as he saw her frown.

"I don't mean permanently," he said quickly. "I mean, do a few things that you like to do. Hit some shows in Vegas. Play the slots or something."

"I don't play the slots. And I don't like shows."

"You don't like shows?"

She shrugged.

"It'll take your mind off things. You have to relax. What do you and Zen do to unwind?"

"Not much," she said honestly. "I mean, we'll watch some basketball or maybe baseball."

"Then go to a Lakers game."

"Oh, watching is such a—"

"No, no, *go*."

"To L.A.? I don't want to go all the way there by myself."

"I'll go with you. I have a season package."

"Thanks, Sleek, but—"

"Up to you. But really, you have to cut loose a bit. Relax. Slow down. I remember when I first left active duty. I was like a jackrabbit, practically bouncing off the walls. And the ceiling. I didn't know what to do with myself. Finally, I gave myself an order. Relax."

"And that did it, huh?"

"Sure. One thing Marines are good at—following orders." He smiled, then reached for the check. "Whereas you Air Force zippersuits never heard an order you didn't think was an optional request, right?"

**Iasi Airfield,
northeastern Romania
25 January 1998
1600**

THE MEGAFORTRESS SHOT FORWARD, ROLLING DOWN THE concrete expanse toward a sky so perfectly blue it looked like a painting. The wind threw a gust of air under the plane's long wings, pushing her skyward with an enthusiastic rush. Flying might be a simple matter of aerodynamics, a calculation of variables and constants, but to a pilot it was always something more than just math. Imagination preceded the fact—you had to long for flight before you achieved it, and no matter how many times you gripped the stick and pulled back, gently or with a hard jerk, bracing yourself for the shock of g's against your face or simply rolling up your shirtsleeves for an afternoon's spin, there was always that moment of elation, the triumph of human spirit that set man apart from every other being. Flying was a triumph of the soul, and a pilot, however taciturn he might seem, however careful he was in planning and replanning his mission, savored that victory every time the plane's wheels left the ground.

Dog and his copilot, Lieutenant Sullivan, remained silent as they took the plane skyward. They hadn't flown together for very long, but the missions they'd been on had forged a strong bond between them. They had one thing above all others in common—both knew the *Bennett* as they knew their own hands and legs. The trio of men and machine worked together flawlessly, striding nose up in the sky, spiraling toward 20,000 feet.

With all systems in the green, they set a course to the southwest, flying in the direction of Bacau.

"Flighthawk commander, are you ready for launch?" asked Dog.

"Roger that, *Bennett*," replied Zen, sitting below in the Flighthawk bay. "I'm showing we have just over ten minutes to the planned release point."

"Affirmative."

"Beautiful day."

"Yes, it is," said Dog, surprised that Zen would notice, or at least take the time to mention it. Generally he was all business.

They turned the aircraft over to the computer for the separation maneuvers. Dog watched his instruments carefully as the Flighthawks dropped off the wings one at a time. The Megafortress continued to operate perfectly.

"*Hawk One* is at 10,000 feet, going to 5,000," said Zen. "Preparing to contact Groundhog."

Dog acknowledged. Groundhog was Danny Freah, who was introducing one of the Romanian units to the procedures required to interface with the planes. They planned on splitting their time this afternoon between two different units, going over the rudiments of working with the aircraft.

The Megafortress had two large air-to-ground missiles on its rotating bomb rack, but it was unlikely these would be used; even though they were very precise, there was too much chance of collateral damage. The Flighthawks, however, could provide close air support with their cannons if called in by the ground soldiers.

The focus of the mission was to provide intelligence: The Megafortress would use its J-STAR-like ground radar to follow troop movements or even vehicles, while the Flighthawks would provide real-time video of the area where the troops were operating. Though the Whiplash people could use their smart helmets to receive the video instantly, security concerns and numbers meant the Romanian troops would have to use special laptop units instead. Dog worried about their ability to receive the streaming video under battlefield conditions, but that was just one of the many things they'd have to work out as the deployment progressed.

With the Flighthawks away, he checked with his radar operators to see how they were doing. The men sat behind him on the flight deck, each facing a console arranged against the hull of the plane. On the right side, Technical Sergeant Thomas Rager manned the airborne radar, which was tracking flights within 250 miles. On the left, Technical Sergeant Jerry "Spiff" Spilani worked the ground radar. Rager had flown with Dog before; Spiff was new to the crew, though not to the job.

"Not too much traffic down there for rush hour, Colonel," said Spiff. "We have six cars in a five mile stretch."

"You sound disappointed," said Dog.

"Colonel, where I come from, we can get six cars in ten feet," answered the sergeant.

"And they're all stolen," said Sullivan.

"Generally." Spiff was a New Yorker. From *da Bronx*.

"Groundhog's on the line," said Sullivan, his voice suddenly all business. "Right on time."

On the ground in northeastern Romania
1630

DANNY FREAH ADJUSTED THE VOLUME ON THE SMART helmet's radio, listening as the Romanian lieutenant completed the exchange of recognition codes with the *Bennett*. In person, the lieutenant's pronunciation was nearly perfect, but the radio equipment made it sound garbled. The lieutenant repeated himself twice before Dreamland *Bennett* acknowledged.

"OK," said Danny. "Let's get some data from the Flighthawk."

The unmanned aircraft streaked a thousand feet overhead, riding parallel to the nearby highway. Danny listened to the Romanian and Zen trade information. The Romanian lieutenant had trouble understanding Zen's light midwestern drawl, but he was able to see the video from the small plane on his laptop without any problem.

As planned, the lieutenant asked Zen to check out a road a mile south of them; they did that without a problem. Then the Romanians called in a mock air attack on a telephone substation about a hundred meters from the field they were standing in. This too went off without a hitch. The Flighthawk dipped down above the Romanian position, straightened its wings, then zoomed on the cement building, which had been abandoned some years before.

Rather than firing his cannon, Zen pickled off a flare. It flashed red in the fading twilight directly over the building.

The Romanian soldiers cheered.

I must be getting old, Danny thought. They all look like kids.

**Aboard the *Bennett*,
above northeastern Romania
1700**

ZEN PUSHED THE FLIGHTHAWK THROUGH ANOTHER TURN, then dipped its wing to fall into another mock attack. The hardest part of the whole exercise was understanding the Romanians' English.

They weren't very good yet at estimating distances, but since he could use the actual GPS coordinates from the laptops as well as the Flighthawks' sensor to orient himself, finding the target wasn't particularly difficult.

After what he'd had to go through on his last mission, though, what was?

What do you do for an encore after saving the world? he mused.

It was an arrogant, self-aggrandizing thought—and yet it was true, or at least more true than false. Their last mission had stopped a nuclear war; you couldn't top that.

But life went on. There were still enemies to fight, conflicts to solve. Whether they seemed mundane or not.

There were also problems to solve and annoyances to overcome. Zen had decided to wear the MESSKIT instead of the "old" chute. It felt bulkier around his shoulders—not enough to interfere with flying the Flighthawks, but enough that he would have to get used to it.

The Romanian ground controller called for a reconnaissance flight over a nearby village. Zen located it on the Megafortress's ground radar plot. A cluster of suburban-type houses sat south of the main road, the center of town marked by a fire station and a small park. He wheeled the Flighthawk overhead, low and slow. The houses, built of prefab concrete panels, looked like the condo development he lived in back home.

They made him think of Breanna. He shut down that part of his mind and became a machine, focused on his job.

Switching on his mike, Zen described what he saw, four-sided roofs atop sugar-cube houses aligned in eight L's around the crest of a hill. He described two cars he saw moving into the complex, the row of parked compacts at the far end of the lot. He saw two people moving on the lawn below the easternmost house: kids kicking a soccer ball around.

"Very much detail," replied the ground controller.

"Thanks," he said. "Next."

UP ON THE MEGAFORTRESS'S FLIGHT DECK, DOG TURNED the controls over to his copilot and got up to stretch. In remaking the plane so that it had a sleek nose rather than the blunt chin the B-52 had been born with, the flight deck had been extended nearly twenty feet. Calling it spacious would have been an exaggeration, but the crews had considerably more elbow room than in the original.

Dog walked to the small galley behind the two radar operators, poured himself a coffee from the zero-gravity coffeemaker—one of the Dreamland engineers' most cherished and appreciated inventions—then took a seat next to the ground radar operator to see what things looked like from his perspective.

"Place looks pretty peaceful," Spiff told him. "You sure they have a revolution going on here?"

"Don't let that fool you," replied Dog.

"No, I won't, Colonel. But we could be looking at the Vegas suburbs here. Minus the traffic. Kind of makes you wonder why these people want to fight."

Dog went across the aisle to check on Rager, who was monitoring airborne traffic around them. The rebels weren't known to have aircraft; Dog's main concern was that a civilian plane might blunder into their path inadvertently. The commercial flight paths to and from Iasi lay to the north and east of where they were operating.

"Here's something interesting on the long-range scan," said Rager, flipping his screen display to show Dog. "These two bad boys just came into the edge of our coverage area."

Two yellow triangles appeared in the lower left-hand corner of the screen. Rager hit another switch, and the ghost of a ground map appeared under the display, showing that the planes were south of Odessa over the Black Sea, 273 miles away.

"Just sitting there," said Rager. "Doing a racetrack pattern."

"Ukrainian?"

"No. Russian. Computer, ID contacts Alpha Gamma six-eight and Alpha Gamma six-nine."

Small boxes appeared next to the yellow triangles; they looked like dialogue balloons in a comic strip.

```
MIG-29
RS
ARM——4AA11, 2AA10
```

The computer's tags identified the aircraft as Russian MiGs carrying four heat-seeking AA-11 Archer or R-27R missiles and two radar-guided AA-10 Alamo or R-27R missiles.

"Russian air defense," said Rager. "I think they're shadowing us."

"Long way from home."

"Yeah."

"You sure they're watching for us? They're pretty far away."

"True. But if I wanted to sit in a spot where I thought I couldn't be seen, that's where I'd be, just at the edge of our coverage. They may not think we can see them," Rager added. "Two hundred and fifty miles is the limit of their AWACS ships."

"Do they have one out there?"

"Can't tell, but I suspect it. Maybe another hundred miles back. This way, if we come in their direction, it sees us and vectors them toward us."

"Keep track of them."

"Not a problem, Colonel."

Dog went back to his seat. If Rager's theory was correct, the Russians must have been alerted to the Megafortress's flight by a spy at Iasi.

"Ground team's done, Colonel," said Sullivan as he strapped himself back into his seat.

"All right, folks. We're going to knock off," said Colonel Bastian. "Danny, job well done. We'll talk to you in the morning."

"Thanks, Colonel. Groundhog out."

"Set a course for Iasi, Colonel?" asked Sullivan.

"No. Let's do a couple more circuits here. Then I want to break the pattern with a dash east."

"The MiGs?"

"Let's see how they react," said Dog.

Dog told Zen what was going on, then prepared to make his move. He waited until they were coming south, then jammed the thrusters to full military power and turned the plane's nose hard to the east, heading toward the Black Sea. Given their position and the circumstances, it was far from an aggressive move—but the MiGs reacted as soon as they were within 250 miles.

"Turning east," said Rager. "One other contact—Tupolev Tu-135—I see what's going on now, Colonel."

"Where are the planes?" asked Dog. Rager's theories could wait.

"They're all turning."

Dog flicked the long-range radar feed onto his display. The Russian planes were definitely reacting to him; all three contacts had headed east.

"The Tupolev is tracking our radar transmissions," said Rager. "That's how they know where we are."

The Tu-135—a Russian aircraft similar in some ways to a 727—was outfitted with antennae that detected radar waves at long range. It could detect the Megafortress a few miles beyond the EB-52's radar track because of the way the waves scattered at the extreme edge of their range. There wasn't much that could be done about it, aside from turning off the radar.

"All right," said Dog. He put the plane into a casual turn back toward Iasi, as if they hadn't seen the Russians at all. "Now that we know the neighbors are Peeping Toms, there's no sense calling them on it. Let's get back to the barn for the night."

Bacau, Romania
1825

GENERAL LOCUSTA OPENED THE FOLDER AND BEGAN running his finger down the list of regimental and battalion commanders and subcommanders, mentally checking off each man he thought he could count on once he made his move. His division commanders had already been taken care of, with promises and bribes. But in some ways these men were even more crucial—they were closer to the troops, and would be directly responsible for acting when he gave the word. All but a few owed their present positions to him, but he knew that was no guarantee they would fall into line. It was important that the groundwork be properly laid.

Tonight he would make three calls, all to men whom he didn't know very well. In each case he would have another reason for calling—something he hoped would cement the commander's loyalty.

Locusta picked up the phone and dialed the commander of his Second Armored Regiment, Colonel Tarus Arcos. He caught the colonel eating dinner.

"I hope I didn't disturb you," Locusta said.

"Not at all, General," lied the colonel. "How can I help?"

"I wanted to update you on your request for new vehicles. I have been arguing with Bucharest, and believe we have won, at least the first round."

"That is good news."

Locusta continued in this vein for a while, taking the opportunity to badmouth the government. Then he asked about the colonel's mother, a pensioner in Oradea.

"Still sick, I'm afraid," said the colonel. "The cancer is progressing."

Locusta knew this; one of his aides had checked on her that very afternoon. Still, he pretended to be surprised—and then acted as if an idea had just popped into his head.

"I wonder if my own physicians at Bucharest might be able to help her," he said, as innocently as he could manage. "They are among the best in the country."

The colonel didn't say anything, though it wasn't hard for Locusta to guess that he was thinking it would be difficult to pay for special medical attention; seeing a specialist outside of your home region was not easy to arrange.

"I think that this would be a special service that could be arranged through the army, through my office," added Locusta after just the right pause. "One of my men can handle the paperwork. A man in your position shouldn't have to worry about his mother."

"General, if that could be arranged—"

"There are no ifs," said Locusta grandly. "It is done. I will have it taken care of in the morning."

"I—I'm very, very grateful. If I can repay you—"

"Repay me by being a good soldier." Locusta smiled as he hung up the phone.

Near Tutova, northeastern Romania
1830

DANNY FREAH POKED HIS FORK INTO THE RED LUMP AT THE middle of the plate, eyeing it suspiciously. His hosts' intentions were definitely good, but that wasn't going to make the meal taste any better. He pushed the prongs of his fork halfway into the lump—it went in suspiciously easily—then raised it slowly to his lips.

He caught a whiff of strong vinegar just before he put the unidentified lump into his mouth. But it was too late to reverse course—he pushed the food into his mouth and began chewing.

It tasted . . . not bad. The vinegar was mixed into a sauce that was like . . .

His taste buds couldn't quite find an appropriate comparison. He guessed the lump was actually a piece of beef, though the strong taste of the sauce made it impossible to identify. In any event, it was not inedible, and much better than some food he'd eaten while on deployment.

"You like?" asked Lieutenant Roma, the leader of the Romanian army platoon Danny was working with. Roma had watched his entire taste testing adventure from across the table.

"Oh yeah," said Danny, swallowing quickly. "Very tasty."

Sitting across from him, Boston suppressed a smile.

"More?" offered Roma.

"No, no, my plate's still half full," said Danny. "Plenty for me. Sergeant Boston—he probably wants more."

"Hey, no, I don't want to be a pig," said Boston.

"Pig?" said the lieutenant.

"Oink, oink," said Boston.

"Animal?" Lieutenant Roma's pronunciation made the word sound like *anik-ma-mule*.

"It's an expression," said Danny. "When you eat more than you should, you're a pig."

The lieutenant nodded, said something in Romanian, then turned to the rest of his men and began explaining what Danny had said. They all nodded earnestly.

The Romanian platoon was housed in a pair of farmhouses south of Route E581, about three miles from Tutova. From the looks of things, Danny guessed that the buildings had been requisitioned from their owner or owners fairly recently. The walls of both were covered with rectangles of lighter-colored paint, presumably the spots where photos or paintings had hung. The furniture, old but sturdy, bore the marks of generations of wear. The uneven surface of the wooden dining room table had scrapes and scuff marks at each place setting, and the sideboard was topped by a trio of yellowed doilies, used by the troops as trivets for the serving plates.

Dinner included a helping of local beer for each man. The tall glass of golden pilsner was not enough to get anyone drunk, but it did add a pleasant glow as the plates were cleared. Danny, Boston, the platoon lieutenant, and the NCOs retreated to a nearby room to talk over plans for the next few days. Danny intended to stay with the unit for another day at least, so he could get a feel for how it operated in the field. At that point, he'd leave Boston to complete the training and move to the Romanian Second Army Corps headquarters, where he would set up a temporary school. The most promising men from this unit would accompany him as assistant instructors. He hadn't worked out all the details yet, but he thought he would send Boston to some of the units in the field to judge how the training was actually working.

Some of the younger men spoke very good English, and when their lieutenant excused himself to take a phone call,

Danny asked them to describe where they'd grown up and what their childhoods were like. Most came from small rural villages in the southwest. To them, this part of Romania was almost a different country, more closely associated with neighboring Moldova than Romania.

Before they could explain the reason, Lieutenant Roma returned, his face grim.

"There has been a sighting of a guerrilla force three kilometers from here," he said. "Muster the men."

Bucharest, Romania
1900

STONER REALIZED HE HAD MADE A MISTAKE SPEAKING OF revenge to Sorina as soon as the words came out of his mouth, but it was too late to take them back. All he could do was brood about it, replaying the conversation in his mind as he struggled to find the key to her cooperation.

Sorina Viorica wasn't motivated by revenge, nor by money, the two most likely motivations for a spy. She wanted justice, though her sense of it was distorted. She could rail about a woman starving to death in the streets, but not do anything practical about it, like sharing her sandwich.

She'd railed against her movement, now taken over—in her eyes, at least—by the Russians and fools. But was that enough to make her betray them? Because it was betrayal, as she had said.

Certainly as long as she thought of the movement as a just one, she would not move further against it.

The Russians were a different story. But her knowledge of them was limited. Or at least, what she thought she knew was limited.

Stoner spent the day trying to flesh out the tiny tidbits she had given him, running down information on the Russians and their network in the country. The military attaché, like all military attachés, was suspected of being a spymaster. He had worked in Georgia, the former Soviet Republic, possibly encouraging the opposition forces there before coming to Romania eight months before.

Right before the first CIA officer's death.

A coincidence?

Stoner spent the afternoon with a man who claimed to be the only witness to one of the deaths, a town police chief who had just moved to the capital and claimed to fear for his life. The police chief had been down the street when the car bomb that killed the CIA officer exploded. The American was on his way to meet him to learn about the guerrillas, and the chief was filled with guilt, thinking the bomb had been meant for him. According to the chief, there was no doubt that the guerrillas had planted it. Despite gentle probing by Stoner, he never mentioned the Russians, and when Stoner brought them up directly, the chief seemed to think it was a ridiculous idea.

After the interview, Stoner returned to the embassy. He'd asked for access to NSA taps on Russian communications from the country. This was not a routine request, but the nature of Stoner's business here facilitated matters. One of the desk people back at Langley had been assigned to help review the information. She'd forwarded some of the most promising intercepts, starting with a year ago. Paging through them, Stoner realized there was little direct evidence of anything. What was interesting was the fact that the number of communications had increased sharply after the new attaché arrived.

Not a smoking gun. Just a point of interest.

There was still considerable information to sort through. Stoner decided to leave it to his assistant in Langley. He emerged from the secure communications room as perplexed as ever, sure that whatever was going on lay just beyond his ability to grasp it.

* * *

IT WAS ALREADY DARK, HOURS LATER THAN HE HAD THOUGHT.
He caught a ride over to the center of town, then took a cab
to his hotel, checking along the way to make sure he hadn't
picked up a tail.

Coming into his hotel room, he caught a glimpse of
his face in the mirror opposite the door. His eyelids were
stooped over, making his whole face sag. He needed to
sleep.

First, a shave and a shower.

Though the room was one of a block that the Agency had
under constant surveillance, he checked for bugs. Satisfied
that it was clean, he went into the bathroom and started the
shower. Hot steam billowing around him, he lathered up and
began to shave.

He was about halfway through when his sat phone rang.

"Stoner," he said, answering it.

"What are you doing for dinner?"

It was Sorina Viorica.

"I don't know," he told her. "What do you suggest?"

"You could meet me. There's a good restaurant I know. It's
near the Bibloteque Antique."

"Sure," he said.

"IT IS NOT SO EASY TO TELL YOU WHERE THEY ARE," SORINA
Viorica told him as they waited for their dinners. "You will
kill them. Not you, but the army."

There was no sense lying to her. Stoner didn't answer.

"They were once good people. Now . . . " She shook her
head. "War changed everything."

"Maybe you don't need to be at war. Maybe you have more
in common with this government than you think. It's a democracy."

"In name only."

"In more than name."

She drank her wine. The short hair sharpened her features. She was pretty—he'd known that from the moment he saw her, but here in the soft light of the small restaurant, he realized it again. She'd gone out and gotten herself some clothes—obviously she had money stashed away, wasn't as poor as he'd thought. She wore a top that gave a peek at her cleavage, showing just a glimpse of her breasts. When they left the restaurant, he noticed how the red skirt she wore emphasized the shape of her hips.

They went near the Sutu Palace, once the home of kings, now a historical museum. It was a cold night and they had the street to themselves. Except for the bright lights that flooded the pavement, they could have been in the eighteenth or nineteenth century, royal visitors come to see the prince.

They walked in silence for a while. He knew she was thinking about what to do, how far to go with it. Eventually, he thought, she'd cooperate. She'd tell him everything she knew about the guerrilla operations.

But maybe none of it would help him fulfill his mission.

"So you come back to Bucharest often?" he asked.

"Not in two years."

"You seem to know your way around."

"Do you forget the places you've been?"

"I'd like to. Some of them."

She laughed.

"Do you go back and forth a lot?" he asked her.

"I have been in Moldova for the past year. And on a few missions."

Stoner wanted information about the missions, but didn't press. It had grown colder, and the chill was getting to her. He pulled off his jacket, wrapped it around her.

"Are you married, Stoner?"

"No."

"Would you like to be?"

"I never really thought about it," he lied.

"Are men really that different from women?"

"How's that?"

She stopped and looked at him. "I can't believe you never thought about getting married."

Stoner suddenly felt embarrassed to be caught in such a simple lie. He was working here, getting close to her—and yet felt ashamed of himself for not telling the truth.

They walked some more. He asked about the missions, but she turned the questions aside and began talking about being a girl and visiting Bucharest. He tried gently to steer the conversation toward the guerrillas, but she remained personal, talking about herself and occasionally asking him questions about where he'd grown up. He gave vague answers, always aiming to slip the conversation back toward her.

After an hour they stopped in a small club, where a band played Euro-electro pop. Sorina Viorica had half a glass of wine, then abruptly rose and said she wanted to go to bed.

Stoner wasn't sure whether it was an invitation, and he debated what to do as they walked back to the apartment. Sleeping with her might help him get more information. On the other hand, it felt wrong in a way he couldn't explain to himself.

She kissed him on the cheek as they reached the door of the apartment, then slipped inside, alone.

He was glad, and disappointed at the same time.

Iasi Airfield, northeastern Romania
2100

COLONEL BASTIAN SAT DOWN AT THE COMMUNICATIONS desk in the Dreamland Mobile Command Center and pulled on a headset. He typed his passwords into the console, then leaned back in the seat, preparing to do something he hadn't had to do in quite a while—give an operational status report to his immediate superior.

The fact that he didn't much like General Samson ought to be besides the point, he told himself. In the course of his career, he'd had to work for many men—and one or two women—whom he didn't particularly like. It wasn't just their personality clashes, though. The truth was, he'd had this command, and now he didn't. Even having known that Dreamland would either be closed or taken over by a general, he still resented his successor.

The best thing for him to do—and the best thing for Dreamland—was to move on. As long as he was here, the friction between him and Samson would be detrimental to the unit and its mission.

"Colonel Bastian, good morning," Captain Jake Lewis, on duty in the base control center, said to him through the headset.

"It's pretty late at night here," said Dog. "Twenty-one hundred hours."

"Yes, sir. You're ten hours ahead of us. Soon your today will be our tomorrow."

Dog frowned. Somehow, the captain's joke seemed more like a metaphor of his career situation.

"Would you like to speak to General Samson?" asked the captain.

"Absolutely," lied Dog.

"Stand by, Colonel."

Dog expected Samson to be connected via the special phone up in his office. But instead the general's face flashed on the screen. Obviously he'd been in the command center, waiting for Dog to check in.

You couldn't blame him for that, Dog decided. He would have done the same thing. A lot of what Samson did, he would have done.

Differently. But what was bugging him was the fact that it was Samson doing it, not him.

Jealousy. Yes. He had to admit it.

"This is Samson. What's going on over there, Bastian?"

"Good morning, General. We've completed our first day of working with Romanian ground soldiers. There were some language glitches, but all in all it went well."

"What kind of glitches?"

"Nothing critical. A little hard sometimes to understand what they're saying, and I imagine vice versa."

"That's it?"

"No. I wanted to alert you to something that should be passed on to Jed Barclay and the White House."

Samson's scowl made it clear that he'd be the judge of that.

"While we were up, a flight of Russian MiGs flew over the Black Sea and part of the Ukraine. I believe they were shadowing us. They appear to have been working with one of their Elint planes to get an idea of where we were. I took a hard turn toward them and they vamoosed. I'm not positive, of course, but—"

"What do you mean, you took a hard turn toward them? You went into Moldova?"

"No, General, I didn't. I stayed inside the country's boundaries and flew in the direction of the Black Sea. But they were watching me closely, and it seems to me they didn't want to be noticed."

"Don't overanalyze it. What sort of planes?"

"Two MiG-29s, configured for air-to-air intercept. There was a Tu-135 just beyond them. We were too far to get comprehensive details. I didn't want to go out of Romanian airspace."

Dog watched Samson step over to one of the nearby consoles in the command center, consulting with one of the men there. Finally he looked back in the direction of the video camera attop the main screen in the front of the room.

"What else do you have?" asked Samson.

"Nothing else. I was wondering when the *Johnson* will arrive."

"Englehardt and his crew took off an hour ago," said Samson. "They should be there tonight, our time."

"Once they're here, I expect to start running two sorties a day. We'll stagger them—"

"I don't need the details. Carry on."

The screen blanked. Dog leaned back in his seat. He was sorry now that he'd agreed to take on the mission. He should just have gone on leave—he was more than entitled.

Rising, he took off his headset and pulled back the curtain to call the Whiplash communications specialist. As he did, the console buzzed, indicating an incoming communication.

It was Danny Freah.

"Colonel, we have something up," said Danny as soon as he punched the buttons to make the connection. "Report of a possible attack in a village southeast of us. We could use some Flighthawk coverage."

"We're on our way."

Allegro, Nevada
1105

BREANNA PULLED UP AGAINST THE SIDE OF THE POOL, catching her breath. Her heart was pumping ferociously, the beats so fast she didn't count them. Fearing she was far over her targeted pulse rate, she took a deep, slow breath, savoring the oxygen in her lungs. Then she went to the side and pulled herself out.

"Hell of a workout," said one of the club trainers, a white woman in her mid-thirties with the unfortunate nickname of Dolly, though she didn't seem to mind it. "You were swimming up a storm."

Breanna nodded, still catching her breath.

"You OK, girl?" asked Dolly.

"I'm fine." Breanna forced a smile. She loved to swim, and

the water workouts were easy on her knee, but her ribs ached from the vigorous strokes.

"You trying to prove something?" asked Dolly.

"Why?"

Dolly laughed. "I think you just broke the record for the 10K free-style."

"Just that I'm in good shape."

"No doubts there."

Breanna smiled, then grabbed her water bottle and the small towel she always took with her during a workout.

No doubt there.

All she had to do was convince the doc. Maybe she'd bring him along tomorrow.

She'd just reached the locker room when she heard her cell phone ringing. She opened the lock and took out the phone, opening it without looking at the number.

"This is Breanna."

"I got those tickets. Meet me over at the county airport at four."

"Tickets?"

"To the Lakers, remember?"

"Oh, Sleek. Um, OK. Sure. Where?"

Sleek Top leased part of a small Cessna that was kept at the Las Vegas airport; they'd take it to L.A., where the Lakers were facing Kings later that evening. He told her where to meet him.

"We'll grab something to eat at the game," he said. "I'll have you back home before midnight."

"Great," she said. "I'll see you then."

Near Tutova, northeastern Romania
2115

THE ROMANIAN PLATOON TRAVELED IN FOUR 1980S VINTAGE Land Rover III three-quarter-ton light trucks, and a pair of much older UAZ469B jeeplike vehicles. The former were badly dented and the latter were rusted, but their engines were in good order and the troops wasted no time moving out, driving down the highway in the direction of the reported guerrilla sighting. The gas pipeline was about fifteen miles to the northwest, and Danny wondered if the report wasn't the result of a mistake or perhaps hysteria until he saw the glow of a fire in the distance.

"It's the local police station," Lieutenant Roma told him, leaning back from the front seat of the UAZ. "They make these kind of attacks all the time."

The police station was located across from a church in a cluster of six or seven buildings just off the main road. The station was one of three wooden buildings nestled together, and the flames that had been started by an explosion had set the other two buildings on fire.

The Romanian lieutenant split up his force, using about half to secure the road on both sides of the hamlet. The rest came with him as he went to investigate the attack.

The men leaped out of the trucks as they arrived, shouting at the people in front of the burning buildings and telling them to get back. Everything was chaos. There were a dozen civilians, some crying, some screaming, others stoically using pails in a vain attempt to put out the flames.

A man in a soot-covered police uniform materialized from the right of the buildings, his face burned to a bright red by the heat. He had something in his arms—a doll, Danny thought at first. And then as he stared, he realized the doll was a human child who'd been pulled out of the building too late.

Tears streamed from the policeman's eyes, and Danny felt his stomach weaken.

Lieutenant Roma was talking with an older man near the steps to the church. The man spoke in almost a whisper, his head pitched down toward the ground, as if speaking to his shoes.

Roma listened for a while, then nodded. He moved away from the church, toward Danny.

"There were twelve," he told him. "They may have taken a policeman hostage. They blew up the building with no warning."

"Where'd they go?"

Roma shook his head. "They have the police car, the ambulance, and may have taken a truck as well. Someone heard tires screeching on the back road there." He pointed to the side street, which ran to the southeast. "It would make sense that they would go that way. They'll avoid the highway."

"Let's get after them."

The lieutenant frowned. Danny realized he wasn't hesitating out of cowardice—there was no local fire department, and he was debating whether anything could be done to stop the fire.

It was already far too late. Fed by the wood that had dried for more than a hundred years, the flames climbed into the night sky. The back of one of the buildings crumbled to the ground. The fire flared, but without wind to spread it across the street, it would soon run out of fuel, choked by its own ravenous hunger.

Thicker, heavier parts of the buildings—rugs, appliances— began to melt rather than burn. Acrid smoke spread across the road, stinging everyone's nose and eyes.

"Yes, let's go." Roma turned to the man and told him in Romanian that they would be back. Then he looked at Danny. "Are your people ready to help us?"

"They should be in the air any second."

**Aboard the *Bennett*,
above northeastern Romania
2124**

ZEN TOOK OVER THE FLIGHTHAWK AS SOON AS IT WAS launched, juicing the throttle and heading toward the GPS reading from Danny Freah's radio. The infrared camera in the Flighthawk's nose showed a docile, almost dreamlike landscape of empty fields broken only occasionally by small clusters of houses. It seemed impossible that there was a war here, but Danny's voice when he checked in sounded as grim as if he were in the middle of hell itself.

"We're traveling on local Road 154," said Danny. "They have a police car, an ambulance, and maybe a pickup truck. There may be a hostage."

"Roger that," said Zen. His rules of engagement required him to get permission not just from Dog, but the Romanian Second Army Corps commander before firing—unless the guerrillas were shooting directly at a Whiplash team member.

In that case he'd obliterate whatever he felt was a danger and ask questions later.

"Check the highways nearby, just in case," added Danny. "But we think this is the road they took."

"Yeah, we're on it."

Romanian road maps had been uploaded into the computer's memory. Zen gave a verbal command and the computer projected the map on the screen. After highlighting his position, it flashed an arrow on the highway Danny had mentioned, a long, winding road that ran from the larger highway to the south.

The road was about thirty miles away. Zen adjusted his course, turning so he would bring the road into view just south of Danny's location. Then he pushed the plane lower, his eyes locked on the view in the screen.

The road ran for about three miles, taking a few gentle S-turns past farm fields and ending at a shallow creek and woods. There were no vehicles of any kind along it. The infrared camera didn't show anything warm in the vicinity. Zen rechecked his position, then took another pass, slowing the Flighthawk down to get a better look.

Spiff, operating the ground radar, reported that the highway was clear, except for a fire truck responding from a neighboring town.

"Danny, are you sure this is the road?" Zen asked as he flew the Flighthawk north, passing over the army vehicles.

"It's their best guess."

Zen pulled up, taking a moment to consult the radar image of the ground. The odd thing about this road was that it didn't connect to any other roads; it was essentially a dead end, albeit a very long one, flanked by numerous barns and some isolated farmhouses. If the guerrillas had used it, they were almost certainly hiding somewhere.

Near Tutova, northeastern Romania
2131

ADRENALINE WAS BOTH A CURSE AND A BOON. TOO MUCH and you started to lose your sense of judgment, rushed into things without taking the wisest approach. Too little and you lost your edge, holding back when you should attack.

Even for Danny Freah it was a difficult balance. The dark night, the unfamiliar territory, and most of all his role as an observer rather than a leader, made it more difficult to walk the tightrope. His heart sped; his head told it to slow down.

Even though Zen had said the road was empty, Lieutenant Roma insisted on driving to the very end. When they reached it, he got his troops out and had them cross the creek, searching the woods and nearby fields. Danny, watching the infrared feed from the Flighthawk on his smart helmet's visor, could tell that the woods were too sparse to hide any of the vehicles. When he told the lieutenant, the Romanian replied that a few months back after a similar attack the troop had chased a small unit of guerrillas across a stream nearby and trapped them in the woods.

A nice story, thought Danny, but one that had no bearing on their present situation.

"They always go back across the border," said Roma. "They are cowards and head in that direction."

"But if they took a police car and the other trucks, shouldn't we look for them? They must be hiding in one of the barns we've passed, waiting for daybreak to launch another attack."

"They will abandon them somewhere," said the lieutenant.

"Why take something so obvious as a police car or an ambulance unless you're going to use it?" asked Danny.

"We have only the mayor's word that they took a police car. Sometimes they say things like that because they hope the government will give them new vehicles. That is what I think is happening here—it's a small village; there may not even have been a police car, let alone an ambulance."

Roma had left two of his men back near the village, and between them and the Flighthawk, it was unlikely that the guerrillas would be able to double back without being seen. But the allocation of resources bothered Danny's sense of priorities. When one of the soldiers thought he saw tire ruts on the other side of a shallow stretch of the stream, Roma ordered most of his men to cross the field and search, a decision that would not only waste time but fatigue the troops unnecessarily, Danny thought. He radioed Zen, who took a low, slow pass overhead.

"The terrain goes up pretty sharply at the end of the field," Zen reported. "I could see maybe a jeep getting in and through there, but not a car, let alone an ambulance."

"How about a pickup truck?"

"Yeah, I guess if it's four-wheel drive. But I don't see anything up there on the infrared. It'd be pretty easy to spot."

"You see tracks?"

"Those might be a little harder, but no, nothing obvious."

"Keep looking, all right?"

"I'm on it."

While Roma's men continued searching the area, the Romanian lieutenant checked in with his division headquarters. The border guards had been alerted, and another company sent over to the hamlet that had been attacked. Five people had died in either the explosion or the subsequent fire; two others were missing. It wasn't clear whether they had been taken hostage or were still somewhere in the smoldering ruins of the buildings.

When the search of the field failed to turn up anything, Lieutenant Roma called his men back and began a systematic search of the buildings they'd passed. The soldiers split into groups so they could cover each other as well as prevent an escape.

The first barn was quite a distance from its owner's house, and Roma didn't bother asking permission before inspecting it. After sealing off the driveway and posting lookouts on the other three sides, two men with submachine guns and a third with a grenade launcher took up positions opposite the large door, which was mounted on a track of wheels that allowed it to be pushed to the side to open. On the count of three, a pair of soldiers shot off the locks and hauled it aside, the runners squeaking and the men huffing as they pushed, then dove to the ground for cover.

Except for some old farm equipment and a few bales of hay, the interior was empty. The house didn't have a garage; after a precursory check of the owner's small Fiat parked in back, the troops moved on.

The second barn was right next to a house, and because of the proximity, the lieutenant decided to alert the owner to the search. After his troops surrounded the place, the Romanian and Danny walked up the creaky wooden steps to the front porch.

Danny had a premonition of danger. He edged his finger against the trigger housing of his MP5 as a light came on inside. A plump woman in her early fifties answered the door, wearing a bathrobe. For a moment she seemed confused. Then she turned angry and began scolding the lieutenant. Roma ignored her, signaling for his men to proceed. They shot off a lock in the nearby barn, hauled the door open, and began their search.

The woman shouted angrily. Roma turned his back on her, signaling for a squad to search inside the house. Enraged, she swung her fist at the back of his head.

Danny grabbed her arm before she connected. She screamed even louder, then spun and tried clawing at his face and bulletproof vest. He pushed her as gently as possible back inside the house. She squirmed against him, flailing with her fists, her fury unleashed. Afraid that she was going to grab his pistol, Danny went to push her away with his left arm and inadvertently smacked her across the forehead with the MP5. The woman staggered back, slapping her head against the doorjamb and then slipping to the floor. He reached out to grab her but was too late; she fell in a heap on the floor, stunned.

Two of Roma's men who had run up to assist grabbed the woman and dragged her farther inside. They pushed her into an upholstered chair. One pointed his rifle at her face and barked something in fierce Romanian. The rest of the squad began searching the house.

Danny stayed downstairs, unsure whether he would be needed or not. The woman sat in the chair, her eyes narrow slits and her mouth clamped shut. She looked as if her insides were literally boiling, her forehead reddened from the effort to keep from exploding.

The whole house shook with the heavy footsteps of the men searching above. Danny moved to the side of the room, watching an alcove that led into two rooms in the back. One of the rooms was a kitchen; a small vase of plastic flowers sat in the middle of the table between two candles, almost as if the woman were expecting a romantic evening.

"Nothing," said one of the soldiers to Danny in English as he came down the steps.

He nodded. The soldier began questioning the woman in Romanian, but she clamped her mouth shut. As the other men came downstairs, Danny decided he'd be of more use outside, and went to see what was going on.

He'd stepped off the porch and was just about to contact Zen when he heard a scream and a crash inside the house.

The soldiers filed out quickly. Danny went back and looked into the room. The woman lay on the floor on her back. Slowly, she rolled over and started getting to her feet. He was about to go help her but the expression on her face stopped him. She was afraid he was going to kill her, and he realized the kindest thing he could do was simply back away.

OUTSIDE, THE BARN AND NEARBY GROUNDS HAD BEEN searched without anything being found. Danny checked in with Zen, then walked back to the troop trucks.

Roma was already there, talking to his commander. More troops were being sent to help with the search.

"I think one of your men hit the old lady in the house," Danny told him, explaining what he'd heard.

"You saw what she was like," said Roma. "Many of these people are like that."

"Still—"

"You had to hit her yourself."

"I grabbed her so she wouldn't hit you."

Roma turned and ordered his men into the trucks.

"Aren't you going to do anything?" Danny demanded.

The lieutenant didn't answer.

Danny grabbed his arm and spun him back toward him. "Listen, Lieutenant. You can't just let your men push around civilians."

Roma looked down at his hand, then back at him.

"I'll ask what happened," Lieutenant Roma said.

"Good."

Danny got into the back of the jeep. Sitting there, he started to doubt that Roma would actually ask his men what had happened. Even if he did, it was likely nothing would come of it.

Yes, he had pushed the woman himself—but only to pro- ·
tect the lieutenant, who would have been hurt otherwise. Everything else was an accident.

Maybe it didn't look like that from Roma's perspective. And maybe the lines he was drawing were too fine to be practical.

**Aboard the *Bennett*,
above northeastern Romania
2201**

"TWO MORE CONTACTS OVER THE BLACK SEA, SAME AS before," Rager told Dog as they circled above the area where the guerrillas had attacked.

"MiGs?"

"MiG-29s. Configuration: two AMRAAMskis, four small missiles, probably infrared AA-11 Archers," said Rager. AMRAAMski was slang for the Russian R-77 radar-guided antiair missile, a weapon somewhat similar to the American AMRAAM. AA-11 Archer was the NATO designation for Russia's R-73 short-range heat-seekers. "They're running a racetrack pattern 263 miles to our east."

"All right. Thanks."

"We going to take another run at them?" asked Sullivan.

"We have better things to do," Dog told him. "We'll ignore them as long as they keep their distance."

"What if they don't?"

"Then that will be their problem."

Near Tutova, northeastern Romania
2207

THE NEXT BARN THEY CAME TO LOOKED AS IF IT DATED FROM the medieval ages. One of its stone walls had caved in, and the rear of the roof was gone. The soldiers searched it anyway, using flashlights to sort through the shadows.

A smaller outbuilding sat behind it. This too was made of stone—large, carefully cut rocks the size of suitcases, piled like a complicated jigsaw puzzle beneath a sharply raked wooden roof.

The door, though, was metal. And new. And ajar.

Danny knelt down near the entrance, covering the soldiers as they went inside. The building wasn't big enough to fit a car, yet it reeked so badly of gasoline that his nose stung.

One of the soldiers emerged from the shed holding a small gas can. It was empty, as were the dozen others scattered inside. One had apparently spilled; the dirt floor was still muddy.

"Pretty recent," said Danny, toeing his boot through the residue.

Back outside, the soldiers had finished going through the main building without finding anything and were now fanning out to search the nearby area. The yard was rutted with tire tracks, but there was no way to tell how recent they were.

A stream ran at the edge of the property, thirty feet from the building. Danny walked over to the shallow water, examining the rock-strewn bed. Though only an inch or so deep, the creek was nearly eight feet wide, more than enough for a car or small truck to drive down.

Were there tracks in it? He couldn't be sure.

"Where does this go?" Danny asked Roma when the lieutenant came over to see what he was doing.

Roma shook his head and took out a map. Danny reached to the back of his helmet and clicked his radio on.

"Zen, that streambed behind the buildings where we are—can you check it out?"

"Stand by, Groundhog."

Roma located it on his topo map and showed it to Danny. The stream ran about a hundred yards before swinging by another road.

"I'd better send some men around to cut anyone off," said the lieutenant, picking up his radio.

"Groundhog, this is Flighthawk leader. The stream runs down near a road that parallels the road you're on."

"Roger that. We're looking at a map right now."

"There's a culvert farther up and then it goes back to the highway. I've looked up and down, can't see anyone nearby."

"You think a car could drive down it?" Danny asked.

"Hard to tell. It looks relatively level. There are a half-dozen properties along the way that have buildings the size you're looking for."

"Can you get low and slow and give me a feed?" asked Danny. "The stream first. The lieutenant's going to send some men up it."

"Yeah, roger that."

Zen took two passes as Danny watched. It looked clear to him, though there were one or two places where someone might have been able to hide in the thick vegetation. Danny told Roma about them and started up with the men.

His suspicion that the guerrillas had used the creek as a road cooled as they went. While it looked flat from above, it gradually grew rockier and deeper, harder and harder for a car to pass.

The point man halted, then pointed to something on the bank.

Tire tracks veered up along the side.

"Flighthawk leader, we think we found the spot where they came off," said Danny.

"Roger that, Groundhog," said Zen.

A second or so later Zen came back on the line, his voice tight.

"Four, five figures coming through the field to your north. They have a heavy machine gun. Twenty yards."

A split second later, the machine gun began chewing up the night.

Aboard EB-52 *Johnson*,
above northeastern Romania
2210

ZEN'S MOMENTUM TOOK HIM PAST THE GUERRILLAS BEFORE he could fire. As he turned back, he launched an illumination flare to silhouette the attackers for the Romanians. Then he pushed the Flighthawk's nose down, zeroing in on the machine gun. He sent a stream of 20mm rounds into the machine-gun spot. Two or three shadows began moving to his left, apparently running away.

"*Bennett,* we have contact on the ground," Zen told Dog over the interphone.

"Copy that, Flighthawk leader."

"Spiff, you see any vehicles moving on the roadway or behind that field anywhere?" Zen asked the radar operator.

"Negative."

Turning back for another run, Zen realized he had lost track of where the Romanian soldiers were. Danny's GPS unit showed his location just south of the now mangled machine gun, but tracers were flying in every direction around him.

"Groundhog, I can't get a good fix on your team's position," said Zen. "Where do you want me?"

"Stand by."

"Roger that," he answered, frustrated that he couldn't do more.

Near Tutova, northeastern Romania
2213

ONE MOMENT DANNY HAD EVERYTHING SORTED OUT IN HIS head—where the guerrillas were, where the soldiers were, where he was. Then it was as if the world had spun upside down. Everything around him was jumbled. He couldn't tell who was firing at whom. Both the guerrillas and the Romanian soldiers had AK-47s, and even in harsh light thrown by the Flighthawk's illumination flare, telling the running figures apart was next to impossible.

Someone ran up from the stream and yelled at him in Romanian. Danny yelled back in English, not understanding a word.

The soldier twisted toward the barn and began firing. Danny couldn't see his target, but apparently the soldier hit it, because he jumped up and started running in that direction. Following, Danny got about four or five yards before tracers zipped so close he could practically feel their tailspin.

He threw himself down, then crawled to the soldier he'd been following. The man had been hit in the head four or five times. The bullets had ripped most of his skull apart.

A fresh salvo of gunfire flew from the barn. Danny flattened himself against the ground, using the dead man's body as cover. The bullets were heavy caliber, and they tore up the ground in little clumps as they sprayed across the field.

"Zen, you see that machine gun twenty yards from the barn?" said Danny.

"I'm on it. Keep your guys away."

Inaudible above the din and rendered invisible because of its black skin, the Flighthawk seemed to be a lightning bolt sent by God Himself. The earth reverberated as a tornado of dirt and lead swirled in a frantic vortex where Danny's enemy had been. Gun and gunner disappeared in the swirl, consumed by its fury.

The ricochets and shrapnel missed him, but not by much. A few hit the dead man in front of him, ripping his already torn body still further. Bits of cloth and flesh splattered over Danny, sticking to his uniform.

The gunfire across the battlefield abruptly stopped. Danny turned toward the stream and yelled for the lieutenant, whom he thought would be there by now, but he didn't get an answer.

He began making his way toward the barn, moving cautiously. He came upon another soldier, facedown in the field. As he checked to see if the man was alive, a shadow moved to his right. Danny raised his submachine gun to fire, stopping only at the last second when he saw what he thought was a helmet, the sign of a soldier.

"I'm Captain Freah!" Danny shouted. "The American observer. The American!"

The figure answered with gunfire.

Two bullets hit Danny's side. He spun to his right, sprawling on the ground. Though the carbon-boron cells in his body armor gave him considerably more protection than a standard bulletproof vest would have, he could practically feel the welts rising at the side of his chest.

Danny pulled himself around, catching his breath and trying to think of something he could say to get the man to stop firing.

He couldn't return fire—he'd lost his MP5 when he fell.

Finally, the bursts stopped.

Danny watched as the shooter rose and began moving across the field, apparently thinking he'd killed him. As the man passed close by, Danny realized it wasn't a helmet he'd seen; the man was wearing a watch cap.

Danny waited, not daring to move until the man was behind him. Then he leaped up, twisting around and throwing himself on the guerrilla's back. He rode the man to the ground, then grabbed the man's rifle and began battering his head with the stock. The man tried to roll and fend off the blows, but Danny swung harder. He battered away, anger and adrenaline fueling a bloody revenge.

By the time he got control of himself, the guerrilla was dead, his face a bloody pulp.

Danny knelt next to him, watching as someone ran up from the direction of the stream. It was Lieutenant Roma.

"Are you all right?" he asked.

"Yeah." Danny got up. "If you pull the men back, I can have the Flighthawk hit the barn."

"There may be hostages," said the lieutenant. "I don't want to strike blindly."

As if on cue, another machine gun began to rake the field from the second story of the barn. Danny put a fresh box of ammo in the gun he'd taken from the guerrilla and began moving to his right.

"Where are you going?" yelled Roma.

"I'll flank it, get an angle. You draw his fire from here."

"No. You stay. My men will take care of it."

"Draw his fire," insisted Danny. "I only need a few seconds."

Danny leapt up, charged to his right a few yards, then dove back to the ground before the machine gunner could bring his weapon to bear. In the meantime, Lieutenant Roma had begun firing. As the bullets swung back toward Roma, Danny lurched up on all fours and scrambled along the ground until he came to a slight rise. He crawled behind it and crept up along a narrow rift formed by a tiny stream that ran only after very heavy rains. He could see the machine gun's tracers, but not the gunner inside the building, hidden by the angle.

Before he could decide whether to go back a little and try from another spot, Danny heard a loud hiss in the field. He threw himself back down into a ball, rolling into a fetal position as a rocket-propelled grenade exploded in the machine-gun post.

He stayed like that for a full minute before he unfolded

himself. The Romanian soldiers began moving forward in the dark.

"American!" yelled one.

"I'm over here!" answered Danny. A sergeant ran toward him. Danny saw three or four figures running past the barn; by the time he realized they were guerrillas, it was too late to shoot.

Lieutenant Roma joined him as his men worked their way toward the barn. There was still sporadic gunfire, but nothing as intense as it had been just a few minutes before.

"We have reinforcements on the way," Roma said, his voice tight with anxiety. "We're cutting off the road near the highway. Then we'll tighten the noose."

"How many troops are coming?" Danny asked.

"A company. Two. Whatever can respond. I don't think there are many more guerrillas," he added. "And those who are left may not have the stomach to keep fighting."

"They have plenty of stomach from what I've seen."

**Aboard EB-52 *Bennett*,
above northeastern Romania
2217**

ZEN SPOTTED TWO FIGURES RUNNING FROM THE REAR OF the barn toward a building across a dirt road a hundred yards away. As he circled around, he saw someone else near the building. Suddenly, one of the walls seemed to give way. A small pickup truck emerged—it had broken through a garage-style door—and headed toward the road. The man nearby threw himself into the back. The two others ran and did the same. Another vehicle, this one a car, followed.

"Danny, I have a pickup truck and a sedan, mid-size, coming out of one of the buildings across the road, about a hundred and fifty yards north of your position," said Zen.

"Roger, we heard it."

"I can nail them."

"Negative. They may have hostages. Follow it for now."

Zen slipped the Flighthawk farther along the road. The Romanians had forces on the highway about three-fourths of a mile away, though there were several places the guerrillas could turn off. He tucked back, then decided to try and spook them by flying toward them low and fast, pickling a few flares into their windshields as he pulled up.

As he came out of the turn and started in, he spotted a small bridge over a stream ahead of the vehicles and got a better idea.

The bridge was little more than a few wooden planks over a culvert pipe. He climbed a few hundred feet, then pushed in, twisting the Flighthawk so its nose pointed almost straight down at the road surface. He mashed the trigger of his cannon, then waggled his plane left and right, chewing the wood up with his bullets.

The pickup appeared as Zen cleared. His attack had damaged the bridge so severely that it slid sideways as soon as the truck started across. The vehicle skidded but managed to get to the other side as the bridge collapsed behind it.

The car that was following, however, was stranded. Seven men hopped out and ran across the culvert to the truck. From the air, it looked like a circus routine, though without the humor.

"Truck got across the little bridge," Zen told Danny. "Six, seven guys getting out of the car, crossing. They're in the back of the pickup."

"Stand by."

The pickup drove about ten yards and then stopped. Everyone spilled out and began running toward a nearby house.

"Danny, they're going toward a building. I see no one that looks like he might be a hostage."

There was a pause as Danny conferred with Roma.

"See if you can stop them," Danny said finally.

Zen laid down a spray of cannon fire across the lawn of the

house. Three or four men fell, but the others were too spread out for him to target in a single run. He circled back quickly, but by the time he brought his guns to bear, all but two had made it into the house.

Whether they had hostages before, Zen thought bitterly, they had them now.

Near Tutova, northeastern Romania
2220

THE POLICE CAR AND AN AMBULANCE WERE IN THE BARN.

So were two policemen. Both had been shot through the head.

Lieutenant Roma quickly regrouped his men, organizing them so he could surround the house where the guerrillas had gone. He seemed to realize that his fears about hostages had probably led to others being taken. Or maybe his somber mood came from the fact that the guerrillas had killed two and wounded four of his men in the field outside the barn.

Danny remained silent as they drove to the house. Half a dozen soldiers had already set up positions near it without drawing fire, but when the guerrillas saw the truck, they began shooting ferociously.

"Time is on our side," said Roma after they took cover. "We will have them surrounded as soon as our reinforcements arrive."

Had the guerrillas mounted a concentrated attack on one of the flanks, they might have been able to break through. But within ten minutes another platoon of soldiers arrived; a few minutes later, another.

The house sat in the middle of well-cleared plot of land, with good lines of fire for the army soldiers as they clustered behind vehicles and other cover. There would be no way for the guerrillas to escape this time. Their only hope would be some sort of negotiated surrender.

Along with the reinforcements, senior officers began to arrive: first a company captain, then a major; before an hour passed, a colonel arrived and took charge.

Roma introduced him to Danny as Oz, without reference to his rank. He had a brush mustache and eyes that sat far back in his skull.

"This is something new," Oz told Danny. "Ordinarily they don't take prisoners. But then we usually don't catch them like this. We are grateful for your help."

"That's why we're here."

"There are five girls in the house," said Oz. "The neighbors say they have a grandmother and an uncle living with them as well. From five to fifteen. Girls." The colonel shook his head. "Innocent people."

"Maybe you can get them to release them."

Oz frowned. "One of my men has already tried calling the house. No answer."

"Can we wait them out?"

"What other choice do we have?"

About a half hour later two armored personnel carriers arrived. Oz climbed into the rear of one, then the two trucks slowly advanced onto the front lawn, stopping about twenty yards from the house. The guerrillas made no effort to stop them, and, as far as Danny could tell, didn't appear at the windows.

The rear ramp of the vehicle Oz had gotten into slammed open. The colonel emerged, a microphone in his hand.

"What's he saying?" Danny asked Roma as Oz began to broadcast a message.

"Telling them they have to surrender," said the lieutenant. "He's giving them a phone number they can call to talk to us."

The colonel paused, evidently waiting for an answer. When none came, he repeated his warning and plea.

This time there was an answer—an explosion so violent it knocked Danny to the ground.

**Aboard EB-52 *Bennett*,
above northeastern Romania
2235**

EVEN THOUGH ZEN KNEW BETTER, THE EXPLOSION THAT rocked the house was so intense that for a second he thought the *Bennett* had unleashed a missile on the building. The fireball rose over the Flighthawk.

"Colonel, you see that?" Zen asked.

"I have it on screen," said Dog dryly.

"They blew themselves up. Shit."

"All right, Zen. Tell Danny we're standing by."

**Near Tutova, northeastern Romania
2237**

BY THE TIME DANNY RECOVERED, THE FIREBALL HAD FALLEN back into the ruins. Smoke and dust filled the air. All he could hear was the low rumble of the motor from one of the personnel carriers; the other had been choked and stalled by the air surge of the explosion.

Then the screaming began. A loud wail went up, as if all the world had begun to cry at once. A dozen men had been hit by shrapnel and were seriously wounded. Another two or three had been killed outright.

What remained of the house was on fire. The glow turned the night orange, casting long shadows around the yard. The Romanian soldiers began to move toward their comrades who had been wounded.

"Groundhog, are you all right?" asked Zen.

"Groundhog. Affirmative."

"What the hell happened? It looked like a piece of hell opened up."

The only thing Danny could think of was that the guerrillas had been carrying plastique explosives with them, and augmented their power with something they found in the house, natural gas, maybe.

"I heard there were kids in the house," Danny told Zen, still in disbelief.

"God."

"I'll get back to you."

Though he didn't have a med kit, Danny was a trained paramedic and realized he could be of more use helping the wounded than lamenting what had happened. He threw off his helmet and ran toward the bodies scattered along the lawn. Most were near the armored personnel carriers, lulled by the bulk of the big trucks into thinking they were safe behind them.

The first man he reached had been hit in the leg by a large piece of metal. The wound wasn't deep. Danny checked for little shards or metal splinters up and down his thigh; when he didn't find any, he made a bandage from the man's handkerchief and had him press down on it to stop the bleeding.

The next man was dead, killed by a large piece of wood that had slit his neck and its arteries wide open.

Oz was sitting on the ground behind the APC, dazed. The shock had thrown him off the open ramp of the carrier and he'd struck his head. His pupils seemed to react to the flashlight Danny shone in his eyes, but that didn't necessarily rule out a concussion, and Danny told him he'd have to be checked by a doctor. Oz nodded, but still seemed dazed.

Lieutenant Roma walked up as Danny rose.

"You see what kind of people we're up against, the criminals," said Roma. He had tears in his eyes. "Devils. Worse. Killers of children."

"It's horrible."

"They're slime," said Roma. "Cowards."

"Yes," said Danny.

Roma crumpled.

Danny knelt and saw that he'd been struck by something hard, a brick maybe, that had caved in the right side of his head. Blood trickled from his ear.

"Roma? Roma?" he said.

The lieutenant didn't answer. He wasn't breathing. He had no pulse.

Danny started CPR. A Romanian medic ran up; they worked together for a minute, two minutes, then five.

When ten minutes had passed and both men could no longer pretend there was still hope, they looked at each other for a moment. Then slowly Danny rose and went to see if there was someone else he might help.

IV

Burnt Wood and Flesh

Stoner rubbed the sleep from his eyes as he looked at the photo of the house and the aftermath of the guerrillas' explosion. There was a torso in the foreground. The other photo showed a baby's arm clutched around a doll.

The American ambassador to Romania pushed the rest of the photos toward the far side of his desk, no longer able to look at them. The ambassador, rarely seen in public without a tie, wore a hooded yellow sweatshirt and a pair of old jeans, as if he were going to work on his car when they were done.

"Pretty gruesome, I'd say." The ambassador shook his head. "Bastards."

"Yeah," said Russ Fairchild, the CIA station chief. "This is what they're up against."

"Was it the Russians or the guerrillas?" asked the ambassador.

"Had to be the Russians," said Fairchild. "That much explosives?"

Stoner leaned forward and took the rest of the photos. Fairchild was probably right about the source of the explosives. But the description of the operation he'd heard from the Dreamland people made it sound too amateurish for Spetsnaz.

He flipped through the pictures, which had been taken

by the Romanian army on the scene. The guerrillas were in pieces, their bodies shattered when the explosives blew.

Stoner found a severed leg. He slipped the picture onto the ambassador's desk.

"They were guerrillas," he told the others. "See the shoes?"

"God," said the ambassador, reacting to the gruesomeness of the shot.

"An old Puma," said Fairchild.

"The Spetsnaz people who came after me had new boots," explained Stoner. "Besides, the Russians would have tried to shoot their way out."

Fairchild nodded. The ambassador seemed to be in shock.

"Can I have these?" Stoner asked, rising.

"By all means," said the ambassador. "We can print more."

"Mark?" Fairchild called after him as Stoner started down the hall. "Stoner—where are you going?"

"I should be back tomorrow," he said.

Dreamland
25 January 1998
1810 (0410 Romania, 26 January 1998)

SAMSON PACED BEHIND THE CONSOLE NEAR THE FRONT OF the Dreamland Command Center, impatiently waiting for the connection to the White House Situation Room to go through. He'd put the call in ten minutes earlier, and had been standing by ever since.

Dealing with the National Security Council and the White House was still new to him, and try as he might, Samson couldn't help but feel a little excited. And nervous. He'd had Mack Smith prepare a PowerPoint presentation, complete with images from the explosion. The photos were dramatic, illustrating again what the Dreamland people—*his* people—were up against.

And by extension, what a good job he was doing commanding them.

"Connection with the White House," said the specialist at the station to his right.

Samson raised his chin and looked at the main screen. Instead of a video feed of NSC head Philip Freeman, however, Jed Barclay's face came up.

"General, sorry I was late. The President called me into a meeting."

"Yes," said Samson, trying to hide his disappointment that he was dealing with a kid barely out of his teens instead of Freeman himself.

"Do you have an update?"

"I have the report from Colonel Bastian regarding the guerrilla attack," said Samson. "The Dreamland units tracked the guerrillas and helped detain them. As a matter of fact, I have a presentation—"

"Yes, sir. I was wondering if there was an update on the Russian aircraft. You'd told me about that earlier."

"There's not much more to tell," said Samson. "They had contacts at a very long distance. Bastian believes there are spies in Iasi that watch them take off."

"OK."

"I have images from the Flighthawk of the guerrillas exploding the house," said Samson. "I had them prepared for the President. If you'd like to see it—"

"We got some photos from the embassy an hour ago," said Jed. "So I think we're good. They came from the army. Pretty gruesome. That's pretty much all we need."

"OK."

"I'm sorry, I'm late," said Jed. "If you want to upload the report, I can check it out when I get back."

Samson fumed. What was the kid late for? A date?

"I'll have my aide do it," said Samson frostily.

"Oh, there was something I wanted to mention to you," added Jed. "Kind of on down low."

"Down low?"

"Between us. There was a discussion today relating to the B-1 laser project. Apparently some members of Congress were asking the Pentagon what was going on with it."

"What questions?"

"You'll have to sweat the specifics through channels, General. I didn't get the details myself, but the tone was, uh, um, hard-nosed. Like they wanted to kill the plane completely. Seems the B-1 has a bad reputation."

"Unjustly."

"Well, the reason I'm mentioning it is, the President was looking for an update."

"It's right on schedule," said Samson. Then he remembered that in fact it was a few weeks behind. "More or less on schedule. What is the President's concern?"

"I really can't speak for him," said Jed. "But, uh, you know with the way Congress is, um, funding . . . "

Samson got the message. Well, at least Jed was good for something. And maybe Freeman had purposely had the kid talk to him, so his "fingerprints" weren't on the warning.

"I just thought you'd like the heads-up before someone from the Pentagon calls," added Jed.

"Yes, yes, actually—thank you, Jed. Good information. I owe you one."

"Uh, yes, sir." Jed signed off.

"Where the hell is Mack Smith?" Samson thundered.

MACK SMITH STARED AT THE MOUNTAIN OF FOLDERS ON HIS desk for a moment, then picked up the phone.

"Mack Smith."

"Is this General Samson's chief of staff?"

"Yes, sir."

"I figured you'd be working late. This is Robbie Denton. Colonel Denton."

"Oh yes, Colonel Denton."

The name was vaguely familiar. Mack quickly flipped through the folders. Darby, Denton . . . ah, Denton was the man General Samson had tapped to take over Combined Air Wing 1, the new designation for the Megafortresses and other aircraft and personnel when on a Whiplash deployment.

"Colonel, good to hear from you," bellowed Mack. "All right. Glad I happened to be working late tonight. A real fluke. Now, as far as security procedures go, I'm afraid we're a little anal about the process. The first thing you need to do—"

"Listen, Major, I'm going to save you a little time here. I've had second thoughts on the job."

"S-Second thoughts, Colonel?"

"Actually, I never really wanted to take it in the first place. I love what I do now. It's the best job in the world. I just had a hard time telling Terrill that the other day."

"Um—"

"He's a force of nature," Denton told Mack. "That's why they call him Earthmover."

"Colonel, you really want to tell him this yourself."

"No, no, that's why I asked for you. I was his chief of staff back when he was in Strategic Air Command," added Denton. "I don't envy you."

"Oh."

Mack dropped the handset on the cradle. Samson wasn't going to be happy; by Mack's count, Denton was the third person he'd offered the job to. Part of the problem was that Samson only wanted proven overachievers, all of whom already had high-profile jobs to begin with. But they were also men he knew personally, which meant they'd served time under him . . . and therefore knew that working for Samson wasn't exactly a holiday.

As he could testify firsthand.

He got up from his desk. There was no question of going home—he had a week's worth of work that had to be finished by the morning. But he was hungry and could use a break.

The phone rang again. He started to leave anyway, thinking he'd let it roll over to voice mail, then saw that the light indicated it was an internal call.

"Mack Smith," he said, picking it up.

"General wants you down in Dreamland Command ASAP," said Lieutenant Stephens, the com specialist on duty there. "Actually, faster than ASAP."

"Tell him I'm on my way," said Mack.

Maybe he's going to compliment me on my PowerPoint presentation, he thought as he walked briskly down the hall to the elevator.

Perhaps. But "good" and "job" were two words that Samson rarely put together, except as a preface to an order for more work. If Samson *did* like the report, he would probably tell him to make a hundred copies each with personalized comments and have them sent out by midnight to everyone in the Pentagon.

The ride down to the secure command center was so quick Mack felt a little light-headed; he regretted not grabbing something to eat earlier. He nodded at the security sergeant standing in front of the door, then pressed his palm against the reader. The doors opened.

"Where have you been, Mack?" growled Samson from down near the center screen.

"Going through some reports, General. How'd the White House briefing go?"

"Fine," said Samson in a voice that suggested the opposite. "What's the status of the B-1 program?"

"Pretty much what it was the other day. Program head is due sometime next week and—"

"What are we doing in the meantime to get it back on schedule?"

"It's not really that far off, General. In some respects—"

Mack stopped short. Samson's eyebrows furled and his cheeks puffed out. Had he opened his mouth just then, he would have looked like a grizzly bear.

And not a particularly happy one.

"What I mean, General, is we're moving it right back to schedule, as you directed," said Mack quickly. "We do have the pilot shortage to deal with."

"Why don't we have pilots, Major?"

"Well we do, but in terms of being checked out—"

"That's your solution?"

"I'm working on it, General."

"That's not a good enough answer, Major. You've been working on this for days."

Hours at least, thought Mack.

"General, I can't just shanghai pilots from other projects or units. Even once the budget line—"

"Why *not* shanghai them?"

Mack blinked.

"I don't care what you do, Major. Find a solution. Get the program back on schedule. I want the B-1s on line. I want to tell the White House tomorrow that they're ready to go operational. I want to tell them to gear up the production line."

"Well, they are ready to fly, General, that's not—"

Mack stopped speaking as General Samson walked up toward him. It wasn't just his face that looked like a grizzly bear now.

"There's one thing you have to understand when you work for me, Major," said Samson, his voice barely above a whisper. "I don't like excuses. I don't like explanations. Results. That's what I like."

"Yes, sir."

"Get it done, Mack." Samson's voice was almost inaudible. "Get it done."

"I'm on it right now, General."

Los Angeles Forum, Los Angeles
2132

THE LAKERS WERE DOWN BY TWO WITH EIGHT SECONDS TO go when Kobe Bryant took the ball in bounds. He looked across court, saw that Rick Fox was covered, then turned down toward the key.

Shaquille O'Neal had just drawn double coverage. Kobe hesitated just a second, as if he was going to scoop the ball up for O'Neal anyway. And then in a flash he was running toward the foul line. As he reached the paint, he jumped high in the air. The ball twirled off his fingertips as the buzzer sounded.

Rimming the hoop, the ball fell into the basket with a swish.

A referee ran from the scrum near the backboard, his hand in the air. Kobe had been fouled.

"Oh my God," said Breanna. She'd spent practically the whole fourth period on her feet, as the Lakers had mounted a stop-and-start comeback after trailing by fifteen. And her knee felt *fine*.

"Great game, huh?" said Sleek Top, next to her.

"Fantastic."

Kobe went to the line for the point that would win the game. He bounced the ball a few times, bent his knees, then bounced it again. Finally, he lifted it, raised it toward the basket, and let it go. The ball spun sharply, hit the glass and slapped in. The crowd shouted at the top of their lungs. Sleek Top grabbed Breanna and hugged her.

"What a game!" he yelled in her ear. "What a game!"

The fans were slow to leave the arena, but once in the hallway there was a mad rush for the exits and the cars. Sleek Top led Breanna around a line of cars to a row of men holding signs for private taxis. Recognizing one of the drivers, he pointed at him and then started to follow, ushering Breanna along.

Breanna was still in the glow of the game when they got into the back of the Lincoln. She was thinking how jealous Zen was going to be that he'd missed it.

"Great seats," she said to Sleek Top.

"Yeah. I don't know what happens next year when they open the Staples Center. I may go to the back of the line. But for now, gotta enjoy it."

The driver eased into the line of cars waiting to get out.

"Want to go and get a drink?" said Sleek Top. "A little nightcap?"

"How are you going to fly home?" said Breanna.

"We could stay over and leave in the morning," he said, putting his hand on her knee.

His touch brought a dozen other hints into focus.

Oh no, she thought. How did she miss this? How could she be so stupid?

She took his hand off her knee. Gently, but firmly.

"I think you have the wrong idea," she told him.

"Really? You sure?"

"Very."

"Doesn't have to be anything serious."

"You're a nice guy, Sleek, but no. No thanks."

He gave her a brave smile, the sort she hadn't seen since well before she got married. She felt a pang in her heart. But she wasn't about to cheat on Zen.

"No hard feelings?" he asked.

"Never happened."

"Hawthorne Airport, same as usual," he told the driver. "I'll get you right around to the hangars."

"Great," said Sleek Top, still wincing a bit.

Bucharest, Romania
26 January 1998
0732

STONER HAD TO POUND ON THE DOOR BEFORE SORINA Viorica answered.

"Stoner?" she called from inside.

"Open up."

She worked the locks and pulled the door open. She was wearing a sweatshirt over a thin cotton nightgown.

"You need to get dressed," he told her.

"What?"

"Come on. We have to go."

She took it the way he thought she would—as a warning that she had been found. Her sleepy expression changed instantly. Quietly, she turned and went inside, changed and started to throw her things into a bag.

"You won't need a bag," said Stoner. "We have to move quickly."

She came out wearing the dark clothes he had first seen her in.

"You should look a little less . . . " He searched for the word. "Militant."

Without saying anything, she turned and went back inside. She came out a few moments later wearing a thick brown sweater over the dark pants, along with a red patterned scarf. It softened her look and made her look prettier, though Stoner tried not to notice.

He found a cab within a block of the apartment.

"Train station," he said in English.

The man said in Romanian that he didn't understand.

"Which train station, Mark?" Sorina asked.

She told the driver; when they reached the station, she bought the tickets. They made the train just as it was boarding.

"Where are we going?" she asked as it pulled out.

"You bought the tickets."

"Yes, but the town—"

"You'll see," Stoner said, and refused to tell her anything else.

Sorina became more nervous at each stop as they headed north. "Are you giving me up?" she asked finally.

He looked at her, looked into her pretty eyes, then shook his head.

"What then?"

"You'll see," was all he would say.

Bacau, Romania
0750

DOG GAVE HIS CREW THE MORNING AND EARLY AFTERNOON off, but the long night mission he'd just completed didn't earn him any extra rest; he had to report to a meeting of the local Romanian army commanders with the defense minister in Bacau at 0800. Fortunately, the base commander was going there as well, and Dog was able to hitch a ride, slumping in the backseat and half sleeping during the thirty minute drive.

Word of his pending Medal of Honor had apparently been making the rounds, and his overnight e-mail included a number of congratulations from people he hadn't heard from in years. With each message, he felt more and more phony.

No, phony was too strong a word, but he certainly didn't feel as if he merited the award—less now even than before. He'd done what he had to do—there was no choice involved, as far as he was concerned.

Was that what made you a hero?

No, he thought. But pointing that out to people would make him sound even worse.

The meeting was held in a former school building near the center of town, a brown-brick structure that dated from the mid-nineteenth century and had first been used as a music academy. The original builder had created a mosaic of musical notes and instruments on the foyer and hallway floor, and the ceiling's chipped plaster sconces were in the shape of musical scrolls.

Armed soldiers guarded the entrance and stood in bunches along the halls; they wore combat fatigues and their guns showed signs of wear, the wood furniture scraped and dented. This made the soldiers also seem like part of the past, and Dog felt as if he were walking through a newsreel of World War II.

Danny Freah had beaten him to the meeting room and was standing near the front of the room, arms folded, staring down at a map unfurled over the table. The large-scale topo map showed not only where the guerrillas had hit the night before, but where they'd made raids in the past. Dog noticed that the attacks clustered south of the highway, and that most of them formed a rough arrow pointing from Moldova; there were more attacks near the border, the cluster narrowing as it moved eastward. There were a few attacks outside the cluster, most notably the attack on the pipeline, which was well to the north.

"How you doing, Danny?" Dog asked. "Get any sleep?"

Danny shook his head. "You should have seen what they took out of the house, Colonel. Parts of bodies. It was pretty awful. Worse than Bosnia."

Danny looked at him as if expecting him to say something, but Dog didn't know how to answer. It sucked, plain and simple. Some of the younger guys had a saying, "Embrace the suck," meaning that you had to somehow find a way to deal with it. But the more horror you saw, the harder it became to come up with any sort of saying that put it to rest.

"They're still not sure how many guerrillas were involved," said Danny. "Body parts were all mixed up together."

Dog shook his head.

"They know there are camps over the border," said Danny. "They ought to attack them there."

"I agree," said Dog.

"Maybe you should suggest it. They aren't listening to me."

Everyone around them snapped to attention. Dog turned in time to see General Locusta and two of his aides enter the room. Locusta also looked like he hadn't slept; there were deep purple rings around his eyes, making his face look almost like a hound dog's.

Locusta had barely reached the front of the room when the defense minister, Fane Cazacul, arrived. A tall, aristocratic-looking man in his thirties, he wore a finely tailored black suit and smelled vaguely of aftershave. He nodded at Locusta; it was clear from their body language that the two men could barely stand each other.

The general opened the meeting without any preliminaries, talking in rapid Romanian about the evening's events. He was clearly angry, though since he wasn't speaking English, Dog could only guess what he was saying. Several of the men in the room shifted uncomfortably as the speech continued; they seemed to be singled out by the general for criticism. After twenty minutes of this, the general ran out of steam. He glanced around the room, gesturing as if to ask whether anyone had anything to say. When no one spoke up, he looked at Dog.

"This is Colonel Bastian, of the U.S. Air Force," he said, speaking first in English for Dog's benefit, and then in his native Romanian. "His men assisted last night, though they were not able to stop the attack. Perhaps next time."

The general sat down. The defense minister looked at Dog, apparently waiting for him to say something.

"I am sorry about the deaths last night," Dog said. "I see what monsters you are up against. Anyone who would kill innocent children—there can be no mercy."

The men nodded.

"I'm sorry that I don't speak Romanian. I'm not even sure my English is all that good," continued Dog. He meant that as a joke, though he was the only one who cracked a smile. He continued, reminding himself to speak slowly and distinctly. "Beginning today, we will have aircraft up around the clock, helping survey the border areas. Captain Freah and his men will help prepare—"

The defense minister raised his hand a few inches, his forefinger extended as if to ask a question.

"Sir?" prompted Dog.

"Will two aircraft be enough?" the minister asked in English. "In light of this attack, I am sure we would welcome more."

"The number isn't up to me, sir, but I will definitely ask for more," said Dog.

Apparently feeling that the Americans were being criticized, the colonel whose unit had been responsible for surrounding the house began explaining that the Dreamland team had played an important role in finding the guerrillas.

"We believe they were intending another attack today," said the Romanian. "Perhaps they would have hit a school, or a bank. The Americans helped us a great deal."

"One thing I don't understand," said Danny, interrupting. "Why don't you guys attack their bases? Hit them where they live?"

General Locusta shot an angry glance at Cazacul, then rose, saying something in heated Romanian before stalking from the room.

"He said, 'That's the first thing that anyone's said that makes sense,'" whispered the Romanian general who'd accompanied Dog to the meeting.

"I DIDN'T MEAN TO CAUSE TROUBLE," DANNY TOLD DOG after the meeting broke up. "It just seemed pretty obvious."

"Don't worry about it. The politics are complicated. Obviously Locusta and Cazacul don't like each other. The general told me that Locusta wants to go over the border, but the government is afraid it will start an incident that will get out of control."

"It's already out of control," said Danny. "I talked to Mark Stoner this morning. The CIA officer we worked with in Asia."

"Sure, I know Stoner."

"He's been assigned special duty out here. He thinks the Russians are involved somehow."

"In this attack?"

"No, not directly. But he wanted samples of the explosives if I could get them. He thinks that probably came from them."

Dog nodded.

"They could send scout teams across the border and watch for them," said Danny. "Or better, follow the guerrillas after an operation and track them down."

"That's their call." Dog rubbed his forehead. "If they mount an operation, we won't be able to support it. Our orders are explicit. The border is off limits. And you're included in that."

"We have to get the rules changed."

"Copy that," said Dog.

Bacau, Romania
1103

THE GUERRILLA RAID ON THE VILLAGE POLICE STATION AND the guerrillas' subsequent decision to blow themselves up left General Locusta in a foul mood. It was probably true, as his aides insisted, that a much more serious attack had been averted; clearly the guerrillas were planning to do serious harm. But that was of small consolation. Coming so soon after the attack on the pipeline, politicians in Bucharest were raising questions about his ability. If he was stripped of his position, his entire plan would crumble.

The Russians were no doubt behind this. They were more trouble than they were worth. As for the Americans . . .

Well, at least they had the right idea about what should be done. Though they were a problem as well.

The general was mulling the difficulties on the way back

to his headquarters when he received a text message from a Yahoo address declaring that the state oil company's stock was going to split and that it would be wise to invest as soon as possible.

The message looked like a routine piece of spam, but in fact it had nothing to do with oil or stock. It was from the Russian military attaché, Svoransky, asking for an immediate meeting.

Asking or demanding?

Locusta preferred to think the former, but the arrival of a second message twenty minutes later drove him to cancel his afternoon schedule. He called a number ostensibly registered to the Romanian information ministry but which in fact forwarded his call to a machine at the Russian embassy. He named a time—2:00 P.M.—and hung up.

Locusta got up from his desk and began pacing, thinking about what he had done—not now, but months making contact with the Russians, using them to advance his dream of running Romania the way it should be run, of establishing the country as the most important in Eastern Europe.

From the start, it had been a deal with the devil. But what other choice did he have?

He needed to extricate himself somehow, perhaps with American help.

But wouldn't that simply be making matters worse?

The only solution was to move ahead with the coup as quickly as possible. Then these complications could be untangled.

Locusta hoped that Svoransky would send another message, saying that the meeting was too far from the capital for the Russian to make, giving him a perfect excuse to call it off. But no message came; the meeting was on.

Two hours later, Locusta told his aides that he wasn't feeling well and was going home for a nap.

"Perhaps I'll take a ride in the country," he added off-handedly, as if it wasn't his intention all along.

He stopped at his house, a modest cottage on a large piece of land owned by a family with royal blood. The housekeeper had come and was just finishing; he told her not to worry about him, that he had just stopped by to feed his cat. The woman, a portly grandmother type who had been employed on the estate in one capacity or another since she was a teenager, nodded approvingly, then went back to work as he got out the kibbles to fill the pet's bowl.

There was something soothing about the mewing of a cat. Locusta waited on his haunches as the pet scampered into the kitchen, rubbing its side against his bent leg as a thank-you before digging in. He gave it a scratch behind its ears, then rose. He told the housekeeper she was doing a very good job. With one last stroke of the cat's back, he walked out to his car and drove toward the highway.

The peace the cat brought dissipated by the time he was halfway to the small café where they were to meet. Ordinarily, he felt comfortable at the restaurant, which was run by a distant relative in a town about thirty miles southwest of Bacau, but today he felt awkward, moving as if his clothes were a half size too small.

He was ten minutes early, but Svoransky was already there. And not alone.

"This is Major Jurg," said Svoransky, gesturing to the dark-haired, ruddy-faced man in a poorly cut gray suit who sat next to him, nursing a glass of vodka. "He is a good man to know."

"I'm sure," said the general, pulling out his chair. It was the first time since they had been meeting that the attaché had brought a companion.

Svoransky signaled to the waiter. "Stew?" he asked Locasta.

"I'm not very hungry this afternoon."

"A drink, then?"

Locusta asked for some bottled water.

"That was a desperate attack yesterday evening," said Svoransky.

"A dozen of my men were killed," said Locusta. "The only consolation is that all of the criminals died as well."

He looked up as the waiter returned with his glass and the bottle of carbonated spring water. He sipped it slowly, waiting until the server had again retreated.

"My explosives experts believe the criminals may have had as much as a suitcase worth of plastic explosives," said Locusta. "I wonder where they would have gotten that."

"I would guess from the Iranians," said Svoransky smoothly. "They have made a habit of selling such items very cheaply."

"I would think that a chemical analysis would show that it came from Russia," said Locusta, staring at Major Jurg.

Jurg stared back.

"Russian? *Nyet.* We would not sell to criminals. Of course, items can always be obtained on the black market. Over that we have no control."

"You had nothing to do with the attack, I presume," said Locusta, his eyes still locked with Jurg's.

"General, please," said Svoransky. "Your voice is rather loud. I thought you chose this place to be discreet."

"The death of my men bothers me. A great deal." Locusta leaned across the table toward Jurg. "I was especially bothered the other evening to find my men were killed in an attack on the pipeline."

"Casualties must be expected in a war," said Svoranksky.

"I am not fighting a war," said Locusta. "Yet."

Svoransky had the good sense not to answer. It seemed to Locusta that Jurg had a smirk on his face, but if so, he'd covered it with his glass.

"What precisely is it you want to talk about?" Locusta asked.

"The Americans are an extremely arrogant people," said Svoransky. "Pushy and interfering."

"They are our allies," said Locusta.

"The government's allies only. I hope. You would not mind seeing them suffer an embarrassment, I think."

"What sort of embarrassment?"

Svoransky shrugged. "An attack?"

"My people are defending their base," said Locusta.

Svoransky turned to Jurg and began speaking in Russian, presumably translating what he had just said, though it seemed to Locusta that Jurg had understood. Jurg's stubble and dark skin made him appear crude, but he wore a gold watch on his wrist—an expensive watch, Locusta thought.

The man must be a member of the Spetsnaz. Very likely he was in charge of the squad that had killed his soldiers at the pipeline; it was even possible he had been on the raid himself.

Locusta worked to suppress his loathing. All he had to do was raise his hand and his cousin would come from the back with a gun. Or he could be more subtle, wait until the meeting was over, then have their car blown up.

But it would be foolish. Svoransky's superiors might hate Voda and the government, but they would not stand idly by while their agent was assassinated. They would change sides in an eye blink.

"Perhaps your people could be moved," suggested Svoransky finally.

General Locusta turned toward Jurg. "What exactly do you want, Major?" he asked in English. "Be specific. And have the courtesy to speak to me directly."

"We want two things," said Jurg, switching to English. "We want to embarrass the Americans, as Mr. Svoransky has said."

"Embarrassing them is one thing. An attack while my men are guarding them is very difficult."

"Not if you help."

"I do not need to be at war with the Americans."

Locusta started to rise. Svoransky grabbed his arm. "You misunderstand," he said. "Your men will not be involved. All they need do is look the other way."

"I doubt that can be arranged."

"You owe us quite a bit, General," said Jurg.

Locusta's anger flared, and for a moment he considered what would happen if he punched the major. The man was shorter than he was, but built like a wrestler, thick around the neck, with large forearms and a chest like a barrel.

If he decked him, there would be a moment of elation, then consequences.

"I owe you nothing," said Locusta. "And I will owe you less if there is an attack on the base."

"General, our relationship has been profitable and surely will be more so in the future. You do not want Romania to be a member of the EU, or NATO. Nor do we. You want to be president—we find that very acceptable."

"What's your point?" snapped Locusta.

"The point is, we will do as we please," said Jurg. "You will have to accept it."

As a young boy, Locusta had struggled to control his emotions. He had gone to great lengths to learn the discipline needed to push away his anger and clear his head for logic. As a twelve-year-old he had stood in his parents' kitchen, his hand over the burning wick of a candle, testing how long he could leave his fingers there despite the pain. His goal had been to recite the times tables backward from twelve times twelve while holding his hand above the candle. It was a game as much as an exercise, but it had served him well. When his anger threatened to careen out of control, he often thought back to the candle and the sensation of heat at his fingertips, and regained control.

"I will accept no more casualties at your hands," he said coldly as he rose.

"General, who said anything about casualties?" said Svoransky. He put his hand out and touched Jurg on the shoulder. "A way will be found to embarrass the Americans without involving you. We just want you to be aware of it. My companion and his people won't even be involved."

"Don't contact me again," said Locusta.

"Now now," said Svoransky. "Remember, we are friends."

The words impaled themselves in Locusta's consciousness, playing over and over as he drove himself back to his Second Corps headquarters.

Near Tutova, northern Romania
1400

IT TOOK ROUGHLY SIX HOURS FOR THE TRAIN TO GET FROM Bucharest to the station near Piatra Neamt. Sorina Viorica spent most of the time sleeping. She lay against Stoner's shoulder, the weight and her scent pleasant despite everything he told himself.

"We need a cab," he said to her when they got to the platform.

"A town like this won't have a taxi."

"Then we'll hire a driver."

"Where?"

"The stationmaster will know," said Stoner, heading toward the ticket office. "He'll have a brother-in-law or a friend in need of work."

It turned out to be a sister, which was fine with Stoner. He gave her the address he'd written down.

The woman read it and glanced at him, a worried look on her face. Stoner nodded solemnly, then fanned the ten twenty-dollar bills he'd concealed in his fist.

The address belonged to the house that had been blown up. It took nearly an hour to get there. When they arrived, the police and a small contingent of soldiers were still guarding it, but they were able to drive up the road and park a short distance away, close enough to see the ruins.

And smell them. The scent of burnt wood and flesh still hung in the air when they got out of the car.

Stoner led her toward the house. Rags covered with blood lay on the front lawn.

"What is this?" Sorina Viorica asked.

"Your friends did this," he told her. "The ones you don't want to turn in. The dregs who are left. Six children died. This is their blood. Girls, one to ten years old. Or maybe there were seven. The remains were so mangled, it's hard to tell."

"Look." Stoner pulled the photos from his pocket. "See if you can tell which were the bombers and which were the victims."

Tears streamed down Sorina Viorica's face. She started to look at the photos, then pushed them away and ran back toward the car.

Allegro, Nevada
0508

BREANNA THREW OFF THE COVERS AND GOT OUT OF BED, wincing a little as she walked toward the bathroom.

"Time to get up, time to get up," she told herself, throwing on the shower.

She'd had only a few hours sleep, but she was determined to get her rehab session over with, then get over to the base, kick butt on the physical and whatever other bs the doctors threw at her, and get herself back on full duty.

Full flight duty. *Flying.*

She was back. During the entire Lakers game she hadn't thought about being hurt once. Her head felt fine. Her legs, ribs, arms—there were still bruises and a few creaks in her joints, but she was A-okay. There was no reason she couldn't get back in the air.

Zen was back. Mack was back. Her father was back.

The only difference between her and them was her gender. And that was absolutely *not* going to make a difference.

The cold water hit her like an electric shock. She resisted the urge to pump it up to hot, instead lathering and moving as quickly as possible. She'd do her hair after her workouts.

Sleek Top had been quite the gentleman after the game. He was such a sweet guy that she hated hurting him. If it weren't for Zen . . .

Her teeth chattered as she hopped out of the shower. She pulled a towel around her, more to ward off the cold than to actually dry herself, and walked out to the kitchen to get Mr. Coffee working. Then she went back to the bedroom to get dressed.

She was getting back in action, all the way back. There was no other goal, and no rest until that goal was achieved.

Bucharest, Romania
1810

"I WILL TELL YOU WHERE THEY HIDE IN MOLDOVA," SORINA said in a quiet voice on the train back to Bucharest. "But I must do it in my own way."

"You can do it any way you want," Stoner told her.

"They were not always so . . . "

Her voice trailed off. She couldn't find the right word. He could think of several—ruthless, despicable, gutless—but he said nothing.

They were sitting opposite each other in a first class car, the space between them divided by a table. Sorina Viorica got up and slid next to him. Then, clutching his chest, she began to sob.

* * *

THE NIGHT WAS A SLIDE DOWN A LONG SLOPE, PREORDAINED. He brought her back to the apartment and started to leave; she looked at him and took a step, and from that moment he no longer resisted, no longer had another self, a professional self, to stop him.

He'd had occasion to use sex as a weapon, or, more accurately, as a means to an end several times in his career. This wasn't like that. It was considerably more dangerous. It was real.

He slipped into bed with her, moving quietly, softly. Then his hunger grew. Making love, it became insatiable.

He fell asleep with Sorina in his arms, his last thought that he had crossed a line that should never be crossed.

Dreamland
1030

THE LAST FIVE MINUTES WERE SHEER HELL. BREANNA FELT as if her legs were going to fall off and her lungs were about to collapse within her chest.

But she kept running.

She kept running because she was coming back, and nothing was going to stop her.

She leaned forward, pushing the soles of her sneakers against the treadmill surface, pushing and pushing as she struggled to finish the stress test. When she'd started, she thought of it as a race, and pitted herself against the clock. Now it was just survival, a race against the growing ache in her muscles, against pain that surged from her bones.

She was going to make it. She had to make it.

The buzzer sounded but she continued to run, comprehending that it was over yet unable to transmit the message to her legs.

Simply collapsing was not an option—the doctor was right behind her, taking it all in.

Gradually, she got her legs to slow. Her breathing was still labored, but as she slipped into a walk, her breathing began to ease and the pounding of her heart grew less intense.

Her knee was throbbing—running put a great deal of pressure on the joint—but it held. She stepped off the machine, trying to appear as nonchalant as possible.

"Well?" she asked the doctor. "What do you think?"

He didn't say anything. Instead, he motioned her toward the curtained examining area at the back of the room.

"You're going to check my blood pressure?" Breanna asked as he took the cuff from its little shelf on the wall.

"Of course."

"Didn't those machines tell you everything you need to know?"

He shrugged. Clearly he was determined to give her a hard time.

"And?" she said pointedly.

"There's no doubt that you have a healthy heart, Captain," he said. "And that in general you're fit."

Breanna started to smile.

"That doesn't mean I'm clearing you to fly," he added. "Your knee doesn't hurt?"

She shook her head.

"Hold out your arm," he ordered.

Breanna did so. The cuff felt hard against her bicep. She tried to relax. The doctor took the reading, frowned again, then let the pressure off.

"Well?" she asked.

"It's all right."

"How all right?"

"Diastolic, seventy. Systolic 115."

"That's 115 over seventy, right?"

"Yes."

"Which is normal."

It was actually the highest Breanna could remember her blood pressure being, but it was in fact well within the normal range. The doctor had no alternative but to declare her fit for duty—active duty, active flying, back in the air.

Back! Back! Back!

But not quite.

"You need General Samson's approval," he said.

"What?"

"Procedure. The wing commander has to sign off. The wing commander hasn't arrived, so you have to go to General Samson."

"You don't want me to fly, do you?" she said.

"I think you need more rest, yes," he said. "And I'd urge you to take a couple of weeks off."

"I don't want to take time off."

"Why the hell not?"

"Because I don't."

"You're being stubborn."

"Where does that fit on your medical chart?"

The doctor shook his head. "The truth is, I can't hold you back. I know, and you know, that if you'd taken this same test a couple of months back, you wouldn't have been huffing at the end. I also know you did a lot better on it than probably half of our pilots. Physically, you've definitely recovered from your ordeal. I should write a paper on your recovery." He smiled, trying to soften his sarcasm. "But . . ."

He took out his stethoscope and twirled it around his hand.

"But what?" asked Breanna.

"That coma bothers me."

"You call it a coma. I was just tired and asleep. My body had to heal."

"Listen, Breanna. I haven't known you that long. I know you're driven. I appreciate that. And you've achieved a hell of a lot. I know it must have been twice as hard for you because you're a woman. But really, you should take it easier. Slower. If you were Jeff—"

"What would you tell Zen?"

"I'd tell him to slow down, too," said the doctor. "Listen, if you do get approval from the general, would you please try to take it easy? Just a little?"

Breanna threw her arms around him joyfully.

"I will," she said. "Now do you have papers for him or what?"

Dreamland
1103

AS A RULE, GENERAL SAMSON DIDN'T LIKE MARINES. THEY tended to be too full of themselves for his taste. But Marty "Sleek Top" Siechert was a *retired* Marine, and while the Marines had a saying that there was no such thing as an ex-Marine, Samson considered that his separation from the service and the intervening years—Sleek Top was close to fifty—had sanded some of the edges off.

Colonel Denton's decision not to take the spot as wing commander under him—a career killing move if ever there was one—forced Samson to make some compromises. Naming a retired Marine pilot head of the B-1B/L program was one of them. But he wanted to move the colonel he'd tapped for the B-1L/B project over to wing commander, and, just as important, he needed the B-1s ready to hit the flight line yesterday.

"Heading the program is a big responsibility, General," said Sleek Top as they finished a walk around *Boomer*. "And I was under the impression that you wanted all active military heading programs."

"You are military," said Samson.

"I'm retired, sir."

"A bit young to be hanging up the saddle."

"I meant, I'm a civilian, General."

"Yes, yes, I know that," said Samson. "I've considered it.

But you're my man. The B-1s—we need them operational. The Pentagon is pushing for a demonstration very soon. Congress is very keen on this, and the President himself likes the aircraft. It will be a good spotlight for your future career."

"There's nothing really holding them back," said Sleek Top. "The basic air frame has been tested and retested. They're not that much different than the standard B-1Bs in terms of overall systems. The laser, of course, and the engines are more powerful, but the core of the computer system was adapted from the Megafortress, and we know that works. All that's necessary is to complete the testing cycle."

"Then get moving."

"General, that's not quite as easy as it sounds. For one thing—"

"How did Bastian get the EB-52s operational?" said Samson.

Sleek Top laughed.

"What's so funny?"

Sleek Top shook his head. He looked as if he had a goldfish in his mouth and it was tickling his tongue.

"Out with it, Marine," demanded Samson.

"Well, Colonel Bastian—" Sleek Top interrupted himself to chuckle. "Colonel Bastian made a habit of putting the weapons right into the mix, officially approved or not. His whole theory was that the real tests didn't happen until they were on the battlefield anyway, so he'd send the geek squad out with the planes, get everything in motion. Sometimes it blew up in his face, of course, but mostly it worked. Then when the Pentagon came around asking questions, he'd roll out the results. Had them eating out of his—"

"How close is close?"

"Excuse me?"

"The B-1s. What would happen if they went into combat?"

"Well, uh—"

"If Colonel Bastian were here and he suggested it, what would you say?"

"I'd say . . . " Sleek Top thought about it for a moment. "I'd say that if you had enough pilots, there'd be no problem. But I'm the only pilot regularly assigned and—"

"Get the planes ready. I'll find the pilots."

"General, you just found one," said Breanna Stockard.

Samson turned around and saw Breanna standing behind him, a broad grin on her face. She'd been listening to most of the discussion.

"Captain, good morning."

"General, I need you to approve my flight fitness report, sir. I'm ready to get back in the air."

"You think that's a good idea so soon?" asked Sleek Top. "You were in some pretty heavy action."

"I'm ready. I just passed a stress test."

Breanna handed Samson a folder with her medical report. The general opened it and took a quick glance. At the top of the page—excellent health.

There were typed comments at the bottom: "Although Breanna Stockard is physically in top shape and appears to have recovered from her ordeal off the Indian coast, I would still recommend that she take a few weeks off . . . "

Doctors, thought Samson. Always finding excuses for people *not* to do things.

He looked up from the folder. Breanna was a good-looking woman—not that he would let himself be influenced by that. But she was definitely in good shape, and her record spoke for itself. The after-action reports, even though they'd been written in terse, matter-of-fact prose, read like war novels.

Of course, she was also Colonel Bastian's daughter. But you couldn't hold the sins of the fathers against the offspring.

"You're in good shape?" he asked.

"Sir, I'm ready to kick butt. Can I fly?"

"Damn straight you can fly." Samson shut the folder abruptly. "Get this over to my office, get it signed off by the chief of staff. I'm looking for big things out of you, Captain."

Tears were brimming in Breanna's eyes. That was the one thing about women that Samson couldn't entirely handle—they got emotional at the drop of a hat.

"Carry on," he told her, and spun away.

**Bucharest, Romania
27 January 1998
0900**

STONER WOKE TO THE SMELL OF COFFEE. HE JERKED OUT of bed, grabbed his watch. He'd slept for nearly ten hours. He hadn't been out that long in ages.

He pulled on his clothes and went to the kitchen. Sorina Viorica was there, cooking something in a frying pan. She'd taken a shower or a bath while he was sleeping; the scent of her soap filled the room.

She'd done something else, as well—dyed her hair jet black.

"Hello there," she said.

"You did your hair."

"Black, yes. The color of an outcast."

He went to her, not knowing what to expect, either of himself or her. She folded her body to his willingly; his complied without hesitation.

"We have a lot to do," he said.

"Yes, but first we should eat," she said. "I bought some eggs."

Iasi Airfield, Romania
1305

"Hey, Colonel, another message incoming," yelled Sergeant Lee "Nurse" Liu, who was handling the communications desk at the back end of the Dreamland Command trailer.

Dog sighed and turned back around. He'd been hoping to take a nap before the night's sortie, but one thing or another had interrupted him since returning from the Romanian command meeting.

"It's a private phone call, Colonel," said Liu, rising.

"Phone call? From the States?"

"No, sir. Sat phone. Encrypted too."

Dog sat down at the terminal and put on a headset while Liu slipped discreetly to the front of the trailer.

"This is Bastian."

"Colonel Bastian, this is Mark Stoner. Do you remember me?"

"Sure I do, Mark. How are you?"

It wasn't likely he'd forget. The CIA officer had helped save Breanna after action in the Pacific more than a year before.

"I'm fine, Colonel. As it happens, I'm working on a job in your neck of the woods. I can't go into detail at the moment, but I'd like to speak to you personally as soon as possible. This afternoon."

"Why don't you come here? I'm in Iasi."

"I'd like to stay out of the city if I could. I have a place picked out that's not that far from you. Could you be there around three-thirty?"

"I can try."

"It might be best to wear civilian clothes, if you could," said Stoner. "And have a civilian car. You shouldn't tell the Romanians where you're going."

Near Dolcina, northeast Romania
1420

STONER KNEW COLONEL BASTIAN WELL ENOUGH TO TRUST him, but that didn't mean the Romanians didn't have him under surveillance. So he was careful about choosing their meeting place.

With as little help from Sorina as possible, he selected a village that was small enough to watch but not so small that doing so would attract attention. Dolcina was about twenty minutes northwest of Bacau, and it had two outstanding assets: first, there was no police department or army detachment in town, and second, there was only one road in and out.

An hour before the colonel was due to arrive, Stoner double-checked the tavern he'd selected for the meeting. There was still only one regular at the bar, an old woman who sat in the corner and mumbled to herself while sipping Pernod, probably from the same glass he'd seen two hours before. Walking around the building, he found a garbage can and used it to boost himself onto the roof, where he surveyed the local street and the dozen or so buildings nearby. If anyone was watching him, they were well hidden.

He stayed on the roof until Colonel Bastian arrived. Then he waited another ten minutes before calling the bar from his sat phone.

"I wish to speak to a man named Tecumseh, if he is there," said Stoner in the Romanian Sorina Viorica had carefully rehearsed with him.

"Tecumseh?"

"Yes."

The bartender asked him something in Romanian that Stoner didn't understand; all he could do was repeat what he'd said before.

There was silence. Then just as he thought he'd have to climb down and go inside himself, Dog came on the phone.

"This is Tecumseh."

"Sorry for the intrigue, Colonel. I need you to drive down the street, out of the village. Continue for exactly two kilometers, then pull off the road."

Stoner killed the connection. Then he crawled to the front of the roof, watching as Dog left the bar and got into his car.

No one seemed to be following him. Still, Stoner waited another few minutes before climbing down. When he did, he trotted in the opposite direction, going back toward the highway to the abandoned gas station where he'd left his motorcycle.

Sorina Viorica had already left.

Not exactly the way they had planned it. He hoped she hadn't had second thoughts. Or worse, that he'd missed a setup.

He had to hit the electric starter twice before the bike would turn over. Once it was humming, however, the single piston engine sounded as smooth as a V-8. He revved the bike onto the roadway, circled once again to make sure he wasn't being watched, then headed toward the rendezvous.

DOG WATCHED THE ODOMETER CAREFULLY. AS SOON AS it reached two kilometers, he pulled the car onto the shoulder, leaving it idling as he looked around. There were empty farm fields to his left and right. No one was in sight.

Undoing his seat belt, he took his service Beretta pistol out of his belt, checked it, then put it down between the seat and the transmission hump next to him. It was months since he'd used it, and then it had been on an indoor range. He wasn't a particularly good shot and hoped he didn't need it.

A cloud of dust appeared in the field to his left. Dog thought about getting out of the car, then decided against it.

The dust swirled, then settled to reveal a motorcycle. Dog rolled down his window, watching as the bike came toward him. Its driver wore a helmet with a dark face shield.

Dog slumped down, using the dashboard for cover, waiting as the motorcycle came closer. He put his hand on the gun.

The bike suddenly accelerated, passing by in a blur. He watched in his side mirror as it veered off the road behind him, then began circling back from his right. He rolled down his window and waited as it drew near. His hand was still on the pistol, now in his lap.

The motorcycle coasted next to him and stopped. The rider leaned down.

"Who are you?" demanded the driver.

Dog was surprised. The voice, muffled by the helmet, was foreign and belonged to a woman.

"I'm waiting for someone," he said.

"For who?"

"A friend. Mark Stoner."

Another bike appeared in his rearview mirror. This one came straight down the road. The woman who'd stopped glanced back but stayed on her motorcycle as the second bike drew near the driver's side of the car.

He'd had Liu check the voice pattern of the call earlier, so Dog was sure he'd been talking to Stoner. But now his paranoia grew, and his imagination spun out of control.

He could slip the car into gear and accelerate, get the hell out of there.

Shoot the motorcyclist on his right first.

The second bike stopped on his left.

"Colonel, I'm sorry for the precaution," said its rider, leaning close to the window. He pulled up his face shield, revealing himself. It was Stoner.

"It's all right, Mark. What's going on?"

"Just a second."

Stoner slipped the bike forward, then parked on the other side. The woman had gotten off her bike, and she joined Stoner as he slipped into the backseat of the car.

"My friend has some information that will be very valuable," said Stoner after he shut the door. "But if she's seen meeting you, there are a number of people who could cause problems."

"OK," said Dog.

"The location of the guerrilla stronghold is over the border," said Stoner.

Dog knew this was valuable information, and immediately guessed why the woman didn't want to be seen—she must be a guerrilla herself.

"I don't know how I can help," he said.

In the mirror, Dog saw Stoner put his hand on the woman's thigh, stopping her from moving toward the door.

"You can pass the information on in a way that it can't be traced to her," Stoner said. "And, there is a condition."

"What's that?"

"Asylum in America."

"You'd know more about that than I would," said Dog. "I'm just a pilot."

"You are very famous," said the woman. "I recognize your face from the television. You are the head of Dreamland."

Dog nodded. This wasn't the time or place to explain the current chain of command.

"I can take care of the technicalities, once she's out of the country," Stoner said. "Getting her out of the country—that's where we'll need your help."

"Why?"

"Because if I were to go into an airport," said the woman, "I would most likely be recognized. If you don't trust Mark—"

"I trust him."

"Can you do it?" Stoner asked.

If the woman weren't in the back of the car, Dog would have explained his hesitation. Transporting a guerrilla well known enough to be on a watch list wasn't exactly part of his mission brief. He could just imagine what General Samson's reaction would be.

On the other hand, knowing the location of the guerrilla strongholds would be very valuable information.

"I can probably come up with something," he said finally. "Assuming she keeps her end of the bargain."

"There will be no problem with that," said Sorina.

"Why are you betraying your friends?" asked Dog.

He saw her face in the mirror. There was pain, and then a mask.

Was it all an act? Or had she debated that very same question?

"The Russians have taken over the movement. There are some devoted revolutionaries, but most of the operations now are being directed by Moscow. The things they are doing turn my stomach."

Dog glanced in Stoner's direction. The CIA man's expression made it clear that he didn't want him to keep asking questions. To the spy, reasons or motivations weren't important; results were.

But to Dog, the question was everything. People didn't give up their friends easily, even if the rest of the world thought it was the right thing to do.

"The Russians know that I am against them," Sorina went on. "They would kill me as gladly as the Romanian army or police."

"And in America you can have a fresh start?" said Dog.

"I don't want to go to America. Get me to Turkey."

"I don't know if I can get you to Turkey."

"Across the border, then, to any European country. I can move on from there."

"Where are the hideouts?" asked Dog.

"Not until I am safe," said Sorina Viorica. "When I am safe, then I will say. Only to Mark."

Iasi Airfield, Romania
1830

DOG'S MESSAGE TO DANNY WAS VAGUE TO THE POINT OF being cryptic, though only if you knew the way Colonel Bastian normally did things. It had been passed along by one of the aides at the small unit where Danny was working with the Romanian soldiers.

OFFICERS MEETING 1830, HERE. PLEASE BE PROMPT.

Danny's curiosity was piqued further when he saw Colonel Bastian waiting for him on the tarmac when the Osprey touched down.

"Hey, Colonel, what's up?"

"You eat dinner yet, Danny?"

"Didn't have a chance."

"One of the Romanian officers told me about a restaurant in the city. Let's go."

"You think that's a good idea?"

"I do."

Dog didn't give any further explanation, and in fact remained silent on the drive. Danny, who hadn't seen much of Iasi, found himself staring at the buildings. Like much of Eastern Europe, the city at first glance seemed drab, still hungover from the days of Soviet bloc domination. But if you looked long enough, the gray and brown tones gave way to color in unexpected places. There were signs for Coca-Cola, along with billboards advertising Sony televisions and Italian fashions. White facades on new houses, blue stones, an office building with a dramatic, sweeping rise—the city was shaking off the gloom of the old era like a spring daffodil poking through rotted leaves.

The restaurant was another surprise. Large and modern, it could have been located in any American city. The food was Italian, and not bad—Danny ordered spaghetti and meatballs for the first time in months, and cleaned the plate.

"So, eventually you're going to tell me what's going on," Danny said to Dog as he finished.

The colonel pushed away his plate. He had only picked at his food.

"I talked to Mark Stoner today. And a friend of his."

Danny listened as Dog told him about the meeting. His first reaction was anger: He felt the colonel should have told him what was going on beforehand, and not taken the risk himself. But it was hard for Danny to be mad at Dog, and he knew how welcome the information about the location of the guerrilla training camps would be. He also knew from talking with Colonel Oz that Locusta had authorized at least two spy missions over the past few months, without results. The Romanians didn't have access to spy satellites; even if they did, Danny knew that small groups of rebels could prove frustratingly difficult to observe or even detect.

"You think that's a good trade?" he asked. "Sneak her out of the country in exchange for the information? She may be a murderer herself."

"I don't know," said Dog. "The truth is, it's probably not up to me."

" 'Probably'?"

Dog smiled. "Definitely not up to me. Hard letting go, I guess."

IT WAS A LOT HARDER LETTING GO THAN DOG WANTED TO admit, certainly to himself. Was it just the power? Or had he grown so used to cutting through red tape and bureaucracy that the necessity of working through channels and responding to the proper chain of command tired him out?

He would have preferred to think it was the latter. But faced with the need not just to report to Samson, but to ask permission to proceed, he realized it was mostly the former.

Before they left the restaurant, Dog and Danny worked out a plan to assure that the woman would tell where the guerrilla hideout was after she was flown out of the country. It wasn't very complicated—Danny and one of his men would stay with her; she would communicate the information to Stoner, and then they'd wait until Stoner confirmed that the information was correct before letting her go.

After Sergeant Liu made the connection, Dog sat down in the seat at the com console, leaning back while he waited for the officer on duty at Dreamland Command to get the general. He was surprised when, rather than Samson, Mack Smith's face appeared on his small screen.

Mack's voice boomed in his headset: "Colonel, how are you?"

"How are you, Mack?"

"Surviving. Barely. Between you and me, Colonel . . ."

"Yes?"

"Between you and me, I want to get back on the flight line yesterday."

"Wish I could help you there, Mack."

"So do I. What's up?"

"I have something I need to talk to the general about."

"Shoot."

"I have to talk to him personally."

"Might as well talk to me," said Mack. "Shit rolls downhill."

"You sound tired, Mack."

"Didn't get much sleep last night, Colonel. Or the night before. Or any night. So what can I do for you?"

"You can get the general on the line."

"Yes, sir."

"SO WHAT THE HELL IS SO DAMN IMPORTANT THAT YOU GET me out of a meeting with my science department?" said Samson, his snarling voice snapping onto the line. There was no visual; he was using the encrypted phone in his office.

"The CIA has developed an asset who knows where the guerrillas are hiding in Moldova," said Dog calmly. "As part of the deal to get the information, they want us to fly the source out of the country."

"What?"

"Yes, sir."

"And they came to you directly?"

"It happens that I've worked with the CIA officer before," said Dog.

"You have?" Samson asked, this time without the sharp note of surprise. "Yes, of course you have. But can we trust him? Does he really have the information?"

"I met the asset. I think we can."

"*You* met the asset? Who authorized you to do that?"

"I didn't realize that was going to happen," said Dog. "In any event, General, I wouldn't have come to you with this unless I was thoroughly convinced it was both real and a benefit to our mission here. I wouldn't waste your time, General. I know you have better things to do than hold my hand."

"Hmmmph."

Dog outlined the plan that he and Danny had worked out, then suggested that the asset be flown to a U.S. base in Turkey, the country she'd requested.

"How do you want me to proceed?" he asked when he'd concluded.

"Do nothing until you hear from me."

"Not a problem. Also, the Romanians are asking for more support. The defense minister said he would go through the embassy, but I thought I'd give you a—"

Dog stopped speaking, realizing Samson had already hung up.

White House Cabinet Room
1206

ROBERT PLANK WAS A RICH MAN, BUT HE HAD A CERTAIN air of nervous danger about him.

Maybe, thought Jed Barclay as he watched him speak in the Oval Office, the millions he'd made had been seeded by some criminal activity that he would do anything to keep from being exposed.

Plank's sharply tailored suits showed off his wide shoulders and thick chest, and he looked to be strong enough to take on any two or three men who confronted him. His speech occasionally betrayed the urban landscape he'd grown up in; as a very young boy, he had lived only a few blocks from the White House, in one of the poorest and at the time most dangerous sections of Washington, D.C.

For most government officials—especially those whose appointment had been so blatantly political—Plank's occasional and unconscious sprinkle of four-letter words along with his habit of speaking bluntly would be serious defects. But in his case, they were assets, enhancing his reputation as a no-nonsense, seat-of-the-pants CIA director.

Plank was also a skilled politico, even if he'd never spent a day as an elected official. As he continued to brief the President on the CIA's successful recruitment of a guerrilla turncoat, Jed was impressed by the director's ability to subtly insert himself into the story. Jed knew the details as well as Plank—he'd gotten them from Stoner himself. So he knew that the guerrilla had initially offered contact, not the other way around, and that Stoner's primary interest lay in getting more information on the deaths of his comrades. But Plank packaged up everything as if finding the guerrilla base was his idea in the first place. He all but said that he knew the guerrilla movement was ready to crack, and had therefore handpicked one of his best international agents, plunking him down at just the right time, in just the right circumstance, to achieve a breakthrough.

It was difficult to judge how much of the act the President actually bought. Certainly Martindale, who had appointed Plank, knew that he'd gotten the job not because he was an excellent spymaster—Plank had worked on the analysis side of the Agency before going into private business. And given that he'd known Plank for many years, Jed assumed that he appreciated the CIA director's ability to put himself in the spotlight as well as anyone.

The only hint that Martindale might not be paying complete attention was the pen he twirled in his fingers—a sign, Jed knew from two years of observation, that he was getting bored and wanted the speaker to get on with it.

"The Russian connection is the most intriguing aspect of the entire affair," said Plank. "If we can obtain real evidence of it, the countries that have been feuding in NATO and the EU will realize how badly they're being played."

"That's a wonderful theory," said Freeman, the National Security Advisor and Jed's boss. "But the only thing that's going to stop their fighting is a reduction in the price of natural gas. The futures have gone up another twelve percent in the commodities markets over the past day even though the last guerrilla attack wasn't aimed at the pipeline."

"Once we expose the Russians' involvement, the attacks will stop," said Plank.

"Once the *Romanians* expose it," said Secretary of State Jeffrey Hartman. "If we do it, no one will believe it."

"One thing I'm concerned about are these Russian aircraft," said the President. He leaned forward on his desktop to look at Jed, who was sitting at the end of the row in front of him. "Recap that for us, Jed."

"Very briefly, Russian planes have shadowed the Dreamland Megafortresses on every flight," said Jed. "They've stayed roughly 250 miles away, as if they don't want to be detected. That's the published range of the radar, although depending on the circumstances, it can see a bit farther."

"We'd do the same if they were operating in our area," suggested Hartman.

"I think what they'd like us to do is go over the border," said Secretary of Defense Chastain. "The Russians have a defense treaty with Moldova. They could contend they were coming to their aid."

"I don't see what that gets them," said Hartman.

"Another twenty point bump in the price of natural gas," said Martindale.

"I agree," said Plank. "That's why we have to move on this. The agent would accompany the Romanians on the raid. This way he would gain information relating to the deaths of our people in Romania."

"Assuming the information is to be had," noted the President.

Plank gave Martindale a little smile, acknowledging that he'd been caught exaggerating, or at least polishing the apple.

"The price of natural gas in Europe is now double what it was last winter," said Freeman. "If the attacks on the pipeline continue and the supply is cut down completely, it will triple. And there'll probably be shortages."

"Urging the Romanians to go into Moldova is going to send alarms throughout Europe," said Hartman. "We cannot let them use our forces there."

"If we simply give the information, but keep our aircraft on the Romanian side of the border, what's the problem?" asked Chastain. "You see what beasts these guerrillas are. Killing children."

"That incident gives the Romanians some cover," said Freeman. "But I wouldn't send our people over. Not even the spy."

"If he doesn't go, he can't get the information," said Plank.

"All right," said Martindale. "Give the information to the Romanians. Our people stay out of Moldovan territory. They don't engage in the fight. That is an absolute order. No one crosses the border, or fires over the border."

"My man?" asked Plank.

Martindale looked at Freeman, but the National Security Advisor said nothing.

"Let him go," said Martindale. "But . . ."

The pause that followed was significant. If anything happened to the officer, he would not be acknowledged. Plank nodded.

"And the request for additional support," continued Martindale. "Can we do that?"

"I would leave that up to General Samson, sir," said Secretary Chastain. They'd discussed the request briefly at the beginning of the meeting. "His plan was always to beef up the force."

The President nodded. "Make it very clear that we are not to go over the border into Moldova."

"What if our people need to defend themselves?" Chastain asked.

"I wouldn't give Colonel Bastian that big a loophole," said Secretary of State Hartman. "We've seen what he's done with that in the past."

Martindale folded his arms and sat back in his chair.

"Colonel Bastian is not in charge of Dreamland anymore," said Chastain.

"No, but he's their point man. He's the one on the scene," said Secretary Hartman. "And he has an itchy trigger finger."

"No more than any of us do," said Chastain. "They have to have the right to defend themselves."

"They can defend themselves only if attacked in Romanian territory," said the President. "They cannot fire or attack over the border. They can't even fly over it. Understood?"

Chastain hesitated. "I can see circumstances where that might put them in grave danger."

"Which would you rather have?" asked Hartman. "A dead Megafortress crew, or world war?"

"It wouldn't come to that," said Chastain.

"No," Hartman agreed, "but Russia could go ahead and bomb the pipeline directly. Then we'll have a worldwide depression and the end of NATO."

"I hope that's not our choice," said the President.

Bacau, Romania
2320

WITH THE DETAILS WORKED OUT, STONER STAYED NORTH, waiting for word from Washington on whether his plan would be approved.

A small part of him—an insignificant, tiny slice—hoped it wouldn't be, at least not immediately. He wanted a few more days with Sorina Viorica.

He wanted more than that.

As soon as Fairchild relayed the OK—and the conditions— Stoner shut that part of himself away and called General Locusta at his corps headquarters. Locusta's aide was reluctant to even bother getting the general—until Stoner said he had definitive information on the location of the guerrilla camps in Moldova.

"Where are they?" Locusta snapped when he came on the line.

"I'll be at your headquarters in an hour. We'll talk," said Stoner. He killed the transmission, giving Locusta no time to respond.

Stoner had read everything the Agency had on General Locusta, but like most CIA briefs on military officers in Eastern Europe, it offered little beyond his résumé, lacking insight into the man. Locusta was an infantryman by training; among his military honors was a marksmanship badge, earned as a lieutenant. He was well-regarded as a general officer, though considered abrasive by the defense minister and the president.

Locusta seemed to have been marked for greater things from the time he joined the army as a twenty-one-year-old lieutenant, fresh out of university. He'd received training in Russia as a young man and had been posted there for about a year in the early 1980s. He'd also toured Great Britain, Spain, and Italy as part of Romania's initiative to join NATO.

His family had connections to Ceausescu, the former dictator. That had hurt them in the years following Ceausescu's fall, but not so severely that the family wasn't well off now. Locusta himself had some property, though not great wealth.

Nothing in the report told Stoner what he wanted to know: the odds that Locusta would put a knife in his back just for the fun of it.

They were about fifty-fifty, Stoner guessed, after he finished telling the general about the guerrilla camps in Moldova. Average.

Locusta sat silently for nearly a minute after Stoner finished. Most of his aides had left for home hours ago; it was so quiet in the corps HQ that Stoner could hear the clock ticking on Locusta's desk.

"How did you find this information out?" said the general finally.

"I can't get into the exact methods we use," replied Stoner. He pulled over one of the seats—a metal folding chair—and sat down.

"Then how can I judge how accurate the information is?"

Stoner shrugged. "I guess we'll have to find out together."

"Together?"

"I want to go on the raid."

"Why?"

"I think the Russians are helping the guerrillas. I think they may have been responsible for killing some of our people, and this will help me find out."

Another man might have asked if Stoner didn't trust him, but the general accepted the explanation without comment. That told Stoner that the general understood the value of seeing things for yourself, that he was a man who liked to act, rather than have others act for him.

Interesting pieces of information, though not immediately helpful.

"So you have a spy?" asked Locusta.

"I can't get into specifics."

"Where are the camps?"

"I don't have that information yet. There are two, and they're within fifty miles of the border."

"Practically half of the country is within fifty miles of the border."

The two men locked gazes. Stoner held it for half a second, then blinked and looked down, wanting the general to feel that he was his superior. He glanced back, then away, underlining his submission.

"I cannot commit troops to move across the border on vague hints," said the general.

"I'll have the information when the operation starts, not before."

"Nonsense."

Stoner smiled in spite of himself. Locusta was right; Stoner could get the information from Sorina as soon as she was safely out of the country. But Stoner wanted to verify that it was correct before letting her go, and she wouldn't agree to any delay.

Not that he didn't trust her.

"This is of no use to me," said Locusta. "Get out of my office."

Stoner rose silently and walked out, turning down the hall. He went out to his motorcycle. He had his helmet on when one of the general's aides ran from the building, flagging his arms.

"Perhaps the general was, acted, hastily," said the man, a major. "Not hastily but in anger. The criminals have caused us, have killed many people. Sometimes it is difficult to act rationally when dealing with them."

"Sure."

"Your information comes from a criminal?"

"I believe my information is good information," said Stoner. "But the only way to actually find out is to test it."

"You cannot use your planes to verify it?"

"The planes are not allowed over the border."

"Satellites?"

"If we knew where it was, we could get pictures," said Stoner. "But we've looked at sat photos before without finding anything. I imagine that's happened to you."

"If an attack were to be launched, would the aircraft assist then?"

Stoner shook his head. "The Dreamland aircraft cannot violate Moldovan airspace."

"Give me a phone number." the man said, "and I will call you in a few hours."

Bacau, Romania
2234

GENERAL LOCUSTA WATCHED FROM HIS WINDOW AS THE American started his motorbike and drove away.

Locusta had no doubt the American's information would prove to be correct. Two of his soldiers had smuggled an American spy over the border a few days ago; this was obviously the fruits of his labor.

And their blood.

Fifty miles from the border. Much farther than the information their own spies had obtained, and at least a partial answer to the question of why his men had failed to find out themselves.

Though another part of the answer was that the rebels had been useful to Locusta, an excuse to build up his force. Now he no longer needed them.

Or the Russians.

Or the Americans, for that matter.

This was his opportunity: the perfect diversion. It supplied a ready-made excuse for mobilizing his units and commandeering the few helicopters available outside the capital.

And he couldn't wait much longer.

There was a knock at the door. The major he had sent after Stoner, Anton Ozera, appeared in the threshold.

"In," said Locusta, gesturing.

Ozera closed the door behind him.

"What did he say?" asked Locusta.

"His source is one of the criminals. There will be no help across the border."

"But the information is good," said Locusta. "He's convinced of that or he wouldn't want to go along."

"The problem is, the Americans do not know the criminals as we do."

Locusta smirked. "I think they know them well enough."

The fact that a turncoat was willing to give the Americans information showed the terrible state the movement was in. They had failed to win the support of the people, and would now wither and die.

With a little help, of course. And as long as the Russians were removed.

"We could use the attack as a diversion," said Ozera. "It would explain the mobilization of forces."

"Always, Ozera, we think alike," said Locusta.

"Thank you, General."

"Your men?"

"We could strike in an hour. If the target was the president's northern home. The capital, as I said—"

Locusta raised his finger, and Ozera stopped talking. They had discussed the difficulties of striking Voda in the capital many times; the assassination itself would be easy, but the contingencies that would necessarily follow would be difficult to manage.

The general picked up his phone. "Connect me to the president's personal residence. It is a matter of great urgency."

He leaned back in his seat, waiting. He knew Voda's personal habits from experience; the president would be up even though the hour was late.

Sure enough, Voda came on the line within a few minutes.

"Mr. President, I have very important news," said Locusta.

He explained what Stoner had told him. As always, the president listened without comment or interruption. Only when Locusta fell silent did he speak.

"If there is a definitive location, I will review the plans and make my decision," he said.

"I will bring the plans personally to you," said Locusta. "Only . . ."

"Finish your sentence."

"I have two thoughts. One is that I would like the assault to proceed rapidly, so that word of this turncoat does not leak out. And two, if I were to come to the capital, it is possible spies would alert the guerrillas. The Russians have been very busy."

"Yes." Voda paused a moment, thinking. "You suggest I come to your headquarters?"

"That too might generate some unwanted rumors." Locusta pretended to be thinking. "If you were at your estate in the mountains . . ."

"It's hardly an estate, Tomma. Merely an old farm."

And one that you love to visit, Locusta thought. He had met the president there many times, and had his own unit of troops nearby to provide additional protection.

"When would we meet?"

"If you were there tomorrow afternoon?"

"My aide will call you with the arrangements in the morning," said Voda.

Locusta gave Major Ozera a broad smile as he hung up, then rose and went to the door. In the hallway, he bellowed for his chief of staff.

"I want plans for an assault inside Moldova," he told him when he appeared. "Two sites to be hit as hard as we can."

"Where, General?"

"We won't know the precise locations until a few minutes before the assaults themselves. Plan for a large action against several buildings. Expect several hundred guerrillas."

"But the president—"

"I'll deal with the president. You prepare the plans. We will make the attack tomorrow night."

**Aboard EB-52 *Bennett*,
over northern Romania
2330**

THE MEGAFORTRESS HIT A STACK OF TURBULENT AIR, shuddering as she turned through the darkening sky over northern Romania. Dog tightened his grip on the stick, easing her through the rough patch of sky.

"Russians are back, Colonel," said Rager, watching the airborne radar behind him on the *Bennett*'s flight deck. "Right on schedule."

"Has to be the most boring assignment in the world, shadowing us," said Sullivan. "Watching as we go around and around and around."

"Nah. They should try working the ground radar here," said Spiff, referring of course to his own job.

"I thought I heard snoring back there," said Sullivan.

"I have to get my z's in while Colonel Bastian's flying," replied the radar operator. "Life's too exciting when you're at the stick."

"Ha-ha-ha."

DOWNSTAIRS ON THE FLIGHTHAWK DECK, ZEN PUT *HAWK One* into a bank south, waiting as the Megafortress got into position to launch *Hawk Two*. Tonight they were scheduled to work with two platoons, one near where the guerrillas had attacked the other night, the other over the gas pipeline. The two areas overlapped, and the Megafortress's patrol circuits had been plotted so the mother ship would be roughly equidistant to the two smaller planes throughout the night.

The computer would help fly the planes, of course, and the Flighthawks could operate on their own if necessary. But as an old school combat pilot, one who had come to the program from fighter jets, Zen mentally projected himself into each cockpit. It was a bit of a challenge to cover such a disparate area—a good challenge.

The first platoon was scheduled to call in at 2400—midnight in civilian time. The second would make contact a half hour later. In the meantime, Zen put the robot planes through their paces, surveying the ground with their onboard infrared cameras. The farm fields, fallow because of the winter, looked like calm patches of the ocean, their furrows of light waves barely breaking the surface. Houses glowed in the darkness, their chimneys bright with heat.

"Bennett to Flighthawk leader. What's your status?"

"Both aircraft are completing their orienting runs, Colonel," said Zen. "I have nothing but green on my boards. Systems are looking good."

"Bennett," acknowledged Dog.

Zen hit the preset button on his joystick control, and the visual in front of him changed from *Hawk One*'s forward camera to *Hawk Two*'s. He thought of it as "jumping" from one plane to another.

Hawk Two's views had more mountainous terrain, but the overall impression—of a quiet, peaceful night—was the same. For the sake of the Romanians below, Zen hoped it stayed that way.

UP ON THE FLIGHT DECK, COLONEL BASTIAN LET SULLIVAN continue to fly the aircraft while he reviewed the mission's flight plan. There were a few sharp cuts involved to stay close to the Flighthawks as they patrolled, but otherwise the route looked like an elongated racetrack that had been squeezed in the middle.

If things got hot tonight, Dog would be able to scramble

Lieutenant Englehardt and the *Johnson* to help out. The plane had arrived a few hours before, and while the crew could use some rest, it was already prepped for an emergency takeoff.

Dog still wasn't sure what additional aircraft, if any, would join them. It was a decision he was frankly glad he didn't have to make himself. Many people thought a force as large and powerful as the U.S. Air Force had nearly unlimited resources, but the truth was that there was always a heavy demand, not just on the planes, but on the men and women who flew them. Dog couldn't fault Samson for taking his time sending more planes—because of the recent action in India and the demands of the test programs, there were in fact only four other EB-52s currently in full flight condition at Dreamland, and none were radar ships. Dreamland's planes were supposed to be on call to air defense units in the U.S.; the bottom line was that there weren't enough ships to go around.

If Samson actually got the money he'd been promised, there would be more, but Dog knew that would inevitably mean more missions to fulfill—and the resources would once more be stretched.

"One of those MiGs just changed direction, Colonel," said Rager. "Contact one on your screen. Coming toward us."

Dog saw it on the radar display. The MiG's wingman was turning as well.

"They're lighting afterburners."

"Probably blowing the carbon out of their arses," said Sullivan. "The Russians are particularly constipated this time of year."

The planes were roughly 250 miles away, traveling at about 500 knots or nautical miles per hour. Lighting their afterburners—essentially dumping a lot of fuel into the rear of the engines to make the planes go fast—would quickly increase their speed up over the sound barrier. Still, they were a good distance away; it would take at least ten minutes and probably a little more before they were close enough to pose a threat to the Megafortress.

Assuming they were interested in doing that.

"Flighthawk leader, our friends are at it again," Dog told Zen.

"Yeah, Colonel, I'm looking at the radar. What are they doing?"

"Probably testing to see how we'll respond," said Dog. "Plot an intercept for *Hawk One* near the border just in case."

"Done, Colonel."

Dog checked the radar image. The radar in the Russian fighters—or whatever was guiding them—wouldn't be able to see the Flighthawk at this range.

Three minutes later the MiGs were still running hot in their direction. Their speed was up over 1,100 knots. They'd switched their afterburners off—if they left them on too long they'd quickly be out of fuel—but kept their course steady.

"Contacts one and two looking at the border in a little over five minutes," said Rager.

"Let's show them we know they're on their way," said Dog. "Sully, open the bomb bay doors."

"On it, Colonel."

The plane shook with the vibration of the bomb bay doors swinging open. The Megafortress had six AMRAAM-plus Scorpion missiles loaded for air defense, along with two smart bombs. Dog wasn't aligned perfectly to fire them—his track was roughly perpendicular to the MiGs—but he could easily bring them to bear if the situation warranted.

By now Romania's ground radars along the seacoast had spotted the MiGs, and the antiaircraft missile batteries along the eastern border of the country were being alerted. The defenses dated from the mid-sixties, however, and would be of little concern to the MiGs if they crossed.

"Two minutes to the border, Colonel," said Rager. "They're— Shit! Weapons radars activated."

"Relax," said Dog. "ECMs, Sully."

The copilot activated the Megafortress's electronic counter measures, jamming the frequencies used by the MiG's radar missiles to home in on their target.

"Colonel, I can set up a better intercept over the border," said Zen.

Dog's orders specifically forbade him to send any of his aircraft over the line, and in fact directed him to "actively avoid contact"—which could be interpreted to mean that he should run away if the MiGs got any more aggressive.

He understood why, of course—the U.S. wanted to avoid giving the Russians even the slightest pretense for coming to the aid of the rebels. But he still bristled.

"Stay on our side of the line," said Dog.

"Roger that."

"Colonel, I have a fire indication! Missile in the air! AMRAAMski! Two of them."

"What the hell?" shouted Sullivan.

Dog dipped his wing, turning so he could "beam" the enemy radar and make it harder for the missiles to track him. The planes were a little more than thirty miles from the border, and the Megafortress was another forty from that. They were just at the missile's effective range, maybe even a little beyond it.

"Missile one is coming for us," said Rager.

"Colonel, you want to take them?" said Zen.

"Negative," said Dog tersely. "Button us up, Sullivan."

"Yes, sir."

The closed doors made it easier for the Megafortress to maneuver.

"Zen, put *Hawk Two* between us. Look for the missile."

"Roger that, Colonel."

Dog turned the Megafortress again, pushing hard to get

away. What the hell were the Russians doing? Trying to start World War III?

"Missile one—off scope," said Sullivan. "Missile two—gone."

"They self-destructed, Colonel," added Rager. "MiGs have turned." He gave a bearing and range—they were under fifty miles away.

"Stand down," said Dog. "Excitement is over, gentlemen. Let's get back to work."

"What was it all about, Colonel?" asked Sullivan after they had returned to their patrol route.

"They're trying to rattle us. It's an old Cold War game. First one to blink loses."

"Did we blink or did they?"

Dog frowned.

"Let's get back to work," was all he said.

Dreamland
1204

ONCE A PILOT LEARNED THE BASICS OF FLYING, HE OR SHE could in theory fly anything. It was a little like learning how to ride a bicycle or drive a car—once the basic physical and intellectual skills were mastered, going from one cockpit to another wasn't all that difficult.

Of course, when you were a pilot who operated at the very top of the profession, who flew planes at the cutting edge in extreme situations, you did more things with your aircraft than the weekend flier puttering from small town to small town in his Piper. And when you were among the most elite members of the subspecies, your expectations of yourself as well as the plane were extremely high. They didn't change just because you were in an unfamiliar cockpit. Yes, you could strap just about any plane onto your back and take a nice, nonchalant orientation flight, not push the bird or yourself very hard without a very steep learning curve. But that wasn't the way a top test pilot operated.

No, an elite pilot pushed a new plane and herself to the max. Which was where the frustration came in.

Breanna tried hard not to curse as *Boomer* gave her a stall warning coming out of the turn. Supplying more throttle, she powered through the maneuver, holding her position tightly to the ghosted course suggestion on her heads-up display.

"Good. I'm ranging. Locked. Ready to fire," said Sleek Top.

Sleek Top was sitting in the pilot's seat. Under normal circumstances, the copilot handled the targeting duties, but both consoles were fully equipped and either pilot could comfortably fly or control the weapons.

"Climbing," said Breanna, sighing as she turned toward her next mark.

"You're doing good, Bree."

"Uh-huh."

"You don't think you are?"

"I guess."

Sleek remained silent as they worked through the rest of the exercise. Breanna didn't have a lot of time in either "stock" B-1Bs or the B-1B/L, but the plane was easy to adjust to compared to getting used to sitting in the second officer's seat. The world looked very different from the right-hand seat.

But if that's what it took to get back in the air, that's what she would do.

They finished off with a mock refuel. Breanna could have had the computer fly the plane through the rendezvous—and on a combat mission, that might have been the preferred option—but it felt like cheating. She held steady, eased up to the boom, and hooked in almost as easily as if she were flying an EB-52.

"You are a hell of a pilot, Breanna," said Sleek Top as they turned back toward the runway to land. "Hell of a pilot."

"For a woman?"

"Nah," he said quickly. "For anyone. You picked up the fine points really fast."

"I'm still working on it. I know I have a way to go."

"Listen. About last night—"

"It was a great basketball game."

"I meant—"

"It was a great basketball game," she repeated. "Maybe Zen and I can join you at another. He's an even bigger fan than I am."

"I'd like that," said Sleek Top. "Very much."

Dreamland Command Center, Dreamland
1229

"THEY *FIRED* ON YOU?" SAID SAMSON. HE COULD FEEL HIS anger rising as he paced in front of the large screen at the front of the Dreamland Command Center.

"They launched missiles in our direction. I took evasive action. They blew up the missiles maybe twenty seconds after launch, over the Black Sea. I assume their plan all along was to spook us."

"These Russian bastards," said Samson. "We ought to shoot them out of the sky."

The general glanced at the screen. The video caught Dog's head jerking right as he glanced in the direction of his co-pilot. Samson felt a twinge of jealousy—he wanted to be in the air himself.

Let those Russian bastards try to spook him. Just let them try.

"I'm sorry, General," said Dog, turning his face back toward the camera in front of his station. "I missed what you said."

"Nothing. You have something else?"

"Negative. Very quiet on the ground so far."

"And you did nothing to provoke the Russians?"

"All we did was take our station. At no time did any of our ships go over the border."

"You better be giving me the whole story here, Bastian. If I get my head handed to me on this, yours isn't going to be worth a nickel."

Dog didn't say anything.

"I'll get back to you," said Samson.

"General, if there's a mission in Moldova, I'd like permission—"

"What part of what I just said don't you understand?"

"It's all crystal clear," said Dog.

The screen blanked.

That was the problem with Bastian, thought Samson. Even when he was in the right, you had to be suspicious of him. He was a cowboy, always looking for a chance to blow something up.

Still, when he was right, he was right.

"Get me the White House," the general told the communications specialist. "Tell them it's important."

White House
1550

JUST IN TIME FOR HIS COUNTRY'S EVENING NEWS PROGRAMS, the German chancellor had responded to the latest round of Russian price increases by threatening to cut off gas shipments through its pipelines to France unless the French paid Germany a special transshipping fee. The French had responded angrily, and now all of Europe seemed at each other's throats. The Italians, who had seen unemployment rise to nearly twenty percent of the workforce in the past two months, were even talking about leaving NATO and the European Common Market.

The National Security Council had called an emergency

meeting to discuss the latest developments. Freeman had Jed come along to make it easier for him to keep up-to-date. The meeting was winding down when Sandra Collins, one of the NSC duty officers, appeared at the door and waved her hands frantically to get his attention. Jed waited for the Undersecretary of State to finish what he was saying—though he used a lot of words, his opinion basically was that the Italian threat was an empty bluff—then excused himself and went to the door.

"General Samson at Dreamland," whispered Collins. "He says it's urgent."

Jed went across the hall to the secure communications center, nodding at the duty officer as he went to one of the stations. He sat down at the desk, typed in his password, then put his eyes into the retina scanner. A few seconds later, General Samson's face appeared in his screen.

"General, what can I do for you?" asked Jed.

Samson frowned. Jed knew from their past communications that Samson expected to be talking to Philip Freeman every time he called. But the National Security Advisor had given specific orders that *all* Dreamland communications, including those that came through Admiral Balboa at the Pentagon, were to go through Jed, and while Samson surely had been told, he hadn't really gotten the message.

And probably never would.

"Jed, the Russians fired on one of our aircraft," said Samson.

"The Russians?"

"Those MiGs that were shadowing Bastian. And he did nothing to provoke it. Now I want permission to shoot those bastards down, and I want it now."

"Um, General—"

"My people have to be able to defend themselves. Even Bastian. The orders have to be changed to allow them to do that."

"The President was pretty specific about them staying out of any sort of situation—"

"Then you get him on the phone so I can talk to him," said Samson.

"I'll do what I can, General. But, listen, the situation over there is pretty volatile. It may seem like it's just a dispute over gas prices, but—"

"Don't tell me how volatile it is. My people are on the front line here. I need to protect them."

"Yes, sir. Understood."

THE NSC MEETING HAD ALREADY BROKEN UP AND JED'S boss was gone. By the time he caught up with him, Freeman was at lunch up at the Capitol, dining in the Members Dining Room as the guest of Larry Segriff, who, besides representing Wisconsin as its senior representative, was head of the Foreign Relations Committee.

Freeman saw Jed walking toward him. "Am I late already?" he said, glancing at his watch. "I just got here."

"Actually, um, Sally made a mistake on the schedule." Jed smiled at Segriff, trying to seem genuine as he offered an excuse. "You were supposed to be in a meeting with the President on the gas situation in Europe. She thought lunch was tomorrow."

"I'm not going to keep you, Phil." Segriff started to wave him away. "Go ahead. We'll have lunch a different time."

"Thanks, Congressman. I'm really sorry. It's good to exchange ideas."

"Yes. I'll have my secretary set something up."

Jed followed Freeman out of the room. At least a dozen pairs of eyes followed them as they left.

"Good, Jed. I think he half believed you," said Freeman.

"I thought—"

"You did fine. What's up?"

"One of the Dreamland aircraft was fired on by the Russians," Jed told him.

"What?"

"It looks like it was meant to intimidate them. In any event, General Samson wants permission to fight back."

Freeman set his lips together in a deep frown as they got into the limo for the short ride back to the Executive Office Building.

Within an hour Jed was sitting next to his boss in the Cabinet Room next to the Oval Office, briefing President Martindale on what had happened.

Martindale ordinarily took even the worst news calmly, and it was generally hard to read his emotions.

Not today. He pounded the table, then ran his hand back through his white hair so violently that it flew into a wild tangle.

"What the hell are the goddamned Russians up to?" he thundered. "They want a war? They want a goddamned war?"

The reaction caught both Jed and his boss off guard. They exchanged a glance.

"I don't know that they want a war, exactly," said Freeman. "I think they're pushing, to see how far they can go. How far we'll go."

Martindale's face flushed. He looked at them for a moment, and as Jed stared at his profile he realized how tired the President appeared, and how old he had become. The last few weeks had been a great triumph—but also an enormous strain. Whatever held his temperament together had been stretched to the breaking point.

"Yes, of course that's what they're doing. Pushing us. Pushing me."

Martindale began to relax, becoming more his old self.

"We do have a couple of options, Mr. President," said Freeman. "We could send the Dreamland people to support the operation in Moldova."

"No. That's what they want. That's what this is about—to

try to provoke us." The President rose. "This isn't just about the price of the natural gas. Oh yes, that's part of it. Definitely part of it. But there's more. They want to break up NATO. Look at the quarreling that's going on. And what do you think will happen to our bid to expand NATO if we're seen taking sides like this?"

"We are taking sides," said Freeman. "We have to take sides."

"Yes, but with restraint. They want to make us look as aggressive as possible. They know we're riding high right now." Martindale shook his head. "Moldova is still off limits."

"OK," said Freeman.

"Um . . ."

Martindale turned to Jed. "What's that 'um' about, young man?"

"Sir, um, the Romanians have been asking for more support. They say two planes, even Megafortresses, aren't enough."

"What does Samson say?"

"Uh, I guess I don't know exactly."

"Find out what his plans are."

"Can the planes defend themselves?" insisted Freeman.

"They are to avoid provoking the Russians at all costs," said Martindale. "No offensive action. Period."

"But—"

"Colonel Bastian will know how to interpret that order. Make sure it's relayed to him."

**Dreamland
1300**

ONCE MORE, SAMSON FOUND HIMSELF BRISTLING AS HE talked to Jed Barclay, angry that the President wouldn't speak to him directly.

"Um, just that the President wants to know if you have an adequate force in Romania," explained Jed.

"Tell him we have more planes getting ready to fly as we speak," Samson said. "They'll be taking off this evening."

"Very good."

"Can we hit the Russians?" asked Samson.

"Actually, the President does not want American aircraft in Moldovan airspace. He thinks the Russians are trying to provoke us."

Samson folded his arms.

"His orders were, this is a direct quote: 'They are to avoid provoking the Russians at all costs. No offensive action. Period.' He wanted that relayed to Colonel Bastian."

"Very well. Dreamland out."

Samson dropped the phone on its hook.

"Chartelle!" he said loud enough to be heard in the outer office. "Get Mack Smith in here. Now!"

"Yes, General," said the secretary.

Mack appeared a few minutes later. The major had apparently been eating lunch, because a small bit of ketchup clung to his chin.

"Mack, I want our B-1B/Ls en route to Romania by tonight."

"The B-1s, General?"

"Is there an echo in this room?"

"General, the B-1 project—"

"Spit it out, Major. Let's have your objections in plain language."

"Yes, sir. It's not an objection, it's just—even with Breanna—I mean, Captain Stockard—I'm still one pilot short. We have Sleek Top, Jack Kittle, and Breanna. That's one short—and to be honest, I don't know if you can push Sleek into combat."

"If he volunteers, he can go."

"Well, I don't know that—"

"Have you ever heard of a Marine who didn't volunteer for combat?"

"Um, no sir. But even so, you're still one short."

"No, we're full up. I'll fly *Boomer*." Samson rose. "Get the others into my office right away. I don't care where they are. Get them. *Now*. We have a job to do."

V

Voyeurs at the Edge of Battle

———

**Dochia, Romania
28 January 1998
0500**

IT WAS THE LAST TIME HE'D SEE HER.

They'd lain in bed all night, not talking, only their sides touching. Stoner slid away from her now, unsure of himself.

Had there been real emotion from the very beginning, lust, or gratitude because of her help? Something vulnerable and simple, frail, unworthy of a spy?

No matter how you steeled yourself—how you *stole* yourself away, hid the vulnerable part of the soul that everyone had behind a wall, in order to do your job—there was some small slither of humanity left, some piece of flesh vulnerable at the edge.

Stoner pulled on his pants, slipping in the button at the waist. They were loose. He always lost weight on a mission. Another week and he would need a belt.

Shirt on, he unrolled a fresh pair of socks and sat on the bed, his back to her.

Temptation lingered, her perfume and his sweat mixing in the stuffy room.

He took his shoes, ignored his chance for one last glance, and left.

A HALF HOUR LATER, STONER TURNED HIS MOTORCYCLE off the main road just north of Bacau, riding down a narrow dirt trail that formed a horseshoe between a farm field and the road. Danny Freah was already waiting, sitting in a borrowed Romanian jeep. Stoner drove past quickly, checking the area, then spun back, kicking up dirt and rocks as he skidded to a stop next to Danny's window.

"How goes it?" asked Freah. He was dressed in civilian clothes, jeans and a heavy jacket.

"I'm OK. You?"

"This Romanian coffee could wake the dead," said Freah, holding up a plastic travel mug.

"One of Locusta's aides called me last night," Stoner told him. "They're going ahead with the raid tonight. Assuming they get approval."

"Yeah, I heard. Locusta's chief of staff called Colonel Bastian." Danny took a sip of the coffee, wincing as he swallowed. "You think their president's going to approve?"

Stoner shrugged. He had no idea. If he had to, he'd sneak into Moldova himself and check on the sites. It'd be far more dangerous, but in some ways much easier: He wouldn't have to worry about anyone but himself.

Danny took another pull from the coffee and once again made a face.

"If it's so bad, why are you drinking it?" Stoner asked.

"I guess I like the pain," said Danny. He laughed softly.

Stoner pulled a blank piece of paper from his shirt pocket. "You got a pen?" he asked.

Danny handed him one and he wrote out the directions to the house where Sorina was holed up.

"She's expecting you in an hour," Stoner said. "Be careful. She's pretty tough."

"Mind if I ask you a question?"

Stoner tensed, expecting that Danny would ask if he'd been sleeping with her.

Would he lie?

No. Tell the truth. No sense not to.

"Aren't you freezing your buns off on that motorcycle?" asked Danny.

Stoner tried not to show his relief that the question wasn't the one he expected.

"It's handy. And it's what I have."

"If there were time, I'd ask to take it for a spin."

"Next time I see you," said Stoner.

"Deal."

"Good luck, Captain."

"Same to you. I don't trust Locusta much."

Stoner smirked, but instead of answering, he revved the bike and started in the direction of the Romanian army camp.

Dreamland
27 January 1998
1900 (0600 Romania, 28 January 1998)

BREANNA FELT HER HEARTBEAT RISE AS *BOOMER*'S BIG engines cycled up, their massive thrust sending a rhythmic shudder through her spine as the afterburners lit. Despite the immense thrust, the big plane seemed to hesitate ever so slightly, her wheels sticking for a brief instant to the concrete pavement.

And then everything let go and she felt herself pushed back in the seat as the B-1 rocketed forward, quickly gathering momentum. Wind swept beneath the aircraft's wings and *Boomer* lifted off the ground, her nose pushing upward like the proud head of an eagle taking flight.

"Retract landing gear," said General Samson, sitting next to her in the pilot's seat.

"Cleaning gear," said Breanna as she did just that.

The big plane continued to climb, moving through 2,000 feet, through 3,000, through 4,000. Airspeed shot past 360 knots. It was a jolt compared to a Megafortress's takeoff, but by B-1 standards it was almost lackadaisical. Breanna told herself to stop comparing the planes and just fly.

There was a tickle in her nose. She hoped she wasn't getting a cold.

"*Big Bird* to *Boomer.* I have you in sight," said Sleek Top from the other B-1B/L. His voice was so loud he drowned out the engines.

"*Boomer,*" acknowledged Samson. "How are you looking?"

"Purring like a kitten, General," responded Sleek. "We have your six."

"Roger that."

"First way marker in ten minutes, General," said Breanna. "Systems are in the green. Fuel burn is a little lighter than originally computed."

"Hmmmph."

"We have a bit more of a tailwind," said Breanna, explaining the difference.

"Good, Captain. Stay on it."

Not too many pilots would have been miffed that they were getting better mileage than expected, but that was Samson. His tone tended to be a bit gruff, but it wasn't anything Breanna wasn't used to from her father. In many ways the two men were similar—no wonder they couldn't stand each other.

GENERAL SAMSON CHECKED HIS COURSE ON THE COMPUTER screen. While he'd flown this B-1 during an orientation flight a few weeks before, it still felt a bit odd. In nearly every measurable aspect, the plane was superior to the "stock" B-1Bs he was used to. It was faster, a hair more maneuverable, and could fly farther without refueling if the tanks were managed properly—which was almost a given, since the computer did the managing.

Boomer's internal bomb bays were taken up by the laser, but the weapon's comparatively lighter weight meant a heavier bomb load could be carried on the wings and fuselage. In this version, the aircraft didn't need the offensive and defensive systems officers; their jobs were completely replaced by the computer. The computer could even take over most if not all of the piloting tasks—not that Samson was about to give it the opportunity.

Still, there was something about *Boomer* and its sister ship, *Big Bird,* that bothered him. It was almost too slick, too easy to fly. It wasn't going to keep a pilot on his toes the way an older ship would.

But what the hell. It was good to be flying again, and even better to lead a mission. Samson knew there'd be flak from above at some point, but if Colonel Dog Bastian could do it, so could he.

Maybe it would earn him a new nickname: the Flying, Fighting General.

Now *that* was the sort of thing that helped you get confirmed as Chairman of the Joint Chiefs of Staff.

Bucharest, Romania
28 January 1998
0900

ALIN VODA'S POLITICAL CAREER HAD STARTED IN THE MOST unlikely way when, at age seven, a family friend gave him a trombone. It was a worn instrument, with many scratches and two dents in the playing tube; the bell of the horn had been pushed slightly to one side. Even an accomplished musician would have had trouble coaxing a winning sound from the instrument. But it lit a fire in Voda's brain. He took lessons at his local elementary school, and within a few months had devoured the teacher's small store of sheet music. His notes, strained by the condition of the old horn, did not always have the best tone, but Voda's enthusiasm for the music burned so hot that it infected anyone who heard him.

His teacher happened to have a better trombone in storage, and one day decided to loan it to Voda, letting the boy play it first at school, and then, within a week or two, at home. The sound of the instrument was a revelation, and Voda's passion, already great, doubled. By the end of the school year he could play at the level of a competent teenager, and certainly practiced as much.

During the summer vacation, Voda returned to his own instrument, and immediately felt its limitations. It was not just the sound of the battered horn; trombones played in a relatively limited range, and while there was much to be mastered, it already seemed to the eight-year-old that the range would be too limited for his imagination. He was thinking and dreaming in notes.

Wild riffs played through his head. If a painter might be said to see the world in colors, Voda had come to hear the world in music. He pestered his parents—poorly paid workers for the state—to find him a piano. Even a used instrument was out of the question, but the same friend who had given him the trombone had a brother who was a janitor at a local school. Thanks to his job, he had the keys to the basement where the music room was, and one day the friend arranged for the brother to meet Voda and his mother so the boy could plunk on the piano.

Within a few minutes, Voda had figured out how to transpose the notes he played on the trombone to the keyboard. His playing was not good by any means; the piano itself was old and some of the keys fidgety, so none of the songs were recognizable except to Voda. But again, it fired his imagination.

He pestered his parents and the friend to allow him to return. A week later, he was able to coax a melodious version of a Romanian folk song from the instrument; after about fifteen minutes of playing it back and forth, his mistakes morphed into a pleasant improvisation, his mind hearing the notes as they might be, not necessarily as they had been originally intended.

The music attracted the attention of the school's principal, who happened to be working upstairs in his office. When he came down to investigate, he was surprised to see a thin, somewhat undersized eight-year-old at the keyboard. While the janitor and Voda's mother froze in fear that they were about to get into trouble for sneaking into the building, the principal strode to Voda. When the boy finished, the older man—a modest amateur pianist himself—began asking questions about the song and, eventually, about Voda's training, or rather, lack of it.

From that point on, coincidence no longer played a part in Voda's musical career. Admission was arranged to a special school in Bucharest, where he had access to some of the best teachers in the country. While the routine of becoming a true artist—the endless hours of practice and study—often bored Voda, it did not dull his love of music. He continued to throw himself into the work, making his fingers produce the notes he imagined in his head.

The teachers were divided over whether the boy should be considered a true "prodigy" or simply an extremely talented and gifted young man. Initially, his public concerts were limited to small performances at the school. He did not particularly stand out at these, not only because of the talent surrounding him on the program, but because the pieces he played tended toward the obscure and difficult. But those who knew what he did in the practice rooms never undervalued his talent, and pushed him to improve.

At fifteen, Voda discovered Mozart. Naturally, he'd played many Mozart pieces over the years and had a general understanding of the great composer's work, but until then he never understood the music the way an artist must understand it. Ironically, the moment came while playing the overture for *Don Giovanni,* not generally considered a pianist's showpiece when compared to the rest of Mozart's oeuvre. As he began the third measure, the notes suddenly felt different. For Voda, it was as if he had pushed open the door of a fabulous mansion and strolled in, suddenly at home.

His first performance of a Mozart piece at the school—

Sonata K 310—was a sensation. The small audience leaped to its feet when he concluded, and applauded so long that he had to do an encore. Within weeks he had his first concert outside the school's auspices; by the time he was eighteen, he was touring the country, playing on his own. He visited Russia and Warsaw. With classical music much more popular behind what was then the Iron Curtain than it was in the West, Voda became an emerging superstar and a national hero.

And then, when he was twenty years old, he made a mistake that changed his life. He played the folk song that the principal had overheard him play at the very beginning of his studies.

It was a second encore after a performance in Bucharest that mostly consisted of Mozart sonatas. It did not fit the program in any way. He hadn't thought of the tune in years, and certainly hadn't played it, or even planned to play it, since his education began.

There was a good reason not to. The Romanian government, in one of its periodic fits of paranoia, had banned all nationalistic movements and displays. The move was really a crackdown on dissidents, whom the government believed were using nationalistic sentiments to stir resentment against the regime. For whatever reason—some critics of the government believed it was looking for more backing from the Soviet Union—the ban extended to all the arts, and extended so far that a musical play based on a folk tale cycle was canceled two days before its opening in Bucharest: the day before Voda's performance.

It was never completely clear, even to Voda, why the song came into his head that evening, or why he allowed it to flow from his brain to his fingers. Perhaps he intended it as a protest against the state, though he had never harbored such political feelings before then. Maybe it was just misplaced nostalgia. In any event, the crowd heard it as a political statement, and their response was beyond anything he could ever have imagined. Had he stood up and declared himself king at the end of the concert, they would have gladly taken him on their back and carried him to the castle.

He did nothing of the sort. He bowed, went to his dressing room, and later walked to the small apartment he kept a few blocks away. He was sleeping soundly at two in the morning when a troop of policemen broke in and arrested him. He was held in jail for six months, put on trial secretly, and sentenced to six years imprisonment for "treasonous behavior."

It was there that Voda found his second career. Unlike music, politics was for him a difficult and unfriendly art. He came to it reluctantly, at first puzzled by the way other prisoners looked toward him as a leader. What they saw as an act of resolute defiance against overwhelming odds, he still viewed as a confused and confusing mistake. Only gradually did he come to understand the principles the dissidents were risking their lives for.

Democracy had never seemed magical to him. Surely a man should have control over his own life, but how far should that control extend? Used to long days of practice and grueling performance schedules, Voda didn't think it should go very far.

When he was let out of jail at the end of his sentence, Voda found that he was no longer allowed to perform. He began moonlighting in small venues as a poorly paid piano player performing covers of popular songs. As long as he did not use his real name and stayed away from classical music, he remained unmolested by the authorities. The gigs paid enough for a very modest apartment, and kept food on the table, though it had to be supplemented by dinners at the cafés where he played.

With his days largely free, Voda drifted toward the dissidents he'd known in jail, meeting them occasionally for coffee or a walk around town. Gradually, he began doing small things for the freedom movement—nothing brave, nothing outlandish, nothing even likely to earn him time in jail.

Until, in a fit of pique at a government decree against another musician who had dared play a piece by an American composer at a public concert, Voda gave an impromptu outdoor concert at Piata Revolutiei—Revolution Square, in the center of the city. For an hour, playing on a poorly miked upright piano, he serenaded the city with a selection of Mozart pieces he hadn't played in public for years. By the time the police moved in, the crowd had grown to over 10,000. Men, women, and children pushed and shoved away the first group of policemen who tried to drag him off. Water cannons were brought in; Voda continued to play. His last song was the overture of *Don Giovanni*. The music continued to soar in his head even as the clubs beat him over the back.

Two of his fingers were broken in the melee, though it wasn't clear whether it had been done purposely. This time he was put in jail without a trial.

That was in April 1989. Eight months later a far larger crowd gathered at Piata Revolutiei to denounce and chase out the country's dictator, Nicolae Ceausescu. Voda was released from jail a few days later. He stood for parliament and was elected. From there his rise to president seemed almost preordained. Voda felt as if it was his fate—an increasingly heavy fate as time went on.

The end of the dictator brought considerable problems to the country. The guerrillas were a sideshow in many ways, annoying, deadly, but more a distraction than a real threat, at least as far as he was concerned. The economy needed to be jump-started. The manufacturing sector was stuck in the 1940s or worse, and agriculture was so underinvested that horses were used to plow fields. Ethnic differences that seemed nonexistent under the dictator became extremely divisive, fanned by politicians trying to boost their own careers.

Foreign relations were a nightmare. Russia pushed hard to bring Romania into its sphere of influence. Voda saw the country's future residing with the West, but deep-seated prejudices among many of the Europeans, especially those in Germany and France, had caused their politicians to drag their feet. On a personal level, Voda couldn't stand most foreign leaders, whom he thought were bigots and thieves. Even the Austrians tried to cheat Romania when the gas pipeline deal was brokered. At times, Romania's only true ally seemed to be the United States, which was pushing for it to join NATO. But even the U.S. could be fickle.

Voda got along personally with the American ambassador, who claimed to own the CD he had recorded when he was just twenty-one. He had met President Martindale twice, not nearly enough to form a real opinion of the man.

By the time he was elected president, Voda had been involved in politics long enough to have made many enemies. A whole section of the opposition viewed not only him but democracy itself as suspect; they would gladly bring back a dictator in a heartbeat—so long as he agreed with their positions, of course. But the worst were his old dissident friends. Most felt they, not he, should be the head of state.

The president's relationship with the military was, at best, difficult. He'd appointed Fane Cazacul as defense minister only in an attempt to placate some of the minor parties whose support was useful in parliament. Cazacul had his own power base, both in the military—with which Voda had problems— and in politics. But Cazacul was in many ways inept when it came to running a department; he had squandered much of the defense budget that Voda had worked so hard to get passed. Still, Cazacul commanded the loyalty of a number of generals, mostly in the western part of the country, and Voda had no choice but to keep him on.

Voda did not count General Locusta as an enemy, but he did not fully trust him either. Locusta was far more competent than Cazacul, and though nominally the equal of Romania's three other lieutenant generals, was clearly the leading light of the General Staff. He also clearly wanted more power— a natural ailment among military men, Voda believed, and perhaps among all men in general. For that reason, as well as financial concerns and problems with Cazacul, Voda had hesitated to send Locusta the additional troops he wanted to fight the rebels. But the attacks on the pipeline trumped everything else; he knew he needed to protect the line or lose considerable revenue.

Voda also realized that the gas crisis was having a serious effect on Western Europe and NATO. If he did not preserve the pipeline, his chances of having Romania join the alliance would probably be crushed.

His hopes of joining NATO led Voda to resist Locusta and others when they suggested sending troops across the border in Moldova to battle the rebel strongholds. But the events of the past week—the attack on the pipeline and the vicious, cold-blooded killing of the family near Tutova—demonstrated that he must take decisive action. More important, the Americans were signaling that they not only approved, but would assist, albeit in a very limited way.

"You are far away," said his wife, Mircea, sitting next to him in the back of the sedan as they drove from Bucharest. "Are you already in the mountains? Or listening to music in your head?"

Voda smiled at her. He hadn't told her about Locusta's call or the real reason for his spur of the moment vacation weekend, though he thought she might have some suspicions.

"Music," he replied.

"Mozart?"

"A combination of different things."

He had met Mircea after being released from prison the first time. She'd been a dissident and had an excellent ear for politics, but not for music.

Mircea gave him a playful tap.

"When you see Julian, then your attention will be with us," she said, referring to their eight-year-old son, who was to meet them at their mountain home near Stulpicani with his nanny. "Until then, you are a man of the state. Or of music."

"Both." Voda smiled, then looked out the car window, admiring the countryside.

Dochia, Romania
0905

"YOU CAN PUT THE GUN AWAY," DANNY TOLD THE SHADOW in the hallway behind the open door. "I'm Danny Freah."

"Let me see your hands," a woman replied.

Danny held his hands out. "How many black guys you think there are in Romania? Black Americans? Up here? Looking for you?"

"Keep the hands where I can see them."

"Usually we say please." Danny raised his arms higher. "We have only a half hour to make the rendezvous. A little less."

The shadow took a step forward, and the woman's features became more distinct. She was about five-six, not much more than 110 pounds. Dark hair, green eyes, hard expression.

"Like I said, we have less than a half hour. And we have some driving to do."

Sorina Viorica took another step forward. The pistol in her hand was aimed squarely at his face.

"Where's your gun?" she asked.

"I don't have any."

"I don't believe you. Unzip your coat."

Danny slowly complied. He'd left his service pistol in the car, unsure what the local laws were about civilians carrying them.

"Turn around," she told him.

Danny sighed but complied again. He held his coat up. She took two steps toward him—he knew he could swing around and grab her, knock the weapon out of her hand. But there was no sense in that.

She patted him down quickly. A light touch—she had done it before.

"Why aren't you armed?" she asked, stepping back.

"Because I thought it would be unnecessary," he said, turning back around.

"All right. Let's go."

"Don't you have a bag?"

"I have everything I need."

Danny led her out to the street, crossing quickly. Sorina hung back, checking her surroundings, making sure she wasn't being set up. Inside the car, she pulled her jacket tight around her neck, though the heat was blasting.

"Do you have a cig?" she asked.

"Cigarette?"

"Yes."

"I'm afraid I don't."

She frowned, looked out the window.

"I haven't smoked in years," she said. "But today I feel like it."

"You want to know the itinerary?"

"Mark explained it."

"I'll be with you until I hear from them. Myself and another one of my men."

She shrugged. Danny watched her stare out of the side of the car, her eyes focused far away.

She turned suddenly, caught him looking at her.

"Have you ever left your home?" she asked. She sounded as if she were accusing him of a crime.

"All the time," said Danny.

"And known you were not coming back?"

"No."

"It's different."

"I'd guess it would be."

She frowned, as if that wasn't the answer she wanted, then turned back toward the window.

It started to snow a few minutes before they got to the field Danny had picked for the rendezvous. The flakes were big disks, circles of white that flipped over like falling bingo chips scattering across the road. Though sparse, they were thick and heavy, slow to melt; as they landed on the windshield of the car they made large ovals, giving way slowly to the heat of the glass.

"An aircraft called an Osprey is coming for us," Danny told her as he pulled to the side of the road. "It can land like a helicopter but flies like a plane. It has some heavy cannon under the nose."

Sorina said nothing.

"I'm just telling you because it can look pretty fierce when you first see it. It's black."

"I've seen things much fiercer than helicopters, Captain."

"You can call me Danny."

She didn't answer.

Danny got out of the car and walked around to the trunk, where he'd left a rucksack with some gear. None of the lights in the houses across the street were on, but there was a glow farther down, near the church and the center of the city. Behind them to the east the thick layer of clouds were preventing the sun from opening the day with a grand display, tinting its rays dark gray and obscuring the horizon.

"The weather is my future," said Sorina. And then she continued speaking to herself in Romanian.

Danny felt no pity—the memory of her friends' massacre remained vivid—but he was curious about her. He wondered why she had decided to help; Stoner hadn't said.

Most likely, he thought, it had to do with money. Yet her austere air and simple clothes seemed to indicate a person not moved by material possessions.

Revenge? Perhaps. Or maybe she'd traded her life. But she moved like a person already dead, a wary ghost waiting for her ride to oblivion.

He heard the heavy *whomp* of the aircraft's rotors in the distance.

"They're coming," he said.

Sorina stared toward the glow of the church, opposite the direction of the Osprey as the plane came in. Just as he turned to start for the rear ramp, Danny saw her reach her finger toward her eye. But he couldn't tell in the dim light if she was brushing away grit or a tear.

**Presidential villa,
near Stulpicani, Romania
1300**

GENERAL LOCUSTA STUDIED THE LAWN AND SURROUNDING property of President Voda's mountain retreat. It had been quite some time since it was farmed, and Locusta guessed it had never been very profitable. The property rose sharply behind the house and fell off across the road in front of it; there were large rock formations, and tilling the fields had to be difficult. With the exception of the front lawn, trees had long ago taken over whatever had been cultivated.

The driver stopped in front of the house. Locusta got out, taking his briefcase with him. A man in a heavy overcoat watched him from the front steps. He was a bodyguard, though his weapon was concealed under his coat. In accordance with Voda's wishes, only the president's personal security team was stationed at the house. Locusta had a company of men a half mile down the road, ready to respond in an emergency.

Or not, as the case might be.

"The president is waiting in the den," said Paul Sergi, meeting the general outside the door of the house.

"Very good," said Locusta, ignoring the aide's arrogant tone. Sergi, Voda's chief assistant and secretary, had never gotten along with anyone in the military.

Inside the house, Locusta turned to the left instead of the right. As he corrected his mistake, he caught a glimpse of

Voda's son, Julian, constructing some sort of contraption out of a set of Lego blocks. The boy whipped it upward—obviously it was meant to be some sort of airplane or spaceship, for he made whooshing noises as he moved it through the air.

Locusta smiled at the boy, then felt his conscience twinge. He hadn't realized the child would be here.

It was a brief twinge. These were the fortunes of war.

Sergi knocked on the study door, then pushed it open. The president was working at his desk, his wife standing next to him. Locusta gave her a feigned smile—he would have no qualms about her death; her record as an antipatriot was very clear.

"General, thank you for coming," said Voda, rising. He glanced at his wife as he extended his hand to shake.

"I'll leave you men to talk," said Mircea. She gave Locusta a patently phony smile as she left.

Voda sat in one of the chairs at the side, gesturing for Locusta to take the other. The seat was old, its leather well worn, but it was very comfortable.

"What do we have?" said Voda.

"As I said last night, the American agent has given us a general area, and promises precise locations once we are ready to strike," said Locusta. He opened his briefcase and took out a map. "I believe the information will be good, but of course it is a matter of trust. If we trust the Americans."

"Do you?"

"The agent seems knowledgeable. So far the Americans have been helpful. In these matters, there is always the possibility of error. We do have to accept that."

"Yes," said Voda.

He looked at the map. Locusta's staff had highlighted about a dozen possible areas, all about fifty miles from the border. The plans to attack were general, and had they not fit so well with Locusta's real goal, he would have demanded wholesale revisions.

"We will compensate for the uncertainty by adding force," said Locusta. "I have commandeered every available helicopter."

That did not amount to much—there was a total of thirty-two at last count. A good portion of the force would have to sneak in by truck.

Voda put down the map. "I have been speaking to the American ambassador this morning," he said. "He indicated they would have no problem with our going over the border against these targets. He also warned again of secret Russian involvement, and mentioned the incident with the plane."

"Will they send their aircraft over the border?"

Voda shook his head.

"They are not afraid to risk our lives," said Locusta, "but not their own. Very brave of them."

"Why would the Russians fire at the Americans, then blow up their missiles?" asked Voda.

"Because they are children." Locusta shrugged. "With airmen, it is a strange thing, Mr. President." He got up, anxious to work off some of his energy. "Fighting, for them is very . . . theoretical, I guess we would say. They almost see it as a game."

"It's not a game."

"Very true. But they must display their feathers, like a prize rooster. They want to convince the Americans they are not afraid."

"Will they attack us?"

"No," said Locusta quickly. He had not considered that possibility.

"If Russian commandos were responsible for the attack on the pipeline, then perhaps they will be at the camps when we attack."

Ah, so that was where this was going. Voda was looking for a reason to call off the attack.

"Who said the Russians attacked the pipeline?" asked Locusta.

"The ambassador suggested it was a possibility."

Locusta made a face. "Absurd. If the Russians had attacked, we would not have been able to repair it so quickly."

Voda nodded. Everyone believed in the invincibility of the Russian army, notwithstanding evidence to the contrary, like Afghanistan and Chechnya.

"The Russians—and the Americans as well—act like children. The top commanders cannot keep control of their men. That is the problem with too much democracy," Locusta added. "There is a lack of discipline even where it should be steel."

Voda looked at the plans. Even if he did not approve them, Locusta would move against him. But the general preferred to strike this blow against the guerrillas now, just before the coup. Not only would it set them back for weeks, if not months, but he could easily disavow it if there were too many diplomatic repercussions.

"How many civilian casualties will there be?" asked Voda.

"We can't worry about that."

"There will be casualties."

"Every precaution will be taken."

"Proceed," said Voda.

"Thank you. I will return when the mission is complete, and deliver my report in person. Assuming you will still be here."

"Yes. We'll be here for a few days. Mircea loves the mountains. And so do I. The pace is quieter."

Locusta smiled. He knew that once here, the president would be reluctant to leave.

"Will you stay for lunch?" asked Voda. "It should be ready by now."

The invitation took Locusta by surprise, and for a moment he was actually touched.

It was a very brief moment.

"I'm afraid that there are details to be seen to," Locusta said. "With regrets."

"Another time," said Voda. He extended his hand. "Good luck."

"We will eliminate the criminals," replied the general. "I will return before dawn."

Iasi Airfield, Romania
1521

THE FLIGHT FROM DREAMLAND TO ROMANIA WAS UNEVENTful, but Samson still felt drained as he came down the B-1B/L's ladder.

Too bad, he thought. There were a million things to do.

"Ready for some chow, General?" asked Breanna Stockard, coming down the ladder behind him.

"Microwaved hash wasn't good enough for you?"

Breanna made a face. Among *Boomer*'s newfangled amenities was a microwave oven and a refrigerator. Samson had liked the hash, though clearly his copilot hadn't.

"Back in my day, Ms. Stockard, we would have killed for a hot meal in the cockpit."

Breanna made another face. "This is your day, General."

Damn, I like that woman, he thought as he headed toward the Dreamland Command trailer.

Bacau, Romania
1540

DOG NODDED AT STONER AS HE WALKED INTO THE CONference room at the Romanian Second Army Corps headquarters. The CIA officer stood with his arms folded, watching as two of Locusta's colonels took turns jabbing their fingers at a map spread over the table at the front of the room. They were debating some point or other about the mission.

"Colonel, would you like some tea?" asked a lieutenant in English.

"Coffee, maybe."

"Very good."

Dog edged toward Stoner. Nearly three dozen officers were crowded into the room. Dog remembered a few from the other day, but it was difficult to put names with faces.

"Danny's all right," Dog told Stoner. He'd spoken to the captain just before leaving to come to the meeting.

Stoner nodded.

"You sure you're going to get the truth?" Dog asked.

"I wouldn't be here if I wasn't."

GENERAL LOCUSTA PUSHED THE DOOR OF HIS STAFF CAR open as it pulled in front of the building, springing out before the car stopped. He was ready to do battle—not just against the criminals and murderers, but against the political regime that made it possible for the criminals and thieves to thrive. Everything was in motion.

He hadn't felt this sort of energy since he was a very young man. The day seemed more vivid, the air crackling. Even the building had a glow to it.

The guards snapped to attention. Locusta smiled at them—there was no suppressing the grin he felt.

"Gentlemen, today is an historic day," he said as he entered the meeting room. His officers stepped back to clear his path as he continued toward the front, speaking as he went. "Tonight we will strike the criminals where they live. I expect nothing less than a full victory. We must be bold, we must be swift, and we must be resolute."

The general turned the meeting over to Colonel Brasov, who would have charge of the mission. Brasov, nodding at the American CIA officer, said the attack area had been narrowed to two ten-mile swatches fifty-seven miles from the border. Each camp was small, housing from one hundred to three hundred guerrillas.

Brasov's attack plan called for strikes by six companies on each hideout, giving them at worst a two-to-one advantage against the rebels. They would be ferried across the border in helicopters that had come up from southern Romania earlier that day, and in trucks that would cross into Moldava between two border stations to lessen the chance of detection.

There would be no direct air support, but the Americans would be able to use their sensors to monitor the attack areas from Romanian territory.

Locusta watched the hollow-eyed CIA officer as Colonel Brasov spoke. Stoner stared as if his face were rock, betraying no emotion; not fatigue, not excitement, not boredom.

Locusta thought it was possible that he was being used and the troops would find no guerrilla hideout. Possibly they would even be ambushed, though Brasov's preparations were designed to meet that possibility and turn the tables on the guerrillas if it occurred.

Whatever happened, thought Locusta, the path was set. By this time tomorrow he would control Romania.

STONER STUDIED THE TOPO MAP, EXAMINING THE AREAS where Sorina Viorica had said the attacks should be concentrated. He could make a pretty good guess where the camps were within those squares, and suspected that Brasov had as well. One was centered around a mine abandoned sometime in the 1920s. The other, less obvious, was a farm isolated from the nearby settlements.

"Did you want to add anything, Mr. Stoner?" asked Colonel Brasov.

"You were very thorough. There should be evidence of Russian involvement at these camps. There may even be a few Russian agents or soldiers," added Stoner. "So I would be prepared. Very, very prepared."

**Dreamland Command Trailer,
Iasi, Romania
1700**

GENERAL SAMSON HAD ARRIVED BY THE TIME DOG RE-
turned to Iasi. He'd told Dog he was coming, of course, and
Dog tried hard not to interpret Samson's arrival as yet the
latest example of his distrust.

It was hard, though.

"So, what are the Romanians doing?" Samson asked without other preliminaries when Dog reported to him at the
Command trailer.

Dog outlined the overall Romanian plan as well as their role
in it. The EB-52s would give advance warning of any large troop
movements without going over the border, though of course
real time video from the Flighthawks would be impossible.

"You think they'll pull it off?" Samson asked.

"If they can handle the logistics side. They only have about
thirty helicopters, and they're fairly old. The problem will be
getting enough men in the field quickly."

"I'd feel better if we could go over the border and support
them directly," said the general.

Samson's remark caught Dog by surprise. "I agree with you,
General. Maybe we should make that point to Washington."

Samson seemed to consider it, but then reverted to his
career officer mentality, anxious to protect his stars. "No.
We'll carry on as is. I've brought two B-1B/Ls with me."

"Yes, sir, you explained that."

"They can get into the mix as soon as it's appropriate.
We'll fly them in tandem with a Megafortress. If you think
that's a good idea."

Now Dog was *really* surprised. Was Samson asking for
his opinion?

"They may be useful," said Dog. "Depending on the
circumstances. If they were able to pinpoint a target on
the ground—"

"That's exactly what I was thinking," said Samson. "I want to see if these fancy lasers are really as good as they're advertised."

"If we were supporting the Romanians, they'd have a real role," suggested Dog, taking one more shot at encouraging the general to argue with Washington about the absurd restriction in their orders.

"No. No. That will come in time," said Samson. "I'm sure there will be plenty of changes in the future."

**Aboard Dreamland Osprey,
above the Black Sea
1900**

THE SUN HAD ALREADY SET BY THE TIME THE OSPREY NEARED its rendezvous north of the Bosporus Strait at the southern edge of the Black Sea. The Bosporus was like a funnel, sending a never-ending flow of ships down from the lake, past Istanbul on their way to the Sea of Marmara, and from there to the Mediterranean, the Suez, the Atlantic.

Ideally, Stoner would have found an American warship for Danny and his "companion" to transfer to, but the U.S. Navy rarely found it necessary to enter the Black Sea, and no ship could be diverted in time. Instead, the CIA had arranged for Danny, Boston, and Sorina Viorica to be disembarked on a tanker sailing south toward Istanbul; they'd ride south and slip off near the city.

"That's our ship there, Captain," said the Osprey copilot, pointing toward a small collection of dim lights in the distance. "We'll be over her in a minute."

"Thanks."

Danny turned to Boston and motioned with his head. Sorina was sitting in the middle of the bench on the starboard side of the aircraft. She was so light her body barely made an impression in the stretched fabric sling that formed the seat.

"We'll be going down," Danny told her. "Can you fast-rope?"

He pointed to the side. Besides the rear ramp, the Dreamland Osprey had a side door that slid open like a traditional rescue helicopter, allowing a boom to be swung out so passengers or cargo could be lowered.

"Rope?" asked Sorina Viorica.

"Can you slide down the rope to the ship, or should we lower you by harness?"

Sorina looked dubious.

"It's all right. We'll winch you down," said Danny. He had to yell to make himself heard over the engines, which roared loudly as the aircraft settled into hover mode. "We'll put you in a sling. Boston, you hear me? We'll get her in a sling."

"That's what I figured you'd want to do, Cap."

Danny got a harness for her and held it out. Sorina didn't look scared, exactly, but clearly she didn't like the idea.

"It's either this or we fly into the airport," said Danny. "We can do that."

She'd already vetoed that idea. Still, she made a face as she pulled the safety harness on. The harness provided more protection than a standard sling.

Meanwhile, the flight engineer—the only crewman on the flight besides the two pilots—came back and punched the automatic door opener. A red light came on and the door began sliding toward the rear of the aircraft. Wind swirled through the cabin.

"You going first or last, Cap?" asked Boston. Like Danny, he was dressed in civilian clothes: jeans, a heavy sweater, and a dark down vest.

"I go first. Then send Sorina. You come down behind her."

"Gotcha."

"Wait till I make sure everything's kosher."

Though the ship had only its normal navigational lights on, it stood out clearly against the darkness of the sea. A small flashlight began blinking on the forward deck near the bow. The Osprey dipped slightly to the left, then corrected, leveling itself about twenty feet from the deck, moving sideways to keep pace with the ship.

Twenty feet wasn't much for an aircraft, but it was a long fall for a man. The Osprey tucked a few feet lower, nudging toward fifteen. Danny grabbed the rope, then pushed off, shifting his weight as he quickly dropped to the deck.

The dim yellow glow of the ship flashed around him; rather than falling, Danny felt as if the tanker was coming up to get him. He landed with both feet, picture perfect, though this was more a matter of luck than skill on the tanker's rolling deck. He took a half step to his right, steadied himself, then spotted one of the crewmen coming toward him.

The man looked as if he had a gun in his hand. As Danny started to reach for the Beretta hidden below his vest, his eyes focused and he realized the man was only carrying a walkie-talkie.

Boston had already started lowering Sorina. The sling spun slowly as it descended, and though the journey wasn't very long, Sorina looked dizzy when she stepped onto the deck. As soon as Danny released her from the harness, she slipped down, and needed the sailor's help to get back to her feet. It was the first time since they'd met that she seemed vulnerable—or maybe not vulnerable, but at least human.

Boston shot down the line after her, bouncing away from the rope as easily as if he were doing a dance routine. He had a small rucksack with him; inside were two MP5 submachine guns in waterproof plastic sacks.

Not that they should need them. But . . .

The sailor led them back toward the superstructure of the ship, located near the stern. The first mate was waiting on the starboard side, in front of a closed door.

"You have to stay outside," he told Danny. "The crew should not see."

Danny thought that was a ridiculous precaution—surely

the crew had seen the Osprey hanging over the bow—but he was in no position to argue. The mate led them along the railing to a coiled rope ladder.

"When the signal is given, you can descend," the mate told him. "We will be two kilometers from Istanbul." The mate was Indian, and between the wind, the engines, and the retreating Osprey, his words were difficult to understand.

"How long?" asked Danny.

"Thirty minutes. Sometimes there are patrols," added the mate. "If this happens, you must get off the ship immediately."

Boston shot him a look that said no way. With assorted adjectives.

"Not a problem," Danny lied.

The mate left them, walking around the front of the superstructure, perhaps to emphasize that the door nearby was locked. Danny led the others toward the stern, stopping just aft of the superstructure in a darkened spot where he could see across to both sides of the channel.

"Why'd he say we had to jump?" Boston asked. "Are we being set up?"

"I don't think so," answered Danny.

"I don't like this bullshit," said Boston. "It's cold, Cap."

"Not too much I can do about the weather, Boston. Don't tell me you haven't had worse."

"Oh, I've had worse." He leaned on the rail. Sorina was standing a few feet away, gazing at the water. "I don't trust her either, Cap. She's got to be planning something."

"Like what?"

"Something."

They'd run a metal detector around her back at Iasi before boarding the Osprey; she didn't have any weapons.

"Maybe she has second thoughts," said Boston. "I would if were her. And third and fourth. She's giving up her own people."

"Boston, shut your mouth," said Danny.

"Just sayin' the truth, Cap."

Danny walked over to Sorina Viorica. She'd raised the direction of her stare somewhat, and was now gazing at the dark outline of shore as the ship entered the channel. There was a small Turkish warship tied up near the cliff; from this distance, it looked as if everyone aboard were asleep.

"You ready to talk?" Danny asked.

"At the train station." Sorina continued to stare at the opposite bank.

"It's going to take a while. Why don't we just get it over with?"

"So you can arrest me?"

She flung her head around. Her eyes shone with fierce anger.

"I'm not going to do anything to you," Danny said. "I'm going to let you go. That's the deal. You tell me where the targets are, I put you on the train."

"I put myself on the train."

"However you want to do it."

She turned back to the water.

The ship had been alone on the Black Sea, but once in the strait, company was plentiful. Several ships sat just outside the navigation channel, stopped for one reason or another. A large, well-lit ferry was just pulling out from a town on the eastern side of the passage. It had obviously been rented for a party, and the sound of music wafted across the water. Danny watched the passengers dance in what seemed like slow motion, their world a million miles from his.

"Another navy ship over there, Cap," said Boston. "Moving."

Danny looked at the eastern shore to their south, following the sergeant's finger. A 150-foot patrol craft was moving out from the shadows, curving in their direction. A 72mm gun turret dominated the front deck.

"Think the Romanians sold us out?" asked Boston.

"They don't know where we are."

Danny looked toward the western shore. It was under a mile away. Both he and Boston could swim that distance, but maybe not Sorina.

And the water would be very, very cold.

"Worse case, that's a life raft up there," said Boston, pointing to a rigid-sided inflatable raft lashed to the side of the superstructure a deck above them. "Or should we take that thing there?"

"That thing" was a lifeboat, which would have to be swung out on its davits. The raft would be easier and less noticeable.

Damn, Danny thought.

Damn. Who the hell gave us away?

A searchlight from the patrol boat cut across the waves, heading toward the hull of the tanker. Danny motioned for the others to move behind the superstructure, where they couldn't be seen. He kept his post, watching the searchlight move in a slow arc back and forth across the water, cursing to himself and considering his next move.

He'd use the tanker as a shield. Would the patrol boat come up alongside? Or would it put down its own boats to board them?

Not very long ago he had worked with a Navy boarding team. Danny tried to remember their procedures. They'd used only one boat, but they had air support to watch in case anyone tried to run away.

The patrol boat continued toward them, its search beam growing stronger. There must be a place to hide inside the ship, he thought. But what sense would that make if the crew was ready to give them up?

Sorina stood near the rail, her expression as stoic as ever.

"How well do you swim?" Danny asked her.

She shook her head.

"You understand the words?"

"I understand," she told him. "I cannot swim."

The searchlight arced upward, sweeping the bow and then the superstructure.

"All right, get the raft," Danny told Boston. "See if there's some sort of rope with it, something we can use to lower her."

"This is part of your plan?" asked Sorina.

"We're ad-libbing."

Boston climbed up over the catwalk above them, examining the raft and how it was held to the ship.

"Don't throw it over yet," Danny told him. "Wait until I tell you."

He trotted aft, planning—once the patrol boat closed in, it would be harder to see them going over.

The boat's searchlight caught the corner of his eye as he cleared the end of the superstructure. It seemed brighter than any light he'd ever seen, a star exploding in his face.

The searchlight swung upward. Danny thought for a moment that it had somehow caught Boston working on the raft, but of course he was out of view. The light moved to the north, toward another ship.

The patrol boat was headed toward that ship, not theirs.

Danny watched for another minute, making sure.

"All right. We don't need the raft," he yelled to Boston. "Not yet, anyway."

THE TANKER MOVED MORE SLOWLY THAN THE MATE HAD predicted, and it was nearly an hour before they got close enough to the city to see its lights. The Blue Mosque sat on a hill at the tip of the oldest quarter, glowing yellow in the distance, spotlights illuminating its dome and minarets.

A long string of ships sat in the water to the east of the mosque, some resting before moving northward or to the west, others waiting to unload cargo at the docks, which were out of sight beyond the jutting land. A train poked along the shore, heading in the direction of the sultan's palace and the ruins beyond, ferrying workers to their late night jobs and returning others home.

The Indian mate appeared from inside the ship, popping out on deck as if sprung there.

"Time," he said loudly. "Time. You must go."

Boston climbed up and undid the raft, lowering it from a pulley set on the stanchion.

"You are taking our raft?" asked the mate.

"You didn't expect us to swim, did you?" asked Boston.

"Our raft."

Danny stepped over to the mate. "Is this a problem?"

"Yes."

"How much?" said Danny.

"Big."

"That wasn't what I mean." He reached into his pocket and took out a roll of American bills. Quickly, he peeled off five hundred dollar bills and gave them to the mate. "That makes it a small problem, right?"

The man looked embarrassed. "No, big problem. You cannot have the raft. It belongs to the ship. Big trouble if you take it."

The mate tried to give the money back but Danny wouldn't take it. Finally he dropped the bills and they scattered over the deck.

Boston had already gotten the raft into the water. Sorina Viorica was standing nearby, watching the bills flutter away in the wind but saying nothing.

"No—you cannot. No."

"I'm taking the raft," Danny told him.

The mate shook his head.

Enough, thought Danny. He pulled out his pistol.

The Indian moved back, shocked.

"I'm sorry, but I'm taking the raft," Danny told him. "There is no F-ing way we're swimming. Sorina, Boston—go."

The Romanian took hold of one of the ropes and climbed over the rail. Boston followed. The Indian mate continued to stare at Danny, his eyes wide with surprise.

"Thanks for your help," Danny told him, reaching over and grabbing the line. "We appreciate it."

He tucked the pistol into his belt and started down. He hadn't had a chance to put his gloves back on, and the wet rope cut into his palms. After a few feet he considered dropping but stuck with it, hands burning. He felt a hand on his leg and lowered himself into the raft, which bobbed beneath his weight but remained afloat.

"Did you shoot him?" asked Sorina as Danny settled in.

"No, I didn't shoot him."

"You cannot corrupt everyone," she told him.

"I didn't want to corrupt him. I just didn't want you to freeze to death in the water."

Boston started the small outboard at the stern of the raft. The high-pitched sound was so loud, the sides of Danny's head began to vibrate.

Istanbul straddled the Bosporus, its eastern and western precincts connected by bridges and ferries. The train station where they were headed was on the eastern bank. Boston circled to the north, crossing behind the tanker and then heading toward the shore. But as they approached, blue lights appeared on the highway above the water. A police car flashed southward. A moment later another one came north, then pulled off the road almost directly opposite them.

Boston cut the engine. "What do you think, Cap?"

It was unlikely that they were waiting for them, but Danny didn't want to take any chances.

"Let's land on the other side," he said.

"You got it, Cap."

Boston spun the boat around, starting out slowly and then picking up speed. A large cruise ship sat docked to the north on Danny's right as they came across, its deck and cabins a yellow glow against the pale black of the night.

"Bring it into that marina?" Boston asked, leaning forward and shouting in Danny's ear.

"No. Somebody might be watching in there. Go up the shoreline a bit, to my right. That way." Danny pointed.

"Probably have some sort of security near that cruise ship."

"Don't get that close. The marina will probably have somebody there too. We want to be in the middle."

Boston found a clump of rocks near what looked like an abandoned field, but that Danny realized was a park when they were about five yards from shore. Despite the cold, a pair of teenage lovers huddled together on one of the benches, oblivious not only to the boat but to the rest of the world.

Sorina hopped out as the raft began to slide sideways back toward the water. Danny jumped out behind her, trotting forward and grabbing her arm.

"I'm not running away," she said. Though she kept her voice soft, she managed to make it sound like a hawk's warning hiss.

"I didn't think you were," Danny told her.

"You don't have to lie, Captain. It doesn't suit you."

Boston, ruck over his back, joined them. By now the two teenagers had broken their embrace and stared at them as they walked past.

"We have to get across," said Danny. "There's a bridge this way."

They began walking, Sorina and Danny in the lead, Boston trailing nonchalantly, the pack over his shoulder. The area mixed small apartment buildings with clusters of commercial buildings in between. They picked their way uphill, following a side street that veered away from their destination, then found themselves in a tangle of streets that were so narrow they would barely rate as alleys back home. A taxi passed on the boulevard just as they reached it. Danny started to hail it, then remembered he hadn't gotten any local money yet. It was too late anyway—the driver was already past.

"This way," he said, pointing to the left.

He checked his watch. It was 2105—five minutes past nine. They were supposed to call at 2130.

A block later he spotted a bank. Stoner had given him a credit card to use for a cash advance or whatever incidentals he needed; Danny slipped his hand into his pocket to make sure it was still there.

"Let's see if there's an ATM," he told the others, nudging Sorina toward the street.

Sorina hesitated.

"They have cameras in the machines," she said. "I don't want to get close."

"Right." He hadn't thought of that. "You stay here with Boston."

Inside the bank's vestibule, he slid the card into the machine and began punching the PIN number. Just as he hit Enter he realized he'd used his PIN, not the one Stoner had given him. He cursed himself, then waited for the machine to tell him he had made a mistake.

The screen stayed blank. It seemed to have eaten his card.

Be patient, he told himself, stifling the urge to punch the machine. *Just be patient.*

Finally the card spit out. Ignoring the Turkish words on the screen, since he had no idea what they said, Danny put the card back into the machine and typed the right PIN. A few seconds later a screen came up, again in Turkish, asking how much money he wanted.

Fortunately, the numbers were familiar. He pressed the largest denomination: a thousand liras.

Boston and Sorina started walking as soon as they saw him come out. Danny trotted to catch up. He suddenly felt cold—the vestibule had been heated.

"Look for a taxi," he told Boston when he got close. "We're behind on time."

Aboard EB-52 *Johnson,*
over northeastern Romania
2120

ZEN BANKED THE FLIGHTHAWK NORTHWARD, SKIRTING THE Moldovan border by less than ten feet. There was no way to gauge where the line would have been on the ground, much less in the air, and he knew that the Moldovan air defense radar couldn't spot the Flighthawk if it flew right in front of the dish. But Colonel Bastian would know, and the mission tapes would reveal the incursion. And that's what counted.

The Romanian forces had just boarded their helicopters a few miles to the southeast. Zen could see them on his sitrep or God's eye-view radar—little bumblebees starting in his direction.

"Force Bravo is en route," he told Dog.

"Roger that."

"Any sign of our Russian friends?"

"Negative."

"Hopefully, they got that out of their system yesterday," said Zen. "Or maybe they fired the only missiles they had."

Northeastern Romania
2130

THE SOLDIERS GAVE STONER AN AK-47 AND FOUR MAGA-zine boxes of ammunition. He checked them, then sat on the bench next to Colonel Brasov as the helicopter—an Aero-spatiale Puma—skimmed over the ground at treetop level toward Moldova.

The wound in his leg had been a dull, low-level pain, pushed to the back of his consciousness over the past few days. Now the pain spiked, as if provoked by the geography.

Colonel Brasov clapped him on the back. "We are a few miles from the border, Mr. Stoner," he said. "Now would be a good time to find out where we are going."

Stoner glanced at his watch. "It should only be a minute or two."

Istanbul, Turkey
2130

THERE WAS A FLOOD OF TRAFFIC AHEAD, CARS, BUSES, and people descending from the tourist area along Istiklal Caddessi. Danny, Boston, and Sorina had walked for nearly fifteen minutes without seeing a cab.

"Wait for the trolley, or go across?" asked Boston.

Danny looked at his watch. The trolleys, modern two-car trains, passed every twenty minutes or so.

"It's time for us to call," he told Sorina.

"Only from the station," she insisted.

"Let's walk across the bridge," he said.

He took Sorina's arm, steering her around a cement toadstool placed to prevent cars from going up on the sidewalk. During the day, both sides of the bridge would be crowded with fishermen, even during the winter months. At night, though, the entire bridge was relatively empty. A few tourists and a pair of aging lovers stared out at the water from the rails.

Danny hurried along, trying to remember the layout of the streets on the opposite shore. The train station was to their left, a few blocks from the ferries. They could walk, but it would be faster with a cab.

Taxis tended to congregate near the foot of the bridge, where there was a tram stop as well as nearby ferry stations and a large mosque. He saw a short line of taxis across the way, but to get there they'd have to cross a solid wall of cars zooming along the highway.

A sign indicated an underground passage near the end of the bridge.

"This way," he said, pointing left and nudging Sorina with him.

The stairs opened into a tunnel lined by shops. The walkway itself had been turned into a bazaar. Dealers hawked a variety of wares from blankets. Everything from baseball caps to 1970s vintage television sets was on sale.

A knot of people appeared before them. Suddenly, Danny found himself in the middle of the swarm, unable to move.

Sorina Viorica slipped from his grasp. Danny edged to the left, following her, but a river of people were descending a set of stairs nearby and the crush separated them. She turned to the left, heading up the stairs; he pushed his way through, momentarily losing her. He became more forceful, shoving to make sure he could get through.

Sorina ran up the stairs. Danny followed, barely able to see her. An elderly woman spun a few steps above him, tumbling into him. He pushed her aside as gently as he could manage, struggling upward.

Sorina was gone.

Danny cursed to himself. He reached the open air and took a step, ready to bolt as soon as he spotted her.

She was sitting on her haunches, leaning against the cement wall of the entrance to his right, breathing hard.

"I can't take it," she said, looking up at him. "So many people."

"Cap?" said Boston, coming up behind him.

"Make the call," said Danny, holding the phone out to her. "Go ahead."

Her face was pale, her lips thin. But she shook her head.

"The station," she insisted.

"Here's a taxi!" yelled Boston.

Northeastern Romania
2144

EVERYONE IN THE HELICOPTER STARED AT STONER, WAITING. They were hovering near the border, waiting to proceed.

"Where are our targets?" asked Colonel Brasov.

"I'll find out in a minute," Stoner told him.

"You said that fifteen minutes ago. I have no time for these games."

Stoner didn't reply. There was no sense saying anything until he heard from Sorina.

The colonel turned around to one of his men and began speaking in loud, fast Romanian. Stoner caught a few words, including an expression he'd been told never to use because of its vulgarity.

Had she played him? Or did she simply have second thoughts?

He hoped it was the latter. He didn't like to think he could be fooled.

But everybody could be fooled. Everybody.

The sat phone rang.

Stoner continued to stare out the front of the helicopter's windscreen for another second, then reached for the phone.

Istanbul, Turkey
2145

"I'M SORRY WE'RE SO LATE," DANNY TOLD STONER WHEN he answered the phone.

"It's all right."

Two trains were coming in, pulling head first into the platform. Danny stepped forward, watching Sorina punch the buttons on the automated ticket machine. She'd already bought four tickets; she was trying to make it hard for them to trace her.

"He's on the line." Danny held the phone out to her.

Sorina shook her head and reached into her pocket for a piece of paper.

"You tell me *now*," said Danny.

She gave him the paper.

He took a step toward the light and opened it. They were GPS coordinates in Moldova.

"Stoner, plug these coordinates into your GPS," said Danny.

Danny read them off. Sorina stood at the machine, buying even more tickets.

A few yards away, Boston eyed the station warily. There were about a dozen people on the platform, young people mostly, going or coming from a night out; it was impossible to say. Two women in traditional Muslim dresses, long scarves covering their heads, stood together near a small patch of bushes where the trains would stop.

Sorina looked down at her tickets, shuffling through them.

"All right, Captain, we have them," said Stoner. "You can let her go."

Danny held the phone out toward her.

"You want to say good-bye?" he asked.

She hesitated for just a second before shaking her head.

And with that she turned and ran to the nearby train, reaching it just as the door slapped shut to keep her out. She drew back; the doors opened again and she slipped in. Danny watched it pull from the station.

"Hey, Cap, you know what's strange?" asked Boston.

"What's that?" said Danny, without turning around.

"Clock has different times on each side," said Boston. He pointed to the large disk just overhead. "You'd think they could synchronize it."

"Yeah," said Danny, not paying attention as he watched the train disappear around the curve.

Over northeastern Romania
2150

STONER CHECKED THE COORDINATES AGAINST THE MAP
and satellite photos. The camp to the north was a small farm
with a single large barn, an outbuilding, and a few small cot-
tages nearby. Three-quarters of the boundary was formed by
a ragged, meandering creek. The last side of the property
was marked by a road that ran along the base of a long rift
in the hills. The high spot provided a good area for the main
landing; a field about a half mile away would allow a smaller
group to land and circle around the rear of the property. The
trucks, which had already crossed the border and were nearly
thirty miles into Moldova, would arrive roughly ten minutes
after the helicopters touched down.

The second target was a church and related buildings in
the middle of a small town. A single main street zigged
through the hamlet, ducking and weaving around a quartet
of gentle hills. An orchard of small trees and an open field
sat to one side of the church; a row of houses were on the
other. A cemetery spread out behind the church. The easiest landing here would be in the field near the orchard; the
geography would make it difficult to surround the building
before beginning an attack. The trucks would take another
twenty minutes to reach the church; they'd be reinforcements only.

The fact that the target was a church bothered Colonel
Brasov a great deal.

"This will be a propaganda coup if you are wrong," he told
Stoner.

"Yes."

"And if you are right, it is a great sacrilege."

Stoner nodded.

"You will be with me in this group," the colonel told him.
"Our helicopter will be the first down."

"Right."

Again Stoner wondered if it was a setup, if he'd been fooled. Perhaps the charges had been set weeks before and were waiting now for the troops—waiting for him.

Doubt gripped him. He thought about the Dreamland pilots, watching from across the border. He envied them. Their jobs were entirely physical. They could push their bodies to perform, rely on their trained reactions, their instincts. They trained and retrained for different situations, dogfights and bombing runs, missile attacks and low level escapes. But Stoner had no such luxury. There was no way to train for what he did. Knowing how to fire a gun into a skull at close range, to fake a language—these were important and helpful tools, but not the substance of his success. His test had come days before in Bucharest, when he'd stared into Sorina's eyes, when he'd stroked her side, when he'd gauged her intent.

That moment was dark to him, lost somewhere down the gap between the ledges he was jumping between.

"We are ten minutes away," the colonel told him.

"I'm ready," said Stoner.

**Aboard EB-52 *Johnson*,
over northeastern Romania
2152**

ZEN NUDGED THE THROTTLE, PUSHING *HAWK ONE* CLOSER to the last of the helicopters carrying the Romanian troops. The chopper was flying just above treetop level, tail up, moving fast for a helo but slow compared to the Flighthawk.

"Border in zero-five seconds," warned the computer.

"Thanks," mumbled Zen. He pulled hard on the stick, banking away just before crossing the line.

"They have two targets," Dog told Zen, relaying the information passed along by Stoner. "Sullivan is entering the coordinates. Both are a little more than fifty miles into

Moldova. We won't be able to go there, but we can see what's going on."

Dog meant that the radars on the Megafortress would give them a good idea of where the helicopters and the trucks were, and would also allow them to warn the Romanians if a large force of guerrillas or Moldovan soldiers suddenly appeared. But as far as Zen was concerned, they were voyeurs at the edge of battle, watching helplessly.

Bacau, Romania
2155

GENERAL LOCUSTA PUT DOWN THE SATELLITE PHONE AND raised his head, scanning his command center at the Second Army Corps headquarters. He needed to keep his head clear, needed to be as calm as possible. It was coming together beautifully, everything going exactly as he had hoped, as he had planned.

"Colonel Brasov has touched down," announced the captain coordinating communications from the assault teams. "No resistance yet."

"Yea!" yelled one of other officers.

"Who said that?" shouted Locusta.

The room fell silent. The general turned his gaze around the room.

"General, it was me," said one of his lieutenants, rising. The young man's face was red.

"This is not a time for youthful exuberance," said Locusta. The man's forthrightness impressed him and he tried to soften his tone. "We will each of us do our duty. We have jobs to do."

"Yes, General. I apologize."

"Accepted. Get back to work. All of you, work now. We will capture the criminals and make them pay."

Moldova
2155

STONER TIGHTENED THE STRAP ON THE AK-47 AND WAITED as the helicopter closed in on the target in the dark. The pilots had night goggles, but even without them he could see the outlines of the spire in the distance.

Someone began shouting in the back. The helicopter bucked to the side. There was a rush of air.

Now!

Go!

The dim red of the interior lights gave the men just enough light to see as they jumped into the field, the helicopter just touching down.

There was an orange flash near the dark hull of the church, then small polka dots of yellow, tiny bursts of color that glowed into red curlicues.

They're shooting at us, he thought.

She wasn't lying. Thank God.

Behind him, the helicopter moved backward, escaping as a flurry of slugs began sailing through the air. Stoner ran forward, then threw himself down behind the last row of headstones in the large churchyard. Bullets exploded above his head.

The Romanian soldiers began moving up along the graves, yelling directions to each other. Stoner pushed himself to his knees, still struggling to get his breath. The stone to his right exploded into shards, raked by the heavy gun. He threw himself back down, working on his elbows and belly to his right.

The machine gun was in a stairwell next to the church. A low thud shook the ground. The machine gun fire stopped. One of the Romanians had fired a mortar point-blank into the stairwell, killing the gunner.

Someone shouted. Another person, to Stoner's left, shouted back. A flare went off, turning the night white and black.

Six, seven dark shadows ran to the building, jumped down the stairwell. Others came toward them from the road. The mortar fired again; this time it landed short, scattering the guerrillas but not stopping them as they flowed out of the church.

A squad of soldiers had fast-roped down onto the street. They came up now, guns blazing, catching the guerrillas from the rear unawares. Their attack had been coordinated with the mortarman; no shells fell as they worked they way toward the basement stairs.

A loud series of booms followed as the soldiers forced their way inside. A second group, this one from the cemetery, ran up to reinforce them.

Stoner waited, watching. If it was a setup, the place would explode now, booby-trapped.

It didn't. He started in motion again, picking his way through the headstones toward the houses on the other side of the church, guessing that the rebels would be housed there.

The graves were laid out in a haphazard pattern, some very close together, others wide apart, and it took Stoner time to weave his way forward. As he turned to go through a tight cluster, he spotted four or five shadows to the east of the church. His first thought was that he was seeing clothes fluttering in the wind. Then he saw sticks waving with the clothes.

He brought the AK-47 up and fired, screaming as he did.

"The guerrillas! They're coming from the other side of the church!"

He shot the magazine so quickly he was surprised when the bolt clicked open. The guerrillas quickly got down and fired back.

Stoner reloaded, then began moving again, sure he would be killed if he stayed where was. He caught part of his arm on a crumpled rosebush. The thorns ripped his flesh.

He kept going, moving to the left. There was more gunfire now, not only in front of him but behind.

Pulling himself along the ground, Stoner felt his hand scrape on cement. He'd come to the path that ran along the east side of the church and went up toward the back of the houses.

The gunfire intensified, rifles flashing back and forth, occasionally interrupted by a grenade blast. Stoner tried to sort out where the forces were. He was facing south, crouched at the corner of the cemetery. The church was in front of him and to his right, a little to the west of his position. The guerrillas had come from a yard to his left.

But the real danger, he thought, was the houses behind him. If there were guerrillas there, they could come in and attack the attackers from the rear. The colonel had detailed a squad to come through the cemetery and head in that direction, but apparently they had been pinned down somewhere along the way.

Stoner turned around so that his back was to the church. Then he began crawling back along the cement walkway.

A line of thin bushes provided some cover to the right, throwing him in shadow. They thickened into a row of hedges after fifteen or twenty feet. Stoner hunkered next to them, trying to listen hard enough to sort the sounds of the night into some kind of sense. But he couldn't hear much over the echoing gunfire behind him.

Stoner rose upright about halfway, just enough to see shadows moving on the other side of the hedges. Dropping to his knee, Stoner sighted the AK-47 along the row of bushes. The cold of the night froze him into position, pushing away time, pushing away fear and even adrenaline. It swathed him in its grasp, and he waited, a stone in the night.

Finally, shadows pushed through an opening thirty yards away. One, two . . . Stoner waited until five had come through, then pushed his finger hard on the trigger, moving across to his left, taking down the black shapes. Cries of pain and agony rose over the fierce report of the gun. The Kalashnikov clicked empty.

Stoner cleared the mag, slammed in a fresh one, and fired in what seemed to be one motion, one moment. The cold of the night intensified, freezing his breath in his lungs as the shouts and screams crescendoed.

His rifle once more empty, Stoner stomped his right foot down and threw himself to the left, spinning amid the gravestones.

He lay on his back, reloading. Stoner heard a rocket-propelled grenade whistle over his head; the sound was more a hush than a whistle, and the explosion a dull thud against the wall of the church.

A second grenade flew past, even closer. But there was no explosion this time; the missile was a dud.

Meanwhile, the squad that had been pinned down rallied to fight the guerrillas near the hedge. The next ninety seconds were a tumult of explosions and gunfire, tracers flashing back and forth, the darkness turning darker. The mortar began firing again, the *thud-pump*, *thud-pump* of its shells rocking the ground.

Cries of the wounded rose above the din. Finally, a pair of soldiers ran forward from Stoner's left—Romanians, rushing the last guerrillas. Three more followed. A man ran up to Stoner and dropped next to him, putting his gun down across his body, obviously thinking he was dead.

"Hey, I'm OK," Stoner said.

The Romanian jumped.

"It's OK," said Stoner. "It's the American. I'm all right."

The soldier said something in Romanian, then got up and followed the others surging into the other yard. Stoner rose slowly. When he saw that the soldiers wouldn't need his help, he turned toward the church.

The trucks had finally arrived, and soldiers were now swarming into the area. The church had been secured; soldiers climbed up the stairs, boxes of documents in their arms. Two guerrillas, bound and blindfolded, sat cross-legged a few feet from the basement entrance. The Romanian soldier behind them raised his rifle toward Stoner as he approached, then recognized him and lowered it.

Stoner pulled his small flashlight from his pocket and shone it into the men's faces, which were bruised and swollen; both looked dazed.

"You speak English?" he asked them, kneeling so his face was level with theirs. "What are your names?"

Neither man said anything.

"English?" Stoner asked again. "Tell me your names."

Nothing.

"I can get a message to your families that you're OK," Stoner said. "If I knew who you were."

Their blank stares made it impossible to tell if they were being stubborn or just didn't understand what he was saying.

Stoner switched to Russian, but there was no recognition. The men were Romanian.

"It would probably be better for you if people knew you were alive," he said in English. "There'd be less chance of accidents."

But the men remained silent.

Two other prisoners had been taken, both of them superficially wounded. Neither wanted to talk. At least thirty guerrillas were dead. The Romanians had lost only three men.

With the church and the immediate ground secured, squads of soldiers worked their way through the nearby houses, searching for rebels or anything they might have left behind. Stoner watched them move down the nearby street, surrounding a house, then rousting the inhabitants. Meanwhile, the papers and a computer that had been found in the church basement were loaded into a truck, to be transported to the helicopters and then flown back to Romania.

"Ah, Mr. Stoner," said Brasov when the colonel found him at the front of the church. "Good information, yes. Good job, American."

"What are you going to do with the dead guerrillas?" asked Stoner.

"They come back with us," replied the colonel. "Evidence. If needed."

"Good. Any of these guys look Russian?"

"You want them to be Russian?"

"Not if they're Romanian."

The colonel shrugged.

"I have you to thank. I was not always trusting you," said the colonel, his English breaking down either because of his fatigue or perhaps his excitement. The operation would make him look very good with the general. "I will not forget."

The colonel went off to check with his platoon leaders, urging them to move quickly. The phone lines in and out of the hamlet had been cut, and a pair of cell phone blockers had been set up near the church at the start of the assault, but there was no way to guarantee that word of the operation wouldn't get out. The troops were to muster on the road in ten minutes; they would ride and march back to the helicopters.

Stoner went back over to the dead men, looking at their shoes. To a man they were battered and old; most wore cheap sneakers. He took a few photos with his digital camera, then went down the steps into the church basement to see what the troops had found. The steps opened into a meeting room about thirty by twenty, punctuated by cement columns that held the ceiling up. A small kitchenette sat at the back. There were a few metal chairs scattered to one side, along with a pair of tables propped against the wall. The place looked like a bingo hall between meetings.

Things were different behind the cheap wood panel wall at the back of the kitchenette. A steel door, pockmarked with bullets, had been pushed down off its hinges to reveal a room stacked with bunk beds. At the far end, tables set up as desks with computers and other office gear had been stripped bare by the soldiers. Paper was strewn everywhere; there were stacks of cardboard boxes in the corner. A pair of

AK-47s and three crates filled with ammo lay nearby. Two steel footlockers were being guarded by a soldier. Stoner guessed they contained weapons; the letters on the top were Cyrillic.

Russian, though that didn't prove much. He took photos anyway.

Quite a bit of blood had been splattered on the floor and walls.

By the time he came back outside, the soldiers were wrapping up, getting ready to leave. Colonel Brasov saw him and walked over, extending his hand.

"Now I hear from my men you are a hero," said the colonel.

"How's that?"

"You stopped an ambush." The colonel pointed toward the back of the churchyard, where Stoner had cut off the guerrillas. "They had a second barracks in that house. You surprised them when they came to surprise my men."

"Yeah, I guess I did."

Brasov slapped him on the back. "You are a funny American. You kill two dozen men, you take no credit."

"I don't think it was two dozen."

"Come on," Brasov told him. "Time for us all to leave. I'll buy you drinks when we are back. Come, come."

Stoner fell in with one of the groups leaving on foot, walking back through the village. The houses were dark. He suspected that the villagers were watching now from behind the curtains and closed doors. Surely they'd known what was going on here. Maybe they were glad to be rid of the guerrillas, or maybe they sympathized with their cause. They were pawns in any event, bystanders whose deaths would not have mattered to either side.

Most of the helicopters had already taken off. The trucks were departing. It was a dangerous time. The operation wasn't over, but it felt like it was, and the adrenaline that had pushed everyone had dissipated. Officers yelled at their men, trying to remind them of that, trying to get them to move quickly, to look alive. But they were slacking too, and the brief but intense fight had left their voices hoarse.

There were less people here than Sorina had predicted. But maybe the evidence he wanted would be in the papers, or on the computer.

Stoner pulled his jacket tighter, suddenly feeling the chill of the night.

Brasov began yelling. The lieutenants started waving their arms, urging the men to board the helicopters immediately.

"What's going on?" Stoner asked the colonel.

"The border stations have been alerted. We have to move quickly."

**Presidential villa,
near Stulpicani, Romania
2155**

"LET'S PLAY SOCCER, DAD."

"Julian, not only is it cold outside, but it's dark."

"I meant in the basement."

Voda looked at his son, then glanced over at his wife, who was reading on the couch.

"I believe it is past your bedtime, young man," Mircea said.

"Papa said I could stay up late all the weekend."

"I did," conceded Voda. While on most matters he considered himself strict, he could not bring himself to enforce an early bedtime, since the night was the only time he had to play with his son.

"Can we play?" asked the boy.

"All right. Let's go."

"Mama too."

"I can't play," said Mircea.

"You can keep score."

She rolled her eyes.

"We can keep score ourselves," said Voda. "Let Mama read."

Julian had already grabbed the ball. "If I win, I get extra time to stay up."

"Even more?" said Mircea.

"And what if I win?" said Voda.

"Nothing. Everyone knows you should win."

Voda told the security man on duty in the hall that they would be downstairs, so he wouldn't be alarmed by odd noises. Then he went down the hall and around to the butler's pantry, where the single door to the basement was located. The stairs, two hundred years old and made of rickety wood, creaked as he came down. The landing was poorly lit, and Voda paused, knowing that his son was lurking nearby, preparing to leap out from the shadows to try and scare him.

"Boo!" yelled Julian, charging at him from his left.

Even though he was expecting him, Voda was a little surprised. He jumped back, amplifying his real shock with a mock expression of horror.

The basement of the old building was a fairly scary place, or at least one that could give rise to the sort of stories common in Transylvania. It was all that was left of the first structure built there, around 1650; it had a dirt floor and very solid stone walls. The original building had burned down or perhaps simply been knocked down to make way for a replacement in the early nineteenth century. It had a footprint three times as large as the original, though it was not nearly so large as the castles and mountain palaces that still dotted the region. Most likely, the house had been built as a summer retreat for a well-to-do but not quite noble family, which is how Voda modestly thought of it now.

"The wine cask is one goal," said Julian, leading his father into the open space behind the stairs. "The workshop is the other."

"Whose goal is the cask?" said Voda, as if he didn't know what the answer would be.

"Mine. You have the door to the workshop."

"It's wider than the wine cask."

"Should we put the cask on its side?"

The barrel was empty, so it would have been easy to do, but Voda declined. He knew that Julian wanted him to protect the doorway because he didn't like to go into the dank space they called the workshop. It was actually a storage area dug out behind the old foundation. Covered with spiderwebs, it had a double wall and led to an old root cellar. There was no electricity in that part of the basement, and the bare bulbs in this part of the basement sent only dim shadows in its direction.

"First one to five wins," said Voda.

Julian put the ball down, faked a kick left, then swatted it against the wall on his right. As it bounced back, he ran and toed it forward. Voda couldn't quite hit it with his foot as it dribbled past him, rebounding softly off the wall near the door. Before he could scoop it up, Julian executed a sliding kick that sent the ball soaring through the open door.

"Goaaaaal!" yelled the boy.

"I do not think sliding kicks are legal in our game," Voda teased. "The ground is too hard. You'll rip your pants."

"Then we can get new ones."

"Clothes do not grow on trees," said Voda, very serious now as he stepped into the darkness to find the ball amid the clutter of the old storeroom. His son's sense of entitlement bothered him. He did not want him to have to suffer, of course, but still, Justin should understand the value of hard work.

There was a pile of barrels staves immediately to the left of the doorway. Their shapes confused Voda, and he thought for a moment that the ball was among them. Finally he realized it must have gone farther in, and began poking forward cautiously, his eyes still having trouble adjusting to the dark. Ducking toward a shadow in the corner that looked as if it might the ball, he found his head tangled in several long strands of a spiderweb. He tried to pull off the threads, but they stuck to his ear and eyelids even after he rubbed at his face with his sleeve.

"Papa?"

"I'm coming, Julian. It's hard to see the ball."

There was a sharp rap and a thud above him.

"What was that?" Voda asked his son.

"I don't know."

There was another thud, this one toward the back of the house. Then a shock so strong that the ground shook.

Voda rushed out of the room.

"Papa, what is it?" The boy's face was filled with fear.

"Go in there," Voda told him. "Go behind the shelves. Go."

"Is it an earthquake?"

"Do as I say, Julian."

"I'm afraid. There's spiders, and—"

"Go. I'll be right back."

Voda had already started for the stairs. The ground was shaking heavily now, and while he could not be sure, he thought he heard the pop of automatic rifle fire. He charged up the stairs just in time to hear Oana Mitca, Julian's young nanny and bodyguard, shouting that they were under attack.

"Mircea!" Voda yelled for his wife. "Mircea, where are you?"

The guard from the hall was crouched near the door, watching the exterior through the small side window. He had unholstered his gun.

"Where's my wife?" demanded Voda, but the man didn't react. Bullets burst through the front of the house, shattering the windows.

"Lights! Lights! Kill the lights!" yelled one of the security people.

Voda ran into his office. He ducked down behind the desk and began working the combination to the small safe. He missed the second number and had to start again.

The tumblers clicked; he slapped open the safe and reached into the bottom, where he had two pistols, one a relatively new Glock and the other an ancient American revolver.

As he rushed from the room, bullets began hitting the rear of the house. The security forces outside were firing furiously; one was firing from upstairs.

Oana Mitca, gun drawn, appeared in the hall.

"Where is my wife?" demanded Voda.

"She's in the kitchen. Mr. President, we are under attack."

"Call the army post up the road," said Voda, rushing past. He yelled for Sergi, his assistant, forgetting that he had left about an hour earlier for a dinner date.

He found Mircea huddled behind the counter of the kitchen with Lienart, the security shift supervisor, who was yelling into his satellite phone.

"We are under attack by the guerrillas," said Lienart, who had already called the army. "Send everyone you have. Send them now!"

"Mircea." Voda grabbed his wife's hand. "Come on."

She looked up at him from the floor. "Why?" she said. "Why are they after us?"

"The army is five minutes away, Mr. President," said Lienart.

Just then a rocket-propelled grenade or perhaps a mortar shell struck the back of the house. The brick walls held, but the blast blew out the glass from the windows, sending the shards flying through the rooms. Lienart ran to the window, peered out, then began firing his submachine gun.

"We're going to the basement," Voda said, pulling his wife with him.

"Go!" yelled Oana Mitca.

"Come with us!" Voda told her.

She hesitated for a moment. Voda grabbed her arm.

"Now!" he said.

Another shell rocked the house. This one landed on the roof and descended into the second floor before exploding.

Debris showered from above, and part of the kitchen wall crumbled. A beam slapped downward, striking the nanny across the shoulder and throwing her to the floor. Voda let go of his wife and ran to her. As he tried to pull the timber off, another shell hit the house. Red flashed through the house, the air filled with dust and smoke.

"Go," whispered Oana.

Voda glanced across the floor, made sure his wife was still there, then reached under the fallen beam. He leveraged his back against it, pushing it upward. Oana Mitca crawled forward, groaning as she came free.

"We need to protect you," she said. Her voice was practically drowned out by the sound of submachine guns.

"Yes, protect us downstairs," said Voda. "Stay with the boy. That's your post."

He pushed her next to his wife, then led them to the door. Just as they started down the stairs, another large round hit the house. The rumbling explosion shook Voda off his feet; he fell down the stairs, tumbling into the women.

They helped each other up. Voda gave his wife the Glock, figuring she would do better with it than the revolver.

"Where's Julian?" asked Oana Mitca.

"This way, come on," said Voda, leading them back to the storage room. He kept flashlights near the entrance to the room, but it wasn't until he started through the doorway that he remembered them. He went back, calling to his son as he grabbed them.

"Julian, Julian, we're here," he said. "Papa's here."

There was no answer. He switched a flashlight on, worrying that Julian had somehow snuck by him and was upstairs. Then he realized he must be in the root cellar around the back of the workshop, unable to hear. He moved through the cobwebs and dust, snaked around the shelves which had once held preserved vegetables, and pulled up the trapdoor.

"Julian?"

"Papa, I'm scared."

"It's OK. Here's a flashlight." He tossed down the light he was holding and lit another. "Down. Come on," he told his wife and Oana, shining the light for them.

Mircea hesitated.

"Julian's down there," he told her.

"Oh, thank God," she said, squeezing by.

"Come on," he told Oana Mitca.

"No. I will stay here."

"The army is already on its way," Voda told her. "They'll be here in a minute."

"Then I won't have to wait long. Here." Oana Mitca dug into her pocket. "My phone."

Voda took the phone. His impulse was to stay with her, but he didn't want to leave his wife and son alone. "You'll be OK?" he asked.

"Alin, please," said the young woman. "Let me do my job."

"Knock twice on the door," he told her. "Twice, then pause, then again. All right?"

She nodded. Voda gave her his flashlight, then squeezed around the shelves. It was hard to see the stone stairs down to the door of the root cellar, and he slipped on the third step, crashing down to the bottom, against the heavy door. He reached for the doorknob and tried to push it open, but it wouldn't budge.

"Mircea!" he yelled. "Mircea, it's me!"

He couldn't hear anything. He pounded on the door, then tried it again. It still wouldn't budge. Desperate, Voda raised the pistol and was about to fire when he heard the loud creak of the door's hinges.

"It's me, it's me!" he yelled, sliding inside.

"Papa!" yelled Julian.

"Alin, what's going on?" asked his wife.

"The army will be here in a second," he said. "How did you lock this door?"

"I didn't. I jammed the hatchet head against the handle."

She showed him. The blade slipped in under the handle, sliding against the spindle and keeping it from turning.

He took the flashlight from Julian. The walls on either side of the door had iron hooks positioned so a board could be placed across it and keep it closed, but there was no board nearby to lock it down with. He glanced around the cellar, looking for something to use. There had once been a set of shelves against the wall, but the wood was long gone; all that remained were the stones that had supported them.

An old rug sat on the floor. Desperate, Voda grabbed at it, hoping it hid boards. Instead, he saw a smooth piece of metal—a small trapdoor they had never explored.

The explosions were continuing, and growing more intense.

"What happened to the army?" his wife asked.

"They're on their way," Voda told her, dropping to his knees to see if he could open the metal. It was solid, but more the size of a grate than a door.

"Papa are we going to be OK?"

"We're going to be fine Julian. Mircea, help me."

"If we're going to be fine, why are we hiding?" asked Julian.

"Help me with this. Let's see how strong you are," Voda told his son, straining to pull up the metal.

Though thin, the trapdoor was very heavy. Finally, with Mircea's help, Voda managed to push it slightly aside, then pushed with his heels to reveal an opening about two feet by a foot and a half.

It was part of an old cistern system, designed at some point in the very distant past to supply water to the house. The walls were overgrown with blackish moss. About four feet down, it opened into what looked like a tunnel.

"We can't go down there, Voda," said Mircea.

"I didn't say we were going to."

He went back to the door.

"I'm going up and getting some of the boards to block us

in," he told his wife. "I'll knock twice, pause, then knock
again. Twice. You'll hear my voice."

"Where is the army?" Mircea demanded. "Why aren't
they here?"

"Just give them time. I'm sure they're on their way," he
said, removing the hatchet. He left her the flashlight. "Lock
it behind me."

**Aboard EB-52 *Johnson*,
over northeastern Romania
2240**

ZEN WATCHED THE LONG-DISTANCE RADAR PLOT, MARKING
the progress of the helicopters as they left the field near the
church. From all reports, the operation had been a resound-
ing success. Both sites had proven to be rebel strongholds,
and the guerrillas taken completely by surprise. Roughly a
hundred guerrillas were killed or captured at the farm; a little
less than half that at the church. Weapons had been stockpiled at both. The church had also yielded a treasure trove of
documents and a computer.

"A lot of activity at border post M-2," said Spiff, operating
the ground radar upstairs. "Looks like the Moldovans have
finally woken up."

Zen switched his video view to *Hawk Two,* which was near
the border post. He was too far to see anything however, and
the terrain and nearby trees made it difficult to get much of a
view of the small guardhouse unless he went into Moldovan
territory—which of course he couldn't do.

"First helicopter is over the line," said Rager, who working
the airborne radar.

Zen felt his body starting to relax. The operation would be
over inside an hour, and they could stand down.

It wasn't that he felt exhausted. It was that feeling of use-
lessness that he wanted to lose.

"Shit—MiGs are back!" said Rager, practically yelling over the interphone. "Afterburners—they're coming west, high rate of speed. Touching Mach 2."

"Here we go again," said Sullivan.

"Colonel, they don't look like they're coming for us," said Rager a minute later. "They're on a direct line for the helicopters."

Moldova
2245

THE INSIDE OF THE HELICOPTER WAS SO LOUD IT WAS HARD to hear Colonel Bastian's voice over the roar of the blades. Overloaded, the aircraft strained to clear the trees at the edge of the field. It cleared the top branches by only a few feet, but continued to steadily rise.

"This is Stoner!" Stoner yelled into the sat phone.

"Stoner, tell your pilot and Colonel Brasov there are four MiGs headed in your direction," said Colonel Bastian. "They're about ten minutes away."

"Four what?"

"Four MiGs. Russian fighters. Get the hell out of there. Get over the border."

"We're working on it, Colonel."

Stoner turned to Colonel Brasov and tugged on his arm.

"There are fighter jets headed in our direction," he said. "They're about ten minutes away."

Brasov's face blanched—he'd said on takeoff that it would take the helicopter roughly thirty minutes to reach the border—then went forward to the cockpit to tell the pilots.

There were thirty soldiers in the rear of the helicopter, along with two of the prisoners, several boxes from the church, and the two footlockers. There were also several bodies stacked at the back. The Aerospatiale was designed to hold about twenty-five men, counting the crew.

Brasov returned, a frown on his face.

"We will stay very low to the ground," he said, shouting in Stoner's ear. "They may not see us on their radar. But it will be tight."

Aboard EB-52 *Johnson*,
over northeastern Romania
2247

DOG SWUNG THE MEGAFORTRESS TO THE SOUTH, PUSHING it closer to the border. The MiGs were definitely heading east in a big hurry, but while they were flying in the general direction of the Romanian helicopters, it was hard to tell if they knew exactly where they were.

"They shouldn't be able to see them on their radar until they're a lot closer," Rager said. "But they *will* see them. Those are Fulcrum C's. Their radar is almost as good as an F-15's."

"Almost as good" covered a wide ground, but Dog wasn't about to argue the point. Even if the radars' look-down ability wasn't up to American specs, the MiG pilots were on a course to fly almost directly over the choppers.

"Stoner, tell the helicopter pilots to cut south," said Dog. He'd decided to use the sat phone to avoid their conversation being monitored by the Moldovans or Russians. "They're riding right on the vector the Russians are taking."

"Copy." Stoner's voice was nearly drowned out by the heavy whirl of the helicopter engines above him.

"Colonel, we can take them down," said Sullivan. "I have an intercept plotted."

"We can't do it, Sully," said Dog.

"Those helicopters are dead ducks if they attack."

Dog didn't answer. He knew that what Sullivan had said was absolutely true—if the MiG pilots decided they were going to shoot the helicopters down, only luck would save them.

And what was he going to do? Just watch?

Dog punched the preset for the Dreamland Command com circuit.

"This is Bastian. I need to speak to General Samson."

"Colonel, he's in bed," said Sergeant Louch, who was handling the communications duties at Iasi.

"Wake him up."

"Yes, sir. Right away."

ZEN BANKED *HAWK TWO* TO THE NORTH, STILL WATCHING the border. The helicopters were about twenty miles from Romanian soil. That translated into roughly ten minutes of flying time. The MiGs, afterburners spent, had slowed to about 800 knots, and were about three minutes' flying time from an intercept.

The helos began changing course, turning south. They were in four groups. One group, which had taken off from the farm, was already over the border and thus out of harm's way. The other three groups, with eight helicopters apiece, were strung out in a semicircle approaching northeastern Romania. The helicopters in each group were flying in slightly offset single file, with the groups themselves forming three parallel hashes as they flew.

The trucks, meanwhile, were moving along a pair of parallel roads to the north. They too could be easily targeted, if the MiGs realized they were there.

One flick of his wrist and a push of his finger on the throttle slide at the back of his control yoke and *Hawk One* would be lined up perfectly for an intercept on the lead MiG. Zen wouldn't even have to shoot it down to protect the helicopters—once he got their attention, he figured, they'd lose interest in everything else.

At least long enough to let them get away.

Surely the colonel was thinking the same thing. Orders or no orders, they had to protect their people. Stoner was in one of the choppers.

Zen pulled back on the Flighthawk's control, adding a little more altitude as he waited for the order to attack.

"WHAT THE HELL IS IT, BASTIAN?"

"We have four Russian MiGs pursuing the Romanian force out of Moldova. I want permission to intercept."

"Where? Romania? You have it."

"No. The MiGs may hit them in Moldova. If I go over the border, I can save them."

"We went over this, Bastian. No. You can't go over the border. No."

"The helicopters will be easy pickings."

"The President's order was nothing over the border. No."

"But—"

"What part of no don't you understand?"

"General—"

"This conversation is done, Colonel. If those planes come over the border or attack you directly, take them down. But you stay on our side of the line. Is that clear, *Lieutenant* Colonel?"

"Crystal, General."

Moldova
2250

IT WAS STONER'S IDEA.

"When its nest is being attacked, a mother bird pretends to be wounded, drawing the predators away," he told Colonel Brasov. "You could do the same—have one of the helicopters peel off, get the MiGs interested, then land. Everyone runs for it—the MiGs come down and investigate. The other choppers get away. We make our way home by foot."

Instead of answering, Brasov went forward to the cockpit. Stoner glanced around the cabin. The troops were quiet now, aware they were pursued. "You are full of good ideas, Mr. Stoner," said the colonel, returning. Then he added, "The Russian aircraft are almost on us."

"How far is the border?"

Brasov just shook his head.

"I would not ask my men to make a sacrifice I was unwilling to make myself," said the colonel.

"Neither would I," said Stoner.

**Presidential villa,
near Stulpicani, Romania
2247**

ALIN VODA CLUTCHED THE REVOLVER CLOSE TO HIS BELLY as he went up the open stairs into the back of the root cellar beneath his house. In his years since joining Romania's government, and certainly in his time as president, he never thought it possible that he would come under this kind of attack. It seemed a fantasy—an evil fantasy, one where the world had turned upside down.

He knew that the guerrillas—the criminals—were evil, but hadn't allowed himself to think they were this evil.

Hubris. And foolishness.

Someone had killed the lights to the basement area. Voda couldn't see into the rest of the basement, and in fact could barely see a few feet in front of him.

The gunfire was louder, closer, right above them—that must be a good sign, he thought; the army had finally arrived.

Should he even bother getting the wood he'd come for? He wanted a piece of the shelves that formed a wall between this corner and the rest of the storeroom. Pulling off a piece, though, would be not be easy.

He put his left hand out, feeling his way, when light flashed through the basement.

"Oana," he started to say, calling for the bodyguard he'd left behind, when there was another flash and a loud bang. The word died on his tongue, his voice stolen by the shock of the sound.

"What?" yelled Oana Mitca.

Before he could answer, Oana began cursing and screaming. Gunfire flashed in the outer part of the basement. There was another flash and Voda felt himself falling, knocked off the slippery stone step to the bottom of the root cellar. He pushed around, pounded on the door.

"It's me," he told his wife, lowering his voice to a stage whisper, forgetting that he'd said he would knock in a pattern. "Open."

The door pulled back. Mircea shined a flashlight on his face.

"I think they're in the basement," he whispered.

They slapped the door closed and reset the hatchet blade into the handle, restoring the makeshift lock.

Voda leaned against the door. For a moment, he despaired. The dankness of the root cellar reminded him of the prison he'd been locked in the first time he played the piano in defiance of the old regime. The thick, musty scent choked him, paralyzing his will, just as it had the first few months he was in jail.

His younger self had been steadied by music. One by one Mozart's strong notes had returned to his imagination and steeled him for the struggle. But that was long ago. He'd left music behind, rarely played now, either in real life or in his daydreams, contrary to what those around him thought.

What would save him now?

"Papa, what will we do?" asked Julian.

Voda saw his son's face across the room, lit by the dim reflection from the flashlight. It was filled with fear, and it was that fear that brought him back from the abyss. In worrying about his son, he remembered how to act.

"You are going to hide with Mama," he said, springing from the door and moving to the metal trapdoor covering the cistern. "Down into this hole. Both of you."

"But it's a well," said the boy.

"You can hide down there," said Voda.

"Alin, what if it's too deep?" asked his wife.

"Come on. Shine the light." He pushed the metal covering fully aside, then squeezed down. The sides of the hole were slimy, but the stones were spaced far enough apart to let him get a good grip.

There was water four feet down, but it was shallow, less than an inch. The tunnel was wider than the hole, and nearly tall enough for him to stand.

"Mircea, the flashlight!"

She handed it to him. Voda shone it down the tunnel. He couldn't see the end of the passage.

Did it lead out? Or was it simply a trap?

Where would you collect rainwater from?

The roof maybe. Gutters. This might just be a reservoir, with no opening big enough to escape through.

Voda tucked the flashlight into his pants and climbed back up.

"Come on," he told his wife. "Let's go."

"I don't want to die like a rat in a hole," she said.

There was a burst of gunfire from somewhere above. Voda turned the flashlight back on and saw his son's eyes puffing up, on the verge of tears.

"We're not dying." He picked up the boy. "Come on. Out this way. I'll be with you."

Even though it was only four feet, it was difficult to climb down with Julian in his arms. Voda slipped about halfway down. Fortunately, he was able to land on his feet, his back and head slapping against the wall.

Julian began to cry. "That hurt," he wailed.

"Come on, now," Voda told his son. "No tears. And we must be quiet. We're only playing hide and seek until the army comes."

Mircea came down behind him, then reached back and started pulling at the metal top to the hole.

"I was going back up," he told her.

"No. We stay together."

Voda handed her the flashlight, then reached up and put his fingers against the metal strip that ran along the back of the cistern's metal top. He could hear, or thought he could hear, voices in the basement.

"Come on," he said, turning to get into the tunnel, but the others were ahead of him. His pants were soaked. He pushed ahead, slipping occasionally on the slime and mud, trying not to think that this was a perfect place for rats.

Lined with stone, the tunnel ran straight for about fifteen feet, then made a sharp turn to the left and began sloping upward. It narrowed as it turned, then the ceiling lowered to two feet. They began to crawl.

"I can stand!" shouted Julian suddenly.

"Wait," said Voda. Then, as the sound echoed through the chamber, he added, "Talk in whispers. Or better, don't talk."

Mircea played the light through the black space before them. They were in a round room about the size of the one they had come down to from the basement. At the far end they found another hole leading upward, similar to the one they had used to enter, though it was about eight feet deep and a little wider. There was a piece of metal on top, again similar to what they'd found in the root cellar.

"Maybe they're waiting above," said Mircea.

"Maybe." Voda climbed up the sides of the well. He thought he knew where he was—the barn about thirty feet from the eastern end of the house, used by the security people as a headquarters so they didn't disturb the family.

Centuries before, water would have been collected from the roofs of the building, piped down somehow, then stored so it could be distributed from these wells, both in the house and in the barn. The gutters or whatever had fed them were long gone, but the reservoir system remained.

Would they be safer in the tunnel or in the barn?

He wasn't sure.

It might be a moot question—the metal panel seemed impossible to move.

He braced himself by planting his shoes into the lips between the stones, then put his hand against the metal, pushing.

Nothing.

"Mama, I need the light!" yelled Julian below.

"Hush. Papa needs it."

"I think there is another tunnel this way!"

Voda climbed back down. Again he slipped the last few feet. This time he landed on his butt, but at least didn't hit his head again.

"Let's see this tunnel," he told his son.

It was narrower than the others, but also ended in an upward passage, only four feet off the ground. It too had a metal panel at its end, and Voda levered himself into position, putting his shoulder against it and pushing.

It moved, but just barely—so little in fact that at first he wasn't sure if it actually had moved or if he was imagining it. He braced himself again, and this time Mircea helped. Suddenly, it gave way, and they both slipped and fell together, bashing each other as they tumbled down.

The pain stunned him; the hard smack froze his brain. He found himself trapped in silence.

"Papa?" said Julian.

"Are you all right, Mircea?" he said.

"Yes. You?"

He rose instead of answering. "Up we go," he said, his voice the croak of a frog. "Up, up."

Gripping the edge of the trapdoor, he levered it open. He pulled himself up into darkness. It took a few moments to realize that he wasn't in the garage at all.

"Give me the flashlight," he hissed down to his wife.

"Voda, we can't stay down here."

"Just wait," he said, taking the light. He held it downward, hoping the beam wouldn't be too obvious if someone outside were watching.

The well had a stone foundation, and came up in the middle of a stone floor. Rotted timbers were nearby, some on the ground, others against the wall. But the ceiling and parts of the wall beyond the wood seemed to be stone. He got up, then saw casks against the wall, covered with dirt. Now he could guess where he was: an abandoned cave about seventy-five feet from the house, at the start of a sharp rise. It had once been used as a storehouse for wine or beer.

And probably for making it, if the cistern was here, though that was not important now.

"Alin?"

He went back to the hole and whispered to his wife. "Come up."

"I can't lift Julian."

Voda clambered back down. He had his son climb onto his shoulders, and from there into the cave. Voda turned back to help his wife, but she was already climbing up.

They slipped the metal cover back on the hole. Did they hear voices coming from the tunnel behind them? Voda didn't trust his imagination anymore.

"We're in the cave, aren't we?" said Julian, using their name for the structure.

"Yes."

"How do we get out?" asked Mircea. The cave door was locked from the outside. There was a small opening at the top of the rounded door, blocked by three iron bars. The space between the bars was barely enough to put a hand through.

Voda went to it and looked out into the night. Compared to the darkness of the tunnel and the cave, the outside was bright with moonlight. He saw figures in the distance, near the driveway and the garage.

They were soldiers, or looked like soldiers. An army truck had pulled up to the driveway. Men jumped out.

Thank God!

But Voda's relief died as he saw two men dragging a woman into the light cast by the truck's headlights.

He recognized her clothes and hair. It was Oana Mitca.

The soldiers dumped her the way they would dispose of an old rag. She lay limp.

Another man came up; an officer, he thought. He had a pistol. Oana Mitca's head exploded.

Why would they kill his son's bodyguard?

"Voda?" whispered his wife. "What's going on? I hear trucks, and I heard a shot."

"There's more trouble than I thought," he said, sliding back from the door.

Aboard EB-52 *Johnson*,
over northeastern Romania
2251

THE MIGs HAD FINALLY REALIZED THE HELICOPTERS WERE to their south. They were ten miles from the closest group. Even if the pilots took their time and waited for the perfect shot, they'd be in position less than three minutes from now.

And still far from the border.

"Why the hell aren't we doing something?" snapped Zen over the interphone. "Colonel, you can't keep us here."

"We have our orders," responded Dog.

Zen checked the positions on his screen. He could get *Hawk One* over the border, tell the computer to take out the lead MiG. Even if the Megafortress flew west, out of control range, the onboard computer guiding the robot plane would take it in for the kill.

He had to do it. He couldn't let the men aboard those choppers die.

If he did that, he knew he'd be disobeying a direct order. He'd be out of the Air Force, maybe even imprisoned.

"Colonel, we *have* to do something."

"No, Zen. Keep the planes where they are. Be ready if they come over the border. If you can't follow my orders, you'll be relieved."

Fuck that, thought Zen.

It was only with the greatest self-control that he managed to keep his mouth shut—and the planes where they were.

ON THE SITREP VIEW OF THE RADAR SCREEN DOG WAS watching, it looked as if one of the helicopters stopped in midair.

"What's going on?" he asked.

"He just popped up, gaining altitude," said Rager. "He's making himself a target. It's a decoy."

Dog saw the helicopter peeling back, trying to decoy the MiGs away. It was a noble idea, but it wasn't going to work—there were too many MiGs.

"Sully, open bomb bay doors. Prepare to fire Scorpions."

"You got it, Colonel."

Sullivan quickly tapped the controls and the Megafortress rocked with the opening of the bay doors.

"Scorpion One is locked on target!" yelled Sullivan.

"Fire. Lock the second—lock them all, and fire."

Sullivan quickly complied.

Not one member of the crew objected. They'd all put their careers, possibly a good portion of their lives, in Dog's hands. They knew the orders, realized how explicit they were: Do not under any circumstance cross the border or fire across the border, do not engage any Russian aircraft.

Under *any* circumstance.

Everyone aboard the *Johnson* wanted to disobey those orders, Dog realized, and would, gladly it seemed, if he led the way.

Was it because he had a Medal of Honor?

They were good men, men who knew right from wrong and valued honor and duty as much as he did; they weren't easily influenced by medals.

Dog checked his radar screen. The first MiG had suddenly jinked back east. Missile one, tracking it, jerked east toward the border.

"Self-destruct missile one," said Dog.

"Colonel?"

"Sully, hit the self-destruct before it goes over the border. Now!"

Dog tapped his armament panel to bring up the missile controls, but it was unnecessary—Sullivan did as he was told. He did the same for missile three as its target also turned east, taking its missile with it.

The last two aircraft continued toward the helicopters.

"Missile two, tracking and true," said Sullivan. There was a tremor in his voice. "Missile four, tracking and true."

"Self-destruct missile two," said Dog as the missile neared the border.

"Colonel?"

Dog ignored him, reaching for the panel and killing both missiles himself.

"Missile launch," said Rager, his voice solemn.

A launch warning lit on his dashboard. One of the MiGs had just fired a pair of heat seekers at the helicopter.

Moldova
2256

STONER GRABBED ONTO THE SPAR AS THE HELICOPTER whirled hard into the turn. The pilot had spotted a small clearing on the hillside ahead. He launched flares in hopes of decoying the Russian missiles, then pushed the nose of the helicopter down, aiming for the hill.

The helicopter blades, buffeted by the force of the turn,

made a loud *whomp-whomp-whomp*, as if they were going to tear themselves off.

Everyone inside the helicopter was silent, knowing what was going on outside but not really knowing, ready but not ready.

"When we get out, run!" Brasov yelled. "Run from the helicopter. As soon as you can, make your best way over the border. It is seven miles southwest. Seven miles! A few hours' walk."

The men closest to him nodded, grim-faced.

The helicopter pitched hard to the left.

"You are a brave man, braver than I gave you credit for when we met," Colonel Brasov told Stoner as the force of the turn threw the two men together.

"You too," said Stoner.

"Until we meet."

Brasov held out his hand.

As Stoner reached for it, he thought of Sorina Viorica, the way she'd looked on the street in Bucharest. He thought of the mission he'd had in China a year before, where he came close to being killed. He thought of his first day at the Agency, his graduation from high school, a morning in the very distant past, being driven by his mom to church with the rain pouring and the car warm and safe.

There was a flash above him and a loud clap like thunder.

And then there was nothing, not even pain or regret.

VI

Fear of the Dead

———

Aboard EB-52 *Johnson*,
over northeastern Romania
28 January 1998
2258

ZEN STARED IN DISBELIEF AS THE HELICOPTER DISAPPEARED from the screen.

"Helicopter *Baker One* is off the scope," said Rager. "It's been hit."

"Confirmed," said Spiff. "Ground radar saw it breaking up."

Zen tightened his grip on the yoke, trying to concentrate on the MiGs. The two that had fired at the helicopter and shot it down were now flying toward the border. If they didn't turn in about thirty seconds, they'd cross over.

He pushed *Hawk One* toward an interception—then got a warning from the computer that the aircraft was nearing the end of its control range.

"*Bennett,* I need you to come south," said Zen. Even with recently implemented improvements to the control communications network, the robot had to be within fifty miles of the mother ship.

"Flighthawk leader, we have to stay near the northernmost helicopter group," said Dog.

"Damn it—the MiGs are *here*," said Zen. "Come south."

Dog answered by turning the aircraft back south, staying near the Flighthawk.

The MiGs started a turn meant to take them back east. But

it was more of a gradual arc than a sharp cut, and it was clear to Zen even before he asked the computer to project their course that they would still cross over the border.

The Russians had fired on the helicopter at relatively low altitude, about 5,000 feet. They'd climbed through 8,000 feet and were still rising. The Flighthawk, by contrast, was at 25,000 feet. The altitude difference represented a serious advantage in speed and flight energy—and Zen intended to use every ounce of that advantage.

He tipped his nose down, studying the sitrep for a second as he lined *Hawk One* up for a double attack. With *Hawk One* touching Mach 1, the MiGs climbed up over the border. Zen twisted his wings, then pulled sharply on his stick, picking the nose of the plane up before slapping over and plunging straight downward. The loop slowed the Flighthawk's forward progress just enough to put it directly above the MiG's path. The Russian's nose appeared in the right corner of the view screen, a bright green wedge slicing through the night's fabric. The targeting piper flashed yellow, indicating that he didn't have a shot yet, but he fired anyway, trusting that the MiG's momentum would bring it into the hail of bullets. He slammed his controls, trying to hold the Flighthawk in position to continue firing as the MiG passed, but he had too much speed for that, and had to back off as the small plane threatened to flip backward into a tumble.

Losing track of his target, Zen dropped his right wing and came around, pulling his nose toward the path of the second fighter. The Flighthawk took ten g's in the turn—more than enough to knock a pilot unconscious had he been in the plane. But aboard the Megafortress, Zen was pulling quiet turns more than forty miles away; he flicked his wrist and put his nose on the rear quarter of the MiG.

This one was a turkey shoot.

The MiG driver had an edge—ironically, his much slower speed would have sent the Flighthawk past him if he'd turned abruptly. But the MiG jock, perhaps because he didn't know exactly where the Flighthawk was, or maybe because he panicked, didn't turn at all. Instead he tried putting the pedal to the metal and speeding away, lighting his afterburner in a desperate attempt to pick up speed.

That only made it easier for Zen. The red flare of the engine moved into the sweet spot of the targeting queue, and he sent a long stream of bullets directly into the MiG's tailpipe. The thick slugs tore through the titanium innards, unwinding the turbine spool with a flash of fire. There was no time for the pilot to eject; the plane disintegrated into a black mass of hurtling metal.

The other MiG, meanwhile, had tacked to the north, still in Romanian territory, damaged by Zen's first pass. Checking the position on the sitrep, Zen brought the Flighthawk back in its direction. He slammed the throttle slide to full military power, plotting an angle that would cut off the MiG's escape.

The small aircraft's original advantages in speed and flight energy had now been used. If the dogfight devolved into a straight-out foot race, the Flighthawk would be at a disadvantage because of the MiG's more powerful engines. Though the smaller plane could accelerate from a dead stop a bit faster because of its weight, once the MiG's two Klimov engines spooled up, their combined 36,000 pounds of thrust at military power would simply overwhelm the Flighthawk.

The MiG pilot apparently realized this, because he had the lead out. But Zen knew that he couldn't stay on his present course, since it was taking him northwest, the exact opposite of where he wanted to go. So he backed off and waited.

He wanted the enemy plane. The desire boiled inside him, pushing everything else away.

It took precisely forty-five seconds for the MiG pilot to decide he was clear and begin his turn to the east. He was ten miles deep in Romanian territory; *Hawk One* was about six miles south of the point where the computer calculated it would cross.

Doable, but tight.

Zen leaned on the throttle, pushing *Hawk One* straight up the border toward the MiG. Then he jumped into the cockpit of *Hawk Two,* which had been patrolling along the route the helicopters were taking. He slid it farther north, positioning it to catch the MiG if it suddenly doubled back.

Back in *Hawk One,* Zen saw the approaching Russian plane as a black smudge near the top of the screen. He jabbed his finger against the slide at the back of his stick, trying to will more speed out of the little jet.

He wanted him. Revenge, anger—he felt something desperate rise inside him, something reckless and voracious. He was going to kill this son of a bitch, and nothing was going to stop him.

The targeting piper turned yellow.

UPSTAIRS ON THE FLIGHT DECK, DOG WATCHED THE MiG and Flighthawks maneuvering on the radar screen. He was stewing, angry at the way Zen had cursed at him, and even angrier that his orders had led to the loss of the Romanian helicopter. Back at Dreamland, he'd wondered what happened to "heroes" at their next battle. Now he knew.

"Colonel, the trucks are nearing the border," said Spiff. "There's a Moldovan patrol about a mile north of them."

"Make sure our guys know that."

"Yes, sir."

"Rager, where are those other two MiGs?" Dog asked the airborne radar specialist.

"Halfway home by now, sir. Probably on their way to get their laundry cleaned."

"How close to the ground troops is that MiG going to be if he gets over the border?"

"A couple of miles. If the ground troops call for support, he'll be close enough to give it."

* * *

THE MiG KEPT SLIDING TOWARD THE RIGHT OF THE SCREEN, edging closer to Moldovan territory as it approached *Hawk One*. Zen leaned with it, willing the plane into the triangular piper at the center of his screen.

The gunsight began blinking red. He pushed the trigger, sending a stream of 20mm bullets over the MiG's left wing. The MiG immediately nosed down and then cut back hard in the direction he'd come from. Surprised and out of position because he'd been worried about the border, Zen had trouble staying with the Russian.

The MiG turned south, breaking clean from the Flighthawk's pursuit. Zen knew he'd hit it earlier, but it showed no sign of damage.

I'm nailing that son of a bitch, he thought, throwing the Flighthawk into a hard turn.

The MiG's tail came up in his screen, too far to shoot—but Zen's adrenaline and anger took over, and he pressed the trigger anyway. The slugs trailed down harmlessly toward the earth.

The MiG driver once more leaned on his throttle and slowly began pulling away. He was still going south; Zen started to tack in that direction, thinking he might be able to cut him off a second time.

The Flighthawk computer warned him that he was running low on fuel, but Zen didn't care. He was going to get the son of a bitch.

Then the computer gave him another warning: His path south was taking him out of control range.

"*Bennett,* this is Flighthawk leader. I need you to come south."

"What's your status, Flighthawk?" asked Dog.

"I'm on the MiG's tail. I almost have him. Come south."

"Negative. We have the trucks approaching the border. We need you to provide cover."

"I'm on his tail."

"Come back north, Flighthawk. The MiG is no longer a player."

"What the hell sense is coming north?" asked Zen. "I can't go across the border if the trucks get in trouble."

There was a pause. A warning flashed on Zen's screen:

DISCONNECT IN TEN SECONDS, NINE . . .

"Come north, Hawk leader," said Dog.

"Colonel—"

"That is a direct order."

It was all Zen could do to keep from slapping the control stick as he complied.

"TARGET THE MIG," DOG TOLD SULLIVAN.

"Targeted. Locked."

Dog looked at the sitrep. He needed Zen to move off before he fired.

The Flighthawk lurched to the right.

"Take him down."

"Fire Fox One!" said Sullivan. The radar missile dropped off the rail. It accelerated with a burst of speed.

"MiG is turning back east," said Sullivan. "Missile is tracking."

Dog brought the ground radar plot on his control board. He had the same situation on the ground as he had in the air—if the Moldovans attacked, he'd be unable to do anything until they came over the line.

"Splash MiG!" shouted Sullivan.

"Close the bay doors," said Dog.

"Colonel, looks like the Moldovan ground forces are going to miss our guys," reported Spiff. "The trucks just got on the highway, heading east. Eight, nine troop trucks. Ten, twelve. Whole force looks like they've caught the wrong scent."

Thank God, thought Dog.

Bacau, Romania
2300

GENERAL LOCUSTA STARED DOWN AT THE MAP BEING USED to track the raid's progress. The appearance of the MiGs had dramatically changed the mood in his headquarters conference room.

"I still can't get them on the radio," said the communications specialist.

"Prepare a rescue mission. Ground and air."

"Standing by, General. The helicopters should be refueled within ten minutes."

Damn the Russians. They would claim that they were merely honoring their treaty with Moldova, but Locusta knew this was actually aimed at him— a pointed reminder that he could not count on the Americans in the future.

As for the Americans . . .

"The Dreamland people. What are they doing?"

"Continuing to engage the aircraft at last report."

"Have them pinpoint the route of the helicopter toward the border."

"Yes, sir."

"Losing one helicopter does not mean the mission was a failure, General," whispered one of his aides as Locusta stalked across the room for coffee.

"Yes," he muttered. His thoughts were split between the operation, the men he'd lost—and the president.

The call should have come an hour ago.

"General, we have an urgent call for you from Third Battalion."

About time, thought Locusta, though as he turned he made his face a blank.

"The unit near the president's house—they're responding to an attack by the guerrillas."

"What?"

"Here, sir."

Coffee spilled from Locusta's cup as he practically threw it back down on the table and strode to the phone.

"Locusta."

"There has been an attack," said one of the captains at the headquarters of the unit assigned to help guard the president. "Guerrillas."

"When? What's going on?"

Locusta listened impatiently as the man related what he knew. The alarm had come in only a few minutes before. Guerrillas had struck at the battalion's radio and the local phone lines around the same time, making it difficult to communicate with the base.

"When did this occur?" demanded Locusta.

The man did not know. The attack had apparently begun sometime before.

"Where is the President?"

"Our troops are only just arriving," said the captain. "We have not yet made contact with his security team."

"Didn't they send the alert?"

"No."

They hadn't been able to—as part of his plan, Anton Ozera had directed his team to activate a cell phone disrupter just before the attack. Like everything else that would indicate the assault was more than the work of unsophisticated guerillas, it would have been removed by now.

"Keep me informed," said Locusta.

He handed the aide back the phone.

"We have another developing situation," he announced.

**Presidential villa,
near Stulpicani, Romania
2315**

VODA WATCHED FROM THE SMALL, GLASSLESS WINDOW OF the cave as two more members of his presidential security team were carried out to the space in front of the barn. They were clearly already dead; their bodies bounced limply when they were dropped.

The men carrying them were soldiers—or at least were dressed in Romanian army uniforms. The fighting seemed to have died down; Voda couldn't hear any more gunfire.

Julian was trembling, either with the cold or fear, or maybe both. Voda pulled him close.

"We're going to be OK," he whispered. "It's going to take us a little while, but we'll be OK."

"What are they doing?" Julian asked.

"I'm not sure."

Lights arced through the window. Voda froze, then realized they had come from the headlamps of trucks driving up past the garage. He rose and looked out the corner of the window. Two trucks had just arrived. Soldiers ran from the back, shouting as they disappeared.

"What's going on?" Mircea asked.

"I can't tell."

"Is the army here?"

"Yes, but there's something odd about it."

"What kind of odd?"

Voda couldn't bring himself to use the word "coup." He watched as two soldiers came into view, walking from the direction of the house. He moved his head to the very side of the window as they took up their posts guarding the bodies yet not hardly looking at them, save for a few glances— guilty glances, Voda thought, though they faced the street, their backs to him.

It was possible that the soldiers had arrived toward the very end of the firefight, with all of his defenders dead, and were unable to tell who was who. Still, the way that the bodies had been handled alarmed Voda. His guards all had IDs, and were wearing regular clothes besides. It ought to be easy to differentiate between them and the guerrillas.

Was he just being paranoid? The only people in this pile

were security people. Perhaps he was mistaking fear of the dead for disdain.

"If the army is here, shouldn't we go out?" asked his wife.

"There's something about it that's not right, Mircea," he whispered. "I can't explain. But I don't think it's safe yet."

"They'll find the tunnel we came through."

"I know."

Voda sat down next to the door, trying to think. Mircea turned on the flashlight. He grabbed it from her and flipped it off.

"What are you doing?" he asked.

"I'm looking around. Maybe there's something here we can use."

"Don't use the flashlight. They'll see outside."

"I can't see in the dark."

"There's enough light, when you get close."

This was true, but just barely. Mircea began crawling on her hands and knees, working her way deeper into the cave. They had been in this cave only once that he could remember, soon after buying the property three years before. There was nothing of use, he thought—no machine guns, no rifles. But at least looking would give his wife something to do rather than stand around and worry that they would be found.

They would be found sooner or later. Most likely very soon—it was only a matter of time before someone figured out that they'd gone into the cistern well.

Could the army have revolted? These men were under Locusta's control. Would they defy him?

Would he launch the coup?

He was certainly ambitious enough.

If the generals, or a general, revolted, would the men in the ranks follow suit? Would they remember what the country was like under the dictator?

But maybe life for them under the dictator was better. They were privileged then, poor but privileged. Now they were still poor, and without privilege.

Voda stood back up and looked through the window. The men guarding the bodies were young; they would have been little older than Julian when Ceausescu died, too young to know how things truly were then.

"Two more," said someone he couldn't see.

Voda slipped his head closer to the side. Two more bodies, both of his security people, were dumped.

"Have they found the president yet?" asked one of the men who'd been guarding the bodies.

Voda couldn't hear the answer, but it was some sort of joke—the soldiers all laughed.

He had to find a place to hide his family. Then he could find out what was going on.

One of the men started to turn around. Voda twisted back against the door, getting out of the way. As he did, Oana Mitca's cell phone pressed against his thigh. He'd completely forgotten it in his scramble to escape.

He took it from his pocket and opened it. The words on the screen said: NO SERVICE.

Frustrated, he nearly threw it to the ground. But he realized he couldn't show his despair to his wife or son, and so slipped it back into his pocket instead.

Voda listened carefully, trying to hear the soldiers outside, not daring to look back through the small window. Finally he poked his head up. All of the men had left.

Voda examined the door, using his fingers as well as his eyes. It was made of boards of oak or some other hardwood that ran from top to bottom. It had no doorknob or conventional lock. He had secured it soon after buying the property, screwing a U-hook into the frame and then putting a simple steel clasp on the door. The clasp went over the hook and was held by a padlock. He'd used long screws to make sure it couldn't be simply pulled aside, and while there was enough play in the clasp for him to feel it move slightly as he put his weight against the door, he doubted he could force it from this side.

"I found a chisel," said Mircea, coming toward him in the dark. "Can we use it?"

The chisel was a heavy woodworker's tool, used seventy or eighty years before to shave notches into wood. It was covered with a layer of rust. The edge was thin but not sharp. Voda turned it over in his hands, trying to figure out how he might be able to make use it.

The boards were held together by two perpendicular pieces at the top and bottom. Perhaps he could use the chisel as a crowbar, dismantling it.

He slid the tool up, not really thinking the idea had any real hope of succeeding, yet unable to think of an alternative.

"Can you use it?" asked Mircea.

"Maybe."

As he began working the chisel into the board, he saw that the door was held in place by a long, triangular-shaped hinge that was screwed into the cross piece. There was one on top and on bottom and they were old, rusted even worse than the chisel.

The chisel tip didn't quite fit as a screwdriver; the screws were inset into the holes in the metal, making them hard to reach with its wide head. Frustrated, Voda pushed the chisel against the metal arm and wood, working the tip back and forth as he tried to get between the door and the hinge arm. He managed to get the tip in about a quarter of an inch, then levered it toward him. The hinge moved perhaps a quarter inch from the wood.

It was a start. He knelt down and began working in earnest on the bottom hinge, deciding to leave the top for last. One of the screws popped out as soon as he pulled against it. The other two, however, remained stuck. He pushed the chisel in, tapping with his hand.

Was it making too much noise?

"Mircea," he whispered to his wife. "Look out and make sure no one is there."

"What if they see me?"

"Stay at the corner, at the lower corner. In the shadow."

She came over. "No one," she whispered. "Oh my God."

She turned away quickly, covering her mouth. Obviously she had seen the dead bodies lying in the grass.

"Did the soldiers kill them?" she asked.

"No, but they dumped them there."

Voda continued to work. The door creaked and tilted down as the last screws popped from the door hinge. Voda steadied it, then stood up.

If he popped off the upper hinge, the door would be easy to push aside; it might even fall aside. But of course the chance of being found would increase.

No. Sooner or later someone was coming through the cistern. They might even be working on it now.

"I can open the door," he told Mircea. "But we must be ready to run."

"Where will we go?"

Voda realized he had begun to breathe very hard.

"Into the woods. Farther up."

"They'll search."

"They'll search here in a minute," he said.

"Someone's coming," she hissed, ducking away from the door's window.

Voda froze, listening. Julian put his arms around his father, hugging him and whimpering. He patted the boy's back, wanting to tell him that everything would be OK. But that would be a cruel lie, easily exposed—in minutes they could all three be dead, tossed on the pile of bodies like so much dried wood. He didn't want his last words to his son to be so treacherously false.

"Alin," said Mircea, tugging him nearer to the window. "Listen."

The soldiers outside were saying that the general was on his way and would be angry. One of them asked for a cigarette. A truck started and backed away, its headlights briefly arcing through the hole into the cave.

One soldier remained, guarding the bodies.

He could shoot him, thought Voda, then pry off the hinge, and make a run for it.

"We could go to the pump house," whispered Mircea. "It's a good hiding place."

The pump house was an old wellhead on the property behind theirs. It was at least two hundred yards into the woods, up fairly steep terrain. It had been abandoned long ago; the house it once served had burned down in the 1970s.

It might not be a bad hiding place, at least temporarily, but reaching it would be difficult. And first they would have to get out of the cave.

A small vehicle drove up and stopped near the other troop truck. He could hear the sound of dogs barking. The guard went in that direction, then returned with two dog handlers and their charges. They walked to the soldier guarding the bodies, then all of them, the guard included, went in the direction of the house.

Quickly, Voda pushed the chisel in against the metal.

"When the door gives way," he told his wife and son, "run. I'll fix it so it looks as if it is OK."

"Where will we go?" Mircea asked.

"The pump house. We'll have to move quickly."

"The dogs—"

"If we can walk along a creek for a while, the dogs will lose us," he said. "I've seen it in movies."

"So have I," said Julian brightly.

His son's remark gave him hope.

The door started to give way at the bottom as he pushed against the hinge. Voda put his leg there, then pried at the top. The screws sprang across the room and the door flopped over, held up only by the locked clasp.

"Come," he hissed, taking out his revolver. He slipped through the opening, looking, unsure what he would do if someone was actually nearby.

Mircea started out behind him. Voda grabbed her and

pulled, then took Julian by the back of his shirt and hauled him out.

"Into the woods," he told his wife. "I'll catch up after I fix the door."

Julian clung to his leg, refusing to go. Voda picked up the door and slid it back against the opening. He couldn't quite get it perfect; the hinges were gone and the clasp had been partly twisted by the door's weight. But it would have to do. He grabbed his son under his arm like a loaf of bread and ran.

He didn't realize there were a pair of guards at the far end of the driveway near the road until he reached the bushes. The men were sharing a cigarette and arguing loudly over something less than fifty yards away. One of them must have heard him running because he shone his light back in the direction of the cave and woods.

Crouched behind the brush at the edge of the woods, Voda held his son next to him, trying not to breathe, trying not to do anything that would give them away. The flashlight's beam swung above the trees, then disappeared.

More trucks were coming.

"OK, up, let's go," said Voda, pulling Julian with him up the slope. He walked as quickly as he could; after twenty or thirty yards he began whispering for his wife. "Mircea? Mircea?"

"Here."

She was only a few yards away, but he couldn't see her.

"Go up the hill," he hissed.

"I hurt my toe."

"Just go," he said. "Come on Julian."

"Alin—"

"Go," he said.

He took Julian with him, carrying the boy about thirty more yards up the slope, picking his way through the dense trees. Below them more troops had arrived. There were shouted orders.

It wouldn't be long before they saw the door at the cave, or followed the cistern and discovered where they had been. Then they'd use the dogs to track them in the woods.

Voda felt an odd vibration in his pocket, then heard a soft buzzing noise. It was the cell phone, ringing.

He pulled it out quickly, hitting the Talk button to take the call. But it wasn't a call—the device had come back to life, alerting him to a missed call that had gone to voice mail.

The phone was working now.

He fumbled with it for a moment, then dialed Sergi's number.

There was no answer.

He hit End Transmit button.

Who else could he call?

The defense minister—but he didn't know his number. Those sorts of details were things he left to Sergi and his other aides.

Voda hit the device's phone book. Most of the people on the list were friends of Oana Mitca, but she also had Sergi's number, and that of his deputy schedule keeper, Petra Ozera. He tried Sergi again, hoping he had misdialed, but there was still no answer, not even a forward to voice mail. Then he tried Petra.

She answered on the third ring.

"Hello?"

"Petra, this is Alin."

"Mr. President! You're alive!"

"Yes, I'm alive."

"We've just heard from the army there was a guerrilla attack."

"Yes. There has been. What else did you hear?"

"The soldier said they were dealing with a large-scale attack. I rushed to the office. I'm just opening the door."

"Who called you?"

"The name was not familiar."

"From which command?"

"General Locusta's. They had just received word from their battalion."

Voda wondered more than ever which side the army was on.

"I want you to speak to the defense secretary," said Voda. "Call Fane Cazacul and tell him I must speak to him immediately. Tell him I will call him. Get a number where he can be reached."

"Yes, sir."

If the defense secretary was involved, he'd be able to track down the phone number. But the dogs would be able to find him soon anyway. Voda told Petra to call several of his allies in the parliament and tell them he was alive. He tried to make himself think of a strategy, but his mind wasn't clear; the thoughts wouldn't jell.

"The phone is ringing," said Petra.

"Answer it."

Voda waited. He heard rustling in the bush to his right—it was Mircea. Julian looked in her direction but didn't leave his father's side.

"It's the American ambassador," said Petra. "He's just heard a report that one of helicopters was shot down over the border and—"

"Get me his phone number. I want to talk to him as well," said Voda.

White House Situation Room
1320 (Romania 2320)

JED BARCLAY RUBBED HIS KNUCKLE AGAINST HIS FOREHEAD, trying to concentrate as the call from the American ambassador to Romanian came through.

"This is Jed Barclay."

"Jed, I need to speak to the President immediately. They tell me that Secretary Hartman can't be disturbed."

"The Secretary and the President are on their way back to the White House," said Jed. "We don't have new information but we do have an idea of where the helicopter crashed and—"

"This is something different. I've just spoken with President Voda."

"You have?" Jed turned to the monitor on his right.

"Yes. He's under attack. Possibly by his own army."

Iasi Airfield, Romania
2320

THE ROMANIANS SCRAMBLED TWO HELICOPTERS IN AN AT-tempt to mount a recovery option on the one that had gone down over the border in Moldova, but as soon as the radar aboard the *Bennett* showed that the Moldovans had trucks at the site, they aborted it. From the Romanian point of view, the loss of the colonel and the soldiers who'd been with him were a regrettable but acceptable trade-off for smashing the rebel strongholds and carrying away important data about the guerrilla operations.

With the mission scratched, fatigue mixed with an unspoken malaise aboard the Megafortress. Dog's crew did their jobs dutifully, but they were clearly disappointed in the outcome of the mission.

And with the decision not to attack over the border to support the Romanians.

"Romanians are shutting down," said Sullivan. "All troops are back over the border. Except for those in the helicopter."

"Thanks," said Dog. "Set a course for Iasi."

Sullivan worked quickly and without his usual wisecracks. They landed a short time later, and after securing the plane, headed to the Dreamland Command trailer for a postflight debriefing.

Though he'd already informed Jed Barclay at the NSC

about the MiGs and helicopter, Dog retreated to the com room to give a written brief. He knocked out a few sentences, inserted the location of the helicopter as well as the MiGs, then joined the others to review what had happened.

Ordinarily, the debrief would devolve into a bit of a bull session after fifteen or twenty minutes, with Sullivan making jokes and cracking everyone up. But tonight no one joked at all. Each of the men typed quietly on laptops, recapping the mission from their perspective.

Sullivan was usually the last to leave—he was a notoriously poor speller and could puzzle for hours over his punctuation—but he was done in five minutes, his report the barest of bare prose. As soon as he was finished typing his summary into the laptop computer, he rose and asked to be excused.

"You can go, Sully, if you're done," Dog told him. "You don't have to ask for permission."

The normally cheerful Sullivan nodded, rubbed his eyes, and left Dog and Zen alone in the front of the trailer.

As Zen hunt-and-pecked his report on the laptop's flat keyboard, Dog cracked open the small refrigerator.

"Beer?" he asked.

Zen didn't answer.

"Zen?"

The pilot pretended he was absorbed in his work. Dog popped the top on his beer, closed the refrigerator and sat down in the seat farthest from the one where Zen was working. Though still angry at the way the major had snapped at him during the flight, Dog decided it was a product of fatigue and anger at losing Stoner, and that it wasn't worth making an issue of it, especially given the fact that his stay with Dreamland was coming to an end.

Dog leaned back in the seat, gazing at the trailer ceiling and the wall of cabinets at the side. It was a silly place to grow nostalgic over, yet he felt the pangs growing. He'd spent a lot of time here—difficult time, mostly, but in the end what he and his people had accomplished had been worth the effort.

"How's it coming?" he asked Zen after a while.

"What do you care?" snapped Zen, without looking up.

"What's wrong with you, Zen?"

"What do you mean?"

"I mean what the hell is wrong with you? You're not like that."

"Like what?"

"A jerk."

Zen put his hands on the wheels of his chair and spun to the side to confront Dog. His face was shaded red.

"Maybe I think you did the wrong thing," Zen said. "Maybe I *know* you did the wrong thing."

"By not disobeying an order from the President?"

"Sometimes . . . "

"Sometimes what, Jeff? It was a *lawful* order."

"It was a stupid order. It killed two dozen men, one of them a friend of ours. A guy that saved your daughter, my wife, a year ago. You don't remember that?"

"We have to do our duty," said Dog softly.

"Our duty is saving people, especially our people. You could have. A month ago, you would have."

"I have never disobeyed a direct order," said Dog.

Zen smirked.

"I have never *disobeyed* a direct, lawful order," repeated Dog. He felt his own anger starting to rise.

"You were always damn good at finding a way around them, then," said Zen. He spun back to his computer.

Dog didn't want to let him have the last word. He wanted to say something, anything, in response. But his tongue wouldn't work.

Maybe Zen was right. Maybe, with Samson taking over, he'd lost a bit of his initiative.

Or maybe heroes started to fade the moment they were called heroes.

Dog couldn't think what to say. That the country's needs were greater than the individual's? Honor and duty were important, but there were situations where fulfilling your duty and maintaining your honor were not the same—were, in fact, mutually exclusive.

Zen finished his report, closed the program and the laptop, then backed away from the table.

"Good night," Dog told him as he rolled past.

Zen didn't answer.

When he was gone, Dog sighed heavily, then took a sip of his beer.

It tasted bitter in his mouth.

"Hey, Colonel, something's going on with the Romanian command," yelled Sergeant Liu from the communications shack at the back of the Command trailer. "They're issuing all sorts of orders, and units are moving all over the country."

Dog emptied the beer in the sink and went back to see what was going on.

"Some of Locusta's units are moving toward Stulpicani, way up in the mountains," Liu told him. "They're talking about guerrillas."

Liu brought a map up on the screen. Stulpicani was a quiet town in the Suceava area of Romania, about eighty-five miles northwest of Iasi. There had been no guerrilla attacks that far north or west, as far as Dog knew.

"They're talking about a presidential retreat," said Liu. "A villa or something."

"Call the NSC right away. Tell them something big is going on. I'll go wake up General Samson."

White House Situation Room
1325 (2325 Romania)

BY NOW THE NSC STAFF HAD ARRANGED A LIVE FEED FROM two Romanian news organizations via their satellites. One feed showed a news program in progress, and since it had not yet been translated, wasn't of immediate use. The other was a frequency used by reporters in the field and at stations around the country to upload raw video and reports to their national headquarters in Bucharest. Jed watched as one feed showed at least a dozen troop trucks moving out of the capital.

The NSC's Romanian translator was sitting at a nearby station, scribbling notes from the video. Jed went over and took a peek at them. The reporter was talking about unexplained troop movements near Bacau.

When the transmission ended, Jed tapped the translator on the shoulder. The woman, a Romanian-American in her thirties, pulled her headphones back behind her raven black hair and turned toward him.

"Have they said anything about guerrilla attacks or the president?" Jed asked.

"No."

"They report on the operation in Moldova?"

She shook her head.

"Watch some of the live broadcast and see if that comes up," he told her. "As soon as the CIA transcripts come in, give them to me, OK?"

Then he went back to his desk and called the National Reconnaissance Office—the Air Force department that supervised satellite surveillance—to see how long it would be before a satellite was available. He was still on the phone with them when Freeman called in.

"The president of Romania thinks the army is staging a coup," Jed told him. "Our ambassador is in contact with him. The Dreamland people just heard that there was a guerrilla attack near the president's house in the mountains. There are reports that the Romanian army is moving in the capital. Big movements, enough to get the attention of the media."

"Is it the guerrillas or the army that's moving against Voda?"

"We don't know. We haven't monitored any official reports of an attack on the president's house and the Dreamland units were not notified."

"What does the defense minister say?"

"We're still trying to get in touch with him."

"You think it's a coup?" Freeman asked.

"Um, I wouldn't, um," Jed stumbled, his stutter returning. "It's too early to say what I think. But it, uh, has that feel. Like in Libya last year."

Jed ran down some of the other developments. Freeman listened without interrupting, then told him to have Dreamland get a plane aloft to monitor the troop movements on the ground and see if they could find out what was going on.

"CIA director was trying to set up a phone conference for 1330," added Jed. "White House chief of staff already knows some of what's going on."

"Where's the President?"

"A reception at the Smithsonian," said Jed. "Secretary Hartman's there too. Due to end at three. Are you going to call him?"

"We'll wait until after the phone conference. I may break away. Alert the chief of staff that we'll need to talk."

Iasi Airfield, Romania
2325

WHEN HE HAD DECIDED TO COME TO ROMANIA, GENERAL Samson had somehow forgotten that the troops were sleeping on cots in a large hangar. Clearly this was not going to be a workable arrangement in his case.

For this one night, however, there was no other choice.

Good for esprit de corps, he reasoned, though his back muscles might never be the same. Worse, he had trouble falling asleep, even though he was dead tired. He'd had one of the bomb handlers rope off a little section for him, stringing blankets as a temporary barrier for privacy, but they did nothing to shut out the noise. The hangar's metal walls and ceiling amplified every creak and cough.

Samson lay awake for hours, staring at the bluish black ceiling high above his head, breathing the stale air that smelled vaguely of exhaust, trying to fall asleep.

And now that he had *finally* drifted off, some jackass was shaking him awake.

Who?

"Who the hell is it?" he grumbled, trying to unstick his eyes.

"It's Dog."

Bastian! It figured.

"What the hell, Colonel?"

"General, something's up," Dog told him. "Troops are mobilizing. There's a report of a guerrilla attack on the Romanian president's house about a hundred miles east of here."

It took Samson a second to process the words. Then he sprang up.

"An attack on the president? By the guerrillas?"

"It may be."

"Get a plane in the air."

"The *Johnson* just took off."

DOG TOLD SAMSON ABOUT WHAT HAD HAPPENED ON THE mission as they walked to the Command trailer. Samson, who didn't know Stoner, did not seem particularly bothered by the loss of the helicopter.

He also wasn't impressed by the downing of the MiGs, which Dog assured him had taken place inside Romanian territory.

"As long as you obeyed orders and didn't go over the border," he muttered, trotting up the trailer steps ahead of Dog.

Sergeant Liu had just gotten off the phone with the Romanian Second Army Corps headquarters. The sergeant confirmed that there was "some action taking place," but told them there was no need for Dreamland units at the present time.

"The hell with that," said Samson. "We should have more than the *Johnson* up. Get the B-1s ready. And your plane, Bastian."

Dog nodded. "The *Bennett* should be ready in an hour. I sent someone to wake up the crew."

"Make it thirty minutes."

Dog couldn't help but smile.

"What?" snapped Samson.

"If I said five minutes, you'd say one."

Samson frowned—but then the corners of his mouth twisted up.

"You expect anything less?" the general asked.

"Jed Barclay on the line," said Liu.

Out of habit, Dog took a step toward the communications area, then stopped. Talking to Washington was Samson's job now.

Bacau, Romania
2335

"WHAT THE HELL DO YOU MEAN, YOU CAN'T FIND THE PRESI-dent?" thundered General Locusta over the phone line. "Where is he?"

Major Ozera did not answer.

"Voda's house is not that big," continued the general. "Where the hell is he?"

"There was considerable damage from the mortars," said the major. "We think he was in the basement somewhere. Some of the timbers have fallen and there was—"

"Find the body. Find the body," repeated Locusta. "What about the bodyguards?"

"They're all accounted for. We think."

"You *think?*"

Even though Locusta was alone in his office, using his private satellite phone rather than his regular line, he knew he had to restrain himself. As thick as the walls were, there was always the chance that he might be overheard if he raised his voice. And besides, a temper tantrum would not help him in the least.

If Voda had escaped, things would be very complicated indeed. But Locusta was in too far now. He'd already given orders mobilizing his units, had instructed his network to begin spreading rumors that the president was dead, and had called his ally in the capital, telling him to call his men out as well.

"Make sure your men are in charge," he told Ozera. "You conduct the search personally."

"Yes, of course. The regular troops have only just gotten here."

"Keep them in the dark. Order them to shoot at anything that moves."

"Yes, General."

"Keep me updated," Locusta said. He hung up the phone. It rang immediately. "Locusta."

"Bucharest," said a male voice. "Done."

The line clicked dead. Locusta hung up again, feeling much more confident. The defense minister had been assassinated. An irritant had been removed.

This was a time for action, not doubt. Locusta rose from his desk, grabbed his satellite phone and strode from the office.

"I am going to the president's house," he told his staff in the conference room. "I will personally take charge of the situation there. Nothing to the media," he added, turning to his public relations officer. "Nothing, official or unofficial, without my express approval."

The man's face paled. Locusta guessed that he had already started feeding tidbits to favored reporters.

The general savored that look of fear as he walked to his car.

Dreamland Command trailer,
Iasi, Romania
2345

DOG FROZE THE INFRARED VIDEO FEED FROM THE *JOHNSON*'S Flighthawk showing the back of the president's house.

"Serious munitions hit that house," he said, pointing at the screen. "Maybe mortar shells, maybe RPG rounds. At least a half dozen."

"The guerrillas could have either," said Samson.

"True." Dog hit the Play button, letting the image proceed.

"Are you seeing this, Mr. Barclay?" asked Samson.

"We see it," said Jed Barclay, speaking from the White House Situation Room. "Please continue the feed. We want to see the area."

More Romanian troops were arriving at a command post set up on the road below the house. From the looks of things, the Romanians believed some of the guerrillas had escaped and they were trying to seal off the area.

"That's what we have, Jed," said Dog. "Anything else new on your end?"

"We're sorting through everything. The CIA station chief reported rumors that the president was dead. We'll be back on with you in a few minutes."

Dog leaned back from the console and glanced at Samson, who was standing against the partition of the communications area. The general's stubble and his combat fatigues were almost jarring; for the first time since they'd met, Samson didn't look like an actor playing the role.

"You think it's a coup?" Samson asked.

"If I had to bet, that's where I'd put my money," said Dog.

"So would I," said Samson.

Dog pulled off his headphones and rose. "Want some coffee?" he asked Samson.

"Yes," said the general.

There was almost always fresh coffee on the sideboard of the trailer's main room, but tonight was an exception. Dog started hunting through the cabinets, looking for the filters and coffee. He was just filling the pot with water when Samson emerged from the communications shack.

"I thought maybe you went into town for it," said the general.

From anyone else, the comment would have seemed a good-natured rib. Samson, however, looked serious.

"Coffee is not my specialty," said Dog.

"Relax, Bastian. That was a joke."

Dog held the pot up, squinting at the numbers to make sure he had the right level of water.

"I hope your eye exam isn't due soon," said Samson.

This time Dog laughed.

Samson, though, had apparently meant the comment in earnest, and gave him a puzzled stare. "Sometimes I don't know how to take you, Bastian," he said.

"Well, General, pretty much what you see is what you get." Dog poured the water into the machine. "If it is a coup, we have to stay out of it."

"I don't know that we have any choice." Samson came over as the coffee dripped through and took a cup down from the cupboard. Then he got one for Dog. "Damn cot wrenched my back."

"I think the beds in Diego Garcia permanently twisted one of my vertebrae," said Dog.

"Good coffee, Bastian," said Samson, taking a cup. "Now let's get those planes in the air."

White House
1345 (2345 Romania)

PRESIDENT MARTINDALE SWIVELED HIS CHAIR TO THE LEFT to get a better view of the video screen. The flat panel screen, some eighty-four inches diagonally, was a technical marvel, thin and yet capable of supplying a picture several times sharper than a cathode ray tube.

Martindale's main technology advisor predicted it would be standard fare in American homes within a decade, but for now, the secure conference room in the White House basement had the only one in existence.

A feed from Romanian television played on the screen, reporting that the defense minister had been gunned down in Bucharest. The body of his assassin—the newscaster called him "a criminal," implying that he was a guerrilla—had been found nearby, apparently shot by the defense minister's bodyguards.

"It's a military coup," said Secretary of State Hartman as the broadcast continued. "There's no other explanation."

He and Martindale had come directly from the reception, and were both still wearing their tuxedos. They were alone in the room with Jed Barclay, who was briefing them on the situation. Defense Secretary Chastain and Admiral Balboa, representing the Joint Chiefs of Staff, were at the Pentagon, linked via a secure video conference line. National Security Advisor Freeman was across the hall in the Situation Room, trying to reach the Kremlin to get an explanation for the interference in Moldova.

"Are you sure the phone call the embassy received is legitimate?" said Chastain. "Anyone could have pretended to be Voda."

"It came on the ambassador's personal line," said Hartman. "And I trust his judgment implicitly. One hundred percent."

"I didn't mean he was lying, just mistaken."

The embedded encryption mechanism made Chastain's voice sound slightly tinny.

"But Art's point is well taken," said Martindale. "We have to keep it in mind as we proceed."

The President rose and took a short stroll behind the large table at the center of the conference room, trying to focus his thoughts and work off his excess energy. His shoulder grazed the wall as he walked. At the beginning of his term, a set of photographs showing his predecessor at work had adorned the paneled walls. Martindale had had them removed, not because they were a distraction or even because of professional jealousy, but because the space was so narrow behind the chair that he often bumped into the photographs when taking walks like this.

"We have to help Voda," said Hartman. "We simply have to."

"Anything we do will be seen as interfering in Romania's internal politics," said Chastain. "And as a practical matter, there's probably nothing we can do."

"We can share the information that he's alive," said Hartman.

"If it's him."

Under other circumstances, the President might have been amused by the role reversal that his two cabinet ministers had undergone: Ordinarily, Chastain was in favor of intervening no matter how complicated the situation, and Hartman was for sitting on the sidelines no matter how clear the case for action. But over the last few days, Romania and the gas line had become so critical to Europe's future that Martindale was hardly in a mood to be anything other than worried.

While he believed that all countries were best governed by democracies, he knew foreign democracies would not always act in America's best interest. It could be argued that a stable Romania was much more important to the United States, and to Europe, than one with a weak and divided government. In the long run a takeover by the military might not be bad; for one thing, it would probably bring a change in spending priorities that would fund better defense to protect the pipeline.

Still, a military coup in Romania would kill any hope for NATO and EU membership, and add greatly to the sense of instability currently sweeping the continent. The new regime might also veto Martindale's tentative arrangements with Voda to utilize bases in the south of the country, where Martindale hoped to shift some forces from Germany to bring them closer to the Middle East and Iran.

"If we say Voda is alive and he turns up dead, we'll be crucified," said Chastain.

"But if he is alive and he needs our help," countered Freeman, "we should give it."

"How?" said Chastain.

"Dreamland."

"Even Dreamland can't take on the entire Romanian army."

"Maybe not," said Martindale, rejoining the conversation. "But they could rescue Voda. If he's alive. If they found him."

Philip Freeman came into the room. He shook his head—the Russians had refused to communicate with him so far. Martindale explained what he was thinking.

"Very dangerous, Mr. President," said Freeman.

"Worth the risk," said Hartman immediately. "We take him out of harm's way, then let the Romanians sort it all out. We'll be the heroes."

"Or the people caught in the middle, catching hell from both sides," said the President. "But let's see if we can do it. Jed. Put us through to Dog."

"General Samson is in charge of the detachment now," said Admiral Balboa, speaking for the first time since joining the conference.

"Yes, my mistake," said Martindale. "Jed, get me the general. But make sure Bastian is there too."

The Russian Embassy,
Bucharest
2345

"LOCUSTA HAS FINALLY MADE HIS MOVE," SVORANSKY SAID into the phone. "Now is the time to strike."

The Russian military attaché put his elbow on the desk

and reached for the vodka he had poured earlier. The only light in his office was coming from the flickering LEDs on his computer's network interface, and from the machine that scrambled his telephone communications to Moscow.

"We have lost two planes already to the Americans tonight," replied Antov Dosteveski. "Your entire program was too provocative."

"The program came from the president, not me," said Svoransky. "I am telling you—if we are ever to strike a lasting blow against the pipeline, the time is now. The country is in confusion. General Locusta has launched his coup and will not be in a position to stop your attack."

"And the Americans?"

"Shoot them down! I cannot fly the planes for you!"

Svoransky slammed the phone down angrily. Dosteveski was a general in the Russian army, detailed by the Kremlin specifically to work with him on the project to disrupt the gas line. Like all too many generals these days, he seemed particularly risk adverse.

Svoransky took a strong swig of his vodka. In the old days, generals gave brave orders: shoot down American planes when they violated Soviet air space, sink a submarine in revenge for sinking one of theirs, crush piddling governments when they stood in the way. Now the men leading the Russian army were afraid of their own shadows.

Dreamland Whiplash Osprey
2347

THE OSPREY FERRYING DANNY FREAH AND SERGEANT Boston back to Iasi was about twenty minutes from touchdown when the call came through from General Samson. Danny took a headset from the crew chief and sat in one of the jump seats next to the cabin bulkhead.

"This is Freah," said Danny, suppressing a yawn.

"Captain, we have a particular tactical situation you may be able to assist with," said Samson. "We're going to need your input on it."

"Sure," said Danny. "We're about twenty minutes shy of landing."

"We want your ideas right now," said Dog, coming onto the line. "Can you talk?"

"Um, sure. Why not?"

Danny listened as Dog described the situation. The president of Romania had apparently been attacked by troops posing as guerrillas and was believed to be hiding somewhere on his mountain property.

"President Martindale wants us to rescue him, as discreetly as possible," said Dog. "But we don't know exactly where he is. And the place is ringed by Romanian soldiers."

"Can you formulate a plan to extricate him?" asked Samson.

"If I knew exactly where he was, maybe."

"The ambassador is working on that," said Samson. "In the meantime, prepare a plan."

"Tell us what you need," added Dog. "Equipment, other information. We'll have it waiting for you when you land."

**Presidential villa,
near Stulpicani, Romania
2354**

THE PUMP HOUSE WAS MORE OVERGROWN THAN VODA REmembered. Brambles covered about three-quarters of the front and side walls. A tree had grown so close that it appeared to be embedded at the back. Hiding here was out of the question.

"We'll rest behind the tree," he told his wife and son. "We'll rest, and then we'll find another place."

"Where, Papa?" asked Julian.

"On the other side of the hill," said Voda. He glanced at his wife. Her expression, difficult to make out in the shadows cast by the trees, seemed to border on despair.

"I'm going to scout ahead. Stay here with your mother," Voda told his son. Then he pointed to a clump of trees. "Mircea. Hide there. I'll be back."

"Don't leave us, Papa," said Julian.

"I'll be right back," he told him. "I won't be far."

Voda was lying—he wanted to use the phone but didn't want either of them to hear how desperate he was. He had to stay positive, or at least as confident as he could, to buoy their spirits.

So far, he hadn't heard the dogs, but that was just a matter of time.

Voda walked in as straight a line as he could manage, stopping when he could no longer make out the large tree that rose from the side of the pump house. He took out the mobile phone and dialed the American ambassador's number. The phone was answered on the first ring.

"I am still alive," he said.

"Mr. President, we will help you as much as we are able to. Where exactly are you?"

Voda hesitated. There were many reasons not to trust the Americans. But there was no other choice.

"There is a pump house behind my property, half hidden in the woods. We cannot stay there very long. There are many soldiers still arriving. I hear many trucks. What is going on?"

"The news is reporting that the defense minister was assassinated by guerrillas," said the ambassador. "They are also reporting rumors of your death."

"Prematurely."

"Our satellites have seen troop movements all across the country. It seems pretty clear that there's a coup, and that the plotters intend to kill you."

"Who is behind it?"

"I don't know, Mr. President. I would hesitate to make a guess without some sort of evidence, and I have none."

It had to be Locusta, Voda thought. It was his area of command, and he was the only one powerful enough to even dare.

"I want you to call General Locusta. Tell him that I know that he is behind this, and that he is to stand down," said Voda. "Tell him . . . "

Voda considered what to say. His instincts told him to be strong with the general—fierce. But perhaps it would be wiser to work out a deal.

"Tell him he must stand down," Voda repeated finally.

"I don't know if that will do much good coming from me, Mr. President."

Voda sensed that was a diplomatic answer—probably Washington had told him not to interfere.

"Are you going to help me or not?" asked Voda, struggling to keep himself from bleating.

"Yes. We will try to rescue you if we can. If you want."

Hope!

"Of course I want," said Voda, practically shouting.

"I want to connect you directly with the Dreamland people who have been supporting your counterterrorist troops. They will help you."

The loud bay of a dog echoed up the hillside.

"Are you there, Mr. President?" asked the American ambassador.

"Give me the number."

"I can connect you, or have them call you."

"No. Tell me the number now. It's not safe for them to call me; the phone can be heard, even when just buzzing. I will call them when I can, in a few minutes. Right now I have to move my family to safety."

**Presidential villa,
near Stulpicani, Romania
29 January 1998
0010**

THE HELICOPTER GENERAL LOCUSTA COMMANDEERED TO get up to the president's mountain house had been used during the Moldovan operation. There hadn't been enough time to completely clean the interior, and spots of dried blood covered the floor. Locusta stared at the blood, brooding. The operation had been successful, though if the Americans had deigned to provide better support, he would not have lost the helicopter with Brasov aboard.

The colonel had always been a problematic officer—a fine leader, but headstrong, occasionally impulsive, and unfortunately as committed to democracy as he was to getting ahead. He would have had to watch Brasov carefully had he lived—so perhaps it was a blessing in disguise after all.

But now that he was dead, Locusta missed him, and mourned the loss of his spirit. He was the sort of man an army needed.

The kind a country needed. Like himself.

A command post had been set up at the intersection of Highway 34 and the road leading up to President Voda's property. There was a field next to the intersection; a pair of spotlights and some small signal flares marked the area for the helicopter to set down.

Locusta sprang out as soon as the pilot nodded to him. Head down against the swirling wind, he ran toward the men standing near the road.

"General, we're glad you're here," said Major Ozera. "The situation is under control."

"You've found President Voda?"

"We expect to shortly. There was a tunnel from the house to a small cave at the edge of the property. We have dogs following his scent."

"Good."

Locusta looked around. About two dozen troops were holding defensive positions near the road.

"You've given orders that anyone found is to be shot?"

"Of course," said Ozera. "As you ordered. The troops have been told that the president is dead and that we're looking for the guerrillas. The special team is with the dogs," he added. "They won't get away."

"They had best not. They have already failed once."

Ozera didn't answer. The "special team" was the hand-picked group of assassins who had made the initial assault.

"Pull as many of the troops back as possible," Locusta told him. "Bring in more weapons, enough to fight a large force. But keep them a good distance away. Have only your men on the property."

"I've brought up everything we had," said the major. "Everything except the antiaircraft guns."

"Bring them. They're very useful."

The Zsu-23-4 mobile antiaircraft guns looked like tanks with four 23mm cannons mounted at the front of a flattened turret. They could be used against ground or air targets, as necessary.

"Our command post should be up at the house," Locusta added.

"Yes. Let me place these new orders, then get a driver."

While he was waiting for Ozera to return, Locusta called his headquarters.

"The Dreamland people keep calling to ask if we need help," said his chief of staff. "What should we tell them?"

"Tell them the situation is under control," said Locusta. "Tell them to remain on the ground. Tell them the situation is very confused, and we don't want them getting in the way."

"They already have at least one plane in the air, General. And we understand more are being readied."

"Tell them I'm traveling to the president's home personally and will confer with them soon," said Locusta. "But emphasize that we do not need them, and do not want them in the air."

"Yes, sir."

"Where is the plane they have in the air?"

"I can check with air defense."

"Do it. Call me back immediately."

"Yes, sir, General."

**Dreamland Command trailer,
Iasi
0010**

"IT'S TOO RUGGED TO LAND NEAR THAT PUMP HOUSE," SAID Danny, pointing to the satellite photo of the area. "But if they can come up the slope a bit, over to around here, we can lower a basket, take them out like it's a rescue. Even in the dark it shouldn't be that hard."

"Can we get in there without being seen?" asked Samson.

"The Osprey is black, so it's hard to see," answered Danny. "But it is pretty loud. I would say the people on the ground would know we're there."

"The President wanted this done without the Romanians knowing we're involved," said Samson.

"I'd like to get in and out quietly too, General," said Danny. "The less people who know we're there, the safer we are. But no aircraft is silent."

"I think we just have to do our best," said Dog. "If they see us, they see us. But we can't not grab him because we might be seen."

"I didn't say we weren't going to do it, Bastian," snapped Samson. He turned back to Danny. "What sort of team will you need?"

"If we can sneak in? I'd say a three man team—Boston, Liu, myself. We don't want too many people because we want to move as fast as possible. For air support, one Flighthawk to show us what's going on, another if things get tight to cover our exit. And whatever else you can throw at them if all hell breaks loose."

"We could run the Flighthawks as a diversion," said Zen. "Do a low and slow approach along the road, have the Osprey come in from the north. That might solve the problem of the noise."

"If it's noise we're trying to cover," said Dog, "let's bring one of the EB-52s down close. That makes a hell of a racket."

"Good," said Samson. "We can use one of the B-1s as well—a nice sonic boom should get their attention."

"I thought you didn't want to be seen," said Danny.

Samson looked at Dog. "I think we can interpret the order to the effect that you're not to be seen," he said. "And take it from there."

"Where do we go when we have him?" Danny asked.

"The American embassy," said the general.

"Is that where he wants to go?"

"Why wouldn't he want to go to the embassy?" asked Samson.

"If I was the president, I'd want to go to my office, rally my troops."

"We can deal with that after we have him," said Dog.

"Bastian's right. Let's just grab him." Samson leaned across the conference table, looking at the Osprey pilots. "How long before you can get in the air?"

"As soon as the aircraft is fueled, we're good to go."

"Colonel Bastian!" Sergeant Liu stuck his head out from the communications area. "The *Johnson* is reporting four MiGs coming hot and heavy toward the Romanian border, straight across the Black Sea."

Aboard EB-52 *Johnson*,
over northeastern Romania
0012

LIEUTENANT KIRK "STARSHIP" ANDREWS TRIED TO IGNORE the pull of the Megafortress as it turned toward the north, focusing all of his attention on the control screens in front of him. His Flighthawks—*Hawk Three* and *Hawk Four*—were just passing through 25,000 feet, climbing toward 30,000. The *Johnson*'s radar was tracking four MiGs, flying in tight formation at roughly Mach 1.2, coming across the Black Sea.

"What's the word on the ROEs?" Starship asked the *Johnson*'s pilot, Lieutenant Mike Englehardt, referring to their rules of engagement—the orders directing when they could and couldn't use force.

"No change. We're not to engage beyond the border."

"These guys are loaded for bear," Starship told him. "They're either coming for us or they're going to hit something in Romania. Either way, I say we take them down now."

"Our orders say no."

"Screw the orders."

"Yeah, we'd all like to, Starship," said the pilot. "But our job is to follow them. We'll get them when they cross."

"By then it may be too late. What's Dog say?"

"It's not up to him."

Starship nudged his control yoke, bringing *Hawk Three* on course for a direct intercept of the MiGs. He could take at least one of the planes down when they came across the border; with a little luck and help from the computer, he might get two. The *Johnson* could shoot down the rest with Scorpion-plus air-to-air missiles.

But by then the MiGs would be in position to launch their own attack, albeit at long range, against either the *Johnson* or the pipeline.

"Radar profiles indicate bandits are equipped with two AS-14 Kedge and free-falls," said the radar operator. "Possibly GPS guided. Aircraft are still proceeding on course."

Free-falls were bombs dropped almost directly over the target; they could be guided to their destination by the addition of a small guidance system that used GPS readings. More deadly were the AS-14 Molinya missiles, known to

NATO as the Kedge. The air-to-ground missile could be guided by laser, thermal imaging, or television. In some respects similar to the American-made Maverick, its range was about ten kilometers—just enough to hit the gas pipeline without crossing the border.

"They'll be in range before the border, or just after it," Starship told Englehardt. "Look, they shot down the helicopter. Things have changed."

"Look, you're preaching to the converted," Englehardt replied. "I'm already on the line with them."

Dreamland Command trailer,
Iasi
0012

"IF THEY'RE CARRYING BOMBS, MY BET IS THEY'RE GOING after the gas line," Dog told General Samson. "They'll do serious damage, a lot more than that guerrilla strike. Given the tactical situation, I'd say we should consider the rules of engagement obsolete. I say we get them right now."

Part of Samson wanted to agree; the other part realized that this was just the sort of thing that could be used to end his career.

"We can always call Washington," suggested Dog.

Samson started to reach for the headset, intending to do just that, then stopped. Bastian was lionized in Washington. Why? Because he didn't stop and ask for permission every time he wanted to do what was right. He just went ahead and did it, consequences be damned.

A good way to end your career if you were a general, however.

But damn it, Bastian was right. If they hesitated now, the pipeline would be blown up. And he would get the blame for that, no matter what else happened.

"Give me that damn headset," he told Dog.

Aboard EB-52 *Johnson*,
over northeastern Romania
0013

GENERAL SAMSON'S GRAVELY VOICE BOOMED IN STARSHIP'S
ears.

"This is Samson. What's your status, Flighthawks?"

"Ready to engage, General. If I can cross the border."

"That's what I want to hear. Shoot the bastards down.
Those are my orders."

The line snapped clear.

"Wow, he sounded a little like Colonel Bastian," said Englehardt.

"Nothing wrong with that," said Starship, changing course
as he laid on the gas.

Like most pilots who had the misfortune to deal with
Flighthawks, the MiG drivers didn't realize they were under
attack until the first flash of bullets streaked across their
windscreens. By then it was too late for the lead pilot. Within
seconds of Starship pressing his trigger, the MiG's cockpit
exploded.

Hawk Three's momentum took it out of position to attack
the second MiG in the formation, as Starship had originally
planned. He jammed his controls, trying to drag the small
plane's nose around to the north to get a shot as the MiG shot
past. But the MiG pilot had gone to afterburners as soon as he
saw the flare of the gun in the night sky, and Starship realized
following him would be pointless.

"*Bandit Two* is by me," Starship told Englehardt.

"Roger that, we see him."

Starship felt the bomb bay's doors opening behind him
as he turned his attention to *Hawk Four,* which he'd aimed
at the other two MiGs. The computer had flown the plane
perfectly, but its human counterpart in the MiG managed to
evade the Flighthawk's first attack, pushing over and twisting

away in a ribbonlike pattern, despite the heavy burden under its wings.

Starship took over the plane from the computer, trying to press the attack as the targeting pipper blinked red, then turned to yellow. Abruptly, the plane squirted upward, throwing the Flighthawk by him in a flash. The maneuver worked, but Starship realized that the weight of his bombs would negate most if not all of his engines' advantage over the Flighthawk. He pulled the robot plane back in the MiG's direction, matching the climb. As he got closer, the Russian rolled his plane over. Starship got two bursts in, then slid on his wing to follow. As the MiG leveled, it ejected his weapons stores and asked the engines to give him everything he had.

"Missiles!" yelled Starship.

"Weapons are AS-12 Keglers," said the radar operator. "He's out of range. They won't make the border."

"*Bandit Three* is out of it," Starship reported. "I'm going after *Bandit Four*."

"Starship, we have two Sukhois coming at us from the north," warned Englehardt.

"Copy," said Starship, filing the information away in his brain. It was too theoretical to act on at the moment.

"Splash *Bandit Two*!" said the copilot, Lieutenant Terry Kung. "Two hits!" The Megafortress's missiles had just taken down the MiG.

Bandit Four had tucked south, away from Romania, but was now coming back north. Starship took over *Hawk Three*, slapping the throttle slide against the final detent as he vectored toward an intercept.

Zen had once described flying the robot aircraft as an act of sheer imagination—that to fly the Flighthawks successfully, a pilot had to see himself in the cockpit. Sometimes, Zen claimed, the illusion became so real he could feel the plane shake and shudder in the air.

Starship disagreed. He didn't feel any illusion that he was

inside *Hawk Three* as it thundered toward the MiG. He didn't think of either plane as a plane at all—they were vectors and flashes on his screen, triangles and dots, with a thick box at the top of the screen showing where the MiG's lethal range began.

The MiG altered course, heading toward the southern end of the box. *Hawk Three* was coming at him from an angle off his right wing. According to the computer, it would arrive at an intercept in exactly fifty-two seconds.

The computer also calculated that Starship would have exactly three seconds on target—enough for a single burst of gunfire.

Probability of a fatal hit: twenty percent.

"*Johnson,* can you take *Bandit Four*?" Starship asked.

"We're being targeted by the Sukhois," said Englehardt. "We have only four missiles left."

"I'll get one of the Sukhois," said Starship.

"Negative. Take the MiG. We have the Sukhois."

Engelhardt's choice was technically correct—the Mega-fortress had to be protected at all costs, and the *Johnson* was in a better position to strike the Sukhois immediately. But in Starship's opinion it was too conservative. Following the book, Englehardt was clearly intending to fire two missiles each at the Sukhois to cover for any malfunctions or screw-ups. One of those missiles could be used against the MiG, with the Flighthawks backing him up.

There was no time to argue. Starship tried to urge some more speed from the Flighthawk, nudging his nose down, but he was already at roughly the same altitude as his quarry and couldn't afford to give up much.

"Intercept in thirty seconds," said the computer.

The targeting pip appeared. It was solid yellow. He wasn't even close to a shot.

The MiG started to turn west, taking it even farther from the Flighthawk. He wasn't going to make it.

He didn't have to shoot the MiG down—not on his first try, anyway. All he had to do was get him to break off his attack.

The Russian had overreacted to the first encounter, going south. Maybe he could be bluffed into doing that again.

Starship pushed the Flighthawk to the right and began firing, even though the piper showed he was still out of range. The change in the angle put his bullets even farther off the mark. But it also made his tracers more obvious—he wanted the MiG pilot to know he was under the gun.

The first burst had no effect, but as he laid on a second, the Russian dipped on its left wing and dove off to the left, heading southwestward.

A warning flashed on Starship's screen as he went after it.

HAWK 3: LOSS OF CONTROL CONNECTION IN TWENTY SECONDS.

"Johnson, I need you to stay with me," he said.

"We have to deal with the Sukhois," said Englehardt.

Starship gave *Hawk Three* to the computer, telling it to stay on the MiG; it would fly pursuit even if the connection was lost. Then he took *Hawk Four* and pulled it south. It was still too far from the MiG to get into a tangle, but he might be able to use it when the MiG came back toward its target.

The *Johnson,* meanwhile, was climbing northward over the mountains, moving away from the Sukhois. The Su-27s were carrying several air-to-air missiles, but as of yet had not targeted the Megafortress.

HAWK 3: CONTACT LOST

Starship flicked the sitrep plot onto his main screen as the Flighthawk separated from his control. The MiG was still running due west. Starship thought, sooner or later, the pilot had to turn north.

Maybe he had a secondary target. Starship reached to his left, tapping the control for the mapping module in the computer. The module could display details on ground features, with identification tags such as highway routes.

"Highlight pipeline," Starship told the computer.

"Instruction not understood."

"Highlight trans-Romanian gas pipeline," he said.

"Instruction not understood."

Frustrated, Starship put his finger on the pipeline that the MiG had been targeting.

"Identify."

"IFC International Pipeline Junction 245A," said the computer.

"Highlight IFC International Pipeline and all junctions."

The pipeline lit in yellow on the map, with small rectangles of color along the way.

There was a block ten miles south of *Hawk Three*—exactly on the vector the MiG was taking.

His secondary target.

"*Johnson,* move west," said Starship.

"We will if we can."

"He has a target to the west. This is it," said Starship, tapping his computer to transmit the image to the pilot's console.

"Missiles in the air!" said the copilot. "Mini-Moshkits— they're homing in on our radar!"

Iasi, Romania
0015

ZEN STOPPED AT THE FOOT OF THE ACCESS RAMP AS HE came out of the trailer.

"Breanna, what the hell are you doing here?" he said, shocked to see his wife.

"Hello to you too, lover." She walked over and kissed him.

"No, really, why are you here?" he insisted.

"I'm here as a copilot on *Boomer,*" she said, pointing in the direction of the plane. "What's the matter?"

"There's no way in the world you should be flying."

"What?"

"Jeez, woman."

"What do you mean, 'jeez woman'?"

"You were—hurt."

"When?"

"Don't give me that. In India."

"So were you."

"You were unconscious for days, for God's sake."

"I was sleeping. The doctors say I'm fine."

Zen shook his head.

"You were on that island as long as I was," she said. Her face had flushed, her hands were on her hips, and her eyes had narrowed into slits. Zen knew she was mad, but he was furious as well.

"I wasn't knocked out in a coma," he told her.

"I'm better now. If you don't like it, tough." She turned and began stomping toward the hangar. Suddenly she stopped, spun around, and said, "And it's good to see you, too."

The people nearby tried pretending they hadn't noticed. Zen wheeled forward, angry that his wife was here, but not sure what he could do about it.

The door to the Command trailer opened, and he turned back as Colonel Bastian came down the ramp.

"Did you see her?" asked Zen.

"Who?"

"My wife."

"Breanna's here?"

"She's copiloting *Boomer.*"

Dog frowned but said nothing.

"You think that's OK?" he asked.

"Did she check out medically?"

"She claims she did."

"It's not up to me," Dog said finally. "Come on. We have to get in the air."

**Presidential villa,
near Stulpicani, Romania
0015**

ALIN VODA KNELT NEXT TO THE PUMP HOUSE, HOLDING HIS
son against his body to warm the boy. He was feeling the cold
himself. At first adrenaline had kept him warm, then fear;
now neither was sufficient as the temperature continued to
drop toward freezing.

The dogs were below them, near the creek. He wasn't sure
how much longer it would be before they picked up their
scent and started up the hill. But even if the dogs couldn't
track them, Voda knew that sooner or later the soldiers would
begin a large-scale search through the woods. The sounds of
trucks moving in the valley below filled the hills with a low
rumble. There must be dozens if not hundreds of potential
searchers.

The Americans had promised to help. Voda wasn't sure
what that promise would yield, but at the moment it was all
he had.

"They're coming up the hill," said Mircea. "What do we do?"

This was as far up the property as either of them had gone;
Voda had no idea what was beyond. But they clearly couldn't
stay here; if they did, they'd be discovered.

"Let's keep climbing," he said.

"Papa, I'm too tired," said Julian.

"You've got to get up!" shrieked Mircea, almost out of
control and far too loud. *"You've got to!"*

"Sssshhh," said Voda. He leaned down and hoisted the boy
up onto his back. It had been years since he'd carried him this
way, long years.

"Are we going to die, Papa?"

"No, no," said Voda, starting to walk. A tune came into his
head and he began to hum, gently, softly. He'd gone at least
a dozen yards before he realized it was the old folk song that
had started him on this path.

Iasi Airfield, Romania
0020

COLONEL BASTIAN'S FATIGUE LIFTED AS HE WATCHED THE ground crew top off the *Bennett*'s fuel tanks. Dog gave them a thumbs-up, then ducked under the belly and watched as the ordies—the bomb ordinance specialists—removed the safety pins and made sure the last Scorpion AMRAAM-plus was ready to be fired. There were four Scorpions and four Sidewinders on the revolving dispenser.

"How's it lookin', boys?" he asked.

"Ready for action, Colonel," said one of the crew dogs. "You want missiles on the wingtips?"

"No time. We have to get into the air."

"Yes, sir."

Not one of the three ground-crew members was legally old enough to drink, but each had a huge responsibility on his shoulders. Dog and the rest of the members of EB-52 *Johnson* were putting their lives in their hands.

"Ready for your walk-around, Colonel?" asked Technical Sergeant Chance Duluth.

"Where's Greasy Hands?" Dog asked. Parsons was the crew chief; Chance was his assistant.

"Chief Parsons is over straightening something out with *Boomer*, Colonel. He sends his regrets."

"Along with how many four letter words?" Dog asked, walking toward the front of the plane.

"Quite a few."

Chance—his name inevitably led to many poor puns—had worked under Parsons for many years. He had inherited the chief master sergeant's fastidious attention to detail, if not his gently cantankerous manner. Where Greasy Hands would frown, Chance would turn his head sideways, smile, and say, "Hmmm."

Dog was anxious to get airborne; the Osprey had already taken off, and the B-1s would shortly. He moved quickly through the preflight inspection, examining the exterior of the plane from its nose gear to the lights atop its V-shaped tail. In truth, he trusted the crew implicitly, and probably could have skipped the walk-around without feeling any less safe. But the inspection was as much ritual as examination, and it would have somehow felt disrespectful to the ground crew not to look over their work.

"Damn good job," said Dog loudly when he was done. "Damn good."

"Thank you, Colonel," said Chance. He'd probably heard that particular compliment a few hundred times, but his face still flushed with pride.

Dog was just about to go up the ramp into the belly of the plane when Zen rolled up.

"Beauty before age," Dog told the Flighthawk pilot.

"Oh yeah," said Zen, backing into the special lift hooks fitted to the ladder. "I'm feeling real beautiful tonight."

As Zen disappeared into the belly, Dog heard Breanna calling behind him. He turned around. She had her helmet and flight gear under her arm.

"Aren't you supposed to be getting ready to take off?" Dog asked her.

"They had a glitch and had to repack the computer memory. I have five minutes to . . . "

Her voice trailed off.

"Something wrong?" he asked.

"I just wanted—to talk to Zen."

"You have something to say to Zen, you better hurry. I'm taking off as soon as I buckle my seat belt."

"Thanks, Daddy." She kissed him and scampered up the ramp.

Dog shook his head. He hated when she called him Daddy while he was working.

ZEN LOOKED UP, STARTLED TO HEAR HIS WIFE'S VOICE behind him.

"What are you doing here?" he said. "Come to see how the other half live?"

"I don't want you mad at me," said Breanna. "I don't want to go on a mission with things between us—with things the way we left them."

"I'm not mad," he said.

"Yes you are. You think I should have stayed home. In bed."

"I do think that," he said.

"And you're mad. I can hear it in your voice. It's angry."

"I'm not mad." But even while saying this, Zen heard his tone. She was right; he did sound angry. "I'm mad a little."

"Just a little?"

He started to laugh. That was the problem with being in love with Breanna—you just couldn't be mad at her, no matter how hard you tried, or how justified you were.

"I guess I'm mad at you, but I'm not really mad at you," he told her. "I do love you. A lot."

She came close and hugged him, wrapping her arms around his head.

"What's with the parachute gear?" she asked, noticing that his emergency equipment was different.

"It's the new gizmo Annie Klondike worked up. I told you about it. MESSKIT."

"Is it ready?"

"More than ready," he told her. "Come on, now, get lost. We gotta get goin'."

"I'm out of here. Kick some butt."

Breanna smiled at him, then disappeared down the ladder to the tarmac.

**Aboard EB-52 *Johnson*,
over northeastern Romania
0030**

THE MIG PILOT, CONFIDENT THAT HE'D SHAKEN THE FLIGHT-hawks and knowing that the Romanian air defenses could not touch him, backed off on his speed in order to conserve fuel for the long trip home. He was at 15,000 feet, descending gradually, no doubt intending to glide right at his target, Starship thought, pop up as he pickled his bombs, then gun north over the border and head home.

As long as he stayed on his present course, *Hawk Four* would meet him exactly eight miles from his target—roughly a mile and a half before the MiG was in range to fire the air-to-ground missiles. And as an added bonus, *Hawk Three* would come back into Starship's control a few seconds later. The enemy plane would be caught between the two Flighthawks, its escape routes cut off.

A perfect plan, except for the fact that the *Bennett* was jinking hard to duck a pair of radar-seeking missiles.

The Russian weapons were Kh-131A radar-seeking mini-Moshkits. Based on the air-to-ground Kh-31P, the large anti-radiation missile used two stages: a standard solid-rocket engine for the first stage, with a jet engine taking over for the final stage. The jet engine was no ordinary power plant; it gave the missile an enormous burst of speed on its final approach, propelling the warhead to Mach 4.5. The acceleration was designed to make the missile more difficult for antimissile systems such as the Patriot to intercept.

There were several ways to deal with mini-Moshkits. Arguably the most effective was the simplest: turning off the Megafortress's powerful radar, to deprive the missile of its target. But doing that would essentially blind Starship, since the Flighthawks relied on the mother ship's radar for everything except firing their guns or scanning very close targets.

Starship left it to the Megafortress to deal with the missile as he concentrated on the MiG heading toward the gas pipeline. The computer's tactical section diagrammed the best angle of attack in his screen, suggesting that the Flighthawk pivot and swoop in directly on the fighter's tail. It was a no-brainer, and yet another example of the advantage the robots had over traditional planes. In a manned plane, the maneuver would knock the pilot unconscious.

Just as Starship reached the point where he had to start the cut, the Megafortress turned hard to duck the missiles. At the same time, the plane dropped about a hundred feet in a fraction of a second. He slammed against his restraints and, despite his pressure suit, felt his head start to float as the mother ship dropped sharply in the air.

Stay on him, stay on him, Starship told himself, trying to hold the Flighthawk to the proper path. The small plane made its turn, jerking its nose hard back toward its right wing, literally skidding sideways in the air. For a brief moment the plane's aerodynamic qualities were overcome by the laws of gravity and motion; it dropped more than two hundred feet, more like a brick than a plane. As the Flighthawk began to accelerate, the MiG popped into Starship's screen.

The pipper went red. The pilot pressed the trigger. Bullets flew past the MiG's right wing. Starship nudged his stick, working the stream toward the body of the target.

"Disconnect in five seconds," wailed the computer.

"Bitch," yelled Starship.

"Unrecognized command."

"Johnson!"

"Stand by to lose external radar," replied Englehardt.

That was about the last thing Starship wanted to hear.

UP ON THE FLIGHT DECK, LIEUTENANT ENGLEHARDT AND his copilot had managed to duck one of the radar homing missiles by their sharp maneuvers. But the other one kept coming, and was now just over twenty miles away.

"Radars are off," Terry Kung, the copilot, told Englehardt.

"Chaff. Turn."

As the copilot fired canisters of metal shards into the air to confuse the missile, Englehardt threw the Megafortress into a sharp turn south, then rolled his wing down, plunging like a knife away from the cloud of decoy metal. The maneuver was second nature in a teen-series fighter; the Megafortress, even with all its improvements over the standard B-52, groaned and shuddered.

The mini-Moshkit following them had a backup semi-active radar, which Englehardt expected would take over once it realized it had lost the signal it was following. If that happened, he hoped the radar would "see" the cloud of tinsel in the air, think it was the plane, and dive on it.

"Still not terminal," said Kung. The flare as the missile fired its hypersonic jet engine would be picked up on the Megafortress's infrared launch warning.

Englehardt pushed the Megafortress lower, then swung back to the east, trying to "beam" the missile's search radar and make it harder for the enemy to see him. But they were too close—he could feel the missile coming in.

**Presidential villa,
near Stulpicani, Romania
0040**

GENERAL LOCUSTA RESISTED THE URGE TO KICK THE DEAD bodies that been placed near the back of the garage at the president's mountain house. It wasn't out of respect for the dead that he didn't. On the contrary, he had no respect for any of the bodyguards, Voda's men all. But the soldiers looking on might not understand.

"These are the only people you found in the house?" he asked them.

"General, it wasn't us who found them," replied the sergeant who was standing with the two other men, both privates. "The special forces men who reached the house first placed them here."

According to Major Ozera, the special unit that had staged the attack had lost a dozen of their own, hastily evacuating them before the regular army arrived. In a way, thought

Locusta, it was good that so many commandos had died: It sharpened the survivors' lust for vengeance, for they had changed into their uniforms and now made up the party of searchers hunting the president.

Locusta walked toward the cave where Voda had supposedly hidden after the initial attack. He examined it, and despite the broken door had a difficult time believing Voda had been here. The cistern system Ozera claimed he had used to escape was closed with heavy metal panels; a weakling such as Voda would never be able to lift them.

The entire back of the house had been flattened by the mortars. More likely the president was buried under there. If the dogs were tracking anything, it was one of the bodyguards who'd been sleeping or had run away out of fear.

His satellite phone rang.

"What is it?" he snapped, answering before the first ring died.

"General, all of the Dreamland planes have taken off from Iasi, including the Osprey," said his chief of staff.

"The helicopter plane?"

"Yes, sir. Air defense reports that the Russians have attacked them near the border, and that at least one Russian airplane has been shot down."

What the hell was going on?

No sooner had the question formed than Locusta realized the answer: The Russians were gunning for the pipeline.

"Are any of our airplanes in the air?"

"Well no, General."

"Get the air force chief of staff. Tell him I want to talk to him personally. And tell him that we need his precious MiG-29s. The Russians are attacking us."

"Yes, General."

"And then find the number or whatever it is that I must call to speak to the Americans directly. To Colonel Bastian, the so-called Dog."

**Aboard EB-52 *Johnson*,
over northeastern Romania
0041**

STARSHIP'S MAIN SCREEN BLINKED AND AN ICON APPEARED
in the upper right corner, indicating that long-range radar was
no longer being provided to the Flighthawks. But the enemy
MiG and the triangular cross hairs targeting it remained at
the center of the screen, provided by the Flighthawk's own
radar.

Compared to the Megafortress's radar, which was as
powerful as the radar in an AWACS, the system aboard the
robot was very limited. But it was fine for the task at hand—
Starship steadied his thumb on the trigger, pushing the spray
of bullets into the MiG's wing.

The MiG's right wing suddenly seemed to expand. A
thin gray funnel appeared at the middle of it—and then red
flashed everywhere. One of Starship's bullets struck through
the disintegrating wing, hitting square on the detonator of a
five-hundred-pound bomb. The explosion that followed was
so severe, the shock waves sent the Flighthawk into a spin to
the left.

And then Starship's screen went blank. He'd lost his connection to the robot.

ON THE FLIGHT DECK ABOVE STARSHIP, ENGLEHARDT LEANED
closer to the instrument panel, willing the big plane away
from the missile. Panic vibrated through his arms and legs;
his throat felt as if it had tightened around a rock. He struggled to control the plane, and himself, jerking back to the
north as the copilot released another set of chaff.

"He's terminal! Big flare!" yelled Kung.

Englehardt tensed, bracing for the impact. He cursed himself—he should have knocked off the radar sooner.

There was a flash to the right side of the cockpit.

The missile?

If so, it had exploded before striking the Megafortress—far enough away, in fact, that the big aircraft shrugged off the shock of the ninety kilogram warhead without a shudder.

What?

. INCOMING MESSAGE flashed on the dedicated Dreamland communications screen. Englehardt tapped the screen with his thumb.

"You're welcome, *Johnson*," barked General Samson from *Boomer*. "Now get that radar back on so we can see what the hell these Russian bastards are up to."

**Aboard B-1B/L *Boomer*,
over northeastern Romania
0042**

BREANNA STOCKARD EXHALED SHARPLY AS SHE LEANED back from *Boomer*'s targeting console. Her head was still spinning—she'd barely strapped herself in for takeoff when General Samson saw that the *Johnson* was in trouble and ordered her to target the missile. Samson had pulled *Boomer* almost straight up, riding her powerful engines to the right altitude for the hit with no more than a half second to spare.

"All right, Stockard, good work." The general's voice was a deep growl. "Now let's get ourselves up north and ready for anything else these bastard Russkies throw at us."

"You got it, Gen."

Samson turned his head toward her. "If you're going to use a nickname, it's Earthmover."

"OK, Earthmover."

"That's more like it, Stockard," said Samson, pushing the plane onto the new course.

**Aboard EB-52 *Bennett*,
over northeastern Romania
0045**

DOG'S COMMENT ABOUT TAKING OFF AS SOON AS HIS RE-
straints were buckled was an exaggeration, but only just. The
Megafortress left the runway just on the heels of the B-1s,
getting airborne in time to use its radar to help orient *Boomer*
to the Russian missile tracking the *Johnson*. Data was shared
over the Dreamland Command network with all aircraft
in the battle package, and in fact could be shared with any
Dreamland asset anywhere in the world.

"Sukhois are turning south over the Black Sea," said
Rager. "Looks like there are two more MiG-29s approaching, though, high rate of speed, very low to the water. You
see them, Colonel?"

"I got them, Rager. Thanks." Dog flicked the Transmit
button. "EB-52 *Bennett* to *Johnson*. Mikey, how are you
doing up there?"

"We're holding together, Colonel," said Englehardt, the
Johnson's pilot. "But we're out of Scorpions."

"Roger that. I want you to go west and cover the area near
the president's summer house for the Osprey. We'll take your
station here."

Englehardt's acknowledgment was overrun by a broadcast
from General Samson, whose scowling face appeared in the
communications screen. Samson's visor was up, his oxygen
mask dangling to the side, his frown as visible as ever. But
to Dog's surprise, Samson didn't bawl him out for usurping
his authority.

"Mike, Dog is right. You get yourself down there and stay
out of trouble. You understand?"

"Yes, sir."

"Sorry, General," said Dog. "That was your call."

"No problem, Colonel. I couldn't have put it better myself.
Now, let's get ourselves ready for these MiG drivers. You

want to take them, or should we give the laser system another field test?"

**Aboard Whiplash Osprey,
approaching Stulpicani, Romania
0047**

DANNY FREAH PUT ON HIS SMART HELMET AND TAPPED INTO the Dreamland database, asking the computer with verbal commands to display the most recent satellite photo of the area where the president's house was located.

The picture was several days old, taken right after the attack on the pipeline, but it was adequate for planning purposes.

From the description that had been relayed to him, Alin Voda was hiding about a quarter mile northeast of his house, near an old structure. But the structure wasn't visible on the map. Danny zoomed in and out without being able to see it among the trees. Finally he backed out, looking for an easier spot to pick him up.

The hill was wooded all the way to its peak. There was a rift on the back slope about fifty feet down, where a drop created a bald spot. The Osprey couldn't land there, but they could fast-rope down, put the president into a rescue basket, and haul him back up.

They'd need some close-in reconnaissance before attempting the pickup, to figure out where the Romanians were. And they'd need a diversion to get into the area.

"What do you think, Cap?" asked Boston, who was standing beside him. "Doable?"

"Oh yeah, we can do it," Danny said, pulling off the helmet. "Just need a little coordination."

He checked his watch. The Osprey was roughly twenty minutes from the mountain house. Hopefully, Voda could hold out that long.

Aboard EB-52 *Bennett*,
above northeastern Romania
0049

THE TWO RUSSIAN AIRCRAFT APPROACHING THE ROMANIAN
coast of the Black Sea were brand new MiG-29Ms, upgraded
versions of the original MiG-29. Equipped with better avi-
onics and more hardpoints, the fighters were potent attack
aircraft, capable of carrying a wide range of weapons. Because they were flying so low, the *Bennett*'s radar was unable
to identify what missiles or bombs they had beneath their
wings, but their track made it clear they were heading for the
Romanian gas fields.

"How are we handling this, Colonel?" Zen asked Dog over
the interphone. He'd already swung his Flighthawks toward
the border to prepare for an intercept.

"You take first shot," Dog told him. "We'll take anything
that gets past you. *Boomer* will knock down any missiles."

"Roger that."

The MiGs were moving at just over 500 knots—fast, certainly, but with plenty of reserve left in their engines to accelerate. They were just under eighty miles from the border, and
another fifty beyond the Flighthawks; assuming they didn't
punch in some giddy-up, Zen knew he had nine and a half
minutes to set up the intercept.

Almost too much time, he mused.

"We have a pair of Romanian contacts, Colonel. Two MiG-
29s coming north from Mikhail Kogălniceanu."

The MiG-29s were the Romanians' sole advanced aircraft.
Older than the Russian planes, they were equipped with short-
range heat-seeking missiles and cannons. It would take considerable skill for their pilots to shoot down their adversaries.

Unless the Americans helped balance the odds.

"Let's talk to them," said Dog. "Sully, can you get us on
their communications channel?"

"Working on it now, Colonel."

Dreamland Command
28 January 1998
1450 (0050 Romania, 29 January 1998)

MACK SMITH HUNCHED OVER THE CONSOLE IN DREAMLAND Command, watching the combined radar plot from the *Bennett* and the *Johnson* that showed where all the Dreamland people were.

The one thing it didn't show was where President Voda might be.

Which, as he read the situation, was the one thing above all else it ought to show.

"What the hell's going on with that NSA chick?" Mack asked the techie to his right. "She get those cell towers figured out yet or what?"

"They're working on it It's not like they monitor every transmission in the world, Major."

Mack straightened. There ought to be an easier way to track Voda.

If the Megafortress types flying over Romania were the Elint birds— specially designed to pick up electronic transmissions—it'd be a no-brainer. They'd just tune to the cell phone's frequencies and wham bam, thank you ma'am, they'd have him.

But with all the high-tech crap in the planes that were there, surely there was some way to find the S.O.B.

The problem probably wasn't the technology—the problem was they didn't have enough geeks working it.

Mack turned around and yelled to the communications specialist, who was sitting two rows back. "Hey, you know Ray Rubeo's cell phone number?"

"Dr. Rubeo? He's no longer—"

"Yeah, just dial the number, would you? Get him on the horn."

Mack shook his head. He had to explain everything to these people.

Aboard B-1B/L _Boomer_,
over northeastern Romania
0053

"GENERAL, THERE'S AN URGENT TRANSMISSION COMING through from Romanian air defense command," said Breanna.

"About time they woke up," said Samson, tapping the communications panel at the lower left of the dashboard. "This is Samson."

"General Samson, stand by for General Locusta."

"Locusta. He's the army general, right?" Samson asked Breanna. "The one who's probably running the coup?"

She didn't get a chance to answer as Locusta came on the line.

"General Samson, I am sorry to say we have not had a chance to meet."

Samson had a little trouble deciphering Locusta's English.

"Yes, I'm glad to be working with you, too," he told him, trying not to arouse his suspicions.

"We understand the Russians are attacking. We have our own interceptors on the way."

"Yes, I've seen the radar, and my colonel is attempting to contact them. We'll shoot the bastards down, don't worry."

"We are obliged. We appreciate the assistance," said Locusta. "Now, we are conducting operations in the north, in the mountain areas east of Stulpicani. You'll please keep your aircraft clear of that area."

Samson decided to employ a trick he'd learned when he was young and ambitious—when in doubt, play dumb.

"This is in relation to the attack on the president's estate?" Samson asked.

"That's right."

"I have an aircraft in that region. We've been trying to get in contact with you," said Samson. "We can provide a great deal of help. We'll catch those bastards, too."

"Your assistance is appreciated but not needed," answered Locusta. "This is a delicate political matter, General. I'm sure you understand."

Sure, I understand, thought Samson—you want to take over the country and don't want any interference from us.

"I'm afraid I don't understand," said Samson. "We can help."

"Whether you understand or not, stay away from the area. I would hate to have one of your planes shot down accidentally."

The arrogant son of a bitch!

"Listen, General—" started Samson, before he realized Locusta had killed the connection.

**Aboard EB-52 *Bennett*,
over northeastern Romania
0054**

WITH GUIDANCE FROM THE *BENNETT,* THE TWO ROMANIAN MiGs were able to change course and set up their own intercept over Moldovan territory.

"Let them take the first shot," Dog told Zen. "But don't let the Russians get by."

"Roger that," said Zen.

He checked everyone's position on his sitrep, then dialed into the Romanian flight's communications channel. They were using the call signs Şoim Unu and Şoim Doi—*Falcon One* and *Falcon Two.*

"*Şoim Unu*, this is Dreamland Flighthawk leader. You read me?" said Zen. The word Şoim was pronounced "shoim."

"Flighthawk leader, we are on your ear," said the pilot.

"I'm your ear too," said Zen, amused. "You know American English?"

"Ten-four to this."

"You want to take both planes yourselves? Or should we divvy them up?"

"We may first attack. Then, you sloppy seconds."

"Where'd you learn English?"

"Brother goes to American college."

His letters back home must be a real blast, thought Zen.

"All right," he told the Romanians. "I'll be to the northeast. If they get past you, I'm on them. You won't see the UM/Fs on your radar. They're small and pretty stealthy."

"What is this UM/F?"

"Flighthawks. They're unmanned fighters."

"Oh yes, Flighthawk. We know this one very well."

Had he been flying with American or NATO pilots, Zen would have suggested a game plan that would have the two groups of interceptors work more closely together. But he wasn't sure how the Romanians were trained to fly their planes, let alone how well they could do it.

The Russian planes were in an offset trail, one nearly behind the other as they sped a few feet above the water toward land. The Romanians pivoted eastward and set up for a bracket intercept, spreading apart so they could attack the Russians from opposite sides.

At first Zen thought that the Russians' radar must not be nearly as powerful as American intelligence made them out to be, for the planes stayed on course as the two Romanians approached. Then he realized that the two bogeys had simply decided they would rush past their opponents. Sure enough, they lit their afterburners as soon as the Romanians turned inward to attack.

Şoim Unu had anticipated this. He bashed his throttle and shot toward the enemy plane.

"Shoot!" yelled Zen.

But the Romanian couldn't get a lock. The two planes thundered forward, the Romanian slowly closing the distance. And then suddenly he was galloping forward—the Russian had pulled almost straight up, throwing his pursuer in front of him.

Frustrated, *Şoim Unu*'s pilot fired a pair of his heat-seeking missiles just before he passed the enemy plane; one sucked on the diversionary flares the Russian had fired and plunged after it, igniting harmlessly a few feet above the water. The other missed its quarry and the flares, flying off to the west before self-detonating.

The Russian had proven himself the superior pilot, but he was no match for a plane he couldn't see. As he turned back onto his course, tracers suddenly flew past his cockpit. His first reaction was to push downward, probably figuring he was being pursued by the other Romanian plane and hoping to get some distance between himself and his pursuer. But he was only at 3,000 feet, and quickly found himself running out of altitude. He pulled back, trying to slide away with a jink to his right.

Zen pushed *Hawk One* in for the kill. As the Mikoyan turned, it presented a broad target for his 20mm cannon. Two long bursts broke the plane in half; the pilot grabbed the eject handles and sailed clear moments before the forward half of the aircraft spun out and corkscrewed into the Black Sea.

"One down," said Zen. "One to go."

Dreamland Command
1500 (0100 Romania)

"THIS IS RAY RUBEO."

"Hey, Dr. Ray, how's it hanging?"

"Major Smith. What a pleasure." Rubeo gave Mack one of his famous horse sighs. "To what do I owe the dubious honor?"

"We're in a little fix down here, and I need your help."

"I am no longer on the payroll, Major. In fact, I am no longer on any payroll."

"We have to locate this guy in Romania who has a cell phone, but we can't seem to get access to the cell tower network, at least not fast enough to grab him," said Mack, ignoring Rubeo's complaint. Geniuses were always whining about something. "And I don't have any Elint Megafortresses. I do have two radar planes, though, and two B-1s. Plus the Flighthawks and an Osprey. I figure there's got to be some way to track the transmission down. Like we cross some wires or tune in somehow—"

"Which wires do you propose to cross, Major?"

"I don't know. That's why I called you."

Rubeo sighed again, though not quite as deeply. "You have Flighthawks in the area?"

"Sure. Four of them."

Another sigh. This one was absolutely shallow.

A good sign, thought Mack.

"Reprogram one of the Flighthawk's disconnect directional homers to the cell phone frequency," said Rubeo.

"Oh sure. Cool. God, of course. How long will it take you?"

"If I were there and with access to the code library, and in a good mood, ten minutes."

"Five if you were in a bad mood, right?"

"The question is moot, Major. When I was fired, my Dreamland security clearance was revoked. We really shouldn't even be having this conversation."

Rubeo wasn't really fired. He had resigned by mutual consent. Forced out, maybe, but not really fired. Fired was different.

But he had a point about the clearance. Mack thought he could waive it on his authority.

Maybe.

What the hell. He was chief of staff for a reason.

"How long will it take you to get here?" he asked. "Or maybe I can send a helicopter—"

"By plane, it will take me six hours."

"Six hours?"

"I'm in Hawaii, Major. I decided to take the vacation I've been putting off for five years."

Rubeo hung up.

Mack wracked his brain, trying to think who he could trust with the job. One of the geeks over at the guidance systems department probably could do it, but which one?

Maybe one of the Flighthawk people.

No, the person he needed was Jennifer Gleason.

Chester, New Jersey
1805 (1505 Dreamland)

JENNIFER GLEASON PUT DOWN THE BOX OF TISSUES AS THE movie credits rolled across the television set. She'd watched Charlie Chaplin's *Modern Times*, and for some reason the ending made her cry.

Even though it was the third time she'd seen the movie this week.

The phone started to ring.

Should she answer it? It almost certainly wasn't for her. Unless it was her mother.

Or Dog.

More likely her mother, whom she didn't feel like talking to.

On the other hand, it might be her sister, whose house she was staying in while recuperating. Maybe she wanted to suggest plans for dinner or ask if they needed something.

Her sister didn't have a cell phone; if Jennifer didn't answer, she'd miss her.

Jennifer pitched herself forward on the couch, leaning on the arm to push upward. By the time she grabbed her crutch, the phone had rung for a second time. Her knee muscles had stiffened from sitting, and even though the distance from the living room to the kitchen was only ten feet at most, it seemed to take forever for her to reach the phone. The phone rang for the fourth time just as she grabbed it.

"Hello?"

"Jennifer Gleason, please," said an official sounding male voice.

"Speaking."

"Stand by, Ms. Gleason."

"Who—"

"Hey, Jen. How's it hanging?"

"Mack Smith?"

"One and the same, beautiful. Hey listen, we have a serious situation here. Do you have your laptop with you?"

"Of course."

"Great. *Greeeaaat.* Dr. Ray says this is super easy to do, with your eyes closed even . . . "

**Aboard EB-52 *Bennett*,
over northeastern Romania
0101**

WHILE ZEN AND *HAWK ONE* WERE TAKING CARE OF THE first Russian MiG, *Şoim Doi* had been hot on the tail of the second. The Russian fighter jock might or might not have been as accomplished as his wing mate, but he was far luckier. Jinking hard and tossing decoy flares as the Romanian closed on his tail, he managed to duck two heat-seekers without deviating too much from his course. *Şoim Doi* pressed on, closing for another two-fisted missile shot. But bad luck—or more accurately, the notoriously poor Russian workmanship involved in manufacturing the export versions of the Atoll missiles—saved the Russian pilot: the lead missile of the Romanian self-detonated prematurely, knocking out not only itself but its brother less than a half mile from the target.

Şoim Doi kept at it, however, following the MiG as it came east and crossed into Romanian air space. Zen, taking over

Hawk Two from the computer, pounced on the bandit from above, pushing the Flighthawk's nose toward the MiG's tail. With his first burst of bullets, the MiG jettisoned two of its bombs, then tucked hard right, then left, trying to pull away.

"Şoim Doi, I'm going to close right," Zen said, pushing the throttle to the limit. "Slide a little farther to his left and be ready if he goes toward you."

"Yes," answered the Romanian.

Zen turned the Flighthawk in toward the Russian and lit his cannon. A few bullets nicked the MiG's tail, but the pilot worked his stick and rudder so deftly that Zen couldn't nail him. He was just about to turn the plane over to Dog when a heavily accented voice warned him off. Şoim Unu had rejoined the fight.

The Romanian flight leader had circled around to the west and managed to get in front of the other planes as they jabbed at each other. He turned in, still pushing the pedal to the metal, and made a front quarter attack at high speed, cannon blazing. Most if not all of his bullets missed, but the spooked MiG driver rolled downward and to the south.

The move took him into the path of the other Romanian. Şoim Doi pumped a dozen or more 30mm slugs into the enemy MiG before he overtook the plane and had to break off.

Though battered, the Russian managed to come back north, pointing his nose in the direction of the pipeline. But there was no escape now—both Romanians were on his tail. The Russian fired his air-to-ground missiles—much too far from the pipeline to strike it—then turned hard to the right, trying to pull one of the Romanians by him so he could open fire. The maneuver worked, to an extent—Şoim Unu started to turn, then realized the trap and broke contact. Before the Russian could take advantage, however, Şoim Doi closed in for the kill. The canopy exploded and the Russian shot upward; by the time his parachute blossomed, his aircraft had crashed to the ground.

**Presidential villa,
near Stulpicani, Romania
0101**

GENERAL LOCUSTA FOLDED THE MAP OVER THE HOOD OF
the car. He was losing time; he wanted to be in Bucharest by
first light. This needed to be wrapped up. Now.

"What's this building?" he asked, pointing to a small
square on the map.

Major Ozera shook his head. "Abandoned. It's small.
One of our teams is near there now. The president is not
there."

"He has to be on the mountain somewhere."

Locusta looked back at the map. He could send swarms
of men onto the hill to find Voda, but he doubted they would
kill the president.

He would have Voda brought to him, take him into the
ruins, then have him killed.

Along with his family, who must be with him.

And the soldiers who found them? He'd have to kill them
too.

Was it worth risking complications?

Not yet.

Ozera and his men would have to do a better job.

The general's attention was distracted by the sound of a
helicopter flying nearby.

"I told you I didn't want the helicopters involved," Locusta
told the major. "Their pilots can't be trusted."

"It's not ours. The sound is different. Louder. Listen."

Locusta listened more carefully, then pulled out his satellite phone.

"Get me the Dreamland people. General Samson. Immediately."

**Aboard Dreamland Osprey,
near Stulpicani, Romania
0105**

"WE'RE ABOUT FIVE MINUTES AWAY FROM THE TOP OF THE hill," the Osprey pilot told Danny Freah. "Where's your man?"

Danny shook his head. He'd checked with Dreamland Command, but Voda had not called the number the ambassador had given him. And the ambassador said that Voda was worried that if they called him, the phone would be heard.

"We can search with the infrared cameras," the pilot told Danny. "We should be able to find them. The night's pretty cold."

"You sure, with all those trees?" asked Danny.

"There's no guarantee. But if they move around—if they want us to see them, we should be able to. I'd say the odds are probably sixty-forty we find them, maybe even higher."

Danny had been on search teams in the Sierra Nevadas at the very start of his Air Force career and he wasn't quite as optimistic. Besides, if Voda was hiding, the people they saw might actually be his pursuers.

"We'll give him another five minutes," he told the pilot. "Let's see what happens."

**Presidential villa,
near Stulpicani, Romania
0107**

TO VODA, IT SOUNDED AS IF THE DOGS AND TROOPS WERE less than ten feet away.

A wind had whipped up, and it blew through the trees like a torrent of water streaking over a high falls. The cold had turned his wife's nose beet red; Julian's hands felt like stones in his. Their fear had stopped providing them with energy. They were at the edge of despair, ready to give up.

Mircea started to rise. Voda practically leaped over Julian to grab her. She opened her mouth; Voda clamped his hand over it.

"Sssshhhh," he whispered in her ear.

She gave him a look that he had never seen directed at him before, a stare that in his experience she'd used only twice during their relationship. Both times, it was directed toward members of the old regime, men who were her sworn enemy.

"We'll get through it," whispered Voda.

She didn't answer.

The men were louder, closer. Or maybe just the wind was stronger, pushing their voices toward them.

The dogs began to bark wildly. Voda reached for Julian with his other hand, pulling him close. He thought of the pistol—should he take their lives to spare them whatever torture Locusta had in mind?

Killing himself would mean dying a coward's death. But it would be an act of mercy to spare his son and wife humiliation and suffering.

Julian shivered against his side.

There was no way he could kill his son; simply no way. Not even for the best reasons.

The barking intensified. The dogs were getting closer.

But they were going in the wrong direction! Confused by the shifting wind, they were doubling back over the trail.

Voda barely trusted the senses that told him this. He waited, holding his breath. Finally, his wife shook her head free of his hand.

"You have to call the Americans," she said. "You have to, so they can find us."

"Yes," said Voda. "Come on, we'll cross over to the other side of the hill while they're going in the other direction. We have to be quiet."

He picked up Julian. The boy seemed even heavier than he had earlier.

"Are you going to call?" Mircea asked.

"I will."

"I hear a helicopter."

Voda froze. "Hide!" he said. "Get as low to the ground as you can."

Aboard B-1B/L *Boomer*,
over northeastern Romania
0108

GENERAL SAMSON HIT HIS TALK BUTTON.

"Samson."

"This is General Locusta. You have helicopters in my area."

"I don't have helicopters."

"Don't lie. I can hear them."

"We have an Osprey standing by in the area where we are operating," said Samson, hedging, of course. "It is a search and rescue craft, ready in case one of our planes—or yours—is shot down by the Russians."

"We believe the criminals have taken prisoners, perhaps the president's son and wife," said Locusta. "They may kill them if they get desperate. Tell your helicopter to back off."

"I can release my aircraft to assist you," said Samson.

"We do not require your assistance."

"In that case, I want it on station for an emergency."

"If your aircraft persists, I'll shoot it down myself," said Locusta.

Presidential villa,
near Stulpicani, Romania
0110

THE CLOUDS HAD CLEARED, ALLOWING THE MOON TO SHINE brightly. Voda saw more of the woods around them, but this wasn't a good thing—it meant the men searching for them would have an easier time as well.

He and his wife and son cleared the crest of the hill and started down. There was a bald spot a few yards from the top. As Voda reached it, his footing slipped. Julian fell from his grasp and both father and son tumbled down against the rocks, rolling about five yards before coming to a stop.

Voda's knee felt as if it had been broken. The pain seized his entire leg, constricted his throat. He felt as if he couldn't breathe, as if his head had been buried in the dirt.

Julian began to whimper. Voda forced himself over to the boy, pulled his arms around him.

"Alin?" hissed his wife.

"Sssssh. We're here. I'll call now." ·

Voda pulled out the phone. His hands were trembling. What if it had broken in the fall? He should have called earlier, no matter the risk.

He pressed the Power button, waiting for it come to life.

If it didn't work, they'd go down the hill, they'd find a way past the soldiers, they'd walk, they'd crawl all the way back to Bucharest if they had to. They would do whatever they had to do, just to survive.

The phone lit.

Voda tapped the number the ambassador had given him. It was an international number—-but it didn't seem to work.

Voda realized he had not remembered it correctly.

"We can't stay here. It's too easy to see us," said Mircea, reaching them.

"We're not going to stay," he told her. "Come on."

He grabbed her side and pulled himself up, thumbing for the number of the ambassador while they started down the hill.

Aboard EB-52 *Bennett*,
over northeastern Romania
0110

"ROMANIAN AIRCRAFT ARE RETURNING SOUTH, COLONEL," said Spiff. "No more Russians. I think we've seen the last of them."

"Don't place any bets," said Dog.

The Dreamland channel buzzed. Samson was on the line. "Bastian."

"Locusta claims he'll the shoot the Osprey down if it flies over the hill," said Samson. "He implied that the guerrillas have the president's son and wife as hostages, and that they'll kill them if we get too close. I think it's a bunch of bull."

"All right."

"What the hell do we do now, Bastian?" Samson asked. "If we can't use the Osprey, how do we get him out? How do we get our people in there?"

"Let's ask them," said Dog.

"What do you mean?"

"Conference everyone in and see what they think."

Samson didn't say anything. He was used to working from the top down—he came up with ideas, and people genuflected.

Dreamland had never worked that way. Neither had Dog.

"All right," said Samson finally. "How the hell do we do that?"

THE PROBLEM WASN'T JUST GETTING THE PRESIDENT OUT— they had to find him first. The *Bennett*'s radar couldn't spot him because of the trees, which would also block the infrared sensors aboard the Flighthawks unless the aircraft descended low enough to be heard.

Zen took Starship onto another channel to give him some pointers for tweaking the filters the computer used to interpret the infrared, even though he knew it was a long shot. The sensors' long-range capabilities were designed primarily to find objects in the sky; they simply couldn't do what they wanted.

By the time they went back on the conference line, Danny was suggesting that he and his men parachute into the hill.

"Even with the moon out, it's still dark enough to jump without being seen," he said. "If we take the Osprey to 25,000 feet, it won't be heard."

"How do you get out of there?" Dog asked.

"There's a spot at the base of the back hill that's not covered by the patrols the troops have set up," said Danny. "We can come down the hill, work our way across and then out. We get across the road, then we have the Osprey pick us up on the other side of this second hill here."

"That'll take hours," said Dog.

"I don't think he's getting out on his own," said Danny.

"General Samson, incoming message from the ambassador," said Breanna.

"Good. Stockard, can you plug me into him?"

It took Zen a moment to realize Samson was talking to his wife. No one spoke, waiting for the general.

"I want this on line. Can you get it on line?"

Zen could hear Breanna explaining in the background that they could conference it, though the quality would be poor.

"Well, do it," said Samson gruffly. "Is everyone listening?"

"We're here," said Dog.

"Stockard, can you get us on line?" Samson asked again.

"It's on."

Zen heard someone breathing in the background.

"President Voda, are you there?" said Samson.

"Yes. The men with the dogs are on the other side of the hill," answered a soft, distant foreign voice. "But there are many soldiers around."

"Where exactly are you?" asked Danny.

"We're on the other side of the hill from my house."

"Below the bald rocks?"

"The rocks? Yes, yes. About twenty feet below them, in the center."

"Good."

"They're coming!" Voda shouted, his hushed voice rising. There were muffled sounds.

Oh God, thought Zen, we're going to hear him get killed.

But they didn't.

"I have to leave," whispered Voda a few seconds later. "We have to move."

The phone dropped off the circuit.

"Stockard, get Dreamland Command to call him back," said Samson. "Osprey—get moving. We'll have him vector you in."

"If we call him and they're nearby, they'll hear and kill him," said Dog.

"Holding made sense earlier," said Samson. "Now we're ready to grab him."

"General, there are Zsu-zsu's lined up all along the roads around the property," warned Spiff, the ground radar operator aboard the *Bennett*, referring to the antiaircraft guns the Romanians had moved into the area. "They'll shoot the Osprey to pieces on the way in, or the way out."

"We're just going to have to risk it," said Samson. "Osprey—we'll help you plot a path."

"I have a better idea," said Zen. "I'll get them."

VII

Flying Man

TO ZEN'S SURPRISE, IT WAS DANNY WHO RAISED THE MOST strenuous objections.

"The MESSKIT was designed to get you out of the aircraft, not haul people around," Danny said.

"No, it was designed to help you guys get around," said Zen. "Annie adapted it to use as a parachute. It's still basically the same tool you started with. Which means it's a lot more than a parachute. We picked that car up the other day, General," he added, making the pitch to Samson himself. "The exoskeleton is extremely strong. To conserve fuel, I'll glide all the way down to the mountain. I fire it up when I get there."

"How do you get out of the plane, Jeff?" asked Breanna. There was fear in her voice—she was worried for him.

"He goes out from one of the auxiliary seats up here," said Dog. "Right, Zen?"

"That's exactly what I'm thinking, Colonel. What do you say?"

"I say it's up to General Samson," said Dog. "But I think it may be our best bet."

"Get moving," said Samson. "Let's do it *now*."

IN OUTLINE, THE PLAN WAS SIMPLICITY ITSELF. ZEN WOULD eject at 30,000 feet, five miles from the hill, far from sight and earshot of the troops below. He'd then glide down to the president and his family, and use the MESSKIT to fly them to another spot four miles away, where the Osprey would arrive to pick them up.

The details were where things got complicated.

Because Zen couldn't walk, he'd to have to land as close to the president as possible. The large bare spot near the crest of the hill would be the easiest place for a rendezvous; if that didn't work, there were two places farther down that might. One was an elbow turn in a dried-out creek bed about half-way down the hill; the opening was roughly thirty by twenty feet. The other was a gouge close to the base of the hill, fifty yards in from the road. The gouge was probably the remains of a gravel mine, and was much wider than either of the other two spots. But it was also very close to a makeshift lookout post set up by the soldiers surrounding the area.

To make the pickup, Zen would need to be in direct communication with the president. The technical side of this was difficult enough: Zen would trade his Flighthawk helmet for a standard Dreamland flight helmet, swapping in the MESSKIT guidance and information system, a piece of software that connected to the helmet's screen functions via a program card about the size of a quarter. He would then hook the helmet into a survival radio to communicate with the *Johnson* rather than the *Bennett,* since it would be easier to coordinate communications aboard the pressurized ship. The *Johnson,* meanwhile, would capture the president's mobile phone call through the Dreamland channel and then relay it to Zen. The need to communicate presented an inherent risk: While they would use an obscure frequency rather than the emergency band commonly monitored, there was nonetheless a chance that it could be intercepted. Its sixty-four-bit encryption would be difficult to decipher, but the radio waves could be tracked.

The field where they would meet the Osprey was well west of the house, and could be approached without running past any of the antiaircraft guns, most of which were closer to the house. Zen would fly by two of the guns, but the radar experts believed that his profile would be small enough, and low enough, that the radar used by the weapons would completely miss him. The guns could be visually sighted, but that took time and would be hard in the dark.

Three trips. In theory, Zen could do it all in an hour, once he landed.

The question was how close together would theory and reality fall.

Voda hadn't called back. The mission would be scrubbed if they didn't hear from him.

As Dog flew EB-52 *Bennett* into position, Zen got out of his specially designed flight chair and slipped to the deck of the Megafortress. Then he crawled to the ladder at the rear of the compartment and climbed to the flight deck.

"Hey, Zen, why didn't you tell us you were on your way?" said Spiff, getting up from his radar station as Zen crawled toward him.

"I didn't think it would be worth the trouble."

"Jeez, let me help you."

Zen knew from experience that the sight of a grown man crawling along the floor unnerved some people, and sometimes he got a twisted pleasure from seeing them squirm as he did it. But Spiff's worried expression took him by surprise, and he let Spiff help him as a way of putting him at ease.

"I just need a hand getting strapped in," he said, pushing up into the seat. "I'm hoping I fit."

As Zen pressed himself into the seat, he glanced up at the outlines of the hatch he was going to be shot through. It looked terribly small.

He turned his attention back to his gear, taking one last inventory. He slapped his hand down to the survival knife in the scabbard pocket at his thigh, then slipped his hand into his vest, making sure his Beretta was easily accessible.

"Let's get this show on the road," he said. "I'm ready to fly."

* * *

"SECURE ANYTHING LOOSE," DOG TOLD THE CREW. "MAKE sure your oxygen masks are nice and snug. Get your gloves on. Not only is it going to get noisy and windy in here, but it'll be cold too."

"We're ready, Colonel," said Sullivan.

"We have to work our way down to altitude gradually. There'll be no rushing," added Dog. "Everybody check your gear one last time, make sure the oxygen is tight and you have a green on the suit system."

He checked his own restraints, then glanced at his watch, intending to give the rest of the crew a full minute.

"Sullivan, you ready?" Dog asked.

"Ready, Colonel."

"Spiff?"

"Good to go."

"Rager?"

"Ready, sir."

"Zen?"

"Roger that."

"All right. Let's find out where the hell our rescuee is," said Dog, tapping the Dreamland Command line.

**Presidential villa,
near Stulpicani, Romania
0130**

A CLUMP OF PRICKLE BUSHES HAD GROWN UP AROUND A fallen tree about fifty yards from the bald spot on the hill. The brush formed an L, with the long end extending almost straight down. Not only did the bushes provide cover, but they also cut down on the wind, which seemed to Voda much stronger on this side of the hill.

The pain in his knee had settled to a sharp throb that

moved in unison with his breath. He passed the cell phone from one hand to another, staring at it. His fingers were numb.

"What's going on?" Mircea asked.

"I'm calling the Americans back," he told her.

Now he couldn't remember any part of the number. He could feel the panic rising in his chest. Part of him wanted to fling the phone down and simply run up the hill. He'd shout, make himself a target, run at the soldiers, let them kill him. It would be a relief.

He wasn't going to do that. He was going to get his family out of there. And then he was going to save his country.

Voda began working through the unfamiliar menus to find recently dialed calls. The number was there.

Reverse the last two digits. That was the problem.

He could just call the ambassador, have him make the transfer again.

He tried reversing the digits first. A man answered immediately.

"President Voda, I'm very glad you're able to call," said the man in a bright, southwestern-tinted American accent. "You are working with some of the best people in the business. We'll have you out of there before you can sing your national anthem."

Voda didn't know what to say, nor did he have a chance as the man continued breathlessly.

"My name is Mack Smith and I'm going to making the communications connections for you. We're going to need you to stay on the line once it goes through. I know you're worried about your battery, but we're in the home stretch now. You're going to be talking directly to the fellow who's going to pick you up. His name is Zen Stockard. He's got a bit of an ego to him, but don't be put off by that. He is one kick-ass pilot."

"You are sending a helicopter?"

"Not exactly. I'll let Zen give you the dope. Now. You ready?"

Voda was confused by Mack's slang as well as his accent.

"OK," he replied.

"Here we go."

There was a slight delay, then a new voice came on the line.

"President Voda, this is Colonel Tecumseh Bastian. Do you recognize my name, sir?"

"Yes, Colonel. You are very famous. You head the Dreamland squadron."

"Yes, sir. I'm in a plane a few miles from the hill where you are. In just a few minutes one of my men is going to pick you up."

"By helicopter?"

"No, sir. We're afraid it would be shot down. What's going to happen is this: One of my men will rendezvous with you on the ground. He'll be wearing a special device that you can think of as a jet pack. He'll fly you and your family one by one to safety."

A jet pack?

"If it will work—" started Voda. He didn't get a chance to finish the thought.

"It *will* work, sir. But we need your help. We'd like you to go to a point where it will be easy to find you. There's a bald spot near the crest of the hill, on the far side of the hill, that is, from your house."

"I can't go there. The soldiers are there."

"All right. We have alternatives."

He heard Dog take a hard breath.

"A little farther down the hill there's a creek," said Dog. "It's either completely dry or just about; it's hard to tell from the satellite photo I've seen. But it's wide, and it takes a sharp turn down the hill and there's an open space in the woods. Can you go there?"

"I—I don't know where it is."

"If you were at the bald spot, it's exactly 232 meters below it, and fifteen meters to the north, which would be on your right if you were looking downhill. Does that help?"

"Yes," said Voda. He could find it simply by going down the hill. The creak bed should be obvious; when they hit it, he would turn right.

"I need you to stay on the line," added Dog. "I know you're worried about being found or running out your battery. But it will help us immensely. We may need you to guide us. I don't want to have to call you back."

Mircea and Julian were huddled against him. He could feel them shaking. If this didn't work, they would freeze to death.

"All right, I'll try," said Voda, struggling to his feet. "We're on our way."

**Aboard EB-52 *Bennett*,
above northeastern Romania
0130**

EVEN THOUGH HE KNEW IT WAS COMING, THE JOLT FROM the seat as it shot upward took Zen's breath away. The shock was so hard that for a second he thought he'd hit the side of the hatch going out. Zen hurtled up into a black void, the sky rushing into his head like the water from a bathtub surging into a drain. The seat fell away, the restraints cut by knives as he shot up, but he didn't notice; to him, the only thing he could feel was the roar in his body, as if he had become a rocket.

A grayish grid ghosted on the visor of helmet. The MESSKIT's activation light began to blink.

All right, Zen thought, let's get this done.

He spread his arms, trying to frog his body. The screen altimeter lit; he was at 32,053 feet, a little higher than he'd expected.

Up until now, Zen had always tried to make his practice jumps last—he wanted to glide slowly to earth. Tonight, his goal was to get down as quickly as possible. So he instructed the MESSKIT to deploy at 10,000 feet, figuring it would be easier to fall to that altitude quickly than to fly to it.

The device didn't like the instructions. It flashed the words BEYOND SAFETY PROTOCOLS on the screen.

"Override," he told it.

But the computer wouldn't. Annie Klondike hadn't wanted to take chances with his life, and so had programmed various safety protocols into the unit that would initiate deployment based not only on velocity, but on time elapsed and altitude drop. Zen was forced to open his wings at 21,500 feet.

He compensated by leaning forward and pushing his arms back, turning the exoskeleton as close to a jet as possible. His descent increased to 25 feet per second before the safety measures kicked in, once more preventing him from dropping any faster.

"This is Zen. *Johnson,* you hearing me?"

"We have you, Zen," replied Lieutenant Englehardt in the *Johnson.* "You ready to talk to President Voda?"

"Yeah, roger that."

"Be advised he's hard to understand. And probably vice versa. Speak as slowly and distinctly as you can."

"Yeah, roger that."

"What am I hearing?" said a foreign voice, distant and faint.

"This is Zen Stockard, Mr. President. I'm going to help you. How far are you from the stream location?"

"I am still looking."

"I'm about twelve minutes away," Zen told him. "Do you think you can find it by then?"

"I will try."

"Stay on the line, all right?"

"Yes, yes."

**Presidential villa,
near Stulpicani, Romania
0130**

"NO, GENERAL. THERE ARE NO BODIES IN THAT PART OF the house," repeated Major Ozera. "Or in any part of the house. The president must have escaped the attack. He has to be on the property somewhere."

General Locusta pounded his fist against the hood of the car. Where in God's name was the son of a bitch? He couldn't do anything until he found him.

Ozera trembled.

"Where is the search party?" demanded Locusta, trying to calm his voice.

"They've moved up the close side of the hill and are now working their way up to the summit. The dogs are having trouble with the wind," Ozera added. "And they got a late start. The cold helps preserve the scent, but there are limits."

More likely the problem was with the handlers, Locusta thought. He retrieved the area topographical map. They'd gone too far. Voda must be hidden somewhere on the hill.

The general's sat phone began to ring. He ignored it.

"Pull the teams back to this side of the ridge," Locusta told the major. "Have them concentrate on the area around that old pump building or whatever it is. There's probably another secret passage."

"Should I add the regular troops to the search?"

"No!" He raised his phone and hit the Receive button. "Locusta."

"General Locusta, I trust you are having an interesting night."

It was the Russian attaché, Svoransky.

"Why have you sent planes to attack my troops?" Locusta boomed.

"Relax, General. They were trying to attack the Americans, not your troops."

"Liar."

Locusta took control of himself. No one, not even Ozera, knew he had dealt with the Russians; he had to be careful about what he said.

"General, please. We should remain civil. We have much to gain from working together. I called to offer help."

"How?"

"I've heard rumors about the president. They say he is dead, but I suspect they are false."

"You suspect?"

Did the Russian have a spy in his organization? Locusta glanced at Ozera. Who else could it be?

No. Svoransky had to be bluffing.

Locusta turned his back and took several steps away from the major. "What business is it of yours if he is dead?"

"None, if he truly is. But I believe he is not. I believe, in fact, he is trying to escape. And that you are looking for him."

The spy might be lower ranking—one of the men on the assassin team, or even the regular army, an officer who was a little too clever for his own good.

Or maybe the bastard Svoransky was simply guessing.

"We have a person at the national telephone company as well," added the Russian. "If you wish, he might be able to provide information about cell phone calls in your area."

"The president hasn't used his cell phone, or his satellite phone," said Locusta. He had taken the precaution of having the lines monitored. "Thanks very much."

"No, he hasn't. But one of his bodyguards has. The woman assigned to his son—she is in the area very close to where you are searching."

**Aboard B-1B/L *Boomer*,
above northeastern Romania
0135**

BREANNA STUDIED THE RADAR PLOT THAT WAS FORWARDED from the Megafortresses, the overlapping inputs synthesized by the computer into a wide-ranging view. EB-52 *Johnson* was flying about two miles west of the Romanian president's house and slightly to the north. The *Bennett* was twenty-five miles south, descending to an altitude where oxygen masks would not be needed. *Boomer* was to the west, getting ready to cover the Osprey as it came north. Dreamland's second B-1, *Big Bird*, was near the northwestern border, on the watch for more Russians, though they seemed to have lost their appetite for confrontation.

The radar also showed Zen, circling down toward the hill. Breanna remembered how angry he'd been—and how he'd given in, kissing her, admitting he was no longer angry.

Don't let that be our last kiss, she prayed silently.

"You're awful quiet over there, Stockard," said Samson, with his usual bark.

"Just making sure where all the players are," Breanna said. "Dreamland Osprey is holding ten minutes from touchdown."

"Good."

Breanna looked out the windscreen. The night was rapidly giving way to day.

Don't let that be our last kiss. Please.

**Near Stulpicani, Romania
0135**

THE CREEK WAS SO NARROW THAT VODA MISSED IT AT FIRST. It wasn't until his wife slipped behind him, tripping over the rocks and cursing, that he realized where they were. He pulled Julian with him as he went back up the hill.

"My ankle," said Mircea. "It feels like it's broken."

"Come on. Lean on me. We have to go in this direction."

Voda braced himself as his wife leaned against him. His knee felt as if it was being twisted, even though his leg was perfectly straight. He took a deep breath and began moving again.

Mircea started to weep.

"Come on, now," Voda told her. "Our rescuers are on the way."

"Mama, come," said Julian. The boy took her hand, but she only cried harder.

"We're almost out," Voda whispered. "We've got just a few meters—look there."

The creek dipped sharply to the left, past two white-barked trees, where he saw the clearing the Dreamland people had told him about.

"We're there," he said into the phone. "Where are you?"

"I'm right above you," said the voice. "Here I come."

There was a light sound in the air, the sort a spruce made when it sprang back after being weighed down by snow. Voda looked up toward the sky and saw a shadow dropping toward him. Had he not been speaking to the man, he would have sworn it was an angel.

Or a devil.

The figure descended toward the rocks, then abruptly fell to the earth, crumpling in a pile.

Voda froze. It was the last disappointment, the last dash of his hopes.

ZEN CURSED, ANGRY AT HIMSELF FOR MISJUDGING HIS altitude and botching the landing. Unlike a radar altimeter, which gave an altitude reading above elevated terrain, the MESSKIT's altimeter told him only his absolute height above sea level. He'd thought he was a few feet higher than he turned out to be as he skimmed in for a landing.

He pushed himself up, repositioning the exoskeleton and squirming around until he was sitting.

"Well, where are you?" he said into his radio. "President Voda? Mr. President?"

There was no answer.

"Hey," said Zen, louder. "Are you there?"

He pulled off his helmet.

"President Voda?" he said in a stage whisper. "President Voda?"

"PAPA," SAID JULIAN. "PAPA, SOMEONE IS CALLING YOU."

Slowly, Voda regained his senses. He heard the voice himself and took a tentative step toward it.

"Here," he answered.

The figure on the ground turned around.

"Hey, come on," said Zen. "Let's go."

Voda let go of Julian and went to help his wife. Ignoring the pain in his leg, he practically carried her to the clearing.

"Why are you sitting?" he asked Zen.

"Because I can't walk. I'm Zen Stockard. You were talking to me on your phone."

"You're hurt?"

"It's OK, don't worry. It's been a long time since I've walked. This device on my back will take care of that. Who's coming with me first?"

"My wife," said Voda. "Her ankle is hurt."

"No, take Julian," she said.

"I'm not leaving you," said the boy.

"Hey listen, guys, somebody has to be first. What's your name, kid?"

Julian didn't answer until Voda tapped him on the back.

"Ju-li-an Voda."

"You ever dream of flying in a spaceship?"

"N-No."

Zen laughed. "Well, you'll be able to tell all your friends that you did. Almost."

There was a noise above them, someone falling down the hillside, cursing in Romanian.

Two hundred yards away? Zen wondered. No more than that.

"All right. No more fooling around," he said. "Mr. President, come on. You first."

"No. My wife and son."

"We all go," said Mircea.

"I can't hold all three," Zen told them. "Maybe two. Come here. On my lap."

Julian began to cry as Voda helped him on. Zen wrapped his arm around him.

"Mrs. Voda. Come on."

Mircea hobbled closer. "I don't understand," she said.

"When I press this button, the engines will activate, and we'll go up. These skeleton pieces along my arm will help hold your weight. I have only one clasp on the harness set here, so we'll secure you and hold your son between us."

The dogs were barking.

"They're coming," said Mircea. She turned away from Zen, but he grabbed her, pulling a belt around her and locking it onto the strap on his chest.

"This isn't going to take long. I want you to hold on tight," he told them. "Very tight. Mr. President, it's going to take me ten minutes to get there, and maybe ten back. Will you be OK?"

"Yes."

"Stay on that line."

Zen snapped the helmet back into place. He attached some wires to the base, then held both hands out and started the jet pack. The sound was like a loud vacuum cleaner. As Voda watched, Zen began to rise. Mircea seemed stuck for a moment, but then she too rose, clinging to his arms. Julian was tight between them.

And then they were gone.

**Presidential villa,
near Stulpicani, Romania
0142**

"THEY'VE JUST HEARD SOME SORT OF NOISE!" SHOUTED the major. "It's the far side of the hill. They're going down."

About time, thought Locusta. But he only nodded and took out his satellite phone. The Russian had driven a hard bargain.

"This is General Locusta," he told the air force officer who answered his call. "I need a no-fly zone across my entire army corps area. That includes all planes, military and civilian."

"The Americans too?"

"Everyone," he said. "Tell them we are at a delicate stage. Tell them we want them to return to their bases. I've spoken to their general, but he is a pigheaded idiot. Complain to the ambassador. Do whatever you must."

He killed the transmission without waiting for a response. The Americans undoubtedly would ignore this latest order, but they would pay heavily for it.

**Near Stulpicani, Romania
0143**

ZEN FELT THE BOY SLIPPING AS SOON AS HE CLEARED THE first set of trees. He couldn't grab him because of the wing assembly, and instead tried to push in his stomach toward him. But that started to pitch him forward.

"Hold on, hold on," he said, though he knew the kid couldn't hear. Mircea pushed tighter, gripping the boy, but even so, Zen felt Julian's weight slipping.

The road was on his left, two or three hundred yards away. Zen turned toward it, then realized he wasn't going to make it.

Where was the cutout from the gravel pit?

To his right?

The kid clawed at him. There wasn't any time—Zen pushed right. The clearing appeared just a few yards away. He leaned forward, gliding to it, then backing off on the power. As he did, Julian slid between his mother and Zen, who cut his power abruptly. All three of them fell together, until at the last second, Zen jerked the engines back to life, preventing another hard landing.

"Let's try again," he yelled, adjusting the thrust from the engine so his feet were hovering just above the ground. "Mrs. Voda, loosen the strap at my arms and string your son through it."

Mircea didn't move.

"Come on now. I have to go back and pick up your husband. Go!"

She still didn't move. Zen started to undo the strap that held her to him, then saw Julian stumbling toward him.

"Come on, Julian," he said. "We have to move so we can help your dad."

The strap, custom-designed to fit Zen's body, didn't have any play in it. The only other thing he could use was the belt that strapped his lower body to the MESSKIT. Loosening it meant he wouldn't have as much control over the device, but there was no way the kid was going to be able to hold on.

Zen slid his hand out from the wing assembly and helped Julian climb up between him and his mother, then undid the lower torso strap and threaded it around the boy's arms, pulling it so tight that it must have hurt, though Julian didn't react. Then Zen hooked it around his chest strap in a knot.

"Hang on," he said, and they started upward once more.

Dreamland Command
1543 (0143 Romania)

MACK PACED IN FRONT OF THE BIG DISPLAY SCREEN. HIS stomach was rumbling and he had a headache. Every time he scratched the side of his head, more hairs fell out. And he swore he saw hives on the back on his hand.

This behind-the-scenes crap was hell on the nerves. Much better to be on the front line actually doing something instead of pacing back and forth and disintegrating miles from the action.

"Jennifer Gleason for you, Major Smith," said the communications officer.

"There we go." Mack punched in the line. "Got it?"

"I do. It wasn't as easy as Ray thought. First I had to code—"

"Yeah, yeah, yeah. What do we do?"

Near Stulpicani, Romania
0145

AS SOON AS HIS WIFE AND SON ROSE INTO THE SKY, VODA remembered that he hadn't kissed them good-bye. He'd never been an overly sentimental man, but he cursed himself as he started down the slope. He might very well never see them again.

Voda followed the elbow of the creek, walking along the rocks for about twenty yards. He could hear the dogs now, barking loudly. He turned and started down. But his weakened knee betrayed him—he collapsed, falling through a spread of prickle bushes.

At least Julian was safe. He could accept death knowing that.

What a strange life he'd had. Mozart and politics.

The Sonata in A Minor, K. 310, began playing in his head. The pace of the music quickening, matching his pounding heart.

Grabbing onto a small sapling, Voda pulled himself up and began walking. The pain in his leg seemed to have fled— or maybe he'd stopped feeling anything at all. Then his feet gave way. He tumbled down five or six yards, smacking hard against a tree.

He pushed to get up, but found he couldn't.

This was where it was going to end, he thought. He reached for his pistol.

It was gone. He'd lost it somewhere above.

**Aboard Dreamland EB-52 *Johnson*,
over northeastern Romania
0153**

STARSHIP SLID HIS HEADSET BACK, WATCHING THE CLOCK dial revolve on the Flighthawk control screen. Finally the hand stopped. The screen blinked, and UPDATE LOADED appeared in the center.

He pushed the headset back into place.

"Ready," he told Englehardt.

"Let 'er rip," answered the *Johnson*'s pilot.

Easy for him to say, Starship thought. If the update screwed up, he was the one who'd lose total control of *Hawk Three*. And knowing General Samson's reputation, it was a good bet he would be paying for the aircraft out of his own pocket.

He and all his offspring, for the next seven generations.

"Reboot C^3 remote, authorization alpha-beta-six-six-beta-seven-four-zed-zed," he said, giving his authorization code. "I am Lieutenant Kirk Andrews."

The computer thought about it for a second, then beeped its approval.

"*Hawk Three* is coming to course," Starship told Englehardt. He banked the Flighthawk out of the figure-eight patrol orbit it had been flying and took it near the hill. He had to stay above 10,000 feet or he'd be heard; he nudged the aircraft to 10,500.

A yellow helix appeared on the screen. The symbol was usually used by the computer to indicate where a disconnected Flighthawk was; now it showed the location of the cell phone they were tracking.

No. It was three miles from the hill, to the south, near an army watch post. It was the wrong transmission.

Starship took the Flighthawk farther north.

Nothing.

"Hey, you sure this guy is on the air?" Starship asked Englehardt.

"We'll have to ask Mack."

"Well, get him on. I'm not picking up anything."

Dreamland Command
1558 (0158 Romania)

"THE CELL TRANSMISSION DIED," THE COMMUNICATIONS specialist told Mack.

"What do you mean, it died?"

"He lost his connection or his battery died. I don't know."

"Call him," said Mack.

"I don't know, Major. We don't know how close he is to the people looking for him."

"Call him the hell back."

"Incoming transmission from the *Johnson*."

"Screen." Mack turned around. Lieutenant Mike Englehardt's face bounced back and forth. Though Mack was sure he'd been told a million times to keep his head still while he spoke, the pilot still jerked around nervously. Good thing he didn't fly that way.

"Major Smith, we're having trouble here with the cell phone from President Voda."

"Yeah, yeah, yeah, I'm on it. Keep your speed pants zipped."

"Major, we're getting a broadcast over the Romanian air defense frequencies you want to hear," said the communications specialist, cutting into his conversation. "Channel Two."

"Stand by *Johnson*." Mack felt the hives on his hands percolating as he flicked into the transmission. "Damn, man. This is in Romanian."

"It comes back in English."

A few seconds later the English version began.

"All planes flying above latitude 46 degree north will immediately cease operations and return to base. This airspace is closed to all military and civilian flights, foreign and domestic. All flights will vacate this space immediately."

"What a load of crap," said Mack. He looked up at the communications desk. "Get me Samson—no wait. Let me talk to Dog."

**Aboard EB-52 *Bennett*,
over northeastern Romania
0200**

MACK SMITH'S FACE SNAPPED INTO DOG'S VIDEO SCREEN.

"Did you receive that Romanian air defense broadcast?" Mack asked.

The sound of the wind in the depressurized cabin was so loud, Dog had to crank the volume to hear.

"We're listening to it now," he said.

"What are you going to do, Colonel? Tell them to shove it, right?"

"I'm not going to tell them that," said Dog. "That's General Samson's job."

Mack frowned.

"He's the reason you have your job as chief of staff, Mack. You got what you wanted."

"Wasn't that a mistake."

"I'll talk to him," said Dog. "I'm sure he's heard it by now anyway."

Dog tapped his screen. His daughter Breanna's helmeted face appeared.

"Bree, I have to talk to the general."

"The no-fly order, right?"

"Yeah."

"He's talking to one of the Romanian air force generals right now. Not that it seems to be doing any good."

"I can wait."

Dog checked his position on the sitrep. They were flying an oval-shaped orbit at 8,000 feet east of the president's vacation house, roughly between it and the border. *Hawk One* and *Two* were in a standard patrol position fore and aft of the *Bennett,* flown entirely by the computer.

Despite the blown hatch, the Megafortress flew a level course, responding to the control inputs flawlessly. As long as they made easy maneuvers and stayed in their pressurized suits, the crew shouldn't have any problems.

"What a bunch of blockheads," said Samson, coming on the line as blustery as always. "Locusta must be behind this."

"Absolutely," said Dog.

"I'll be damned if I'm going to comply."

"Agreed. We only need a few more minutes," said Dog. "Zen is almost at the Osprey rendezvous."

"I better tell Washington what's going on. Someone may get their nose out of joint."

Dog was about to suggest that Samson might not bother to pass the information along for a few minutes, just in case someone at the White House decided they should comply immediately. But he was interrupted by his airborne radar operator, who shouted so loud he would have easily been heard even if Dog didn't have his headset on.

"Colonel! We have more MiGs! A lot of them this time . . . *sixteen!* And they are coming at us like wolves at a pig roast!"

Near Stulpicani, Romania
0205

ZEN FELT A BIT OF STRAIN IN HIS SHOULDER AS HE ROSE over the second hill and started downward. The exoskeleton handled the enormous strains imposed by flying, but the weight of Mrs. Voda and her son was mostly borne by his body. They tugged him away from the wing unit; like an ancient Roman enemy of the state, hitched to a pair of chariots and about to be pulled asunder.

The Osprey sat like a vulture ahead to his right, opposite a small barn. Zen leaned slightly in that direction, adjusting his movements to the extra weight he was carrying.

"Almost there," he yelled. "You'll be on the ground in just a second."

Near Stulpicani, Romania
0205

VODA SAT STARING AT THE SKY, LISTENING TO THE MUSIC in his head. He was lost, done. But at least he had saved his wife and son.

That was a man's duty.

But was it a president's? Should he have put them ahead of his country? Should he have gone and left them to die?

History would have to judge.

His body began to buzz. His leg was on fire.

No, it was the cell phone, vibrating.

He reached for it, took it out.

"Yes?"

"Yo, Mr. President, I was afraid I'd lost the connection for good," said the American, Mack Smith. "You need to keep the phone on."

"I had it on. It must have turned off when I fell."

"Well don't fall anymore, all right? What's going on?"

"They're coming for me. I can hear them nearby. Above me."

"Well hide. Go. Go!"

Yes, thought Voda. There were some fallen trees not too far away. He pulled himself up, then started for them, dragging his aching leg.

As he reached them, Voda realized they wouldn't provide much cover. But they did give him an idea. He stripped off his shirt and tucked it between the tree branches, making it just visible. Then he began moving in the other direction.

The dogs barked nearby.

Near Stulpicani, Romania
0205

"They think they hear him," Major Ozera told Locusta. "It won't be long now."

"I want no more reports until he is dead," Locusta said.

His satellite phone rang. Locusta answered it. It was his aide, back at headquarters.

"General Karis of the Third Division has ordered his troops back to their barracks."

"What?" demanded Locusta.

"That's the only report I have."

Karis was a key ally. Locusta didn't understand what he was doing, except that it was not what they had agreed. The troops would be needed to keep order.

He would have to talk to Karis personally.

"The Dreamland people want to talk to you as well. General Samson—"

"I don't have time for them. Tell them they are to return to Iasi. Things are critical."

Near Stulpicani, Romania
0206

DANNY FREAH WATCHED ZEN DESCEND. THE LANDING wasn't the most elegant he'd ever seen—Zen came down too fast before cutting his power, and the trio collapsed forward like mail sacks thrown from the back of a truck—but it did the trick.

Boston reached them first, pulling Zen upright.

"Man, how'd you tie this?" he asked. He yelled to Sergeant Liu, who was running up with the med kit. "Nurse, where's the knife?"

"Don't cut it," said Zen. "I got one more to go."

Danny knelt down and unhooked Mrs. Voda, then handed her off to Liu. Julian, the president's son, looked at him as if looking at a ghost.

"She's in shock," said Liu. "But OK."

"Get them into the Osprey," said Danny as Boston finally undid the knot. He picked up the boy and gave him to Boston, who cradled him in his arms and began double-timing toward the rotor plane.

"I'll be back in about twenty minutes," said Zen. "Maybe less."

"Wait." Danny grabbed his shoulders. "Give me the MESSKIT. I'll go."

"I got it."

"Zen, they're closing in on him. Voda's going to be hiding. You won't be able to find him."

"We'll just tell him to run to the clearing."

"They're all around him."

Zen lifted his arms to fly. Danny tried to push them down. Zen was too strong and shrugged him away.

"Let's not screw around," said the pilot angrily.

"If you get killed, the Flighthawk program stops," Danny told him. "If I'm lost, it's no big deal."

"It is a big deal."

"Listen, we've been through a lot together. I'm the best person for this job. You know it. Don't let your pride get in the way."

A long moment passed. Then, finally, Zen reached down and began undoing his straps.

**Aboard Dreamland B-1B/L *Boomer*,
over northeastern Romania
0208**

EVEN FOR A PAIR OF MEGAFORTRESSES AND TWO B-1B/LS, sixteen MiGs was a lot to take on. And General Samson's force wasn't in the best position to do so either. The *Johnson* was out of long-range missiles, and had to stay near the hill to help pinpoint President Voda. The *Bennett* had a depressurized cabin and no one to fly its Flighthawks.

But Samson liked challenges. And he had one of the best combat air tacticians alive to help him meet this one.

"Forget borders, rules of engagement, all that other bull crap," he told Dog. "Come up with a plan to kick these bastards in the teeth."

"Missiles engage the leaders, Flighthawks break up the flight, lasers pick them off one by one," said Dog without hesitating. "The sooner we engage them, the better. The *Johnson* stays with the Osprey. We leave *Big Bird* back as free safety while you and I go out over the Black Sea."

"We're on it. Give us a heading," replied Samson.

Near Stulpicani, Romania
0208

VODA CRAWLED ON HIS HANDS AND KNEES UNDER THE narrow rock ledge. It looked like the best hiding place he could find, though far from perfect.

"Still with me?" asked the American on the cell phone when he held it to his ear.

"I'm here," said Voda.

"Your signal is real scratchy."

"I'm beneath a rock ledge." A beep sounded in his ear. "What was that noise?"

"Wasn't on my side."

Another beep.

"My battery is running low," said Voda.

"Our guy is ten minutes away," replied Mack. "Just hang in there."

"They're all around me," whispered Voda. He saw a dark khaki uniform moving through the trees near him. "I can see them. I can't talk anymore."

Aboard Dreamland EB-52 Bennett,
over northeastern Romania
0110

"KILL OUR RADARS," DOG TOLD HIS CREW. "WE'LL USE THE Johnson's. No sense giving them a road map."

It took roughly sixty seconds for the crew to secure the radars. In the meantime, Dog brought the Bennett north, acting as if nothing was going on. As soon as they were no longer splashing their radio waves into the air, he turned to the east and applied full military power, racing toward an intercept.

The MiGs were coming at them at about 1,200 knots. They were just southwest of Odessa, flying around 28,000 feet, a bit under 230 miles away. The MiGs were slowing down—

they couldn't fly on afterburner very long if they wanted to make it home—but were still moving at a good clip. As Dog completed his turn and began to accelerate, the Megafortress and the Russians were closing at a rate of roughly 27 miles per minute.

"Time to Scorpion launch is four and a half minutes at this course and speed, Colonel," said Sullivan. "I can lock them up any time you want."

While Scorpion AMRAAM-pluses were excellent missiles, substantially improved over the basic AMRAAMs, head-on shots at high speed and long range were not high probability fires. Statistically, Dog knew he had to fire two shots for each hit; even then, he had a less than 93 percent chance of a kill.

But if they were going to overcome the overall odds, they had to take chances.

"One missile per plane," he told Sullivan. "Wait until we're just about at the launch point before opening the bomb bay doors."

"Right."

"After the radar-guided missiles are off, we change course and set up so we can pivot behind the survivors and fire the Sidewinders."

"Um, yes, sir. That means getting pretty close."

"Pretty much. Make sure you have enough momentum to fire if they're still moving this fast."

"Um, OK. Where are you going to be?"

"I'm going to go downstairs and see if I can help the Flighthawks take down some of the other planes."

**Near Stulpicani, Romania
0112**

DANNY DIDN'T QUITE FIT INTO ZEN'S CUSTOMIZED ARM AND torso harness; his arms and shoulders were smaller than the pilot's. But this proved to be a blessing—it let him keep his body armor and vest on.

He held his breath as he went over the first hill. There were two roads between him and the president's hiding place. Troops were posted on both, according to the ground radar plot from the *Bennett*. An antiaircraft gun had been moved in as well.

Sure enough, he saw the shadow of the four-barreled weapon to his left as he came over the first hill. He kept his head forward, focused on where he was going.

"I've lost the transmission," said Mack, back in Dreamland Control.

"Just send me to his last point."

"I may be sending you into an ambush."

"Just direct me, Mack."

"All right, don't get your jet pack twisted. Come to 93 degrees east and keep going."

The sound of the jet was loud in his ears, but it was an unusual sound; if the soldiers on the ground heard it, he was by them so quickly, none of them could react.

Danny had put on Zen's helmet, rather than trying to get the smart helmet to interface with the MESSKIT's electronics. But the moon was bright, and he could see the bald spot near the crest of the hill in the distance ahead.

He could also see two figures moving across it—the search party looking for the president.

"Hard right, hard right," said Mack Smith.

He turned, and slipped closer to the ground.

"There's a truck coming on the road. Be careful."

Even though he'd studied the satellite photos and the radar plots from the Megafortress while waiting for Zen, Danny still had trouble orienting himself. He couldn't find the creek elbow where Zen made the first pickup, nor could he spot the wedge that had been the old gravel mine near the base of the hill. He zeroed back the thrust, slowing to a near hover.

"You're ten yards from the last spot," said Mack. "It's on your left as you're facing uphill."

Something passed nearby. A bee.

No, gunfire. There were troops on the road, and they saw him in the air.

Danny pushed himself forward.

"Too far."

"I'm landing," Danny said, spotting a small opening between the trees.

VODA HUNKERED AS CLOSE TO THE GROUND AS HE COULD. He tried not to breathe. The soldiers were ten yards away.

Should he go out like this, dragged like a dog from a hole? Better to show himself, die a brave man—at least the stories of his death would have a chance of inspiring someone.

No. They'd make up any story they wanted. He would become a coward to history.

The soldiers stopped. Voda remained motionless, frozen, part of the ground. The soldiers began running—but to his left, away from him.

DANNY CROUCHED NEXT TO THE TREE, GETTING HIS BEARings. There was a group of soldiers somewhere above him; they had dogs and they were making their way down the hill. But there were also soldiers below him, the ones who had been shooting. How far away they were, he couldn't tell.

"You have to move forty yards to the north," said Mack. "It's almost a direct line."

He picked his way through the brush, but stopped after a few yards. He was making too much noise.

"Thirty-two to go," hissed Mack in his ear. "Let's move."

Shut up, Danny thought, though he didn't say anything. He could see the patrol above, maybe twenty yards away, shadows in and out of the scrub. Six or seven men moved roughly in single file. They walked north to south across the hill.

Danny waited until they had passed, then got up out of his crouch and began moving again, much more slowly this time. He slid through the underbrush as quietly as he could.

"Twenty-five yards," said Mack.

The dogs were barking excitedly above him. He heard shots. The men who were below him heard them too—they yelled to each other and began running up the hill.

He was going to get caught in a three-way squeeze.

"You sure you're right?" he whispered to Mack.

"This is his last spot. His cell phone is totally off the air. Twenty-five yards dead north," repeated Mack. "That's my best guess.

Danny began crawling. The dogs had definitely found something.

After he'd gone about ten yards, he spotted a rock outcropping to his left.

That must be where Voda had been, he thought. He got up and started toward it, walking, then trotting, and finally running.

VODA HEARD SOMEONE COMING. THEY WERE ON HIM NOW. It was the end.

Finally.

He took a deep breath. They might lie about how he had died, but he would know. He would be satisfied with that.

He thought of Mozart, and the folk song.

"Good-bye Julian. Mircea," he whispered, stepping up and out of his hiding place.

A black figure grabbed him and threw him down.

"Ssssssssh," hissed Danny Freah. "They're just above us."

Aboard Dreamland EB-52 *Bennett*,
over northeastern Romania
0115

THE *BENNETT* HAD ALREADY STABILIZED ITS CABIN PRESSURE, so as long as Dog stayed clear of the hatchway, there was little chance he'd be swept out of the plane. Still, the passage to the rear of the flight deck was nerve-wracking, especially with the wind howling around him.

He grabbed each handhold carefully, moving as fast as he dared. When he reached the ladder at the back of the deck, Dog took a deep breath, then dropped to the floor and grabbed the top of the ladder. He felt himself slipping, unbalanced by the plane's sharp maneuvers as it got ready to engage the Russians.

Dog grabbed the ladder rail and climbed down into the compartment. When he reached the deck, he punched the button to close the hatchway, sealing off the lower level and banishing any possibility that he might fly out of the aircraft. He went to Flighthawk Station Two on the left side of the plane, plugged in his oxygen set, and powered up the console.

Dog knew only the general outlines of how the Flighthawk control system worked. There was no way he could pilot the small planes better than the computer, certainly not in combat. But that wasn't necessary—all he had to do was tell them who to hit.

"Sitrep on main screen," he told the computer after his control access was authorized.

The sitrep appeared. The Megafortress was at its center; *Hawk One* and *Hawk Two* were shown as crosses in blue. Dog struggled for a moment, trying to remember how to change the scale so he could see the targets as well. Finally he tried the voice command that worked on his console upstairs.

The screen flashed. When it reappeared, the entire battle area was presented. The MiGs were red daggers at the edge of the screen.

"*Hawk One,* designate target *Bandit Five,*" said Dog.

A message flashed on the screen:

TARGET OUT OF RANGE

"*Hawk One,* suggest target," said Dog.

The computer thought about it, then flashed a yellow line on the screen. It wanted to strike *Bandit Eight,* even though it was even farther away than *Bandit Five.*

"Colonel, we're almost ready to fire," said Sullivan over the interphone.

"Take your shots as soon as you're ready."

"Roger that. Opening bay doors."

Dog tried to block out the sound and the Megafortress's maneuvers. Should he accept the computer's judgment? It didn't quite make sense to him, but Zen often talked about how subtly different the tactics for the Flighthawks were when compared to conventional aircraft.

It came down to this: Did he trust the technology, or did he trust his own judgment?

When he first arrived at Dreamland, it would have been the latter. Now, he knew, he had to go with the computer.

"*Hawk One* targeting approved," he said.

A new message flashed on the screen:

OK TO LEAVE CONTROLLED RANGE?

"Affirmative," replied Dog.

The message remained. The computer had not accepted his command.

"*Hawk One,* authorized to leave controlled range for intercept," said Dog.

ACKNOWLEDGED.

Hawk One pivoted north.

North? What the hell was the computer thinking?

Near Stulpicani, Romania
0116

VODA'S EYES WERE WIDE, CLEARLY NOT BELIEVING WHAT HE
was seeing.

"You're not the same man. You're not Zen."

"No, I'm Danny Freah. Your wife and son are safe. Now
you and I have to get out."

"Is there an army of flying men?"

Danny smiled and shook his head. "Come on."

There were too many trees above them to try crashing
straight upward and out. They'd have to move to a clearer
spot. But going back to where he'd come down seemed too
dangerous.

"Mack, I have him," said Danny.

"Get the hell out of there."

Mack Smith, master of the obvious.

"All right, Mr. President, what we're going to do is move
down the slope until we come to an opening where we can
fly from. Then I'm going to strap you to me and we're out of
here. Right?"

"Call me Alin."

"OK, Alin. Let's do it."

With the first step, Danny realized Voda had hurt his leg.
He put his arm under Voda's shoulder and helped him forward. They had only gone a few yards when he heard the
shouts of the men above.

"Stay in front of me," said Danny.

He raised his gun. A burst of automatic gunfire blazed
through the brush.

"*Johnson,* we need a diversion," said Danny. He grabbed
Voda and pulled him next to him, starting down the slope. "I
have a bulletproof vest, Alin. Stay between me and the bullets.
I know your leg hurts—just do the best you can. Come on."

Aboard Dreamland B-1B/L *Boomer,*
over northeastern Romania
0121

"Do whatever you have to," Samson told Englehardt. "Shoot them up. Just get him to Bucharest."

"Roger that," replied Englehardt. "*Johnson* out."

Samson turned to Breanna. They were still five minutes away from the MiG flight.

"You ready over there, Stockard?"

"Ready, Earthmover."

"What's your nom de guerre?" he asked.

"Sir?"

"Your handle? Nickname?"

"Um. People sometimes call me Rap."

"Don't like it," said Samson, checking his course.

Aboard EB-52 *Bennett,*
over northeastern Romania
0122

The missiles appeared on Dog's sitrep, flashing toward the MiGs. The Russians had not yet seen the Megafortress, nor its missiles. Apparently unaware that they'd been targeted, they continued blithely on course.

Dog turned his attention back to the Flighthawks.

"*Hawk Two,* suggest target."

The computer suggested *Bandit Nine,* far back in the pack.

"*Hawk Two,* target approved."

As soon as Dog acknowledged that the location of the target was beyond control range, the Flighthawk peeled off to the west. This route, at least, was direct and obvious.

"MiGs taking evasive action," said Sullivan over the interphone.

They were, but it was too late. Dog saw Scorpion One and

the lead MiG intersect on the screen. A red starburst appeared, indicating that the missile had hit its mark.

Missiles three and four struck their targets in rapid succession.

Two missed, self-destructing harmlessly a half mile away.

As he watched the screen, Dog realized why *Hawk One* had gone north. Russian air doctrine not only organized the MiGs into four distinct groups, but dictated their routes of escape when attacked. *Hawk One* was perfectly positioned to take out its MiG as the aircraft cut to the north.

But it would have to do it on its own. The words HAWK ONE: CONNECTION LOST flashed on the screen, followed a few seconds later by a similar message for *Hawk Two*.

Near Stulpicani, Romania
0123

VODA STARTED DOWN THE HILL. THERE WAS NO MUSIC PLAYing in his head now, just the rapid drum of his heart and the too-loud rustle of the brush as he pushed his legs across the ground. Danny Freah twisted and turned through the thick branches, pushing this way and that, prodding him through the gray tangle of leafless brush and trees.

Suddenly, Danny stopped short, grabbing him. Voda slipped and fell to the ground.

"Stay down," whispered the American, crouching next to him.

A dozen soldiers were coming up the hill.

"That's where we're going," Danny whispered, pointing to the right.

Voda saw a patch of moonlight between the trees. It was a small clearing, ten or fifteen yards away.

"There should be a diversion here any second," Danny said. "We have to add to the confusion."

Voda couldn't quite understand what he was saying. Danny reached to his vest, then held something out to him. "Two grenades," he explained. "How far can you throw?"

"Throw?"

"A baseball?"

Voda shook his head. He had no idea what Danny was talking about.

"Here's what we're going to do," Danny whispered. "In about thirty seconds there are going to be some flares launched above us. We're going to throw these grenades as far as we can down the hill. They're flash-bangs—they make a lot of noise and light, but they won't hurt anybody. As soon as you throw the first grenade, turn around and run with me to that clearing. When we get there, grab my neck. And hang on. I'll set down as soon as I can and we'll get you in the harness. We'll be OK if you hang on. Just grip me tight. Keep your head down—we'll definitely be hitting branches. All right? Do you think you can hold on?"

No, Voda thought, he didn't think he could. His fingers were frozen stumps.

"Yes," he said weakly.

"Careful, these are primed," hissed Danny, handing him a grenade. "You let go, they'll explode in a few seconds."

Flares sparkled above, a fire show of light.

"Throw!" yelled Danny.

He heaved his grenade, then started to run with the American.

There was more gunfire, explosions.

As they reached the clearing, Danny grabbed Voda with one hand. There was a whooshing sound. Voda threw his arm around the American's neck. As he did, he realized to his horror that he had only thrown one of the grenades. The other one dropped from his raw, numb fingers.

God!

Voda's head spun. Dizzy—something smacked hard against him, grabbed and scratched him.

He was airborne, flying over the trees. The ground lit with a boom and a flash.

VODA'S GRIP WAS SO TIGHT, DANNY STARTED TO CHOKE. HE had intended to put down on the road, but tracers showered all around him, and he knew the best thing was simply to fly. He pushed forward, zipping over the road toward the next hill.

Their feet smacked into the top of the tree branches as he steered the MESSKIT. He kept his head straight, trying to keep his frigid hands steady on the controls.

As they came up over the crest of the hill, he saw the Osprey off in the distance, already in the air. Fire leaped from it—it was shooting at one of the antiaircraft guns.

"Whiplash Osprey, what's going on?" he said, but there was no answer.

He backed off his power. The fuel in MESSKIT was limited; he had very little room to improvise.

The Osprey stopped firing and spun to his left, heading away from him. Danny saw trucks moving on the road below. He veered to the right, back toward the original landing zone.

A tone sounded. He had only a minute of fuel left.

What was the Osprey doing?

Voda groaned.

"We're gonna land!" Danny shouted to him.

They glided downward, skimming over a rooftop and dipping into a farm field fifty yards from the one where Zen had landed. Danny tried to walk as he came in, but Voda was facing backward and they ended up tumbling awkwardly.

Even after the fall, Voda held his grip; Danny had to pry him off and shout at him to get free.

"Whiplash Osprey! Whiplash Osprey!" he yelled into the helmet's microphone as he grabbed his submachine gun. "We're ready for pickup!"

Again there was no response. Finally, Danny realized what

had happened. While he was taking off he'd inadvertently pulled the wire connecting the helmet to the radio from its plug.

He punched it in.

"Osprey, I'm down!"

"Roger, Captain. We see you and are en route. Stand by."

Danny looked toward the house, about 150 feet away. Someone was watching from a lit window at the top.

He heard gunfire, but it wasn't aimed at them or nearby, and he couldn't see who was shooting.

The Osprey whipped toward them, a hawk swooping in for its prey. As it dropped into a hover nearby, two trucks stopped near the house. Figures emerged from the back—soldiers.

"Come on. Here's our taxi," Danny said, turning to Voda.

The president was crouched over on one side, a pool of vomit on the ground.

"Come on, come on," said Danny, pulling him.

The Osprey's wings were tilted upward. It flew like a helicopter, gliding in between them and the house as Danny and Voda ran out of the way to give it more space. The aircraft spun, keeping the gun under its chin pointed at the troops that had come out of the truck, but they didn't fire.

"In, let's go, let's go!" yelled Danny, pulling Voda with him.

Sergeant Liu sprang from the ramp at the rear. He grabbed Voda from the other side and together he and Danny held the president suspended between them. When they reached the ramp, they threw themselves head first into the aircraft as it began to move.

Boston was standing in front of the side door, manning a .50 caliber machine gun. He sighted at the men below but didn't fire; neither did they.

"Button up! Button up!" yelled the crew chief. "We're outta here."

Aboard Dreamland B-1B/L *Boomer*,
over northeastern Romania
0125

BREANNA STUDIED THE TARGETING SCREEN, WATCHING AS THE
MiGs scattered under the pressure of the *Bennett*'s long-range
missile attack. The airborne radar operator in the *Johnson*
was playing traffic cop, divvying up the remaining targets as
the Russian aggressors found new courses toward their target.
Bennett and its Flighthawks were to tackle three planes, *Bandits*
Three, Eight, and *Nine.* That left ten for the B-1s.

"*Boomer,* you have *Bandits Five* and *Six*," said the operator.

"Roger that," Breanna said.

"*Boomer,* you also have *Bandits Ten, Twelve, Thirteen,*
and *Fifteen.* Do you copy?"

"You're adding those," she said, glancing at the sitrep. "We
have *Five,* we have *Six,* we have *Ten,* we have *Twelve, Thir-*
teen, we have *Fifteen. Boomer* copies."

All of their targets were currently headed south, though
they would have to cut back north soon to strike the pipeline.
The closest, *Bandit Twelve,* was seventy-five seconds from
firing range. They were dead-on to its nose.

The trick, though, wasn't taking out just one plane, or even
two. Breanna knew she had to make like a pool player intent
on running the table. If she took too long between shots, one
or more of the MiGs would be by them and dropping their
bombs before they had a chance to shoot them down.

"Earthmover, I need you to come back north," said Breanna, giving Samson not only a heading but a speed.

"Hmmmph," said Samson.

"Did you get it?"

"I got it."

"I need a good, strong acknowledgment," she said, moving
the cursor toward the shot. "I can't guess."

"*Affirmative.* I have it."

"It's just that you mumble sometimes."

"I'll work on it, Captain."

"Good. Laser cycling," Breanna added, pressing the button to arm the weapon. "Preparing to fire."

"Right—acknowledged," said Samson. "Fire at will."

"Engaging. Stand by for laser shot."

"Hrmmph."

Breanna smiled but said nothing.

A massive bolt of energy flew at the MiG, striking a spot just behind the canopy where a thick set of wires ran back from the cockpit. The burst lasted three and a half seconds; when it was finished, the wires had been severed and the MiG rendered uncontrollable.

"*Bandit Ten* disabled," said Breanna. "Targeting *Twelve*."

"Roger that," said Samson.

"Indicated airspeed dropping—increase speed thirty knots—come on, General, let's move it!"

"You better hit every goddamn plane, Stockard," said Samson, goosing the throttle. "I don't take this abuse from just anyone."

**Aboard EB-52 *Bennett*,
over northeastern Romania
0130**

DOG WATCHED AS *HAWK ONE* CLOSED ON ITS TARGET. THE aircraft was still out of control range, but from the looks of the synthesized sitrep view on the radar display, it didn't need his help. It came toward the MiG at a thirty degree angle, pivoting seconds before the MiG came abreast. The turn—many degrees sharper than would have been possible in a larger, manned aircraft—put the Flighthawk on the Russian's tail. If the MiG driver knew he was in the computer's bull's-eye, there was never a sign of it. The plane simply disappeared, disintegrating under the force of the Flighthawk's gun.

Hawk Two had a slightly more difficult time: Its target relinquished its missiles and tried to maneuver its way free. The Flighthawk hung on, following the MiG through a climbing scissors pattern as the Russian pilot swirled back and forth, attempting to flick off his opponent.

Had the MiG pilot satisfied himself with simply getting away, he probably would have made it; he succeeded in opening a good lead as he reached 35,000 feet. But pilots are an aggressive breed, whether they're Russian or American, and the MiG driver saw his chance to turn the tables on his nemesis as he came out of his climb. He pushed back toward the Flighthawk and lit his cannon, dishing 30mm slugs toward the Flighthawk's fuselage and nearly catching the plane as it turned.

But the U/MF, small and radar resistant, made for a very poor target. It jinked hard left, escaping the MiG's path. Only two bullets struck its fuselage, and neither was a fatal blow. The MiG started to throttle away, its pilot figuring that the Flighthawk was committed to its escape turn.

A human pilot would have done that. But not the computer. It jerked the Flighthawk back, shrugging off close to eleven g's to put its nose in the direction of the MiG's canopy. Then it fired a long burst.

That was the end of the Russian plane.

UPSTAIRS, SULLIVAN WAS POSITIONING THE *BENNETT* TO take down *Bandit Three,* which had escaped its earlier AMRAAM-plus.

The MiG had its head down and was running toward northern Romania at well over the speed of sound, not even thinking about defending itself. Sullivan banked as the MiG approached, jamming his throttles to set up a shot toward the fighter's tailpipe.

"Fire Fox Two," he said as the Sidewinder missile clunked off the dispenser. He fired a second heat-seeker, then buttoned up the plane.

Had the Megafortress been an F-15, or if its target had been a less capable aircraft, Sullivan would have nailed it. But even with its uprated engines spooling to the max, the Megafortress simply couldn't accelerate out of its turn quickly enough to get the proper initial momentum for the missile. The Sidewinders tried valiantly to catch up to their prey but they soon lost its scent and self-destructed.

"Son of a bitch," said Sullivan, dejected. "He's by me, Colonel. I'm sorry. Shit."

DOG HAD SEEN EVERYTHING ON THE SITREP. SULLIVAN HAD done a hell of a job, but he sounded as if he was ready to bang his head into the bulkhead because the Megafortress couldn't do the impossible. He was holding the plane—and more important, himself—to an impossible standard.

Same thing I would have done to myself, he thought.

And it would have been just as unfair.

Sullivan had done an incredible job, no matter what scale he was measured against.

It was difficult to be objective when you were used to pushing yourself. High standards were important when so many lives were at stake, but you couldn't let that blind you to your actual achievements.

And that was true of the medal, he realized. He deserved it, not just because it symbolized the efforts of the people around him, but because he had earned it.

"You did fine, Sully," Dog told the pilot. "You did fine. One of the other planes will take him."

White House Situation Room
1530 (0130 Romania)

"TH-TH-THERE'S NO QUESTION ABOUT IT, MR. PRESIDENT," said Jed. "Those are Russian planes, on a deliberate mission to attack the gas pipelines. It—It's the third wave of attacks against Romania."

"Enough is enough," said Martindale. He walked over to the desk manned by the duty officer, but rather than addressing him, picked up the red phone at the side.

It was the so-called hotline to the Kremlin.

"Sir, I have to punch in an authorization code for the call to work," said the duty officer.

"Do it," said Martindale. "Either these attacks stop here or I'm going to launch an immediate counterattack on every Russian air base east of the Urals."

Aboard Dreamland B-1B/L *Boomer*, over northeastern Romania 0145

"LASER CYCLING!" SAID BREANNA.

"Roger!" said Samson.

"Engaging."

The beam of energy from *Boomer*'s belly drilled a small hole in the right wing of the MiG; as the metal disintegrated, fumes in the tank ignited and the wing imploded. The rest of the MiG crumpled into very expensive scrap metal.

"Splash *Bandit Fifteen*," said Breanna. "Double trifecta."

"Perfecta, Captain. Damn good show."

"You weren't too bad yourself, Earthmover." Breanna leaned back from the targeting console. Her neck was so stiff the joints in her vertebrae cracked as she twisted toward the pilot. "That's got to be some sort of record."

"The hell with the record," said Samson. "I'd like to see Congress veto our funding now."

The situation was looking good. Danny and President Voda had reached the Osprey and would soon be off. The *Johnson* was swinging south to escort it.

"*Bennett* radar is coming on line," said Breanna. "It will take a second for the computer to coordinate the feeds."

The images blurred, snapped into focus, then blurred and came back.

"*Bandit Three* is through," said Breanna, examining the plots. "It's flying south. *Big Bird* won't be able to get it."

"Stand by, Stockard. We're going to catch that son of a bitch. And you better acknowledge that with a strong voice."

"Kick ass, Earthmover," she said, bracing herself as Samson torched the afterburners.

**Presidential villa,
near Stulpicani, Romania
0150**

GENERAL LOCUSTA COULDN'T BELIEVE WHAT HE WAS HEARING.

"They're continuing to search," said the major. "But they think the flying man may have take President Voda away."

"A flying man?"

The major shook his head.

It was too much for Locusta. "I'm going to corps headquarters, then to Bucharest."

"But the President—"

"The hell with him. We're too deep to pull back down," said Locusta. "The coup will proceed as planned."

"General, I don't think if he is alive we will succeed."

"Then call me when you've killed him," Locusta said, stalking to his car.

**Near Stulpicani, Romania
0150**

VODA HUGGED HIS WIFE AND JULIAN. BOTH WERE SOBBING. Someone had thrown a blanket over him; someone else handed him a plastic packet that produced heat when he grabbed it. The Osprey circled westward, climbing away from the gunfire.

He knew this was far from over. He had to pull himself up, ignore the smell of vomit on his clothes, ignore the throbbing pain in his leg, and regain control of his country. Now that his family was safe, his duty was clearly to Romania.

"I love you, Julian," he told his son, kissing his head. "And you, Mircea."

They grabbed him, but he pushed them away, rising to his feet.

"I need a phone," he told the Americans. "I need some way of communicating with my people."

ZEN SAT ON THE FABRIC BENCH ACROSS FROM THE ROMA- nian president, nursing a cup of coffee as Voda got to his feet. In barely the blink of an eye Voda seemed to have changed. He no longer had the look of a hunted animal. There was something deeper in his eye, something determined.

"You can talk to anyone you want," said Danny Freah, handing the president a headset. He showed him how it worked. "You're on a special line. Mack Smith will make the connections back at Dreamland."

"Good," said Voda. "We begin by calling the television stations, to let them know I am alive."

Voda looked out the window. He could tell from the moon and the highway they passed that they were heading south. He turned to Danny.

"Is it possible to go over the troops that have surrounded my house?"

"I don't think so."

"Can you get a loudspeaker?"

"The Osprey is equipped with one but—"

"They have to be told that I'm alive. I want to see what their reaction is. Are they for me? Or against me? Are they for a free Romania, or a captive one?"

"No way, sir. I just can't go along with it. They have antiair guns in some spots on the road. Even for us—"

"I believe the soldiers will drop their arms when they hear me. And if not," added Voda, "then I need to know what I'm up against."

"Yeah, but we're not committing suicide."

"If you're just looking to test the reactions," said Zen, "maybe we can overfly some troop trucks farther along in the valley."

"Troops on the outskirts of the action will be acceptable," said Voda.

Danny shook his head. "No way."

"Are you here to help me?" Voda asked sharply. "Or am I your prisoner?"

"You're not my prisoner," said Danny. "But I'm not going to let you do anything dumb."

"Who are you to judge me? You're a captain. I am a president."

"There's plenty of troops stopped along the highway, Danny," said Zen. "We can just pick some away from the antiair guns. It won't be too much of a risk."

"I'll give the order to the pilot myself," said Voda, starting forward shakily.

"Zen, this is nuts," said Danny, leaning down toward him.

"Hey, if the army's not going to back him, he's screwed anyway. He might as well find out now."

"He's already screwed. They were trying to kill him on the hill. This is going to get us shot down."

"Not if we pick the right place."

"No way." Danny straightened.

"I can pull rank," said Zen.

"I'm calling Samson."

"That's an option."

Danny pulled on his headset. Zen reached for his.

**Aboard Dreamland B-1B/L _Boomer_,
over northeastern Romania
0155**

TERRILL "EARTHMOVER" SAMSON HAD FLOWN B-1BS FOR
a long time, but he'd never flown one like he flew _Boomer_. He'd
never flown _any_ plane like he flew _Boomer_—throttle mashed
against the last stop on the assembly, wings pinned back so far
against the fuselage the plane's sides were groaning.

The speedo bolted past Mach 2, but Samson wanted more.
He _needed_ more—the MiG was still three miles out of range.

But it was slowing—popping up.

To make its bombing run.

"You ready over there, Stockard?" he barked.

"I need two and half more miles," she answered. "And,
General, we're too low. We have to be above him."

"The hell with that, Stockard. You're firing upside down.
Ready, Stockard?"

"I'm ready."

Samson held the control stick tightly. Not only did he have
to time the invert just right, he had to be careful coming out
of it—he was down below 10,000 feet, and using altitude to
kick up his momentum.

Eight thousand, going through 7,500, going through 7,000,
going—

"In range!" shouted Breanna.

Samson flipped the aircraft onto its back, turning the laser
director toward the MiG. The energy beam shot out, striking
one of the missiles under the plane's right wing.

Two seconds later the missile's fuel ignited. Shrapnel pep-
pered the MiG's belly. A piece of hot flying metal ignited the
warhead on the missile sitting on the opposite hardpoint.

Flames consumed the MiG so quickly, the pilot couldn't
hit the silk.

Samson didn't see any of it. He was too busy righting the
B-1 and pulling out of its death dive toward the earth.

"Where do I need to be?" he shouted.

"Anywhere you want, Earthmover. Scratch *Bandit Three*."

Samson grinned.

"Incoming message from Whiplash Osprey," added Breanna. "Major Stockard and Captain Freah."

Samson hit the preset. There was no visual; Danny and Zen were on the line from the Osprey. Zen explained President Voda's request.

"Captain Freah believes it might be an unnecessary risk," added Zen. "Right, Captain?"

"I think it's unwise, yes," said Danny.

"You know what, Captain? Just this once I'm going to disagree with you. I'm glad to see that these people have a president with some balls. Let him do what he wants, the way Zen just laid it out. Don't let him get killed."

"Um—"

"You have a problem, Captain?"

"Those two orders are in conflict. Sir. I mean—"

"Let the Romanian president do what he wants," said Samson. "Those are my orders. *Boomer* out."

"All MiGs are down, General," said Breanna. "All our aircraft are good. No casualties. Doesn't look like the Russians got a shot off."

Samson grinned. If some of the Dreamland people were a little full of themselves—well, if *all* of them were a *lot* full of themselves—now he saw why.

"You did a damn good job there, Captain," he told Breanna. "You kicked ass."

"Couldn't have done it without you, sir."

"You got that right," said Samson.

Breanna started to laugh.

"What's that?" he asked. Then he started to laugh as well. So maybe he was a little full of himself too.

So what?

Aboard Dreamland Osprey
over Romania
0205

DANNY PULLED OFF THE HEADSET.

"He's only been here a few weeks," he said to Zen. "And already he's starting to sound like Colonel Bastian. Screw the risks. Get the job done."

"Dog has that effect on people," said Zen.

Reluctantly, Danny went forward and told the pilots what they had to do. The Osprey circled back north, skimming lower. As they came to the main highway leading to the road where Voda's house was, they spotted a pair of small jeeps guarding the intersection. It was about as safe a place as they were going to find.

"It's all yours," Danny told Voda, handing over the headset. "It's set to loudspeaker."

"They'll hear me over the rotors?"

"Yes. We've used it for rescues and crowd control. It's very loud. Wait until the flares get their attention. At the first sign of trouble, we're out of here. So hold on."

VODA TOOK THE MICROPHONE AS THE OSPREY SPED toward the post.

Maybe Captain Danny Freah was right; maybe he was being foolish. Maybe he should just go on to Bucharest, make his speeches to the TV. It would be the prudent thing to do.

But what good would the speeches be if the people weren't behind him? And if he couldn't persuade two dozen soldiers to help him keep Romania free—well then, he had failed as president, hadn't he?

An illumination flare turned the night white. Two or three of the men pointed their weapons at the black aircraft as it hovered close, but no one fired.

"Open the door," he told the sergeant standing near it.

"Shit," said Danny.

But he nodded, and the door was opened. Voda looked down at the men.

"I need to be lower."

The captain shook his head.

"Lower!" yelled Voda.

The microphone caught his voice, and it echoed through the cabin. The Osprey settled a little closer to the ground, close enough, at least, for Voda to see that the soldiers were kids: eighteen, nineteen. To them, the dictator was just some story their parents told when they were bored. They didn't know what it was like to be the slaves of a dictator.

Or free men, for that matter.

"Gentlemen of the army," began Voda, his voice shaky. "This is President Voda. I wish to thank you for your role in helping save me today. Our democracy has passed a great test, thanks to your help. Romania remains free! *Romania for the people!*"

The soldiers didn't react. Voda felt a moment of doubt. Then he leaned out the door.

"Thank you, Romania!" he yelled into his microphone. "We remain a free people, with a great future!"

The soldiers began to cheer. Voda waved so hard one of the Americans had to grab him to keep him from falling out.

"To Bucharest," he told Danny Freah.

"Damn good idea," said Danny. He waved toward the front. The door was closed and the Osprey wheeled back into full flight.

"Hey, Mr. President," said Zen Stockard, sitting across from him. "Whose fancy car is that?"

Voda crossed to the other side of the Osprey and looked out. It was a black Mercedes S series sedan with flags—one Romanian and the other . . .

The other bore the insignia of the Romanian army.

Locusta's car.

"I want that son of a bitch arrested!" he yelled. "Get him, now! Kill him if you have to."

"Now there's an order we can all live with," said Zen.

Southwest of Stulpicani, Romania
0210

LOCUSTA HEARD THE AIRCRAFT BUT WAS CONFUSED. IT couldn't be his helicopter—they were still several miles from headquarters.

A black beast swerved in front of the car. His driver hit the breaks.

It was the Dreamland Osprey.

What the hell were they doing?

SAMSON HAD ORDERED HIM TO FOLLOW THE ROMANIAN president's orders. Still, Danny Freah didn't feel entirely comfortable shooting up the car.

"Get him to stop," he told the pilots. "Fly in front of him, train the guns on him. Then we'll have him surrender."

The Osprey pitched around, settling in front of the vehicle. Voda was on the loudspeaker, talking to Locusta.

"General Locusta," he said in Romanian, "I order you to place yourself under arrest. You are to come with these soldiers. No harm will come to you, unless you try to escape."

"Tell him to stop the vehicle," said Danny.

"General, stop the car," said Voda.

The Osprey was moving backward, its chin guns pointed at the Mercedes. Instead of slowing, the car picked up speed.

"Can he hear me?" Voda asked.

"Yeah, he can hear you. He's just being stubborn. I'm going to mash up his front end and take out his engine. The car is armored, but that's not going to be much of a problem."

"Do it."

"Yeah."

A second after Danny gave the order, the pilot began firing his chin cannon. The Mercedes veered to the side of the road.

INSIDE THE CAR, GENERAL LOCUSTA THREW HIS ARMS FORward, bracing himself as it skidded off the road.

How could this possibly be happening? How had Voda managed to escape—and not only escape, but come for him?

The Americans. Dreamland. The bastards. He'd kill as many of them as he could before they killed him.

He threw open the door and raised his gun.

DANNY SPRUNG FROM THE SIDE DOOR OF THE OSPREY, Sergeants Liu and Boston right behind him. The rear passenger side door of the car opened and a man leaped to the ground, rolled over, and came up firing a 9mm pistol.

The first two or three bullets flew wildly to the side.

Then one struck Danny in the chest, right above the heart.

His bulletproof vest saved him, deflecting the bullet's energy.

A second later Danny threw himself in the air. He couldn't fly without the MESSKIT, but flying wasn't what he had in mind. He came down on top of Locusta, who dropped the pistol under the force of the blow.

Two punches and it was all over. Locusta, stunned, lay limp on the ground, alive, breathing, but undoubtedly a condemned man.

His driver came out of the car with his hands high.

"You're under arrest by the authority of the president of Romania," said Danny.

"Under the authority of the *people* of Romania," said President Voda, picking up Locusta's gun from the ground. He hobbled forward, favoring his injured leg. "It's the people who have sovereignty in a democracy, isn't it, Captain?"

VIII

For Freedom

———

Bucharest, Romania
3 February 1998
1730

THE EVENING BEFORE THE DREAMLAND TEAM RETURNED
home from their deployment, the president of Romania
hosted a special reception for them. When he first heard
of the plan, General Samson began to fret—because of the
rush, he hadn't packed his Class A uniform, bringing only his
battle fatigues and flight suits.

In another command the mistake might very well have
been fatal. But when you headed Dreamland, people
expected you to be a little different. Samson, though perhaps
still not entirely comfortable, realized he was beginning to
adjust.

President Voda didn't seem to care how the Dreamland
people were dressed. He was back in control of his country,
with the northern army corps dispersed and the units under
all new command. General Locusta was in prison, as were
his co-conspirators.

The guerrillas had stopped their attacks, though no one
was sure whether they were simply biding their time or if the
movement had collapsed, as Sorina Viorica had predicted.

The Russians, while not acknowledging that they had tried
to attack the pipeline, had announced that they were appoint-
ing a new ambassador to Romania and overhauling the embassy personnel. More significantly, they had lowered the
price of the natural gas they supplied to Europe.

President Martindale had personally telephoned Samson to tell him about the Russians.

"I'm surprised you went to Romania yourself, General," he said. "I thought your priority was at Dreamland."

"My priority is my people, Mr. President. And my mission."

"I'm glad you did," said Martindale. "You need a sense of what's going on. I like that sort of initiative."

So did Samson. The mission had shown him exactly how much there was to a Dreamland Whiplash deployment, how much it depended on the proper mix of technology and old-fashioned warrior spirit. It had also convinced him that while he still had trouble stomaching Tecumseh "Dog" Bastian at times, the lieutenant colonel deserved every accolade he'd ever received, and then some.

It happened that Samson and Colonel Bastian were seated next to each other at the reception. When the band stoked up following the speeches of gratitude and friendship, President Voda rose to dance with his wife. While he favored his injured knee—the ligaments had been strained but not torn—he still cut an acceptable figure on the floor, moving with a slow, dignified grace.

Dog and Samson found themselves alone at the table.

"So," said Samson. "Have you given any thought to your next assignment?"

"Not really," said Dog. "Maybe I'll retire."

"Retire? Quit?"

"I don't know if it's quitting."

"You know, Dog—if I can call you that."

"Sure."

"You have a *hell* of a lot of experience. And you're being promoted to colonel."

"I can't be promoted for a few months at least."

"Way overdue." Samson waved in the air. "Everyone knows you're going to be promoted. You're on the fast track to general. Assuming you don't quit."

"I don't think retiring is the same as quitting. I don't have anything left to prove," said Dog.

He leaned back his seat. Samson followed his gaze. He was looking at his daughter, who was kissing Zen at the next table.

"No, true. You have absolutely nothing to prove," agreed Samson. "But on the other hand, you have a lot to offer. A lot of commands could use you. Mine, for instance."

Dog turned to him.

"Look, I know we don't get along. Hell, Tecumseh, when I met you, I thought you were a big jerk. I still think that. To an extent. A lesser extent."

Dog started to laugh. It was the same laugh, Samson realized, that he'd heard from Breanna in the plane during the mission, after he'd said that some people were conceited.

It must be embedded in the family genes.

"But we don't have to be friends," Samson continued. "That's not what Dreamland is about. Or the Air Force. Hell, I don't need friends. What I need is someone to run the air wing. Someone with ability. Integrity. Creativity. Balls. A leader."

"I thought you offered that job to someone else."

"Don't worry about that. I've been known to make mistakes. Sometimes . . . " He broke into a smile. "Sometimes I even admit it."

"I THOUGHT DANNY WAS GOING TO SHOOT ME WHEN I TOLD him we should go back and let President Voda talk to the soldiers," Zen told Breanna, finishing the story he'd started before she began kissing him.

"Hey, bullshit on that," said Danny, returning to the table with their drinks. "I wasn't going to shoot you. Throw you out of the Osprey, yeah."

Breanna laughed.

"The president's son tried teaching me Romanian on the way back to the capital," added Zen. "I can say hello."

"Hello?"

" 'Ello."

"That doesn't sound Romanian."

"You think he was gaming me? I paid him a buck."

Breanna laughed, finally realizing that Zen was joking.

"He's a cute kid," she said. She'd met Julian earlier that evening.

"Our son's going to be cuter," said Zen.

The remark froze Breanna. Their son?

Was Zen finally ready to talk about having children?

"Jeff?"

Zen smiled. Before Breanna could find a way to press him, someone tapped her on the shoulder. She turned around and found General Samson standing behind her.

"Captain Stockard, would you care to dance?"

"Um—"

"As long as your husband doesn't mind, of course. I don't need unnecessary dissension in the ranks."

"Dance away," said Zen. "A little unnecessary dissension never hurt anyone."

"I'M GOING TO HIT THE WC," ZEN TOLD DANNY. "WANT anything on the way back?"

Danny shook his head and held up his beer.

"I'll be back."

Danny took a long pull from the beer as Zen disappeared. He leaned back in his seat, thinking about the past few days, thinking especially about Istanbul, and Stoner.

The Moldovans claimed they'd only found three bodies in the wreckage. Stoner's wasn't among them.

Did it mean he was alive?

Undoubtedly not. The photos showed a horrific scene. The helo had crashed at the edge of a swamp; most likely Stoner had been thrown from the wreck and his body was lying somewhere in the mud, submerged.

No one would hold a reception for him; there'd be no fistful of medals. He wouldn't even get a wake. The government would never acknowledge that he'd been on the mission, or even been in Romania, let alone Moldova.

Yet, he'd done as much as they had. More really. He'd given his life.

Danny put down the beer and got up. He'd seen a cute Romanian woman who worked in the defense ministry at one of the tables near the door. Maybe she'd like to dance . . .

DOG WATCHED GENERAL SAMSON LEAD HIS DAUGHTER TO the dance floor. Samson wasn't a bad dancer at all.

Nor was he a bad commander. In fact, he might even be a pretty good one. He'd seemed a lot less controlling over the past few days, more willing to improvise and go beyond the book.

Was it just that he hadn't given Samson a chance at first? Or had Samson started to grow into the role? Was flying *Boomer* responsible? Was the battle? Or was Dreamland?

Maybe all Earthmover needed was time to forget the political bs he'd had to learn once he made general. Maybe the mission had given him a chance to remember what it was he liked about the Air Force in the first place.

Dog picked up his drink. He remembered his own first days at Dreamland. He'd changed as well.

For the better.

And he'd change again, and again, and again.

Because that was what heroes did.